THE NORIEGA
TAPES

LANCE KARLSON

The Noriega Tapes © Lance Karlson 2019

ISBN: 978-1-925834-16-1 (paperback)

Cataloguing-in-Publication information for this title is listed with the National Library of Australia.

Published in Australia by Lance Karlson and InHouse Publishing.
www.thenoriegatapes.com
www.inhousepublishing.com.au

Printed in Australia by InHouse Print & Design.

Acknowledgments

The inspiration for this novel came from the work of those journalists who braved the threats of dictators, rebel groups and the CIA in Latin America to deliver the truth. Special thanks to foreign correspondent Frederick Kempe for his motivation, unparalleled research and captivating storytelling in "Divorcing the Dictator: America's Bungled Affair with Noriega". I wish to also acknowledge the late Gary Webb, whose courageous investigative journalism inspired the protagonist of my novel, and whose "Dark Alliance" series was the subject of intense scrutiny by the CIA until it was ultimately found to be factual. Likewise I wish to acknowledge the work of John Dinges in "Our Man in Panama", Hugh Graham in "Ploughing the Seas" and also Peter Eisner for bringing to paper "America's Prisoner", the memoirs of Manuel Noriega.

I wish to thank my wife Shana for her constant encouragement, my mother Noeline for her honest feedback, Yesenia Estrella for her Spanish translations and the team at InHouse Publishing for their ongoing personable support.

Lastly I wish to acknowledge the extended family of Hugo Spadafora who have continued to keep alive his legacy. His incorruptible and audacious pursuit of Noriega was unrivalled, and although this is a work of fiction, his story is one that I hope to adapt with accuracy and respect.

Prologue

Paso Canoas, Costa Rica/Panama Border.
Friday, September 13th, 1985.

The doctor scanned the crowd as he finished his last cigarette. He stacked a neat pile of coins beside the ashtray, nodding at the waitress before descending the steps of the café. With a glance over his shoulder he turned towards the smoke of makeshift street kitchens, his briefcase a shield against hawkers as they beckoned to exchange wads of foreign notes. Ahead he could see the line for customs, and counted the stalls on his left before slipping from view. Within minutes he had crossed the border, pushing through a grove of banana trees that lined the path into Panama.

Puffs of bright colour burst over the tangled power lines above, and a row of muddy children refused to part as confetti floated and danced between their fingertips. The doctor followed a brindle dog out of the celebrations, remembering that today was the start of a weeklong border festival. It was an unexpected welcome home, but now was not the time to celebrate. With a grimy sleeve he wiped the sweat from his forehead. He wished that he could also wipe away the stares now crawling over his famous Mediterranean features and distinctive sideburns.

The man at the front of the bus shelter had the flattened face of a boxer, with narrow eyes and a leering grin. The smell of his tobacco filled the doctor's mind with unnerving memories as he passed, stopping at a ticket office that was locked behind rusted steel bars and windowpanes peppered with diesel exhaust. The doctor surveyed the empty shelter, avoiding eye contact with the stranger. He watched as an elderly lady shuffled in, licking at her fingers and absently kneading her hair. The stranger continued to stare. Almost instinctively, the doctor's hand began to move over the snub-nosed pistol buried against his thigh. He was about to make eye contact when the shelter vibrated with the wheezing of a battered white bus.

The doctor waited until the lady had ascended the steps of the bus before offering to help her into a seat. She smiled, allowing him to support her by the elbow as the stranger shoved past them and spread out in the back seat.

The bedlam of Paso Canoas disappeared in a swirl of dust and exhaust. The driver wrestled through the gears, urging the bus across a narrow bridge and then upwards into open farmland. Coffee plantations spread northwards to the foot of the Cordillera Central, where the peaks of jagged volcanic bluffs cradled the dark green glow of cloud forests.

The doctor opened his window. The familiar Chiriquí air added to his confidence that the worst was over. His thoughts turned to the journey ahead – the shocked faces, the hugs; the mission. Images of his past flickered over the windows – Panama before Noriega, his days in parliament, the many times he cheated death as a guerrilla fighter in West Africa, in Guatemala, Nicaragua and Costa Rica. But now, with his hair turning grey at the edges, this mission meant more than ever.

The bus rattled over another bridge where a row of fishermen looked up as they pulled nets from the river below. A ridge of palm trees opened into a view of the town of La Concepción. Pick-up trucks filled with vegetables, sugarcane and fish crates crowded the road into a leafy square at the centre of town. The footpaths were bustling with tents and stalls being erected for the start of the weekend markets. The bus edged to a stop beside a cement-rendered dental clinic.

Amongst the crowd were growing clusters of men in military uniform. Locals began to stop and stare, and the street music dulled as the men surrounded the bus. The doctor smiled wryly, shaking his head. There was no way they would attack him with this many witnesses.

The stranger stood up from the back seat, cracking his neck and moving forward. Still shaking his head, the doctor allowed himself to be escorted into the crowd outside. He pulled against the grip on his arm to give the driver's assistant a handful of coins, winking at him, then raised his passport into the air.

"Mi nombre es Hugo Spadafora!" he boomed. "My name is Hugo Spadafora and I am being detained without charge!"

The crowd began to shout and cheer, many of them recognising the famous revolutionary. But the cheering quickly turned into screams as the soldiers locked and loaded their weapons.

By nightfall the town of La Concepción had fallen eerily silent. Within a white military building dark red blood dripped over the edge of an interviewing table. On the table rested a telephone, its coiled cord extended to a solemn face.

"I'm being put through to the General," the face rasped in Spanish.

Other faces watched intently, one of them pushing the doctor's struggling head back into the blood and tightening his gag.

The face with the telephone receiver became taut as a distinctive voice came across the wires. "General Noriega?" the face grated. "We have the rabid dog."

On the end of the line, Panama's dictator paused. His pockmarked cheeks could almost be heard cracking into a smile. He responded slowly, his voice draining into a hiss. "And what does one do with a dog that has rabies?"

.

PART I
SINS OF THE MOTHER

Chapter One

Costa de Miskitos, southern Nicaragua.
September 10th, 1985.

Owen gripped the side of the boat tightly, his glasses becoming fogged as he peered into a twisted web of mangroves. It was the first time that he had heard real gunfire, and the shock was reverberating outwards from his stomach to his fingers, his muscles tensing with each echo in the morning mist. Four men stood beside him, unperturbed by the shots. They had turned off the small outboard motor, replacing their rifles with oars as they slowly patted through the shallows. Their faded baseball caps were wet from brushing the leaves above. Droplets of water ran down their military jackets and onto Owen's guitar case that lay on the floor of the boat.

"Llegamos?" one of the guerrillas whispered.

"Si, si," replied another.

A snapping of mangrove roots brought the boat to a sudden stop. Two of the men leapt out, tying the mooring rope to a gnarled tree trunk and motioning for Owen to follow. Another round of shots rang out, closer this time, and Owen quickly pulled his backpack over his shoulders. He followed the men out of the mud, through a network of clutching vines and onto a narrow track. He struggled to keep up as they dodged between giant ferns and mossy limestone boulders, the thick smell of decaying leaves gradually dissolving into the taste of smoke and burning bacon rind. Images of backyard barbecues in summer beside the pool stole his attention and he breathed in deeply. He pushed through a layer of wet palm leaves and into a large clearing bordered by a series of canvas tents.

Four soldiers stood up from damp log seats around a fireplace, staring and shouting in Spanish.

"Llego el gringo!"

"Donde esta el doctor?"

Owen's stomach began shuddering again. Inquisitive faces guided him through the fireplace to the entrance of the largest tent. The soldier escorting him stopped at the tent flap and cautiously peered inside.

"Doctor?"

"Si?" boomed a voice from within.

Owen's fingers and toes tingled sharply and he carefully wiped back his curly brown fringe. The soldier turned to him and nodded, motioning for him to enter the tent. He dithered, his knees bending, then slowly stepped through.

A dancing kerosene lantern illuminated a carefully arranged interior. Cabinets were filled with files, medical books, first aid kits and plastic medication cases. Two AK-47s were propped against a cabinet stacked with boxes of tobacco and cigars. An old set of scales sat atop a desk covered in bullet shells, clamps, measuring spoons and boxes of gunpowder. A fluorescent light hung from the central tent pole over an elevated stretcher bed. On the bed lay a shirtless soldier, facedown and glancing up painfully at Owen, sweat dripping down his nose. The steady, gloved hands of a doctor moved over the soldier's back holding a pair of tweezers and carefully threading stitches across an open bullet wound. A glass of bloodied bullet fragments sat beside the patient's head along with a large, empty syringe.

Owen gulped. He tried to make eye contact with the doctor's rugged, unmistakable face. It was a face famous across Latin America, and sure to be hanging on CIA pin boards like that of Che Guevara and Fidel Castro twenty years before.

Hugo Spadafora seemed to ignore his visitor as he carefully tied off a stitch and trimmed its stray thread. He gave his patient a friendly slap on the hip, letting him know that he was done. The soldier exhaled heavily, wiped away the sweat from his face and painfully pulled on a torn shirt.

Owen opened the tent flap and allowed the soldier to stagger through. A long silence ensued as the doctor washed his hands in a basin, turned off the fluorescent light and then lit a cigarette. Finally, his fiery eyes met with Owen's.

"Mi nombre es Owen Ellis," Owen stammered. "Um, hablamos por teléfono."

Spadafora slowly breathed out a gust of smoke and smiled. "Don't bother with the Spanish boy, but thank you for trying. Have a seat."

Owen fumbled with a wooden chair as the doctor continued to stand, examining the young man before him.

"So you say that you're a journalist?"

"Yes, well, I'm working freelance at the moment," Owen replied, reaching into his backpack and pulling out a leather-bound notebook and pen. "I've been investigating the La Penca bombing but was told that you recently supplied some information to the Drug Enforcement Administration in Costa Rica."

"This is true," Spadafora frowned. "But I've learned my lesson not to trust Americans. Why should I trust you to do what the DEA will not?"

"I'm not American," Owen replied, a slight smile dimpling his pale cheeks. "I'm from Canada."

Spadafora raised his eyebrows and quickly disguised his expression with a puff from his cigarette. His eyes flicked back and forth between Owen's until he decided that this young correspondent looked too innocent to be lying. "Well amigo, you've got balls coming here, and I trust you are who you say you are. But how did you know about my meeting with the DEA?"

Owen cleared his throat. "I have a source. That's all I can say."

Spadafora smirked, flicking the embers from his cigarette into a yellowed glass jar. "That's what I like to hear. I respect that."

Owen leaned forward uneasily. "So the reason I contacted you – the reason I'm here – is to discuss what you wanted to reveal about Noriega.

I understand that you have evidence implicating him in a drug trafficking operation?"

Spadafora clenched his jaw, his intense eyes glowing in the lambent light. "It's a bit more than that. Everyone knows that Noriega is transporting crack into the United States. The CIA have known it for over a decade, but of course, they aren't willing to do anything about it."

Owen's eyes narrowed. "And why is that?"

"Why do you think? Because the agents are profiting from it as much as Noriega is." His shoulders suddenly relaxed, and the words began flowing freely as if he had been waiting for this opportunity to vent. "I gave the DEA a file of evidence that should have started a wildfire. Transcripts of tapes, flight paths, invoices for front companies, statements of transport times and dates that I received from Noriega's pilot. But are they going to act on it? Of course not, they would rather keep their jobs – and their money."

"And the files, this information, do you still have it? Did you make copies?"

Spadafora squashed the last of his cigarette and reached into a drawer below the ashtray. With a casual toss, a black folder landed on Owen's lap.

Owen struggled to contain his excitement as his fingers flicked hungrily through the pages inside. "You're giving this to me?"

"Of course, you're a journalist, no?" Spadafora's tone had become impatient. "I'm returning to Panama on Friday with another copy, and I could do with some extra press. I'm going to shout the truth through every newspaper headline, and from every radio station until Noriega falls. If the Americans are too scared to act, then we'll see how the people of Panama deal with the truth. But at the same time, I want you to make sure the contents of that folder make it to as many Western headlines as possible."

Owen was frozen with excitement, and a smile gradually split through his taut lips.

"Don't look so hopeful, boy. You won't just be exposing Noriega. If those documents make it into press your name is also going to be against the fall of CIA agents across Latin America, and one in particular." He paused as he rolled another cigarette. "They'll come after you, they'll try to discredit you, and they'll probably try to kill you." He suddenly laughed, as though realising for the first time the risk that Owen would be taking.

Owen ignored the prickles of moisture that were forming around his hairline. "I can do it. I will be heading to Panama City tomorrow, then flying back to Canada next Friday. I'll have an article in press before I get on that plane."

Spadafora coughed and then grinned. "I like your optimism, Mr Ellis, and I hope it will get you further than those before you."

"But," Owen paused, "what did you mean by one CIA agent in particular?"

Spadafora ran a hand through his hair and began pacing back and forth in front of the stretcher, blowing smoke erratically through his nose. "You'll find the name in nearly every file there, I've highlighted it. He – or she – goes by the name of RUBUS, and is Noriega's pawn in the CIA. Every drug flight, every cache of weapons supplied to the Contras, and every fake company laundering Noriega's fortune has the name of RUBUS behind it."

Owen again flicked through the documents, his expression stony with concentration. Indeed, the name had been highlighted, and was surrounded with Spadafora's handwritten annotations. "I'll see what I can find out," he breathed, "and I'll let you know."

Spadafora laughed again. "You'll just give me another call, will you? Don't even think about it, boy. The CIA wires every phone-line between here and Colombia. If you want to contact me after Friday, do it in person. Look for a red door in Casco Viejo, Panama City."

Owen scribbled the instructions into his notepad, his writing even more illegible than usual. Spadafora began loading ammunition into a rifle and muttering under his breath, indicating to Owen that it was time for him to leave.

"Well, th-thanks again," Owen stuttered, packing the notepad into his backpack and tucking the folder under his arm. "I'll make sure –"

"Here, take this," Spadafora interrupted. He reached into a shelf to produce a golden snub-nosed pistol and a box of ammunition. "I'd blame myself if I found out you needed it."

Owen's stance became rigid, and he slowly shook his head. "I'll be fine without that."

Spadafora raised his eyebrows. "A pacifist, hey?"

"You could say that."

The doctor's stare was penetrating, as if recognising something familiar in Owen's eyes. "I envy your naivety, boy. Keep your head down, and I'll see you on the other side of the Canal."

Chapter Two

London Palladium Theatre.
Present day.

Jenna closed her eyes as she launched into her final pirouette. The crowd's cheers lifted her up off the stage as she spun, her twisting body buoyed higher into the swirling kaleidoscope of stage lights, her black ponytail splaying wildly and her feet landing gently in a sea of clapping. Her eyelids flicked open through the mascara and a beaming smile brought another eruption from the standing crowd. She could feel the other dancers and actors emerging onto the stage behind, their arms linking with hers and applauding whispers competing to reach her as they bowed in unison.

"One of the VIPs wants to meet you, Jenna."

Jenna spun her chair around and looked up from her phone, her fingers continuing to text as she met the smiling face of her aging director. "Sure, who is it?"

Miss Hindmarsh's smile became broader, creasing her thick foundation. "Well, I'm not entirely sure. He's from the White House, some sort of senator I think. He's got two bodyguards with him, so he must be important."

Jenna's eyes narrowed. "An American with bodyguards? Wow. Um, do I need to get changed?"

"No, you're fine dear. He will be coming to the after party. Apparently he wants to talk to you about opportunities in America."

Jenna laughed boldly. "Well how could I say no to that? I'll be another five minutes, see you out the front?"

"Okay dear, take your time."

As Miss Hindmarsh closed the door Jenna spun around to her dressing mirror and acted a silent scream of excitement. Bottles of nail polish and hairbrushes fell to the floor as she frantically grabbed at her phone.

Chandeliers glimmered above a crowd of tuxedos, flowing silk dresses and immaculate hors d'oeuvres. Jenna couldn't help grinning as she promenaded into the hall, her caramel skin, black hair and green eyes illuminated by a bold emerald dress.

Miss Hindmarsh raised a bony arm through the crowd, her glass of champagne tilting dangerously. "Jenna darling, come meet him, he's just over here! He's been asking after you all evening."

A tall, white-haired man stood before an archway in which two bodyguards scanned the scene before them. Surrounding the man was a circle of excited faces. The man turned slowly, his blue eyes rising from Jenna's shining heels upwards to her inquisitive face. His pinstriped suit was pulled tightly over a broad barrel chest, and his weathered face was carved into a confident smile.

"Jenna," Miss Hindmarsh grinned, "this is Joseph Thorn, from America."

"Miss Martinez, it is my pleasure."

The American's voice was gravelly, his accent distinct in a crowd of British performers. He reached out an iron handshake, which Jenna responded to with a competitive flutter of her eyelashes. "It's nice to meet you, sir. What brings you to England?"

Thorn's mouth smiled gently while his eyes carefully scanned Jenna's face. "Old ties," he mused. "I don't believe I can do my job without the endorsement of our closest ally, and of course, an escape to the theatre."

"And you're always more than welcome," Miss Hindmarsh chimed in.

"Well, young lady," Thorn continued, "I thought your performance was exceptional, and I am very keen to hear your story."

"My story? How do you mean?"

"Why don't we start with your taste in wine? Champagne, chardonnay, or a red maybe? I'm sure my friend over here can help you out? Let's grab a seat and have a chat. I believe, based on your performance this evening, that I could fix you up with a few contacts back in New York."

Jenna's eyes lit up. "Oh, sure," and turning to the waiter, "just a sparkling water thanks."

"I'll leave you two alone, then," Miss Hindmarsh beamed.

Jenna smiled at her friends staring from a far corner and nervously adjusted the front of her dress.

"So," Thorn started, leading Jenna to a private table behind the archway and pulling a chair out for her, "your delightful director has told me that you are from Panama. Is that correct?"

"Uh, yes," Jenna responded. "But I was born here, in England."

"I see. It's a beautiful country, Panama; I spent much of my early career there. Have you gone back to visit relatives at all?"

"No, no I haven't. My mother went back recently, but I don't have any relatives left there."

"I see, I'm sorry to hear that. And your father?"

Jenna narrowed her eyes.

"Pardon me, too many years in intelligence."

A glass of sparkling water appeared and Jenna gladly took a sip. "No, it's fine. My father was killed there, that's why my mother left. I don't know much about him."

"Oh, I am very sorry. I didn't mean to pry. So tell me, how long have you been dancing for?"

"Ever since I can remember. My mother runs a dancing studio, in Harmiston, where we live."

"Ah, wonderful. So she used to perform professionally as well?"

"Apparently, when she was younger, but not since she came here."

"I see," he smiled. "Well as I was saying, I have some contacts back in New York, my wife being one of them, who are very keen to have some diversity in their shows. I was wondering if you would be interested in any auditions?"

"Of course! Is this for dancing? Theatre? Acting?"

"All of the above. I take it you've never been to America before?"

"Well, no, but I guess it's always been a dream."

He smiled warmly. "Listen, I have your director's details from before, so I will pass those on for you. No promises of course, but I would be glad to have an input in what is already a promising career."

"Wow, thank you so much. Really, that is fantastic!"

"My pleasure. But I'm afraid that I must be off, another party to attend."

"Ha, sounds like a hard life! Well it was great to meet you sir, and I hope you enjoy your time in England."

Thorn smiled dryly. "Oh, I certainly will. Thank you, and farewell."

Jenna watched him walk carefully back through the crowd, his bodyguards shifting a path for him. Just before he disappeared from view he turned, glancing back at Jenna momentarily. Then, in response to the hushed words of his bodyguards, he nodded.

Chapter Three

La Concepción, Panama.
September 12ᵗʰ, 1985.

Owen smiled excitedly as his cousin's voice came across the line. "Sorry for calling your work phone, but –"

"Hang on buddy, just let me close the door. Where are you?"

"I've crossed the border. I'm now in La Concepción. I'll be in Panama City at around eight tonight."

"Jeez man, you're a fast mover. Have you still got the folder that Spadafora gave you?"

"Of course, guarding it with my life."

"Good, good, and have you had a chance to translate much of it?"

"Only bits and pieces so far. I'm going to need your help. I don't suppose you found out anything about this CIA agent by the name of RUBUS?"

"Not as yet, I'm afraid. I'll keep asking though."

"Okay, I better get going. I don't think I'm going to get another chance to eat before I arrive."

"Alright buddy, stay out in the open, and don't talk to anyone. I'll be at the bus station at eight, and I'll organise a hotel for you."

"Sounds great, and thanks again."

"Don't mention it. Hasta Luego!"

Owen left the payphone, pulling his backpack and guitar case out of the booth and trekking into the leafy town square. The smell of flamed pork and pungent fresh fruits swirled around the scores of street stalls where beckoning women held up bright fabrics and wire jewellery. Avoiding the stares and outstretched hands, he stumbled into a table filled with wide-eyed tortoises frozen in lacquer and twisted into crude poses. He shuddered, skipping between the tables and adjusting his glasses.

Standing against a cement-rendered dental clinic was a dark, muscular man with a flattened face and narrow eyes. He watched Owen with a languorous expression, only his eyes moving. He remained so still that Owen wondered for a second if he was a statue performer. He was used to attention since arriving in Latin America, but this stare was more intimidating than inquisitive.

Perched at the other end of the dental clinic, also unmoving, was a soldier in a crumpled dark green uniform. Both men kept up the brazen staring before making what seemed to be eye contact with each other. A fleeting smile from the soldier while he glanced at the other man gave Owen an uncomfortable impression that they were colleagues. Paranoid theories rushed through his mind – were these men enemies of Spadafora who knew that he had the doctor's notes? Or perhaps undercover DEA agents who wanted to question his intentions in Panama? Or simply two locals smiling at each other about the appearance of a clumsy, pale-faced foreigner in their town? All theories made him uncomfortable, and he hastily followed a sign for public toilets.

"Señor, busca un hotel?"

Owen turned to see the flat-faced man following him. A chill scuttled across his sweaty back. "No, no necesito," he replied, continuing to walk around a corner towards the toilets.

A stray dog blocked the path, its yellow eyes staring up at Owen blankly as it chewed on a dusty bone.

"Señor, señor!"

"Esta bien," Owen growled as the man continued to follow. He decided to continue past the toilets in fear that the man would wait outside for him, but the alleyway became cluttered with cardboard boxes and milk crates. The acrid smell of urine filled the air and he covered his nose in repulsion.

Rapid footsteps made him turn, but his reactions were too slow. A sickening crack turned the scene into a blur of red and popping black circles. He lost consciousness, his body limp as it slumped into the cement.

Torn clouds covered the afternoon sun as Owen's eyes slowly blinked open. His glasses were gone, and the side of his head had swollen into a lump that throbbed against a cold concrete wall. Blood had flowed down his neck, and was now crusted over his exposed chest. He tried to sit upright, letting out an anxious groan as he saw the bare skin on his wrist where his father's gold watch should have been. The haziness of his surroundings failed to come into focus as his hands swept desperately over the crumbled stone floor.

Spanish graffiti enveloped a far wall, and as he sat up completely he realised that he lay within the ruins of an old church. His backpack was ripped open beside a tussock of weeds, its contents strewn across the floor.

The sounds of the town centre were a distant drone. As he stared through the holes in the church wall he tried to piece together what had happened. He rose to his feet, stumbling, and continued his search. He could feel his passport tucked into the inside of his jeans, and the pressure of the American notes still hidden in his shoe. But with a gasp of horror and dismay he found his leather-bound notepad – two months' worth of interviews and journal entries – now reduced to ashes beneath the remains of the church's pulpit. His hands flailed through the wisps of charcoal, dizziness threatening to take his consciousness, but he found no sign of the doctor's notes.

He began to sort through his clothes and toiletries, tucking and arranging them fastidiously in his backpack. The padlock for his bag fell out of one of his jackets, the metal now reshaped by the crooked teeth of bolt cutters. His anger was suddenly too weak to hold back his pain. He slumped dejectedly into the ashes, tears stinging at the corners of his eyes.

La Concepción turned a ghostly purple in the twilight as Owen lumbered into the town centre. Ignoring the stares of a few remaining street vendors, he traced his steps from the phone booth through the square and into the alleyway in which he had been attacked. He found a patch of blood on the pavement where he had fallen and the cracked remains of his glasses. He cursed angrily, kicking at the milk crates. A group of young children had gathered on a doorstep behind him, whispering and giggling in the light of a streetlamp.

He ignored the children, wrapping his glasses in a shirt and placing them carefully into his backpack. He turned to leave when one of the girls called out in Spanish.

"Will you play us a song?"

He looked back, puzzled. At that moment, a grubby boy shuffled from the doorway carrying Owen's guitar case.

Owen's eyes widened in shock, his chafed lips stinging as he smiled. "Muchas gracias!"

The boy giggled shyly and looked to his sister for permission to hand the guitar over.

Owen knelt down and excitedly unclipped the buckles of the guitar case. Butterflies streamed through his stomach as he pulled the guitar out and tilted the sound hole into the light. And there, still wedged innocuously inside were the doctor's notes.

Chapter Four

Bridge of the Americas, Panama Canal.
September 13th, 1985.

Owen peeled his face from the bus window as the jungle gave way to a giant yellow-brown waterway that snaked into a mountainous horizon. He adjusted the bandage around his head as he stared wearily over the edge of a grand white bridge. His eyes suddenly widened as he realised what he was seeing.

Scores of cargo ships lined both sides of the canal beside giant loading docks, ominous dark blue cranes and thousands of neatly stacked shipping containers. The steamy Panama City skyline was emerging through the front window of the bus, its white skyscrapers shimmering like a mirage in the afternoon sun.

Owen curled the doctor's notes on his lap and slipped them back into his guitar case, glancing around to make sure none of the other passengers were watching him. He tried to check the time on his watch but instead rubbed sadly at the tan line where it should have been.

At first glance the outskirts of Panama City were indistinguishable from other Latin American capitals. Moustached motorbike riders swerved around brightly coloured rickshaws and stared up into passing buses, their eyes inquisitive at the sight of a gringo on public transport. Once majestic Art Deco architecture was hidden beneath peeling whitewash, barbed wire and rusting metal bars. But like entering a teleport into another country, manicured lawns suddenly appeared beside baseball grounds, and proud American soldiers strutted through car parks full of polished Fords, Chevrolets and yellow ex-county school buses.

Deeper into the city, advertisements for Coca-Cola reigned the rooftops and balconies overflowed with bougainvilleas, chaotic power lines, women taking in washing and curious children wearing American fashion brands. Western businessmen walked briskly around gutters and alleyways wearing tailored white and tan suits, white shoes and, to Owen's amusement: Panama hats.

The bus finally reached its destination in a street of neon electronics advertisements and international banks. Owen stumbled into the crowded street, wishing that he had his glasses to see the passing faces clearly. He pulled his backpack out from the compartment beneath the bus and tried to search through the swarm of exiting passengers.

"I think the bandage suits you, buddy," came a thick American accent.

Owen spun around, his bruised face beaming. Standing proudly before him was the tallest man in a crowd of bustling Panamanians. His blonde hair shone nearly as brightly as the string of medals that adorned his firmly pressed uniform. A golden oak leaf was pinned beside his embroidered nametag, where the capital letters "THORN" gave Owen flashes of his uncle a decade before. He was about to respond to his cousin's greeting when he was buried in a powerful embrace.

"Great to finally see you," Thorn grinned as he placed his massive hands down on Owen's shoulders and studied his face. "And I guess I should be giving your guitar a hug too, hey?"

Owen smiled meekly, his eyes cast downwards. "Thanks again for picking me up, and for staying up on the phone last night."

"Hey, don't mention it, I've always got your back. Now let's get out of here."

Thorn grabbed Owen's guitar case and backpack and marched through a path in the crowd that seemed to magically open up for him. Owen struggled to keep up until they reached Thorn's shining Jeep, parked defiantly in a loading zone.

"I've got you a room in Casco Viejo," Thorn shouted through the roar of a truck as he dropped Owen's belongings in the back and then opened the door for him. "And I've already let the Canadian embassy know that you were attacked. There's nothing they can do, but it's one less thing for you to worry about."

"Jeez, thanks a million," Owen exclaimed as he pulled his seatbelt on.

The Jeep's engine started with a guttural growl, and moved through the growing shadows of Panama's metropolis with an air of arrogance. Sliding on a pair of gold aviators and flicking down the sunshield, Thorn pointed out across the glinting Bay of Panama. "That's Casco Viejo over there, the rocky headland where the Presidential Palace is, so you'll be close to the man himself. He's currently in France though, so I suspect you'll miss him."

"That's probably a good thing," Owen muttered under his breath.

"So, when is your flight out of here again?"

"Next Friday, at this stage. It will be more than enough time to get the article done, as long as no one else comes after the files."

Thorn laughed. "I don't think you were attacked for that, buddy. It's just lucky that no one found them. You said they stole your watch, didn't you? That's probably all they were after."

Owen rubbed at his naked wrist, sighing. "It was my Dad's one, you know, with the gold band?"

"I can't say I remember it. But don't fret, we'll find you another one. The first thing you learn in Panama is to not be sentimental; nothing here lasts."

Owen frowned, staring at the white Presidential Palace and its reflection on the water.

Thorn pushed up the sun visor as a tight avenue full of slums took away the glare reflecting off the water. "So who did the handiwork on that bandage of yours?"

"It was a family in La Concepción. They took me into their house and treated me, then fed me and gave me the phone to call you. Panama isn't all bad!"

"Ha! You're a lucky bastard. I'm surprised they didn't steal the rest of your things while they were fixing you up."

The Jeep rolled loudly across a cobblestone entrance into a mysterious maze of paved streets and colonial architecture. The Presidential Palace was in clear view now, resting proudly at the edge of the bay, its white pillars staring scornfully at the rising Panama City skyline.

The Jeep bounced to a stop in front of an old white tower wedged between two government buildings. Thin French doors stared down from behind boutique balconies and the swaying fronds of giant palm trees.

"This is it," Thorn declared, stepping out. Again, he took Owen's guitar and backpack and led the way into a bright pink foyer where The Rolling Stones prattled from a transistor radio and a rusting fan swung in the round, powdered face of the receptionist.

It took Thorn just a few seconds of Spanish before the lady smiled broadly and turned towards Owen. He was fumbling through his backpack for his wad of American dollars.

"Buddy, it's on me," Thorn smiled. "Just give her some ID and the room is yours."

"Oh right," Owen responded, looking up in surprise. He reached into the front of his jeans where he knew his passport was hidden. "Here you go. And thanks again, Joe, but I'm going to pay for this."

The receptionist took Owen's dog-eared passport as Thorn chuckled. "This place is owned by a friend of mine. Keep your money, the room is free."

Owen was about to respond when a shrill scream rang through the foyer. The receptionist had dropped his passport in horror, and it now lay open on the floor, the photo page staring upwards.

Owen's stomach churned in horror. Someone had slashed a mark over his photograph, the knife piercing through his eyes. He bent over to make out the symbols: "F-8".

"Don't touch it!" Thorn thundered. He pulled a handkerchief from his chest pocket and, kneeling down, carefully wrapped up the passport. He muttered some Spanish to the receptionist as she retreated further behind her desk, then turned to Owen, his expression grave. "When did this occur?"

Owen stammered anxiously. "I-I don't know. It must have happened last night. They must have taken it out and put it back when I was unconscious."

Thorn sighed heavily, staring downwards. After a few seconds, he breathed to Owen, "I've got to go. Get yourself a taxi to the embassy tomorrow and sort out a new passport, and don't tell anyone about this. I'll come by again in the evening. Hopefully I'll have some answers for you."

It was nearly dark when Owen emerged onto his balcony, the bandage discarded and his hair wet from a lukewarm shower. He took a sip from a bottle of Heineken that he found beside the chocolates in his fridge, his face now relaxing with the familiar taste. He watched as the last of the sunset caressed the grand architecture that spanned to the end of the headland, but his attention was drawn to hundreds of slums that gripped the slopes along the bay. Smoke crawled up the hill, bringing with it the smell of burning tortillas, tomato paste and Caribbean spices. The muffled sound of guitars and singing wrestled with the shattering of glass bottles and drunken shouting.

"You'll find me at the red door," he whispered to himself as he scanned the buildings in view.

The beer was gone by the time the sun sank beneath the ocean, taking with it Owen's lingering fears and paranoia. He lit an oil lantern over the outside table, and after carefully organising the doctor's files and a notepad in front of him, he attempted to start his article. But the questions were building up like a stack of unanswered mail each time that he tried to bring pen to paper. Where did he start with all of these notes? What did Spadafora want him to focus upon? Was RUBUS even a real person? And how could he publish this if he couldn't confirm the sources?

He decided to run with his instincts and traipsed out of the hotel's foyer, pulling the hood of his jacket over his head.

The streets were lit brightly enough to make out the colours on each door, but his vision was failing him. For the next hour he traced each street to the end of the headland, his eyes moulded into a painful squint. The cold was beginning to win over his stubbornness when he stumbled into a dark street that was empty except for a homeless man sleeping against the back entrance to a restaurant. A large red door was illuminated by the streetlight opposite the man, bringing a flutter to Owen's chest.

Two alleyways bordering the residence were overgrown with vines and bird's nest ferns that filled cracks in the limewashed walls. Mangled barbed wire separated two storeys of balconies from the alleyways, and giant red windowsills and corrugated iron gutters were caked with salt spray. Owen hesitated, staring up into the dark windows above before knocking loudly.

The windows remained dark, and the rumbling of the door gave a hollow echo from within. Again he knocked, his eyes flicking up and down the street. Two blocks away, a wide troop carrier slowly grunted around a corner, its high beam headlights washing across Owen's face. He stumbled on the cobblestones as he retreated from the door, passed a nervous hand through his hair, and decided to turn back towards the hotel. But as he began to retreat the door creaked open, and a young female face peered out

"Um, buenas noches," Owen stammered, leaning in towards her. "Uh –"

"Tiene una cita? Do you have an appointment?" the lady asked, glancing up and down the street. She was dressed only in black lingerie, and her dark curly hair was tinged purple by the soft light within. She had a pretty face, but the concern in her eyes and the layers of makeup stole much of her beauty, leaving her with an aura of melancholy that made Owen more uncomfortable.

"I-I'm after Doctor Spadafora," Owen whispered. "I was told to meet him at a red door in Casco Viejo."

"There is no doctor here," the lady responded sharply.

"Oh, I see," he murmured. "Well I've obviously got the wrong place."

The cry of a baby came from deep within the house as the lady began to swing the door shut. "He never showed up," she whispered, just loud enough for Owen to hear before the latch clicked shut.

Chapter Five

Soho, London.
Present day.

The last of the students shuffled out of the freshly painted doors, their high-pitched voices fading down the steps to where their mothers waited beneath black umbrellas. The drizzling rain had become heavier through the morning, and was now fingering along the windowpanes of Miss Hindmarsh's dance studio. The growing darkness had turned the inside of the windows into mirrors, and Jenna found herself staring at the reflection of her best friend Tracey as they stretched on the empty studio floor. Their faces were drained from teaching, but relieved to finally be alone.

"So what day do you come back to London?" Tracey asked as she stared back at Jenna's reflection.

"Friday next week," Jenna replied, stretching her feet behind her head and sticking her tongue out.

"Pfft, you look like an idiot. So you'll be here for the photo shoot next Saturday?"

"Maybe, if the photographer isn't the same creep as last time."

"No, it's a different one, still a guy though, so I'm sure you'll be singled out again."

Jenna smirked, flipping her legs back in front.

"Oh come on, you love the attention."

"Whatever," Jenna protested. "You're the one who was sucking up to what's-his-name last time."

"Ha! Unlike you, I am reserved for one man only."

"Yeah, a complete jerk."

"At least he exists. And is not some crusty American politician."

"Hey, that guy was sweet, and obviously has an eye for talent."

"Pfft!" Tracey bounced to her feet, pulling the ponytail out of her blonde hair and making for the change rooms. "Well in that case you should introduce him to your mother. I'm sure she would leave him completely smitten."

"Ha!" Jenna scoffed. "Completely broke as well."

"Aww, don't be harsh, your Mum's an angel. How is she doing, anyway?"

Jenna frowned, tucking her hair behind her ears. "She's okay, still active and everything. She's getting chemo again this evening so I'm going to try to be there. Speaking of which, I'd better get moving. What's the time?"

"You're wearing your new watch, hun."

"Yeah, but it's analogue, and –"

"You're such a ditz!" Tracey shook her head as she pulled her phone from her locker. "It's nearly twelve. Are you staying for lunch?"

"No, I can't I'm sorry. I better run."

Tracey pouted dramatically. "Okay babe, well say hi to your Mum for me, and call me when you get home."

"Will do!"

Jenna felt a wave of excitement as she hugged her friend goodbye, the realisation that she was about to leave London finally breaking through all other distractions. The stress of constant performances had created a void beyond today, and as she slipped on her favourite pair of flats, the images, smells and tastes of home were itching. She couldn't wait to drop the London façade.

The clapping of Jenna's shoes echoed off the cement walls of the underground car park. She spied the cherry red shine of Molly, her Morris Minor, at the end of a row of cars, and reached into her new handbag for the keys. The unfamiliar array of pockets had conspired against her, and she stopped beside a large grey van to pull the bag wide open.

It was more a feeling of being watched than anything that alerted her senses, but it made her pause. She looked up slowly, shadows playing at the top of her vision. Something definitely moved within the back of the van. She kept staring, and the reflection of another car in the back windscreen slowly melded into the pale face of a man staring back at her. He tried to duck out of sight as Jenna silently gaped. She pulled her bag closed and hurried onwards to her car, looking back over her shoulder.

The loud rattling of the keys in Molly's door added to Jenna's nervousness. Once inside she quickly reached across and locked the doors. The old car started with a hesitant shudder, after which Ray Charles began crooning from the wood-rimmed cassette player. The upbeat chorus was too much; she turned down the music and began reversing.

The rain continued through the narrow streets of Soho until it was swallowed by a stubborn layer of grey smog that blended the murky water of the Thames into the industry beyond. Jenna frowned at the view, wiping the sleeves of her jacket across her fogging windscreen and cursing at the crawling traffic. It took another half hour until she was accelerating onto the M40, turning the music over to a pop station and singing along.

Jenna positioned a foam cup of bubble tea beside the steering wheel and tried to break the lid off a plastic bowl of salad. She knew that her mother would be scourging her for trying to multitask while driving, but there something liberating about ignoring safety on the highway. After wiping her lips she flicked her eyes up to the rear view mirror and spotted a large grey van following at a constant distance behind. The windows were tinted, and the driver's face was nothing more than a blur in the rain. She changed lanes, braking and frowning as the van resisted the opportunity to overtake, slowing down even more and ducking behind a lorry.

Jenna veered off the highway and slid Molly between two larger cars to steal a vacant fuel bowser. The van also took the exit and was parking at a nearby fast food restaurant. She stared at it warily as she grabbed the fuel nozzle. The numberplates were an unfamiliar blue, and they were too far away to record. An argument between an elderly couple at the next fuel bowser distracted her attention, and when she turned back towards the restaurant the van was gone.

Industry and suburbia were soon left in Molly's wake, replaced by green paddocks, quaint hedges and bungalows hidden in patches of woodland. The spires of Harmiston's churches and university buildings rose through the mist, and an old grey draught horse leaned against a wooden fence bordering the road. Jenna pursed her lips. That same horse had been leaning on that fence for as long as she could remember. And on the hill to the left was an eternally crumbling barn with half of its roof missing; at the next crossroads were the same faded florist signs that no one ever bothered to take down, and lining the driveways of the next two farms would be yellowing poplar trees. She knew the intricacies of every road and laneway from here to her mother's house, and there was both comfort and derision in knowing that they would always be the same.

She reached into the glove box, pulling out an old tape and sliding it into Molly's cassette player. She drummed her fingers on the steering wheel and sang emphatically, her thoughts turning to the high school friends she had failed to catch up with on her last visit home, and the nights of dancing to live music that awaited this weekend. The bars would be packed with a new cohort of cocky Harmiston boys to torment, and it would be warm enough now to sing through the university grounds after midnight, waking the security guards and then prancing into the darkness of the gardens.

The wind was picking up across the fields in the distance, and the clouds were coalescing into a dark green mass on the horizon. A blade of lightning printed itself over the silhouette of the town, silencing Jenna's singing as she slowed for road works. She pretended to ignore the wink of one of the workers as he zipped up his fluoro rain jacket and glanced nonchalantly into her wing mirror. Her cheeks suddenly smeared into a scowl.

The grey van reappeared like a ghostly sliver around the last bend. It slowed cautiously before the road works. Jenna bashed the dashboard, glaring into the mirror as though her aggression would make the driver turn around.

Was this an obsessed fan, or perhaps someone from the media? She accelerated after the road works and then veered sharply into a gravel driveway lined with swaying pine trees. Her expression remained grim as she watched the van continuing to slow, rumbling as it lowered gears, then juddering on down the road.

"Weirdo," Jenna growled, reversing and then accelerating back the same way in which she had come. She reached for her phone as she stopped again at the road works, debating whom to call, and noticed that she had a text message from her mother. She shot a glance into the rear-view mirror as she opened the text.

"Check Oscar's grave. I love you."

She narrowed her eyes in confusion and held down the call button. Ringing reverberated through the car, but the call went to voicemail.

"Hey Mum, it's me. What's the text about? I'm going the back way. Some weirdo has been following me. Should be there in ten. Love you."

A sign for Caversham Lane finally appeared from behind a row of hedges and Jenna made sure that she was the only car on the road before skidding Molly into the entrance. The lane was more overgrown than she remembered, with straggling privet and grand maple trees that were bending and thrashing in the wind. Dead leaves splattered like insects against the bonnet and collected on the windscreen wipers, but Jenna knew the lane too well to slow down.

A modest wooden house at the end of the lane had been home since Jenna could remember. The small acreage and surrounding orchards nursed memories in every overgrown corner, and the muddy creeks running along the boundary fences had destroyed more than a few of her dresses. It was a previous life that she was embarrassed by, and she had never taken any of her friends from the dance academy back here.

As she revved up the crunching gravel driveway to the back of the house she felt a stab of concern. The back door of the garage was open, and her mother's blue Mercedes was gone. She pulled on the handbrake and stepped out into a growing gale, her hair spraying wildly. Leaving her bags in the car, she skipped up to a small patio where she found that the back door was left ajar, vibrating and slamming in the wind. The smell of tobacco smoke and alcohol choked the back room as she slowly stepped inside, calling out her mother's name.

Chapter Six

An unfinished cigarette smouldered in a coffee mug at the foot of the living room curtains. Beside the mug lay an empty bottle of vodka and a cordless phone. Jenna's concern for her mother stalled her instinct to clean up the mess. She turned around and bounded upstairs.

Her bedroom was exactly as she had left it two months before. Posters of Audrey Hepburn and Katy Jurado adorned the walls, and photographs of her trip across France with Tracey formed a halo over her bed's headboard.

She moved slowly down the hallway, her eyes wide as she peered into her mother's bedroom. A suitcase lay open on the bed, half-packed with clothes and packaged food. The flickering monitor of her mother's computer lay on its side on a desk beside the window. The back of the computer had been pried open.

She remembered her mother's text message, her face contorted as she spun around and hurried downstairs. Throwing the back door open seemed to break the clouds' patience as a deluge of rain shattered like a haystack over the patio roof, needles of water stabbing into the steps below. She groaned. Positioning her jacket over her head, she ran into the tremulous branches of overgrown apple and plum trees that choked the path to the back of the yard.

Oscar's grave was located at the base of a weeping willow where twisted roots were now clawing through the tin fence and into the creek beyond. Jenna's thoughts were tinged with sadness as she thought of the old cocker spaniel that lay beneath the dirt here. She quickly dismissed the flashbacks and peered into the myriad of crevices that were being enveloped with water.

A sudden crunching of gravel added to the hammering of raindrops on the tin fence. Jenna tried to peer through the fruit trees to see who was on the driveway, but the leaves reached too high. Turning back to the tree trunk, she noticed a thick spider web that had been brushed aside, and hastily wedged her hand into the hole that it had covered. Sure enough, her fingers wrapped around a folded piece of paper. She unfolded the note in the protection of her jacket. Her eyes narrowed at her mother's uncharacteristically messy handwriting.

Rafael Cordoba.
Isla de Marfil, Gulf of Batabano, Cuba.
I love you.

Jenna shook her head in confusion, stuffing the note into the back pocket of her jeans and staring fearfully into the gale. A low rumbling reverberated through the ground, followed by the distant drumroll of thunder. She shivered, slipping off her flats and splashing through the mud. Wet leaves slapped at her cheeks as she pushed through the fruit trees and into the open grass beyond. She parted the tousled hair from her eyes and inhaled in shock.

Three police cars blocked the cul-de-sac at the front of the house, their lights flashing off the pine trees beyond. Parked in the driveway were two grey vans, their back doors being pulled open by gloved men in black rain jackets.

Jenna's heartbeat pounded violently as she began to creep around the house. She dropped to her hands and knees and peered through a low privet hedge.

"Miss Martinez."

Jenna spun around. Standing calmly behind her was a stocky man in a black trench coat, his face partly hidden behind a wide black umbrella and his exposed neck mottled with scars. His coarse voice had wrapped around her surname with a distinctly Latino accent, and the wrinkled olive skin of his cheeks had seen far more sun than could ever be found in England.

"What do you want?" Jenna stammered as she rose shakily to her feet. "Who are you?"

The man ignored her, carefully stepping over the hedge and waiting for her to follow him to the front of the house.

"Hey! What is going on?"

The scene became a blur of blue and red flashes, umbrellas and foam coffee cups. The men in black jackets entered the house from the back, unlocking the front doors and pulling open the garage. Jenna's shouts were ignored as the men began marching back and forth carrying desk drawers, files and boxes that they loaded unashamedly into the vans. One of the police officers pulled her away from her desperate grabs at the men, wrapping a plastic poncho around her and escorting her to one of the police cars. He opened a clipboard beside her, explaining to her a search warrant that was quickly dotted with rain. He tried to leave the clipboard in Jenna's hand, but she threw it back at him, shouting with rage and struggling against his wet grip on her arm.

All the while the Latino man watched from the front door. He tucked his phone into his coat and continued to stare at Jenna, ignoring her shouts as he carefully squeezed a capsule of tomato sauce into a brown paper bag. He swallowed his pastry slowly, his nostrils twitching as if tasting the air. When he looked up again the back door of a police car had been shut, and Jenna's cries were being driven into the storm.

Chapter Seven

Panama City.
September 14th, 1985.

Owen's eyes were wide for the photograph, his expression like that of a child caught raiding a pantry at midnight. The flash had reflected off the scar developing from his temple across his forehead, and he decided that breezing through customs checkpoints would be more difficult from now on. He tucked the new passport back into his jeans and asked the taxi driver to turn up the radio.

The news was being read hurriedly, and although Owen's translations were too slow to catch much of what was being said, he was sure that for the entire six-minute newscast Spadafora's name was not once mentioned.

The taxi pulled up before Owen's hotel and he slowly made his way into the foyer, his new passport hopefully a calming agent for the receptionist.

"Buenos dias, señor."

"Buenos dias," Owen smiled back, presenting the new passport to her.

The receptionist glanced at the awkward photograph, took a photocopy and then returned it hastily. Owen was already heading up the stairs when she called him back.

"Señor, tengo su traje. I have your suit."

Owen looked back, puzzled. "A suit? Para mi?"

"Si, si. From Major Thorn. You are going out tonight, to the club, no?" She reached under her desk and pulled out a black tuxedo in fresh plastic wrapping. A handwritten note was attached, which Owen read with raised eyebrows.

Owen, I figured you wouldn't have one. I've rounded up some contacts
for you to meet. You'll find me at the back of the Union Club at 8pm
~ JT.

The usual evening rain was pelting into the alleyways of Casco Viejo by the time Owen scampered out of the hotel. Within a few seconds his ruffled hair was dripping relentlessly onto the new suit. It wasn't until he rounded the corner to reach the entrance to the waterfront club that he remembered his concern for how much his light brown shoes – the only pair that he had – clashed with the jet black suit. A disapproving stare from two doormen brought back the embarrassment. They checked his passport, stared at each other for a moment and then nodded for him to enter.

The building was as grand inside as it was from the street. Suspended above lapping ocean waves and designed around an extravagant saltwater pool, the club was a tribute to Panama's elite. White colonial pillars supported balconies lined with palm trees and white-suited waiters glided between lavish bars. A giant oil painting of Noriega in military uniform hung in the foyer. It may have been Owen's poor vision, but the General's usually pockmarked face appeared to be smoothed over by the artist, and his grandiose posture evoked famously glorified portrayals of Napoleon. Another painting of the late General Torrijos, Panama's previous military ruler, adorned an archway through to the pool. The handsome depiction of the populist, womanising leader was far more lifelike than that of Noriega's. Ironically, thought Owen, it was Torrijos who was now dead.

The rain stopped suddenly and two exotic dancers ventured onto the side of the pool, their bare torsos twisting to the rhythm of a Creole jazz band dressed in red suits.

"Owen, my man! Over here!" The shout came from a table overlooking the bay where three men were framed by the smoke of their cigars.

Still worried about his shoes and the water dripping down his suit, Owen smiled awkwardly as Thorn paraded into the light. The hulking soldier's blonde hair was oiled back, his top few buttons undone and his white sleeves rolled up. He threw an enthusiastic palm into Owen's, his handshake nearly crushing his knuckles. "Thanks for coming, and sorry I couldn't catch up with you earlier."

"No problem," Owen cried over the sound of the band. "I got the passport sorted. So who are these contacts?"

"Come up and I'll introduce you. Waiter, dos cervezas más! Okay, the bulldog on the left is Conrad Ramirez. He's Puerto Rican, works for the CIA and is the one who tipped me off about Spadafora and the DEA, but don't mention you know that. The older bearded guy is Hector Goldstein. You've probably heard of him?"

"No, I don't think I have."

"Don't let him know that. He was a business associate of Noriega's until they had a falling out, but he knows everything about everyone in this city. He also runs a dance studio up on the hill where his daughter trains the dancers you see by the pool."

Owen glanced at the dancers as the younger of the two turned in his direction, but her face was too far away to make out her expression. Most of the men in the club were watching her, and she moved with a coolness and confidence that seemed to make their expressions more intense. Her partner was now sliding between a group of men in front of the band, handing out drinks.

Thorn led Owen into the darkness where the two men stood up to shake his hand.

"Bienvenido," Hector said gruffly with a slight nod, his eyes more focused on the dancers than his new acquaintance.

Conrad's smile was infectious as he warmly shook Owen's hand. "Cigar, compadre?" he asked with lively eyes. He was no older than Thorn, but his brown skin was patchy and his bent nose gave him the appearance of a man who had been in more than a few fights.

"Uh, no, no I'm fine, thanks." Owen smiled uneasily, taking a beer from the waiter and descending into the chair that Thorn had pulled out for him.

"I'm afraid he's not the cigar type," Thorn winked, resting his arm over the back of Owen's chair.

Conrad smiled comically, forcing out a slither of smoke. "So are you sure that you two are related?"

"Apparently," Owen shrugged. His smile quickly faded as he stared across at Hector, who was carefully studying his face while carving the flesh out of a stack of oysters. Owen took a long gulp from his beer, wiping the froth from his mouth and trying to relax.

"His mother was my father's sister," Thorn was explaining. "Although he was brought up in Canada, so perhaps that explains things?"

"I won't hold that against you, amigo," Conrad nodded at Owen affirmatively. "In fact, the further away you were from this clown and his father, the better!"

"Hey now," Thorn retorted. "What are you trying to say?"

The banter was interrupted as Hector tossed an oyster shell into his pile and cleared his throat. "Owen," he began with a baritone rumble, "I understand that Hugo Spadafora has given you a file; a dossier, on Noriega's underworld dealings?"

Owen shot a glance at Thorn, who failed to give any telling eye signals back and buried his expression in his beer. Owen decided to go along vaguely, his stares in Thorn's direction prying for some pointers. "Well, yes, I did receive some documents."

"And you found in those documents some information about a CIA agent by the name of RUBUS, yes?"

Owen shifted uneasily until Thorn broke the silence. "It's okay buddy, these guys know everything."

"Uh, well yes," Owen replied finally. "Um, I don't suppose you've heard –"

"No creo," Hector said firmly. "There are no agents by that name. The codename 'RUBUS' was used by a CIA agent ten years ago whose role was to confuse Noriega's intelligence officers during the Panama Canal negotiations. It turned out, however, that the agent was actually selling recordings of the American negotiators to Noriega. When the Americans found out, the agent was dismissed. Noriega later used the codename mockingly, to let the US know that he had infiltrated them. Now if the codename has appeared in Spadafora's files, I dare say that your doctor friend has been strung along, most probably by Noriega himself."

"But," Owen winced. "Spadafora's main source of information was Noriega's pilot, who was later assassinated after speaking to him. Surely there's got to be something in that?"

"I haven't seen the documents," Hector responded. "So I can't speak with authority, but if you would like me to go through them, I'm sure I can determine what is going on."

"I have not read them also," Conrad broke in, sighing. "But from what I gather from the DEA in Costa Rica, the transportation dates and routes that Spadafora described were looked into closely. It was found that the National Guard was indeed smuggling Panamanian goods into America for sale on the black market – mangoes."

"Oh dear," Hector scoffed, leaning forward and grinning through his thick beard.

"Spadafora may be an infamous guerrilla," Conrad continued with a slight smile, "but I would have to question his skills as an informant."

Owen turned desperately to Thorn, whose head was bowed.

"I'm sorry, Owen," Thorn sighed. "I was going to tell you earlier, but I thought you should hear it from the horse's mouth."

"But somebody was obviously concerned that I had those documents," Owen pressed, "and they tried to steal them from me in La Concepción. You really think that people would go to that effort if they knew the notes were about... mango smuggling?"

"You were robbed in La Concepción for your watch," Hector frowned. "Just like Noriega's pilot, I'd say you were the victim of one of a thousand crimes that will go unsolved in Panama every day."

"And my passport? What they did to it? Joe has no doubt told you –"

"I wouldn't worry about that. Nothing more than some local thieves trying to leave a signature."

Owen finished off the rest of his beer, trying to prevent images of the doctor's files from twisting with his calm expression. He wanted to ask where Spadafora was – why he hadn't yet surfaced in Panama City – but feared another discouraging response. Had the doctor already realised that he wouldn't get anywhere with his research and given up?

"I'm going to grab some more drinks and mingle," Thorn announced, standing up from the table and giving Owen a sympathetic frown. "What can I get you all?"

"Old Parr for me," Conrad said as he spun his empty glass in his hand. "And I think our muchacho needs one too. Oh yes, he does."

"I'll come with you, Joe," Hector said, excusing himself.

Conrad turned to Owen with a benevolent smile as the other two left. "Don't let Hector get you down, my friend, he's a bitter old bastard."

Owen was biting his bottom lip, trying to hide his confusion and disappointment.

"So how long have you been a journalist for?"

Owen continued to look distracted. "I graduated two years ago, and I've been working for a small paper since then. This is the first freelance work that I've done."

"Well don't go thinking that doesn't make you as good as anyone else in the media down here. And if it's any consolation, I've always believed that Spadafora is an honest man. He may have been off target with RUBUS, but I hardly believe that there isn't some truth behind his musings."

"So you think Hector is lying?"

"I didn't say that," Conrad frowned, "but he is stubborn and over-confident. He only gets his information from someone else, and he certainly isn't the 'horse's mouth.'"

Owen studied Conrad's expression as a waiter appeared with the whiskeys.

"The CIA is a giant spider web of information," Conrad continued, his hand gestures becoming animated as he took a sip, "but for every strand of truth, there's inevitably two more lies woven into it."

Owen continued to frown in thought, and found himself staring out towards the lights of the city. "Joe mentioned that Hector was a business associate of Noriega's," he said slowly, turning to face Conrad again. "What exactly was the business he was involved in?"

"Now you're sounding more like a journalist," Conrad grinned, somewhat deviously. "Oh yes, he certainly had dealings with Noriega, as well as Omar Torrijos. Like Noriega, he also earned a wage from the CIA supplying information and technology."

"Technology?"

"Hector was the CIA's main player in trafficking the latest weaponry from Europe to the Contras," Conrad explained. "But he also made his not-so-humble living importing recording devices. He supplies only the best, and Noriega was always his biggest client. You see, Noriega is obsessed with eaves-dropping. He records virtually every conversation he has. He sells some of the tapes to the Americans and the Cubans, and keeps the rest for blackmail."

Owen's excited thoughts were becoming blurred in the haze of the whiskey, and he wished that he had his notepad. "Blackmail? Who has he blackmailed?"

"Everyone," came a gruff voice from the darkness beside them. It was Hector, who had emerged unnoticed from a flight of steps and was adjusting his tie. He took a seat at the table, clapping his glass down drunkenly. "Politicians, diplomats, lawyers, journalists, the CIA; even regular civilians. We all have our secrets, and Noriega knows them all." He slumped backwards in his chair, running a hand through his silver beard. "Since his days as a policeman, Noriega has gained power over his superiors by spying on them. Without that information, he would never have been promoted above a captain."

"And no one has tried to do the same to him?" Owen queried. "I mean, everyone knows that Noriega is crooked."

"Oh yes," Conrad smiled sadly. "But that's exactly the problem. How do you frame someone as corrupt when it's already out there for the world to see? You're going to need to prove more than just a few shady deals with the Cubans. And this is why Spadafora has to prove something big if he wants anyone to listen to him."

"And if he is actually on to something, he better watch his back," Hector said in a foreboding tone. He slowly leaned back, lighting a cigar and turning to Owen. "I've spoken to your cousin. I want you to come to my house tomorrow evening with him. And bring those documents with you."

Conrad eyed Hector suspiciously and questioned him in Spanish. The haze of the whiskey prevented Owen from following their discussion, but he judged from the tone of their voices that they were in disagreement.

Owen turned his attention to the dancers below as they both floated behind a pillar into the darkness. His thoughts were scattered, and it took him several seconds to notice that only the elder dancer had emerged into the light. He began to squint, and slowly made out the silhouette of the younger dancer leaning back and pushing her body up against a man dressed in white. Owen kept squinting, his eyes suddenly widening as he saw that the man was Thorn. His cheek was pressed against her face, and his hand was slowly moving up her thigh.

The dancer eventually drifted back into the light and Thorn slid leisurely along the edge of the darkness. He hopped up the same staircase that Hector had used and emerged beside the table. His nose was noticeably red and he brushed at it uncomfortably.

"I hope these two haven't been ignoring you, have they?" Thorn asked Owen drunkenly.

"Of course not," Conrad reassured. "Owen's been telling us all about how you scammed your ascent through the ranks of the army."

Thorn suppressed a burp and grinned proudly. "It's all lies; my charm and good looks had nothing to do with it!"

"You're a fool," Conrad blurted.

The band had been replaced with an Italian man playing the saxophone, and the whiskey glasses began to crowd the table. Owen felt his balance swaying and his vision distorting, and he tried to exclude himself from the drunken banter that continued flying between Conrad and Hector. He tried to start a conversation with Thorn, but instead found himself leaning clumsily over the edge of the balcony, the smell of the sea soothing his aching head.

It was after two in the morning by the time Owen stumbled into the hotel. The bright pink walls of the foyer were bending and twisting into triangles, making him stagger awkwardly past the front desk. He hiccupped loudly and then snickered at the shapes dancing up the staircase. Grinning cartoon faces burst like bubbles as he held onto the staircase rails, guiding himself clumsily up to his floor. He fumbled for his keys, eventually pushing aggressively at the doorknob until the door creaked open. He switched on the light and stared.

The bed had been turned on its side, the mattress stripped of its sheets and littered with the contents of his backpack. The door to the balcony was open, a gentle breeze tossing the lacy white curtains inwards and brushing over the splinters of his guitar.

Chapter Eight

Harmiston Police Station.
Present day.

"It appears your mother's lawyer must be too busy for you," said the Latino man as he draped his trench coat over a seat and carefully sat down. He stared like a hawk into Jenna's eyes from across the table, his mottled neck rippling as he took a long sip from a foam coffee cup. Behind him, two stern-looking men dressed in pale business shirts occupied the corners of the dull blue interviewing room.

Jenna fidgeted nervously, staring up at the black video camera in the corner and then at the closed metal door.

A grainy photocopied document slid out of a pile beside the man's hand and across the table. "Miss Martinez," he spoke in his distinct accent, "what do you see before you?"

Jenna narrowed her eyes. "It's-it's a birth certificate. It's my mother's."

"And what name is written on that birth certificate?"

"My mother's name – Teresa Martinez. Why do you have her birth certificate? What is this about?"

Another document slid across the desk.

"And this," the man said slowly. He took another sip from his cup and carefully wiped his lips with a napkin. "Whose birth certificate is this?"

"Uh, someone called Eva… Miranda."

"Correct. Now, do you know who Eva Miranda is?"

"I don't know." She shook her head. "I-I've never heard of her."

The man studied Jenna's face carefully. "I see. Now, who is in this photo?"

A black and white image was flicked across the desk. An attractive young woman was shown leaping off a dance floor, her bare torso bearing a distinctive birthmark.

"That's my mother," Jenna stared, the curiosity of seeing her mother in such a pose quickly quelled by the horror of the name written beneath the photo.

"Correct," the man smiled. "That is indeed your mother, before she disappeared from Panama in 1989."

"What?!"

"The birth certificate on your right is a fake. A good one, oh yes, but a fake nonetheless."

"No," Jenna wheezed. "No, no, no. You're not making any sense."

"Fraud is a serious crime," the man sighed, "but that is not why we are here. Twenty-six years ago an arrest warrant was issued for Eva Miranda in Panama. She was to be charged for the murder of a United States marine during the invasion of Panama."

"What?!" Jenna cried again. "No, this is ridiculous. What is this? That's not true! You must have made a mistake."

"Please remain calm," the man continued, his hand motioning for her to stay in her seat. "You do not want to make this situation any more difficult for yourself. Now you are, at the moment, free to leave here at any time. From our perspective you have not committed any crime. And honestly, I don't believe that you have any knowledge of your mother's past. All that I am asking is for you to tell us where she might be."

Tears were streaming down Jenna's cheeks, falling from the base of her chin. She tried to talk, but her words became an incoherent stutter as she began to hyperventilate. The door to the interviewing room opened and a plain clothed officer presented her with a cup of water. He also laid a document next to the Latino man, who picked it up and then consulted with the men behind him.

"Take your time," the Latino man said calmly, still staring at the document before him. "In through your nose, out through your mouth. Let's keep it together here."

"My Mum isn't some kind of fugitive, this is ridiculous. She's a dance teacher, you've got this all wrong!"

"I don't expect you to comprehend this information, Miss Martinez. The only thing we want from you is to know where your mother might have gone? Does she have any close friends in the area? We have an alert out for her vehicle registration, and we have questioned your neighbours, but so far we have no leads. It's not unexpected, of course, as she seems to be very good at disappearing."

"I don't know," Jenna sobbed after a minute of laying her head in her heads. "I don't know where she is. She was expecting me this afternoon; I'm supposed to take her to hospital. She's sick, okay! She's sick, and you can't do this to her!"

The man leaned forward, placing the document that he had received on the table and spinning it around for Jenna to see. "Twelve thirty-three this afternoon you received a text message from your mother. At twelve fifty-four you made a call to her, and left a voice message. Now what, may I ask, was your mother referring to by 'Oscar's grave'?"

Jenna gave the man a hostile stare, her nostrils flaring. Images streamed through her mind: Oscar licking her face, flashes of light as she danced on stage, chandeliers and cocktails, her mother standing and clapping. She pushed herself tightly against the chair, subconsciously protecting the folded piece of paper in the back pocket of her jeans.

"I don't know," Jenna responded, glaring into the man's dark eyes.

"A cat, perhaps? Although I recall from your mother's medical records that she is allergic to cats, isn't she? Perhaps the dog in the photos on your mother's mantelpiece, buried in your back yard, oh yes?"

Jenna struggled to keep a poker face, and she could feel the man's stare boring deep into her swollen eyes. She turned away, inhaling and shaking.

"But your mother wouldn't exhume the remains now, would she? She must have placed something there, a message to you, perhaps. And you were in the back yard when I found you."

"Who the hell are you?!" Jenna exclaimed, standing up from her chair and slamming her palms on the table.

The man ignored her, calmly turning to the men behind him. "Have the yard searched. Look for a large tree; somewhere you would bury a dog beneath. Don't be afraid to excavate."

"I want to talk to someone else," Jenna cried. "I don't know who you are, and I don't trust you. This can't be legal!"

The man sighed, leaning back and taking another sip from his coffee. "The police have organised a counsellor for you, and legal advice is available should you wish to discuss how this matter will proceed when your mother is detained. We aren't here to hurt you, Miss Martinez, or your mother. But that being said, what we have just discussed requires a degree of confidentiality. And I ask, with repercussions for a refusal, that you sign the following clause."

Jenna scowled as another sheet of paper was put before her. She quickly scanned the dot points and shook her head. "I don't understand this. I want my mother's lawyer, and I'm not signing or saying anything until she's here."

"I would sign that if I were you," the man frowned.

She remained silent, keeping eye contact with the man until he turned away.

"Okay then, let's terminate this interview and reconvene after we see to old Oscar, shall we? You're free to go, but your mother's house will have visitors until she decides to show some concern for her daughter's wellbeing."

The men all stood up and made for the door, whispering as they left.

"Who are you people?" Jenna asked spitefully as the Latino man ascended to his feet. "You never even showed me your ID."

The man smiled. He gathered together the documents on the desk, stared again at Jenna, then walked out of the room.

Chapter Nine

El Chorrillo, Panama City.
September 15th, 1985.

O wen stared out the window of Thorn's Jeep as it grunted through the slums of Chorrillo, slowing for a group of teenagers in torn denim to roll past on their oversized bikes. The Jeep sped up again as they passed La Comandancia – the imposing headquarters of the Panama Defence Forces. The ugliness of the guarded concrete prism made Owen wince, and his cluttered thoughts turned to home. He could see his workmates gathering in a small bar around the corner from the office, their notes about local ice hockey games and council elections stained with the rings of their beer glasses. His vision slowly melted into the view he would see from the plane home, and the Jeep's window danced with images of dark green conifers and glacial lakes stretching languidly to the horizon. He could almost feel the chill waiting to greet him when he walked out of the airport, and for just a second he could smell the multi-coloured air fresheners that dangled from the rear-view mirror of his old station wagon. He sighed heavily, thoughts of last night bringing him back to reality and exposing the smoky haze now hovering over Panama's slums and soaking up the afternoon sun.

"Cheer up, buddy," Thorn said suddenly, giving Owen's shoulder a nudge. "It could have been worse – they could have broken into your room while you were there."

Owen continued to frown and stare out the window, his eyes glazed over.

"Oh come on, the files were useless anyway, you heard what Hector said."

"Who else have you been talking to? Who else knew about me, and knew about Spadafora's files?"

Thorn laughed weakly as the Jeep slowed, rumbling uphill into an exclusive suburb overlooking the city. "What are you talking about? I didn't tell anyone else, only Conrad and Hector. And you can trust those guys, buddy, they've been there for me ever since I arrived in Panama."

"But we discussed this," Owen sighed. "This was between you and I; no one else."

"Now hang on, Owen," Thorn spat aggressively, pulling onto the side of the road. "What are you trying to say? That you think someone found out about you through me? That's bullshit, alright, I would never put you in any danger!"

"I'm not saying that," Owen shook his head. "I trust you, you know that, and I wouldn't have gotten anywhere without your leads. But I don't trust those other guys."

Thorn pulled on the handbrake angrily. "Where do you think I get my leads from, Owen? I'm a soldier, not a CIA agent. Conrad and Hector supply me with everything I know, and I trust them with my life."

"But you never told me that before. I only found out about them last night. And I only found out last night that you're seeing one of Hector's dancers. I'm not just a journalist, Joe; I'm your cousin. You've got to start telling me things."

Thorn clenched his teeth. "So you saw me with her, did you?"

"I saw you making out with her in the dark, if that's what you mean."

"What, so I'm not allowed to have some fun without telling my little cousin? Or are you just jealous because you aren't getting any?"

Owen snarled, holding back the expletives ready to flow. He shook his head and folded his arms pathetically.

Thorn scoffed, dropped the clutch and revved the Jeep up the hill.

Hector's mansion was an ominous sight, positioned at the top of the hill between giant fig trees and fenced off like a king's fortress.

The terracotta tile roof was diminished by luminous white cement rendered walls; the glare broken by rows of arched windows and colossal Romanesque pillars that bordered the front doors. The imposing bronze gates were open, and Thorn's Jeep cruised onto a white pebble driveway that circled an immaculate couch lawn, a pond of white lilies and the misting water fountain within.

To Owen's surprise the car park at the side of the house was cluttered with less-than-impressive Japanese hatchbacks and coupes. They seemed to cower self-consciously from a row of grandiose statues that lined a path towards a set of arched wooden doors. He stepped out of the Jeep with a confused expression, and realised that the ground floor at the end of the building was a vast auditorium. Now visible through the open doors was a flock of young dancers spinning in synchronisation across the walls of mirrors within.

"You can't say I don't know the right people," Thorn said with a blank expression, pretending to ignore his cousin's wide eyes. He tucked the tail of his polo shirt into his moleskin trousers and led the way towards the open doors.

Thorn's expression changed as one of the dancers emerged from the closest door, prancing across the lawn with a broad smile, her pink tank top darkened by patches of sweat.

"Look who it is," Thorn chuckled, sliding his aviators back.

The dancer stopped before the two cousins, smiling giddily at Thorn and then reaching her hand out to shake Owen's.

"Owen," Thorn announced proudly, "may I introduce Eva Miranda, the most beautiful girl in Panama. And Eva, this is my cousin, Owen Ellis."

"Mucho gusto, Owen," Eva grinned, her glowing teeth illuminated by her flawless brown skin. Her accent was strong but her voice was demure, and it made her appear all the more innocent than the seductive guise that Owen remembered from the club.

"Hector is upstairs on the phone," Eva explained. "He said for me to give Owen a tour, so please, follow me."

Thorn gave Owen a wink as they both watched Eva spin around and lead the way around the side of the auditorium. The dance music faded as they passed through an archway and into a carefully manicured Mediterranean garden. A copse of Italian Cyprus trees and bay laurels bordered high sandstone walls lined with shrewd barbed wire spirals. The walls blocked a view of the city, but the ocean and its steamy horizon were still visible, giving the impression that they were standing atop the peak of a Greek island. At the end of the garden an oak tree draped Spanish moss over the surface of a granite swimming pool where two children splashed against foam toys. A middle-aged woman in a flowery dress watched the children from behind a shaded table littered with empty wine glasses and the remains of a fruit platter.

Eva greeted the woman in Spanish and then opened her palm towards Owen, introducing him.

"This is Hector's daughter, Sarita," Eva explained.

Owen smiled, nodding towards her.

Eva addressed the children in a high-pitched voice, drawing giggles as they splashed in the water. She turned back to the cousins, her expression still giddy. "They live here most weekends."

"As does Eva," Thorn smiled.

"Well so would I, if I had the opportunity," Owen remarked. "So how long have you been training here, Eva?"

"Uh, two years?" She looked to Thorn for confirmation. "I was doing ballet in town, but things weren't working out, and Hector offered me the job at the club."

Thorn cleared his throat. "A couple of years ago Eva was picked up by the wife of Panama's ambassador to the UK, and she was offered a position at the Royal London Ballet."

"Oh wow," Owen exclaimed. "That would have been amazing. What happened?"

"My father said no." Eva shrugged her shoulders. "He didn't approve of my job at the club either, but it pays more than I can get anywhere else here."

Owen fell quiet, tucking his shirt in more tightly as Eva led them past an aviary full of toucans and inquisitive macaws. The lush walkway then meandered around one of the fig trees visible from the road, through another gated archway and back to the side of the auditorium.

"This is the backstage area," Eva explained as she entered a code into a number pad and pushed open a fire escape.

Owen's eyes took a few seconds to adjust to the darkness. He peered around a row of curtains to see several dancers discussing a routine on the dimly lit stage, then followed Eva through a narrow corridor to a room with black walls and a high ceiling.

"And this is Hector's secret collection of music," Eva announced as she pushed aside a layer of curtains to reveal a vast wall of old records and tapes. "But don't tell him I showed you!"

Owen's eyes widened as he scanned the collection. There were albums of modern American rock bands, musicals and film soundtracks beside dusty records of Beethoven, Tchaikovsky and scores of tapes with Spanish labels.

"Amazing," Owen blinked.

"Not bad, is it," Thorn grinned, shuffling through the curtains.

"Entonces," Eva said, "I think I should take you upstairs. He must be wondering where you two are."

The dimly lit corridors stretched out into the main foyer, where the last of the sunlight filtered through the enormous arched windows, over the polished floorboards and onto a grand cedar staircase. Hung in sequence along the staircase was a series of black and white photographs of male and female ballerinas, and continuing upwards were washed-out images of the Panama Canal during construction.

The voices of young women and clatter of cooking utensils filled the top floor as the trio emerged into an open room. An entire wall beyond a bar and kitchen was made of glass, and gave a view of the ocean that stole Owen's attention. He stood, entranced, and barely noticed the piña colada that Eva placed into his hand or the other young women smiling at him from lounges in front of a vacant grand piano.

"Is that… Is that you, Joe?" came a wavering shout. "You better come here, Joe."

Thorn turned around, his face suddenly tense at the tone of Hector's voice. Eva left the drinks that she was preparing at the bar and followed the two cousins down a short hallway to the entrance of a giant bamboo-lined office that smelt of musty books and cigar smoke.

Hector was sitting behind a desk at the end of the room, his hands hidden in the curly wisps of his grey hair. He looked up slowly as he heard the footsteps outside the door, muttered some Spanish and sighed. His face was pale and he stared blankly – almost eerily – and cleared his throat loudly. "Come in please gentleman, and close the door. Eva, we'll be out in a minute."

Thorn closed the door, his face taught with concern. "What is it, Hector?"

"Please, gentlemen, take a seat. You're going to need one."

Owen's eyes flicked back and forth between Thorn's and Hector's, who seemed to have a way of communicating without talking. His heartbeat was drumming anxiously, and he tightly gripped the carved wooden arms of the chair.

Thorn was the first to break the silence. "They've found Spadafora, haven't they?"

Hector took awhile to nod, maintaining shaky eye contact with Thorn only. He reached for a document lying inside a fax machine, and sent it across the desk. "This has come direct from the autopsy in Costa Rica."

Thorn's face was robbed of emotion as he read the text before him. He began translating aloud, his voice unwavering. "Encontramos el cuerpo el Sabado... The body was found on Saturday by a farmer, two-hundred metres inside the Costa Rican border. He had been wrapped in a US postal bag and dumped in a creek. He… they…"

Owen swallowed loudly as Thorn's voice broke. But he continued, determined to translate the horrific details.

"Habia mucha sangre… Blood was found in his stomach that he ingested while his neck was being severed... The tendons in his groin had been cleanly sliced, to more easily facilitate..." Thorn's face screwed up in disgust, and he skipped the next few lines. "Multiple ribs were broken and there was evidence of torture across most of his body. Several teeth were found on a nearby bridge, but they... they are still searching for his head."

Owen dry retched, his head throbbing in revulsion. He stared at the carpet until he felt his consciousness drifting somewhere above, staring down at his trembling body. He began to breathe in through his nose, sitting up and clenching his fists.

"They also carved this into his back," Hector said gruffly, pulling out a grainy image from the fax machine. He held it up, and Owen retched again – for engraved into the bloody image of Spadafora's naked back was the same symbol that had been carved into Owen's passport: 'F-8'.

"It's the mark of Noriega's hit men," Thorn grimaced, staring into Owen's terrified eyes and shaking his head. "You've got to get out of Panama, Owen, now!"

Chapter Ten

"EJECUTARON A SPADAFORA."

The headline seemed to scream from the newspaper stands of Omar Torrijos International Airport's departure terminal as Owen stumbled through the glass doors. The text gnawed at the corners of his eyes, and the whispers and murmurs in the check-in line all seemed to revolve around the doctor's horrific murder. He tried to focus upon the flight ahead, but the images from his taxi ride were forcing their way to the surface.

Sparks had flown in Panama City early that morning; the newspapers fuelling a wildfire of protests that spilled like petrol onto the guards that surrounded Noriega's Comandancia. Owen's taxi had escaped the flames, speeding him like a fugitive to an exit from the chaos. He had stared at the passing faces with splintered emotions – fear for his own safety gradually overriding his anger at the faceless men behind the doctor's murder. His motivation to continue his article with no notes had slipped away, and now he tried to dismiss the sting of betrayal that seemed to be lingering with an image of Spadafora's headless ghost. He had tried to convince himself to stay – that there was still a story to chase – but Thorn's resistance was unyielding. He had to leave.

It was mid-morning after a long delay that the plane finally lifted itself out of the trauma below. Owen closed his eyes tightly as the pressure dropped inside the cabin, and he kept them closed until the sting of tears dissipated. His eyes were bloodshot when he opened them, and embarrassed by the look from the man beside him, he stared out at the muddy Panama Canal and the larger mountains beyond. He felt himself sucked into the peaks and scarred cliffs, his thoughts scattered. Wiping away the moisture from his eyes, he tipped his seat back and felt himself slowly drifting towards the glorious banality of home.

Chapter Eleven

Heathrow Airport.
Present day.

Dusk was fading into darkness when the woman appeared in the fluorescent glow of the Heathrow car park. Security cameras followed her as she moved towards the crowded departures terminal with an anxious determination, her wavy black hair sticking unceremoniously to her clammy forehead. She wheeled a plush red suitcase with gold buckles that clashed with her frightened expression – like her black fur coat, the suitcase had been bought in a frame of mind that she struggled to empathise with now. It was a disposition that she had paraded for her entire life, but was now scraping away like the last remaining gloss on her scuffed high heels.

The woman stopped at a brightly lit pedestrian crossing, her dark eyes scanning back and forth through the lanes of taxis before proceeding. She passed a handsome silver-haired man in a black suit, but her usual engaging smile was tucked too far behind her anxiety to even give him a flicker of attention. Her walk became a lopsided strut as she yanked the suitcase into her hand. She reached the third lane; her eyes fixed upon the entrance to the departures terminal, and completely ignored the warning shouts to her left.

The gunmetal grey van moved like a silent bullet, its driver skilfully mounting the curb and becoming a blur in the camera footage. A corpulent security officer dropped his Chinese takeaway as his television screen focused upon the empty high heels that remained stationary in the middle of the road. He let out a terrified yelp as he threw his fist into the alarm button.

The woman's body spun through the air like a dog's play toy, wrapping almost comically around a bus stop sign. A small child choked on her scream as she saw the blood gathering at the base of the pole, soon followed by the thud of the broken body.

Chapter Twelve

Jenna curled herself into a ball, her fingertips clutching at her mother's pillow and drawing it closer into her chest. The sombre music crying from the bedside speakers didn't help her determination to remain calm, and the tears quickly soaked through the pillow, the salty taste rubbing against her swollen nose and lips. She reached out, imagining wrapping her arms around her mother, but the wall stared back blankly, and the music continued to draw bursts of trembling and groaning. She usually refused to get close to any man, but right now she would have settled for any strong touch; any protective hand running over her back, pulling her cheeks against the chest of someone who cared.

The police officers had tried to stay, but Jenna's outrage as they broke the news to her of her mother's death had sent objects flying across the kitchen. They retreated, and were now cowering in two vehicles blocking Caversham Lane. Their absence had allowed her fury to subside, and her body was now paralysed with shock, her limbs and hands refusing to move as if gravel had been pumped into the joints. She had managed to unlock her phone and call Tracey, and the cheerful voice at the other end of the line quickly released her tears. Soon after the call, her phone began to vibrate with an assortment of different numbers. Alerts flashed on the screen to show that her online accounts were being flooded with promises to leave London tonight to be with her. She obsessively responded to them all, insisting that she needed to be left alone.

Tracey arrived shortly after midnight, flashing her licence at the police officers and running up the driveway. Her nervous knocking at the front door went unanswered, and when she pushed the door open she found her friend slumped backwards on the floor, her face grey and wincing. Tracey dragged her to the couch and huddled as a flow of incoherent babbling was mixed with outbursts of wailing.

Lopsided after the raid, a tall grandfather clock ticked through the early hours of the morning. Jenna eventually crawled up to her mother's room, trembling and clinging onto her mother's sheets. Tracey followed with mugs of tea, but they went cold on the bedside table. With the light left on they sprawled across the bed, the hours of crying draining them both to sleep.

Mats of frost were melting into the front yard when they awoke. The crunching of ice under cautious footsteps was replaced with the slushing of an army of boots. Tracey gasped as she wiped the condensation from the inside of the window. Jenna joined her, her hair matted across her reddened face. She remained expressionless, watching the police officers trying to set up barricades. But the journalists were determined to get to the front door, and the animated arguments became the focus of bored cameramen.

The splashing of the shower against Jenna's face flushed the red from her eyes, and she watched calmly as the shampoo spun down the drain between her feet. Her thoughts had fleetingly turned to a funeral, to dealing with her mother's friends, then back to seeking answers. She rubbed her towel aggressively against her face before staring deeply into the reflection of her eyes. She didn't know where to start, or who to call, but the flames rising inside her corneas told her that it didn't matter where she began – karma was surely on her side.

Tracey was the first to give in, unlatching the front door and allowing the police to enter. Two female officers took off their muddy boots, hung their hats beside the door and stepped inside to the buzzing of the morning news and the smell of burning toast. Their tense expressions relaxed, and they were about to ask for a coffee when they heard the swearing from the kitchen. Jenna ended a phone call, slamming the receiver onto the bench and glaring at the officers with the wrath of a cornered snake.

"Miss Martinez, we're going to have to –"

"Where are my mother's things?" Jenna hissed. "I want everything back, exactly where it was before. Now!"

"Miss Martinez, I'm sorry to have to ask this, but we will need you to come with us. We may need you to identify the body."

"Did you hear what I just said?" Her voice was hoarse and painful. "Everything you stole, back here, now!"

"Look, we can't do anything until –"

"I've seen the footage on TV, and I don't want to see any more. I'm not going to do what you say until her things are returned, and until you tell me who those people in the grey vans were!"

"I will make a call for you," one of the officers sighed, "but I'm afraid we don't –"

"Don't play games with me," Jenna snarled. "You know who they were, you know who killed her, now talk!"

Another knock at the front door allowed Tracey to escape the tension, and she slipped out of the kitchen with a bowed head.

"I understand your frustrations, Jenna. But I'm afraid we cannot comment on the investigation that had commenced before your mother's accident. Just be assured that the coroner will thoroughly examine the cause of your mother's death, and you will be kept informed with all findings. And the first step for that process is –"

"The cause of her death? She was hit by a van you bell end! They should be investigating who killed her, not how they killed her!"

"And I will make sure they do," came a gruff female voice from the lounge room.

Jenna's eyes lit up as she recognised a stern, grey-haired woman with a straight fringe and stilettos that stabbed like skewers onto the kitchen floor.

"Angela Hunter; Coleman and Bailey," the woman declared, dropping a pile of documents onto the kitchen bench and giving the officers an impatient stare. "You two can leave now. I'd like to have a word with my client."

Angela's stern features softened as she allowed Jenna to give her a hug. "I'm so sorry, my dear," she soothed as the officers left through the back door. "Your mother was a beautiful woman. I'll make sure we get to the bottom of this. Now do you think you're up for going through a few things with me?"

"Sure," Jenna sighed.

Tracey made another round of coffee as Jenna and Angela took seats at the dining room table.

"Your mother had a lot of secrets," Angela said as she arranged a series of documents before her. "And even though I was her solicitor, I won't pretend to know half of them. But I do know that whatever secrets led to her murder involved an investigation that stemmed far higher than the police."

Jenna's aggression returned. "Who were those people?"

Angela sighed. "I believe the information surrounding the investigation is classified. Not even the police know. Whether they were MI5 or another government agency, I can only guess. But given the severity of the crimes that your mother was accused of, it's no surprise that everyone is being kept in the dark. This is serious stuff, Jenna, and it won't move quickly."

"But you don't actually believe my mother killed someone in Panama, do you?"

"I don't know what to believe right now," she said grimly, hesitating before taking a sip from her coffee. "But even if she did, they weren't after her just for that. They were after something in this house, something they thought your mother had in her possession. Do you have any idea what that might be? Did you notice anything different in your mother's behaviour recently, did she try to contact you, leave you any messages?"

Jenna was about to mention her mother's note when something in Angela's gaze made her tense. She glanced at Tracey, whose innocent expression was the only one she could trust right now. "No," she sighed. "I've got no idea. She didn't tell me anything."

Angela frowned. "Well if you think of anything, let me know straight away. In the meantime, there are some issues with your mother's assets that you should be aware of."

"Go on."

Angela leaned forward with a little too much energy. "Because your mother was living under a fraudulent identity, her bank accounts, as well as her life insurance and investments, could also be judged to be fraudulent."

The pink in Jenna's face dissolved into grey. "So you mean, everything she owned could be –"

"But let's not get ahead of ourselves," Angela tried to smile. "All I want you to be aware of is the fact that legally, things are going to get very complicated, and so I'm going to have to adjust my fees accordingly. She did have a will, but I won't be able to go through it with you until a death certificate has been provided from the coroner. And I'm unsure when that will be, given that the coroner may recommend further investigations."

"How do you mean?"

Angela took another sip from her coffee, looking past Jenna's gaze at the mantelpiece beyond. "As you know, this story is attracting wide coverage, and theories are being developed as to who was behind the wheel of that van. The media will also be combing every lead into your mother's real identity, as well as your own. The case may be classified, but as you know, journalists will dig up anything that could make a headline. As a result, I wouldn't be surprised if an inquest is called."

"Well I'm not going to wait around for that to happen," Jenna responded. "I want answers now, and I don't care where they come from. Am I able to talk to the media?"

"I would strongly advise you didn't speak to anyone about the case." Angela turned, facing Tracey. "And that goes for you too."

Jenna narrowed her eyes, her back straightening like an agitated cat.

"And the other thing that you need to be aware of is the state of your mother's finances. To be frank, Jenna, your mother was hopelessly in debt. She lost a considerable amount of money in the last divorce, and as you know, she was an excessive spender. You will be provided with access to her accounts once a death certificate is provided, but I suspect it won't be substantial. I can try to –"

"I don't care about the money," Jenna interrupted, shaking her head and looking out the window. "I don't care about any of this. Just find out who killed her."

Chapter Thirteen

It was the photos that finally made her stop. Jenna slumped beside the cardboard box in the living room, her fingertips flicking through the dog-eared albums. The musty smell of old cardboard added to her nostalgia, and her thoughts drifted into the slow guitar-playing reverberating from her mother's stereo. Having finished unloading the last of the boxes, the police had finally left and the house was empty for the first time in two days.

Jenna's tears rolled down smiling cheeks and she breathed calmly, photos of her younger self in her first tutu reviving memories that had long floated adrift. She flicked past the awkward images of her early teenage years and found an album of her mother and her first husband – a proud Italian man who spent far more than he earned. Her eyes narrowed and she studied the images suspiciously. Another album – the second husband – was less intriguing. This man was pale white, as obese as he was rich, and completely smitten by Teresa's exotic allure. He had been kind to Jenna, buying her extravagant dollhouses that had cluttered her bedroom, but Teresa's affections had always wandered elsewhere.

Jenna pushed the albums back into the box with a sigh. Those men were hopeless lovers, not killers. And they had all moved on after the divorces. What she needed were photos of her mother before she came to England; before Jenna was born. And anything that contained the name Rafael Cordoba.

The police had tried to patch the slices made in another cardboard box, but the fresh masking tape was torn as Jenna's black fingernails ripped into the hidden contents. Again she slumped, slowly pulling out old books by

Dr Seuss, Enid Blyton and Roald Dahl. She flicked through the pages with a chuckle, remembering the twisted dreams and nightmares those stories had invoked. At the bottom of the box was an old pink cassette player, flanked by ballet tapes. Black crosses had been marked on the sides of the tapes, and Jenna studied them with a confused frown.

The final box had been carefully packed, and contained the electronics that Jenna had been looking for. She excitedly pulled out her mother's desktop computer and its cords, a battered laptop, two external hard drives and a stack of USB sticks. After plugging them into the wall, the computers both started faster than expected, and she shouted in frustration as she found that they had both been reformatted. She examined each of the hard drives and USBs, ripping them back out angrily when she saw that they had all been wiped.

She rubbed her temples and slowly typed the name "Rafael Cordoba" into the search bars of each computer. No results. She shook her head and opened up an internet browser to do the same. The computer requested the password for her wireless internet, and just as she was about to type 'Oscar123' a sudden thought stabbed through her eagerness. If the agents had managed to hack her phone messages, then they were surely able to break into and monitor her internet as well. She couldn't allow herself to fall into any traps. Whoever Rafael was he had to be kept secret.

Molly crept quietly through Harmiston's winding streets, sliding inconspicuously into a car space shaded by the Gothic turrets of Carlisle College. Jenna stepped out into the cold wind, her laptop tucked beneath her woollen coat and her hair tied into an austere bun. She strode through the bustling courtyard of the main library and, glancing over her shoulder, slipped through a low sandstone archway into the dark hallway beyond.

Growing up in the company of more than a few students of the university, Jenna had no trouble logging into the college network under a friend's details. She took one last look through the racks of books lining her study table, clenched her jaw and began to type.

"Rafael Cordoba" returned thousands of hits. She pursed her lips thoughtfully, then added the word "Cuba". Ten news articles appeared, and the corners of her tight lips curled upwards. She clicked on an article from a Miami news website and scanned the page with a steely expression.

Cuban Drug Trafficker Escapes Custody

A notorious Cuban drug trafficker has escaped custody in Miami only minutes after his arrest for conspiracy to import 20kg of cocaine into the United States. Rafael Cordoba, 29, who has previously escaped indictments for drug-related offences by hiding in Cuba, allegedly fought off three undercover agents on Tuesday evening before leaping into the water at Sunset Harbor Yacht Club.

"Mr Cordoba had been the subject of a year-long surveillance operation," a DEA spokesman said. "He was detained on board a yacht at Sunset Harbor at 4:30pm, before fighting his way free and jumping overboard. No trace of Mr Cordoba was found after entry into the water, and we are appealing for any persons in the area who may have witnessed the event to come forward."

The DEA spokesman said that approximately 20kg of cocaine was found hidden inside fish heads on the yacht. No other arrests were made, and the yacht club was closed for three hours after the incident while an unsuccessful manhunt was conducted.

Jenna saved the page and continued onto other articles in Spanish. She opened up a Spanish translator and pasted in the text, smiling as she found that Rafael Cordoba was originally from Panama.

Another thought crossed Jenna's mind, and she excitedly typed in "Isla de Marfil, Cuba". Only a few pages were returned, referring to a small fishermen's island that had become the site of an annual trance festival for European backpackers. She searched for a map of the island, shaking her head in confusion as she saw that the only infrastructure was a warehouse, a wharf and fishermen's huts. She ran a hand through her hair, pulling out the bun, then continued to type words that spun though her mind.

"Eva Miranda"

"Teresa Martinez"

"MI5"

"Panama Invasion 1989"

"Manuel Noriega"

"CIA"

"CIA and Manuel Noriega"

"CIA cooperation with MI5"

Her head becoming weary, she made her way to a café and stood in line, staring every so often over her shoulder. As she reached the front of the queue the words of the lady serving her became incoherent noise. She was staring up at the television overlooking the service area, where a news channel was reporting a speech by the US president. Her eyes flickered as a familiar face was shown standing beside a flag in the background. "Just a cappuccino to go," she blurted to the lady, reaching clumsily for her purse and keeping eye contact with the screen.

Back at her computer, Jenna's fingers moved like lightning. She leaned forward, scanning a short biography and frowning.

"Joseph Thorn was born in Kansas, 1954, and grew up as the son of the Republican Governor, Howard Thorn. He played Lacrosse and American football for Yale, graduating six months early with majors in Spanish and psychology and following his father's footsteps into the military. Thorn served in the invasion of Grenada, earning a Silver Star and Purple Heart for capturing four members of the Cuban Special Forces. After two years of training in Fort Leavenworth, he served as a Major in Panama and subsequently as a Lieutenant Colonel, earning his second Silver Star in Operation Just Cause. He was then assigned to the Department of Defence in the Pentagon, managing clandestine missions in coordination with the CIA. Touted as an expert in military strategy and diplomacy, he began assignment in the National Security Council in the White House in 2008. In 2016, he was controversially nominated as the Director of the CIA."

Jenna sighed. It was farcical to think that this man had anything to do with her mother's death. The probing questions at the concert must have just been his way of getting to know her – he had approached her about her dancing performance, nothing more. She threw the foam cup of her cappuccino into the bin, saved all of the articles that she had searched to her desktop and gathered her things.

The shadows had grown across the empty courtyard as Jenna strolled towards her car. The rapping of her boots on the stone pavers echoed off the black windows and steeples, but was joined by a softer pulse of rubber-soled shoes. She stopped in an archway, staring back through the shadows of the Gothic spires. There was no one there.

The grass of an adjoining quadrangle absorbed the sound of Jenna's boots, and she skipped towards another stone archway, ducking into the shadows and staring through a gap in the turrets. She waited for another minute until a group of students passed by, then took a winding route through the courtyards to a leafy garden at the back of the car park. She was about to stroll through the trees when she spotted a bald man in a black windcheater crouching and trying to conceal himself behind a shrub in front of her car. He had his back to her, and studied his phone between glances over the shrub.

She moved silently across the lawn, her pace quickening as she stepped across a mat of crisp yellow leaves. The man spun around, his blue eyes wide with shock, and tripped backwards as the sharp heel of Jenna's boot nailed into the base of his sternum. His lungs were flattened, and his pale, featureless face was twisted in agony as he tried to shout.

"What do you want?" Jenna spat, forcing her foot harder into his chest and snarling. "Answer me! What do you want with me?!"

The man continued to writhe frantically, his ribs juddering underneath Jenna's heel as he broke free. Jenna kicked at him with a scream of both fear and rage, collecting the back of his thigh as he bounded forward like a rabbit from a shotgun, clambering across the car park and into the street beyond.

Chapter Fourteen

The church was overflowing, but there was a vacancy at the funeral that no one else could see. The dance students and their mothers, the neighbours, ex-husbands and family friends – they all knew Teresa Martinez as a brash yet caring dance teacher with a distinctive accent and an ambitious daughter. But they knew nothing of Eva Miranda, or the secrets that brought about her horrific end. And as Jenna's eyes scanned the crying faces at the eulogy, her tears hung tight. She couldn't allow herself to cry – not until the vacant chairs from her mother's previous life were filled – not until they had names and faces, and told the truth about a young dancer from Panama.

At the end of the service Jenna hovered over the coffin like an apparition, the coldness in her eyes freezing the wisps of her black veil. She accepted the hugs and the flowers with a stiff iciness, her black fingernails poised like claws as she hugged those who she didn't trust. She wanted to return the sorrowful smiles to Miss Hindmarsh as she wrapped Jenna in a loving embrace, but it was as though all of her tenderness had been bled out.

"I always envied her," Miss Hindmarsh whispered in her ear. "She was an incredible dancer; the best. Just like her daughter. Come back to London, Jenna."

"I will," Jenna assured, her voice husky, "soon enough."

The media had been blocked from the service, but they appeared like a swarm of wasps as the hearse crawled through the maple trees into the windy afternoon. A group of mothers were more than happy to have their tears recorded, and spoke of their own theories about the mystery woman's death, and what an inquest may find. Only Tracey dared walk with Jenna as she descended the steps of the church, her friend's face darker and more menacing than the looming clouds.

"It doesn't feel right," Jenna sighed heavily. "How can you have a funeral for only half of someone's life?"

"Maybe that's the only half that she would have wanted remembered."

Jenna frowned, continuing to stare into the sombre brigade ahead.

A moustached man in a black suit and thick black sunglasses stood at the base of the steps, his solemn face turned towards Jenna. His closely cropped hair was turning a salt and pepper grey, and he looked genuinely saddened. He clasped his hands at his front and gave Jenna a respectful nod as she passed.

"I've got to get out of here," Jenna breathed to Tracey like a ventriloquist. "I don't know where, but I've got to go."

Tracey wiped away a stray tear and tried to slide her hand into Jenna's black-gloved arm. But Jenna pushed it away, and the fire in her eyes told Tracey to keep the body contact for another time. "I'll come with you," Tracey whispered anxiously. "Let's just take off, you and me, we'll book a plane to France, or Scotland, or Australia."

"That's not what I meant," Jenna responded bluntly. "I don't want a holiday. I want answers."

The scones at the wake were too dry to digest, and the saucers of cream and jam were attracting flies. Jenna gave a slight moue of distaste towards the bustling crowd, and waited for Tracey to start another round of small talk before making an escape to the back of the marquee. She slipped through a flap in the canvas, scanning a quiet grove of maple trees before setting off into the university gardens. Her determined strides turned into a stumbling jog, startling a raven as it clawed into the scraps within a garbage bin. She slipped off her shoes and veil, leaving them on the grass and kicking her feet through the layers of dead leaves that lined a reedy creek. The cold shade opened up into an oval where a cricket match was being played, and she wandered along the boundary rope, ignoring a ball that rolled past her and into a row of hedging.

The sound of a lawnmower drifted across a second oval, and the smell of freshly cut grass joined the aroma of jasmine vines that wove through a picket fence. Jenna ripped at one of the purple flowers, crushing it between her fingers and pretending to ignore the moustached man who had been following her since leaving the marquee.

Chapter Fifteen

Toronto Times office, Canada.
December 8th, 1989.

The postal cart moved through the tenth floor offices with a rattling rear wheel, the acne-scarred delivery boy forgetting again to take it downstairs for repairs. He slowed the cart as he gave the morning stack of envelopes to the editor, who barely looked up to acknowledge him. He moved onwards, squeezing a collection of glossy magazines onto the desk of the promotions director, then stopping beside the desk of a reporter who seemed to spend most of his time abroad. For the last month the desk had been cluttered with annotated images of the fall of the Berlin Wall and a growing stack of mail, but now it was looking more inhabited. In the chair sat a man with a curly fringe, unruly sideburns and a worn tweed blazer. He looked up at the delivery boy, adjusting his black-rimmed glasses and raising his eyebrows as if to say that he was too busy to chat.

"Mail for Owen Ellis," the boy said hesitantly, and dropped a wide yellow envelope on top of the reporter's notes.

Owen finished the sentence that he was typing, took off his glasses and reached for the Stanley knife in his second drawer. His thoughts were still focused on another trip to the European Bloc, and he ignored the Panama postal service stamp on the front of the envelope. He casually sliced through the seal, tipped the envelope up and then froze in shock.

Three black and white photocopied photographs slid onto the desk, followed by a grainy, annotated blueprint of a military building. The colour drained from his face and he quickly shuffled the papers into a crude arrangement in front of him.

The three images were marked in the bottom right corners with dates and times, and were overlain with translucent "CONFIDENTIAL" watermarks. Owen clenched his jaw as he recognised himself in the first image, his young face nervously staring through the branches of a mangrove swamp from his seat in a wooden boat. Surrounding him were four armed guerrillas wearing baseball caps and paddling cautiously, all oblivious to the presence of the photographer.

The second image was also of him. It was a close-up of his face, bloodied and unconscious on the crumbled floor of a church. And the third, making his muscles tighten, was a photograph of his possessions on the floor of the church – his father's gold watch, notebooks and his open passport displayed purposefully on top of his backpack. At the bottom of the image was a handwritten message: "As discussed. No files found, will continue to monitor. Machos briefed on Dr's route – RUBUS."

Owen's face remained expressionless, but his heart was pounding like a jackhammer. His attention turned to the floor plan of the military building in the fourth document. It had been too long since trying to translate Spanish, and it took him a minute to realise that it was a plan of La Comandancia – the headquarters of General Noriega's defence forces. Scrawled in pen over several rooms of the multi-story complex were numbers, circles, question marks, recent dates and initials. On the far right of the blueprint was the plan of the building's basement, where the conspicuous number '1' had been drawn within a circle around a long room beside a staircase. There was no date within the circle, and the room had no label. A large bold question mark had been drawn beside the circle, overlapping with the edge of the photocopy.

Owen began spinning his pen between his fingers and studying the calendar pinned beside his computer. He suddenly stood up, pushed his chair in and marched towards the office of his editor.

Chapter Sixteen

Omar Torrijos International Airport, Panama City.
December 12ᵗʰ, 1989.

Joseph Thorn closed the door of his red BMW and watched the lightning dance like spiders' legs over the black airstrip. The webs of rain held back in time for his cousin to make it across the airport car park, burying his hand in Thorn's handshake as the tempest struck.

"Jump in, quick!" Thorn cried through the lashing rain.

Owen barely had time to admire his cousin's new vehicle before throwing his suitcase into the back and then inhaling the smell of fresh leather seats. Heavy metal roared from the multitude of speakers, vibrating the back windows and giving Owen the feeling that he was about to enter a war zone.

"It's great to see you again, buddy!" Thorn shouted over the music and rain. "Typical of you to only give a day's notice though!"

"I know, I know," Owen grinned as he pulled on the seatbelt and wiped the rain droplets from his spectacles. "Thanks so much for making yourself available. So when did you get this car?"

"Two weeks ago." Thorn took off from the taxi stand, the gleaming alloy wheels skidding on the rippling sheen of the wet bitumen. "She's a beauty, isn't she?"

"Very nice!" Owen agreed, sliding his spectacles back on and running his hand over the dash. "I'm assuming this is your way of rewarding yourself for the promotion?"

"Ha, something like that." Thorn leaned forward to check the traffic at a stop sign and then took off with a roaring of the engine. "How was the flight?"

"Not bad, apart from the turbulence before we landed."

"Well you can expect a lot more of that." He flipped the rear-view mirror upwards to avoid the headlights of the car behind. "Things are about to explode here. That's why I told you not to come, this place is going to be mayhem."

"It can't be worse than some of the things I've seen in Europe."

"Oh yeah? Wait till we get into the city, I'm sure you'll change your mind. Since the coup attempt two months ago Noriega has replaced all of his uniformed soldiers with a brigade of mercenaries from Cuba. They call themselves the Machos del Monte – Men of the Mountains – and they're as wild as their name suggests. Two punch ups with our soldiers already this evening, and it's only a matter of time before someone lets off a bullet."

"So I've heard. But still, I had to come. As I said on the phone, someone here is trying to tell me something."

"Whatever you say. You've always been a crazy son of a bitch, and things obviously haven't changed."

Owen shrugged nonchalantly. "So how are things at work? How is Eva doing?"

"Work is hectic as ever. We're all being kept in the dark on what is going to happen here, so everyone's on edge. I'd rather just have the orders to take Noriega out; it's the waiting and not knowing that keeps me up at night. And as for Eva, well, she's still keeping me up at night too!"

Owen shared Thorn's laugh, shaking his head.

"But seriously, she's great. She's moved in to the new place with me, and I think she might suspect what's coming."

"What do you mean?"

"Have a look in the glove box," Thorn replied eagerly.

Owen's fingers fumbled in the darkness until he pulled out a small navy blue box. "You're kidding me," he cried. Inside was the largest diamond he had ever seen, its glittering white core sucking the light from the passing streetlights and transmitting it into a thousand multi-coloured blades. "That thing must be worth a fortune! How did you –"

"Oh come on," Thorn laughed back. "The US army must treat its colonels better than the Canadians do!"

"I'll say! She's going to die when she sees this!"

"Well I hope not, got to keep her alive long enough to get out of this wretched country."

"Get out? You're leaving Panama?"

"As soon as we get rid of Noriega I'm done. Back to Kansas. But I'm not leaving until the job's done, I've put too much into this. Now, am I taking you back to the same hotel as last time?"

"No, the Marriott, please."

"Oh, look at you now, going up in the world, hey?"

"I can't let my cousin keep showing me up, can I? Work will cover the costs for this trip. When I showed the editor what turned up on my desk he practically threw the plane tickets at me."

Thorn's eyes were narrowed in the light of the dash. "So you didn't tell me on the phone what these documents are? And who you think sent them to you? Because if this turns out to be someone setting you up, I'm going to throw you straight back on that plane, you hear? The Spadafora case is over, and there was never any agent called Ru –"

The BMW lurched onto the side of the road as Owen flicked the photocopied images out of a clipboard. As the car came to a stop, Thorn reached up to turn on the cabin light. He swore, his face contorted.

"They were following me the whole time," Owen said matter-of-factly, his stomach swelling to see Thorn's stunned reactions. "And look at this – it's signed by RUBUS himself. This guy, whoever he is, knew everything. He knew that I met with Spadafora, he knew that I had the files in La Concepción, and he knew where I was staying in Panama City. He also knew when the doctor was going to cross the border."

"This is absurd," Thorn stammered. "I mean, I – this is bad. Hector assured me there was no one by that name, that it was…"

"And why do you think he said that? Why do you think he so strongly encouraged me to back away when I had the doctor's files?"

"No!" Thorn growled. "No, no, no. Someone must have been eavesdropping on our conversations. Someone must have tapped the phones, but not Hector. It can't be..."

"And the plan of the Comandancia? Look at this. Someone has been through each room, ticking them off, searching for something, but they haven't yet found it, or had access to it. Remember what Hector said about Noriega blackmailing his opponents with files and tape recordings? Well, what if he was speaking out of direct experience, and Noriega is blackmailing him or one of his old colleagues in the CIA? If the US somehow manages to extradite Noriega to face drug trafficking charges, then Noriega could use any tapes or other evidence in his defence, and pass the blame for his crimes onto whoever was really behind all of this."

Thorn shook his head with a bewildered expression, flicking the cabin light back off and thrusting the car onto the road. "You have a vivid imagination, Owen. I agree that someone had been watching us back then, but... Look, if it makes you feel better, I'll call a meeting with Hector tomorrow, and trust me, I'll know if he's lying. You're right, there are things to be explained here, but I assure you, I'll get to the bottom of this."

"And I'll be doing exactly the same," Owen responded calmly, adjusting his collar. "And don't bother organising a meeting with Hector, it's already arranged."

The heat of the morning sunlight bore down on the slums of El Chorrillo, drawing the night's rain from the gutters in swirling wisps of steam that circled Owen's ankles. He stepped into the shade of a ramshackle workshop and scanned a line of polished scooters and motorbikes.

"Usted quieres hire un bike?" came the voice of a round, moustached mechanic, sweat soaking through his grease-stained shirt.

"Si, si," Owen responded, reaching for his wallet and passport.

Ten dollars later, Owen's head sweltered in the worn fabric of a bike helmet, and his legs steadied themselves around a white scooter. He took a lap around the block of workshops before speeding down Avenida A, a claustrophobic conduit that dissected the walls of decaying wooden balconies, cracked cement footpaths and power lines that thread through twisted tin roofs. Soon he was staring at the imposing concrete Comandancia, rising up like a jail from the sea of slums. He took two laps around the building and the adjoining block, deciding that any sort of entry would require a small army.

The scooter purred more favourably as it swung past the rich green baseball fields and manicured front lawns in the US-occupied Canal Zone, then wheezed as it struggled up the hill overlooking the city.

The bronze gates of Hector's mansion were shut, and on either side stood heavily armed military guards. Owen doubled back, thinking for a moment that he had the wrong address. He revved the scooter in a wide circle before approaching the guards. One of them raised an eyebrow above his thick sunglasses, but continued staring forward and frowning.

"Uh. Tengo una cita con el Señor Goldstein."

The closest guard stared at him before pointing at an intercom beside the gate. Owen dismounted the scooter, edged forward and pressed the button.

"Si, quién es?" The female voice was sharp and impatient.

"Yo soy Owen Ellis," he enunciated carefully. "Tengo una cita."

The gates suddenly rumbled, overcoming a jitter before grating open.

The guard nodded at him as Owen wheeled the scooter inside. He was about to jump back on when he realised that the scooter's narrow tyres would surely topple on the driveway's white pebbles. Instead he parked it just inside the gate, gathered his notepad and walked stiffly towards the front door.

Hector's daughter Sarita stood tautly at the doorway beside a guard. Owen tried to suppress his unease, taking in the lush gardens and noticing that the dark windows of the auditorium were being overgrown with ivy.

"Owen, isn't it?" Sarita asked with a thick accent.

"Uh, yes, Owen Ellis."

"Yes, I remember you. We met here a few years ago. My father is in el jardin. The garden, I mean. This is his guard Javier, he will take you around."

Owen nodded at Javier and followed him hesitantly around the side of the house. Sarita continued onwards towards the gates, calling one of the guards over in Spanish.

A giant satellite dish had been installed where a row of flowerbeds had once been, and spirals of angel wire were threaded across the top of the garden wall. Owen ducked through an archway into the pool area, where Hector could be seen reclining in the shade of a gazebo. Javier stationed himself at the archway and motioned for Owen to continue over.

A newspaper was stretched over Hector's flowing white pants, and he was coolly puffing on a cigar. He removed his reading glasses as Owen approached, folding the newspaper onto a glass table and slowly standing up.

"Hello there," Owen called.

"You're a man of your word," Hector rasped with a sly grin, dropping his cigar into an ashtray and rubbing his hands together. The glare dancing from the pool flickered over his light grey eyes, giving him a ghostly appearance and highlighting the deep crow's feet stretched across his olive cheeks. He looked frailer than the last time they had met, but his iron handshake quickly brought back Owen's intimidation. "So how have you been?"

"I've been really well," Owen said as he pulled out a chair and sat down at the table. "Busy as ever with work, spending most of my time in Europe at the moment. And you?"

Hector smiled faintly as he reached for his cigar. "I'm always good," he said with a nimble wave of his hand. "So what, you have a woman in Europe do you?"

Owen laughed. "No, no, I've been covering the events in Poland and –"

"I know," he smiled shrewdly. "I was just hoping you had a better reason for going over there than chasing bombs. I read your article on Mazowiecki, and the one you wrote earlier in the year on Tiananmen Square. You're talented, boy, but you're also completely mad."

"I'll take that as a compliment," Owen grinned, his cheeks flushing with red. "So what's the satellite dish for, and the guards out front?"

"You certainly are more of a journalist than last time, aren't you?" Hector coughed as he chuckled, leaning back and stretching his arms behind his head. "I wanted better TV reception. And I sleep better when I know that other people will die before I do."

Owen frowned, trying to gauge the extent of his satire.

"You heard about Giroldi's attempt to oust Noriega a couple of months ago?"

"Of course." Owen's expression suddenly changed. "You had something to do with that, didn't you?"

Hector sighed, staring back at him with languorous eyes as he sucked again on his cigar. "Possibly. Noriega was there for the taking, all we needed was backing from Bush – a few more soldiers – but he chickened out. If you ask me, Bush is scared that Noriega has dirt on him."

"And does he?"

Hector smiled. "Of course he does. Noriega has dirt on everyone."

"Including you?"

Hector looked startled. "Pardon me?"

Owen stared intensely, holding his gaze as he opened his clipboard and arranged the photographs over the table. Hector hardly reacted, staring downwards with a confused expression and rubbing at his eyes. Something about the way he reached for his reading glasses made Owen's shoulders relax, and in that instant he decided that Hector had nothing to do with the images.

Hector rubbed his beard as his eyes flicked back and forth, his fingers shifting each image carefully. "This is serious stuff," he growled. "This is very serious indeed. And you have no idea who sent them?"

"No idea," Owen sighed. "There was no return address on the envelope. Just those documents."

"Hmm. This blueprint – La Comandancia?"

"Yes, that's correct."

Hector removed his glasses and sat back. "Hmm."

"That room – room number one. What's in there?"

Hector smiled meekly. "I'm afraid I'm no longer an inside man, Owen. But if I was to have a guess, I'd say that someone is trying to find Noriega's archives."

"Archives?"

Hector puffed at the remaining stub of his cigar and stabbed out the embers. "Think of it as a library for blackmail. Reel-to-reel tapes, coded messages, photographs, court transcripts, forgotten love letters, medical reports – anything that Noriega could possibly need to bribe and to blackmail."

Owen leaned forward, encouraging Hector to continue.

"This agent, whoever annotated this blueprint, has obviously been trying to break in. Perhaps they've been instructed to do so by the CIA, or perhaps they're trying to get themselves out of Noriega's pocket."

"Okay, but who sent these pictures to me? Who knows all this, and has access to be able to photocopy and send them to me? Someone obviously knows who this agent is, but who is that someone?"

Hector stroked his beard again, sitting back thoughtfully. "This person hasn't drawn you out here for a game, Owen. They obviously have a plan for you."

"You speak as though you know who this person is." Owen turned his head to the side, raising his eyebrows.

"I don't know who they are," Hector shrugged. "But I know their style. I'm afraid I cannot help you more with this; I'm too old to be playing spy games. But be patient, your friend will be in contact."

Owen was unconvinced. After a long silence he decided to take a different approach. "The people that Noriega has in his pocket, does that include you?"

"Excuse me?"

"Why did you and Noriega have a falling out? I've done my own research and as far as I can tell you used to be thick as thieves."

Hector turned away and smiled. He was obviously not offended by the question, but turned back to Owen with narrowed eyes. "During your research, did you find out when the papers started referring to me as a 'former' business associate of Noriega's?"

"I did. It was following the death of Omar Torrijos in a plane crash."

Hector nodded. "And what do you deduce from that?"

"I know that you were a fan of Omar Torrijos. You two were close, and I believe you assisted him in spying on the US during the Panama Canal negotiations."

"That is true. But you do not have permission to write that down."

"And I also believe that the plane crash wasn't an accident."

Hector grimaced as though the memory pained him. "That is also true."

Owen paused, frowning. "Noriega was behind that crash. He organised Torrijos' death so that he could take over as leader of Panama. And you knew it."

Hector breathed in deeply through his nose and sighed. "Noriega wasn't smart enough to make it look like an accident. There was only one man in Panama with the skill to pull that off – me."

Owen gaped. "You caused the crash?"

"You have to understand that Torrijos was not the target. It was meant to be Noriega."

"My God!"

"Noriega was becoming a threat. We had to get rid of him. But he was one step ahead. He had been spying on us for months. And the tape recorders, the bugs and the bomb – I had given him them all. I created that monster, and without realising I was also feeding it."

Owen shook his head in amazement. "So these guards, and the surveillance, this is all to protect you from Noriega?"

Hector laughed. "If Noriega wanted me dead it would have happened years ago. When you've had a past like mine it's the sins you don't remember that are most likely to kill you. Now I've told you enough. You better be on your way. You have more important mysteries to solve than me."

The hazy city glimmered through the bronze gates and a light breeze filtered through the fig trees. Owen breathed the scent of lavender lining the fence, images of his grandmother's house in Canada filling his mind. He turned back, waving another goodbye to Hector as the old man retreated into the house.

The gates began to rumble open, the guards taking no notice as they continued surveying the quiet road. Owen pulled out the keys to his scooter, his thoughts cluttered and churning as he noticed a note wrapped around the scooter's handlebars. He sprung forward fervently, unwrapping the paper and finding a handwritten message:

66 Avenida 4a, tomorrow night, 6:15pm. Follow on foot, don't be seen.

Owen glanced back towards the house, but Hector was already gone. He scanned the grassy front lawn, then quickly wheeled the scooter through the open gate. "Disculpe," he called to the guards, holding up the paper. "Who did this? Who was here?"

The guards ignored him, one of them adjusting his stance and puffing out his chest.

"Hey! Someone was here, you must have seen them!"

Still no response.

Owen shook his head, debating whether or not to return to the house to ask for Hector's assistance. He eventually shoved the note into his pants and with a burst of energy, pulled on his helmet and revved the scooter onto the road. He was quickly sailing back down the hill, suspicions and theories whipping through his mind like the wind that thrashed at his shirt. He was certain he knew the address on the note – or at least that street – but surely it couldn't be the same place.

The scooter moved swiftly through the slums and then onto the cobblestone streets of Casco Viejo, where the rank smell of garbage was replaced with the smell of seaweed and fresh paint. He counted down the avenues and then slid into a narrow street lined with wrought iron balconies and once grand doorways. And there it was – number 66. Just as he had suspected, it was the same red door that Spadafora had guided him to last time he was here.

"Tomorrow, 6:15pm," Owen breathed to himself, stepping off the scooter and removing his helmet. He stared at the door, memories flooding back of the night that the prostitute had greeted him. "Spadafora was meant to come to this house," he whispered as he stared. "But why here? Why a brothel?"

The maroon curtains were drawn on the ground floor, and the windows all reflected the midday sun. The balconies were overflowing with bird guano and cigarette butts, and the rusted guttering creaked in the breeze. As he stared upwards he noticed the curtain in one of the lower windows shift. It was a movement so slight that he wondered if it had moved at all, but the adrenaline still shot through his body. He wheeled the scooter around the corner of the house, trying to move casually.

The alleyway was shrouded in shadow, and as Owen attempted to mount his scooter he let out a short gasp. A small boy – no older than five – was standing directly in front of him, his dark brown face solemn and his black eyes unblinking. Owen hesitated and then pulled the scooter back towards the street. He pretended to ignore the boy, but noticed him brushing past a row of ferns protruding from cracks in the wall and then crouching on all fours beside a barred hole at the side of the house.

Owen pulled on his helmet and started the scooter. The low droning filled the alleyway, and the small figure slowly moved backwards towards the hole. And then, like a hermit crab retreating into its shell, the boy slid through the bars and into the darkness beyond.

Chapter Seventeen

Casco Viejo, Panama City.
December 14th, 1989, 6:05pm.

Owen had eaten an early dinner prior to his ride into Casco Viejo, and the Marriott's marinated squid churned in his stomach as though still alive, dragging his focus from the road ahead and reminding him of the revelations that awaited only two blocks away. He had spent the entire day trying to contain his restlessness, swimming laps of the hotel's indoor pool before racing the scooter up to Pedro Miguel, a small town where the cargo ships squeezed through the narrow Panama Canal locks.

The heat of the afternoon left a salty, humid haze lingering in the narrow streets of Casco Viejo. The sweat filled Owen's helmet with no prospect of drying. He parked the scooter a block from Avenida 4a, shook the sweat from his hair, donned a straw hat and then walked casually towards the red door. The streets and balconies were crowded with locals returning from work and bringing in washing, but Owen could feel that his attempts at blending in were failing. He wished that he could relax, to casually smoke a cigarette beside a doorstep, and to avoid making eye contact with the passing locals. But he had neither the patience nor assuredness of a spy. It had taken four years of university to mould a journalist out of his introversion, and he was now too far down that path to remember how to be a shadow. He leaned stiffly against the wall of a restaurant, adjusting his sunglasses and trying to stare inconspicuously across the street.

6:15pm passed, and the red door remained shut. Owen's presence had attracted attention, and an elderly woman pushing a cart stopped before him with a toothless grin. "Agua de coco?" she wheezed hopefully, the cataracts in her eyes pulling Owen from his concentration.

Owen hesitated. "Puede ser," he said finally, reaching into his pocket for coins.

The old woman smiled as her machete came down violently, slicing the top off a coconut and letting it spin into the base of her cart.

As he placed a straw into the freshly opened shell, Owen noticed a lady in a tight red dress and red high heels strutting towards the end of the block. He stumbled forward, unsure of where she had come from. He took one last glance at the red door and then marched through a cackling group of teenagers. His coconut water splashed onto the pavement.

The lady continued to move in a manner that stole Owen's ability to walk casually. His eyes fixed involuntarily on the gliding movements of her hips and the bouncing of her curly black hair. Unable to make out her face, he crossed to the other side of the road, his strides turning into a jog to see her profile more clearly. He squinted, then decided to fall back to avoid being noticed.

The pursuit continued into El Chorrillo, where the lady's sashay became a furtive glide as catcalls and whistles spilled from the crowded balconies. The unwanted attention worked to Owen's advantage as he ducked unnoticed between the smoke of street stalls and children riding squeaking bicycles. He threw the shell of his coconut into an overgrown alleyway and then gasped as he saw the woman's destination. She glanced behind her, smoothed the hair out of her face and then approached the guarded gates of the Comandancia.

"You're kidding me," Owen panted, watching in amazement as the woman flashed a seductive grin and then walked straight through the gate. She then turned slightly, her hair flicking back purposefully, and stared directly through the fence into Owen's widening eyes. The guards had also turned, but their attention was focused firmly on the swaying of the lady's hips. They grinned at each other, adjusted their weapons and then resumed their places.

Owen continued to move closer to the fence, ducking behind a parked troop carrier and watching as the lady strutted up to the entrance of the military base. She stopped, her stance suddenly becoming diminutive and shy as a short, uniformed figure appeared at the top of the steps. The man took a step forward. The sun washed across his round, pockmarked face.

"Noriega," Owen gasped. He ducked behind the troop carrier as though he was being shot at. He gained his breath and then stiffly moved to the other side of the road. But however he attempted to stand on the pavement his legs trembled, and he decided to take a lap of the block.

He soon found himself on the other side of the Comandancia, clambering up the steps of a grimy lane and into the shadows of an overhanging passionfruit vine. From this vantage point the Comandancia was in full view, and he began to survey the movements of each of the guards. At the rear of the building he noticed a large rubbish skip, and beside it, an emergency fire escape. The gates in front of this area were wide open, and two army vehicles were shifting onto the street to allow a garbage truck to reverse in.

Owen continued to watch as the clouds mingled above the slums, forcing an early twilight and melting the shadows into a lilac gloom. The glow of the streetlamps began to strengthen, creating a ghostly splay of new shadows across the Comandancia's treeless grounds. The guards began to thin out, and those that remained patrolled the fences and chatted loudly on their radios. Owen was about to shift positions when he noticed the emergency door at the back of the building easing open. From the doorway emerged the lady in the red dress, her expression reticent and wary. She strolled across the concrete with a timid smile towards the watching guards, then moved briskly in the direction of Casco Viejo.

Owen realised that he was still wearing his straw hat, and took it off as he clambered back onto the street and followed the lady through the gloom. He wanted to call out to her, to run up beside her and ask who she was, to ask about the note, the photographs – was it her that had sent them? Was she waiting for him to catch up?

The quaint paving of Casco Viejo's roads replaced the broken bitumen of El Chorrillo, and the lady's pace quickened. She rounded a corner into the darkness. Owen sprung forward to reach the corner before she disappeared, but he was too slow. He stood beside a burnt-out sedan, wiping his face with the sleeve of his shirt and deciding that his pursuit was pointless now anyway. He had done what the messenger had asked of him, but what was he to do now?

A rustling of garbage alerted Owen to the figure emerging from beneath a nearby house. The silhouette of a small boy appeared in the moonlight, and he stood defiantly in the centre of the road. Owen hesitated, as though standing in the yard of a taunted guard dog. He was so fixated on the boy's hollow black eyes that he barely reacted when the flash of a switchblade knife whipped around his neck and pressed firmly into his trachea.

Chapter Eighteen

"Don't move," the lady hissed in English, the sleeves of her red dress pressed against the back of Owen's shoulders as she adjusted the knife higher against his throat. The boy watched, his face still hollow and vacant, then evaporated into the darkness.

Owen's body was frozen stiff. His fingers were still trying to hold onto the straw hat, but it fell silently onto the crumbled pavement. He flinched as the lady's icy cold hand snaked into the pockets of his cargo pants. She removed his passport and wallet, and he could feel her skilfully flicking them open between her fingers, her other hand still clutching the knife.

"You have been following me since I left my house, 'Owen Ellis, foreign correspondent.' Explain." Her voice was tense, but her English was enunciated carefully enough to show that she was less fearful than her prisoner.

"I-I was … I thought you were the one who –"

"Who what?" the lady barked. "Speak your language properly."

Owen tried to clear his throat, feeling the knife pinching into his skin. "I received a note, a message to follow you tonight. I thought that maybe you were the one who wrote it, who sent me the photographs?"

There was a long pause before the lady pulled the knife away and pushed the tip against his left kidney. "Walk."

Owen shifted forward uneasily. He could sense the lady scanning the empty street as they rounded a corner and then edged towards the light of the red doorway. The door was resting ajar, and the boy's face appeared from within.

The knife was again removed as Owen shuffled awkwardly into the dim light of a waiting room. Flanked by velvet couches, the violet walls were decorated with erotic gold-framed artwork. From the roof hung small crystal chandeliers, and on a coffee table rested a stack of magazines, a row of phallic candles and a tray of incense. The boy disappeared behind a layer of curtains and the lady motioned abruptly for Owen to follow. He pushed the curtains aside and the lady directed him around a staircase, through a dimly lit hallway and past a drab kitchen where two women in lingerie ate pasta around a tiny television. Another hallway led to an open brown door, through which the lady motioned for Owen to enter.

A long white desk spanned from a chipboard bookcase to a scarred brick feature wall. A cane chair with ruptured cushions was positioned beside a large bay window, in which stark white shutters were drawn firmly shut and reflected the glaring white light of a naked bulb.

"Sit," the woman ordered as she sat cross-legged on the desk. She retracted the knife blade with a frightening flick, reached into her bra for a cigarette and then into the desk behind her.

Owen felt like a student on detention, slinking into the low cane chair and staring up at the headmistress, her face imperious yet seductive in the hissing flame of a match.

"I am used to people following me, Mr Ellis," the lady said as she inhaled the smoke, "but not journalists." She studied his face carefully and then blew outwards, her eyes narrowing. "You came here once before, no? You asked for Spadafora, and I turned you away."

Owen ran a nervous hand through his hair. "Yes, that's, that's right. Again, I was only following instructions. I... wh-what is this place, and who are you?"

"Ha!" The lady scoffed. "You're not much of a journalist, are you?" She flicked the ash from her cigarette and leaned forward. "My name is Maria, and this is not a grocery store. Now if somebody sent you to follow me, I want to know who. Who are they? Talk."

Owen raised his hands. "Like I said, I received a note; it said to follow someone who left this address at 6:15pm this evening. I can only guess that whoever sent me the message wanted me to know that you have a relationship with General Noriega, and that you have access to the Comandancia."

"A relationship?" Maria laughed emphatically. "You think I have a relationship with that animal? Ha! What I do is called work, Mr Ellis."

"But you have access," he responded, finding confidence in the fact that this woman was not going to sell him out to her employer. "To the building – you can walk in there without being stopped." He dug into one of the lower pockets of his cargo pants and removed a photocopy of the Comandancia blueprint. "I was also sent this. I believe that someone from the CIA has been trying to get access to a basement inside the Comandancia. I don't know for sure what's down there but it's possible they're after evidence that Noriega has been using for blackmail."

Maria barely looked at the blueprint before twisting her thick lips into what appeared to be a snarl. She stood up, the switchblade flicking out loudly. "You think you can just use me? Just like Spadafora, you think I will help you get access to Noriega's dirty little secrets?"

"So there is something in there?" Owen pressed through his fear. "And Spadafora? He also wanted to get access to the Comandancia through you?"

Owen's body heaved deeper into the chair as the knife was flung in front of his face. Maria's dark brown eyes were inflamed, and she hovered there for several seconds before retreating slowly, the blade kept open. "I don't know who set you up, but they're playin' games with you. I learned my lesson not to cross Noriega, oh didn't I just! The only reason I have his trust is because he destroyed me, he owns me, and he owns my son. And if you think I'll risk my life again for some gringo fool you can forget it. I've got too much now to lose."

"I wasn't asking you to help me," Owen wheezed, his thoughts racing. "I just need information, I just need to know for sure what's inside that room. Any knowledge that you have can help me. And look, if you do help me, if you do have access to Noriega's files, I can organise protection."

"Protección?" Maria laughed. "The only protection I need is from fools like you! Get outta here, Owen Ellis. Go on, sal de aqui!"

Owen dithered, breathing heavily through his nose as Maria pointed at the door. He finally gave in, rising to his feet and allowing her to shove him out the doorway and towards the right. A narrow hallway turned beneath a worn wooden staircase and then spiralled down a series of concrete steps. The windowless room below was lit with a dusty bulb that flickered over a cellar trapdoor and scores of broken plastic toys. On the other side of the trapdoor was a rusted steel ingress, which Maria unbolted to reveal a passageway back up to the street. Owen moved forward cautiously, then stepped out into the night air, staring back into Maria's scowl.

"If I ever see you here again, I swear I will bury you below this floor. Now go, and don't be seen."

Thorn wiped the remaining Thai curry from his lips and took a long sip from his glass of coke. "I can understand where you're coming from buddy, but organising protection for a prostitute doesn't exactly come under my job description."

Owen nodded, sighing. He pulled a laminated menu from behind a bottle of soy sauce and scanned the desserts menu. "What about your contacts in the CIA? What about Conrad?"

"Look, even if you think you can get this woman on side, do you really think she'd have access to every room in the Comandancia? I've been in there, and you can hardly stretch your arms out without striking a guard."

"But you should have seen the way they looked at her, Joe. Every man inside that fence was enamoured. If anyone can get access, it's her."

Thorn shook his head, smiling sadly. "I think you've been watching too many spy movies, buddy. The only way to get into that building is by force, and that's exactly what we'll do if the button is pushed. The Comandancia will be our first target, and be assured, whatever is in there will be seized."

"Or destroyed."

Thorn smirked, waving down a waitress. "A black coffee for me, and a bowl of ice cream for James Bond here."

Owen scoffed.

"So you haven't received any other notes?" Thorn was staring seriously now, and snapped a toothpick between his fingers. "Any phone calls? Any more thoughts on who could have sent you those pictures?"

"Sorry," Owen shrugged. "Nothing."

"Hmm, well I'm sure that Hector knows more than he's letting on. Keep me in the loop if you hear anything more, okay?"

"Of course."

Thorn stared intensely into Owen's eyes, frowning. "I mean it. I'm uncomfortable with all of this. I feel like you're being set up, and I think Hector is behind it."

"What happened between you two? Last time I was here you idolised him. As did Eva."

"She still does. And so she should. But a few good deeds don't make a man a saint. And it certainly doesn't excuse Hector from his past."

"But you always knew he had a shady past. You were almost proud of acknowledging it! What's changed?"

Thorn shrugged and looked away. "I remember you telling me about those deadbeat journalists you used to work with after you graduated. You remember? Before you came down here for the Spadafora story?"

Owen produced a confused smile. "What about them?"

"Do you still speak to them? Do you even bother anymore, now that you stay at the Marriott?"

"Um. I do, actually. I still keep in touch."

Thorn shrugged again. "Well that's where you and I differ. Hector may have given me a leg up, but he's a liability now. People know about his past, about his stuff-ups in Mossad and the CIA, his arms dealings, and – oh yeah, his wife. And jeez, that's a story you don't want to delve into. I really don't need that association. And neither does Eva."

"Sorry, his wife? What happened to her?"

"Nobody knows. Her body washed up in the Canal when Sarita was a teenager. Most people believe Hector did it. I certainly do. Apparently she was having an affair with Torrijos. Anyway, Sarita went off the rails. She got herself hooked on crack and threw away a career in dancing. So Hector built the auditorium, apparently as an effort to keep her at home and mentor other dancers."

"Well that sounds rather commendable."

"Whatever you say. But remember this: nothing makes you try harder to impress than guilt."

Chapter Nineteen

Harmiston Library.
Present day.

Jenna pursed her lips, her face illuminated in the light of her laptop as she scrolled through the list of flights that left Heathrow at the time of her mother's death. Her pen moved swiftly as she read, the back pages of her diary turning into a complex map of possibilities. She could have typed what she wrote, but there was something cathartic about pen on paper, her emotions articulated in the leaning slant of her handwriting, the bold question marks and arrows helping to untangle the knots in her mind. She read back over the maze of ideas, flipped the diary shut and then cringed at the glittering love heart stickers on the front cover. She ripped them off and flicked them into a nearby bin. Tucking her laptop into her gym bag, she strode towards the sunlight flooding through the library exit.

Curled autumn leaves fluttered lazily through Harmiston's streets, crunching under Jenna's joggers as she marched towards her mother's old dance studio. School had just finished, and the sight of children waiting for buses and prancing across pedestrian crossings softened her ire. She pulled out the keys for the dance hall, but noticed that the doors were already open for an after-school class. She frowned, hoping that there would still be space at the back to grind her emotions into the floorboards. Dancing had become the only means by which her mind could be pulled away from the pain of reality, and her reliance upon the escape was becoming an addiction. She was about to step into the doorway when a voice made her turn.

The man was middle-aged, his hair greying above his ears and his neatly trimmed moustache giving him the look of an old-fashioned academic. A thick leather jacket beefed up his wiry build, but clashed with his dowdy appearance. "Sorry Ma'am," he said in what sounded like an American accent, pushing back his dark sunglasses, "I don't have any change for the parking meter. Am I able to exchange a note for some coins?"

"Uh, sure," Jenna responded hesitantly, pulling her purse back out.

"I'm sorry," the man repeated. "The meters here don't seem to like foreign credit cards."

"That's fine," Jenna smiled, avoiding eye contact. "Here you go."

The man smiled warmly, pushed a five-pound banknote into her palm and took the coins. His mild features and soft green eyes gave him a likeable appearance. The leather jacket, however, made him look like the casualty of a mid-life crisis. He thanked her again, flicking his sunglasses back over his eyes and sauntering towards the parking meters.

Jenna stepped inside, feeding the banknote into her purse and acknowledging the stares of two young dancers who recognised her. Her strides to the back of the hall quickened to avoid a conversation, then came to an abrupt halt. One side of the banknote was marked with thick black ink.

I knew Eva Miranda.
Meet me at the Highgate Motel, Room 43.

Jenna spun back around, her heart pounding. She ran to the doorway, but the man was gone.

Chapter Twenty

Jenna's fingers were trembling as she slid Molly into the dingy parking lot behind the Highgate Motel. She flipped down her sun visor to stare at herself in the mirror. Her eyes were like those of a lost child's, unblinking and cagey. She adjusted her hair before stepping out onto the broken glass that littered the asphalt. The sun was beginning its descent over the red tile roof of the motel, and two jays were fluttering jauntily as they built a nest in a nearby tree.

Jenna stared through the mangled fences surrounding the back of the motel before forcing her legs to move up the shadowy concrete steps. Her legs doubled in weight as she reached the last two steps. She stopped to survey the view below and stepped into a dimly lit corridor. Her mouth was dry as she swallowed, her eyes fixed upon the first doorway on the left. Number 43 – it was written in cracked gold numbers that hung off crooked brass nails. A bizarre feeling of calm swept across her as she stopped before the doorway and raised her hand to knock. But before her knuckles struck the wood the door slowly opened inwards, scuffing along the auburn carpet.

Only the brown leather shoes of the man inside were showing as he hid himself behind the door, waiting for her to enter. The only light in the room came from a small bedside lamp and a dated TV that blared out a news channel; the curtains were drawn and the single bed was undisturbed. A backpack lay on a bench above a bar fridge, and a leather jacket hung on the back of a chair. There was no luggage, and Jenna's racing mind told her that the room had been reserved only for their meeting.

She took a short step forward, staring into the shaded eyes of the man as he waited to close the door. He flicked on the light, exposing a grave expression that had – after many years of frowning – imprinted into his forehead. Subtle crow's feet pulled at the sides of his eyes, and a greying moustache bordered his pale lips. His eyes seemed sadder than they had been outside the dance hall, and his loose fitting white T-shirt seemed a far cry from the gaudy leather jacket.

Jenna's heart was suddenly pounding desperately and she grabbed the door to stop him from closing it. She took a nervous step backwards into the hallway, a strange feeling of pain overcoming her fear and bringing tears to her eyes.

"I'm not going to hurt you," the man said as he retreated back into the room, raising his hands. "I'm on your side. I was a friend of your mother's."

"How do I know you aren't lying?" she asked tautly, her voice breaking. She fidgeted with her handbag, cleared her throat and then uttered, "Who are you?"

The man stepped closer, slowly reaching into his trousers and producing a Canadian passport. "My name is Owen," he said softly, his eyes penetrating into hers, "Owen Ellis."

Chapter Twenty-One

Marriott Hotel, Panama City.
December 16th, 1989.

Owen leapt out of the shower, wrapping himself in a plush white robe and running for the living room phone. The volume of a BBC broadcast had almost drowned out the ringing, and he pressed at the TV remote as he lifted up the receiver. Through the panels of glass before him Panama City spread out like an abstract artwork. The streets from this height appeared empty, and the skyscrapers looked like Lego pieces as they competed with the lush rainforest and fought for space beside the strangely still bay.

"Hello?"

"She said yes!" came the response. "She said yes, buddy!"

For a second, Owen's face was awash with confusion. Then he beamed. "Joe, that's fantastic! That's just wonderful, congratulations!"

"Yeah, I'm stoked. It actually happened last night. I'm sorry I didn't get a chance to call, I was partying with the Joes till early this morning."

"Haha! I bet you were, it's great news."

"So we're free this evening, and Eva was wondering if you wanted to come over for dinner, to have a family celebration?"

"Well, sure. Um, what time?"

"Seven, if you aren't busy?"

"Of course. But I've never actually been to your house. Where is it?"

Owen wrote down the address as he stared at the television screen, his smile fading. The images of Noriega's speech the day before continued to dominate the headlines, and the words of the reporter took over his concentration.

"With rumours of a US backed coup growing, Noriega has declared Panama in a state of war with the United States. He has asserted himself as 'Maximum Leader' of Panama, and has promoted celebrations across the country for 'Loyalty Day' – this now the sixth anniversary of his rule."

Noriega was shown pumping his fist at a crowd, and the madness in his eyes sucked Owen's throat dry. He finished the phone call asking Thorn whether it was safe to even leave the hotel tonight.

"I wouldn't be driving around in a troop carrier," Thorn joked. "Yeah, it's bad buddy, and it's getting worse, but you're not here for the sunshine, are you? Take your scooter; nobody will even blink at you."

Owen tried to keep a bouquet of flowers from being torn as his scooter cruised through the silent evening. He took the highway around the Chorrillo barrios, and stared across at the distinctive figures building roadblocks around the Comandancia.

The Machos del Monte were as wild as Thorn had described. They looked like exaggerated movie villains in their black tank tops, red sweatbands and rugged black beards. They drove enormous 4WDs equipped with improvised machine gun holsters, and climbed aboard the soft-top roofs brandishing machetes and assault rifles.

"This place is insane," Owen breathed as he accelerated into the Canal Zone, where US soldiers were also setting up barricades and moving tensely, their marches out of time as they surveyed the boundaries of their territory.

Thorn's house was located against the jungle in Fort Clayton, a military town that looked as though a Midwest suburb had been overgrown by tropical palms and Spanish moss. Fresh green lawns spread like playing fields between tennis courts and white concrete houses, which flowed languidly across fenceless yards.

Floodlights beamed across Thorn's cement driveway, which was blocked on one side by a box trailer and stacks of iron window bars wrapped in plastic. Owen shielded his face from the glare of the lights as he examined the bars, noticing that the labourer had begun installing them across the front windows. He wheeled the scooter along the wide veranda and chained it to a pillar beside a three-door garage. Gathering the flowers and a bottle of wine, he shuffled clumsily towards the front door where a black security camera bore down at him.

Owen's knock on the door was quickly followed by Eva's strutting figure in the stained glass. She pulled open the door with a welcoming smile, her curled hair bouncing energetically over a tight fitting maroon dress.

"Wonderful to see you again Owen, bienvenidos!" She gave him a kiss on the cheek. "Come in, entra!"

"Thanks, wow, you're looking... Wow, here, I bought you some flowers." And pointing at the ring on her finger: "Congratulations! I'm so happy for you both!"

"Muchas gracias!" she said with a boisterous giggle. "Joe, look at these, aren't they beautiful?"

"Owen, my man," Thorn said as he strolled through a plush sunken lounge to shake his cousin's hand.

"Oh, and some wine," Owen said with a flustered smile, handing the bottle to Thorn.

"Thanks buddy," Thorn blurted with a slightly drunken smirk. "We might crack this a bit later on. In the meantime, have a taste of this Cab Sav from California. Some of the Joes brought it back for me last night. A decade old, worth a fortune."

"Sure, why not."

Owen smiled back at Eva as Thorn shifted them towards the kitchen and then changed his mind, setting down his wine glass. "Come and I'll give you a tour."

Eva turned up the volume of an antique record player as Thorn wrapped his arm over Owen's shoulder and led him into a strangely familiar poolroom. The high, intricately corniced ceiling was speckled with down lights that angled towards the antlered heads of deer, moose and black bears.

"You're kidding me," Owen laughed as he circled the room, shaking his head. "This is the same room as your father's old place. The heads; they're his too, aren't they?"

Thorn was smiling smugly as he leaned against the pool table. "No, no, they're mine. All shot with his Ruger though. You remember that rifle?"

"Uh, no, I don't."

"You used to cover your ears and run every time you saw it, even when my father was inside cleaning it."

Owen smiled uncomfortably, scanning the collection of medals displayed in a hardwood cabinet. "That sounds like me."

"My chest candy," Thorn pointed with a smile. "That's a Purple Heart there." He strutted to the cabinet and opened the glass doors. "And the Silver Star, both from Grenada. That's when you were in College I think. Yeah, it was, because your papa was in hospital for the first time, yeah?"

Owen's eyes flicked downwards and he nodded stiffly.

"Let me show you the other rooms."

"Please do."

The front of the house was occupied by an enormous study with a broad bay window that looked out at the trailer in the driveway. Thorn flicked on the lights and was about to move on when Owen stopped him. "What happened to the window?"

"Ah, yeah," Thorn sighed, standing in the doorway. "Some of the locals I'd say, broke in a week back. Nothing too serious, just bored teenagers."

"That's no good," Owen frowned. "So that's what the bars are for outside, then?"

"Indeed. So how is your friend Maria? Conrad has given me some intel on her, by the way."

"Oh yes?"

Thorn grinned as he led the way through to a sunroom filled with ferns and hanging pots. "She's got quite a reputation. Apparently she had most of Panama's top politicians wrapped around her finger. Before she had the kid, that is."

"Hmm," Owen frowned. "That doesn't change anything. In fact, it only makes her a more valuable asset if she can be coerced."

"But she won't be," Thorn frowned knowingly. "Not unless you have more money than Noriega."

"I don't think money is what she's after." Owen was staring at him with an intense expression, but Thorn avoided his eyes. "I think she just wants her son to be safe."

"Of course it's money she wants, she's a hooker." He turned back down the hallway. "Time for some American beef. I hope you're hungry!"

Owen's thoughts were scattered throughout dinner and he avoided the wine, keen to remain sober. He noticed that Eva was constantly filling Thorn's glass, and was staring at Owen with a strange smile, obviously picking up on his distractedness.

"I understand that you are now teaching," Owen said to Eva. "Are you still dancing yourself at all?"

"Certainly am," Eva nodded, forking out another slab of meat onto Thorn's plate. "And I would still love to dance professionally, maybe in London. Just as soon as Joe decides to sweep me out of Panama."

"You be patient," Thorn slurred. "The sooner we get the go-ahead to blow Noriega's ass out of here, the sooner you can dance around wherever you like."

Owen poked again at his steak. There was something in Eva's stares that didn't feel right.

"Out of wine," Thorn sighed, tipping up a bottle clumsily. "Didn't you say there was more, babe?"

"Yes," Eva said tensely, sitting upright. "It's airing in the study, like you asked. Owen, could you please grab it while I prepare dessert?"

"No, no, I'll get it," Thorn blabbered. "I'll just –"

"Stay there, mi amor," Eva soothed, "and finish that steak. Didn't you say last night that you could eat two pounds in one sitting?"

"Pfft, you see what I'm going to have to put up with here, Owen? God, she's worse than a Colonel."

"It's fine," Owen grinned. "I'll get it for you."

The hallway lights were glaring after the candlelight of the dining room, and Owen tightened his eyelids as he rounded a doorway into the study. He flicked on the light and walked towards a tall filing cabinet where the wine was perched beside a black and white photograph of Thorn's father. His attention was drawn to the imposing face as he reached for the wine, and he almost missed seeing a small note protruding from beneath the bottle. He picked it up slowly, his fingers unsteady as he recognised the handwriting.

Second drawer. Control yourself.

Beneath the note was a small golden key. Owen's heart was pounding as he leaned back to stare down the empty hallway. He rested the wine on the desk and carefully crouched beside a set of hardwood drawers. A lump in his throat seemed to press into his windpipe, and his hands were shaking as he slid the key into the lock.

The drawer rolled forward on well-oiled brackets. Inside, a black Beretta pistol lay over a neat stack of enlarged photographs and documents. Owen's hands flailed through the images, his body convulsing in horror. They were the originals of the photographs that he had been sent in the mail, yet there were more. Far more. And behind them, resting over a leather-bound folder was a sight that ripped the air from his lungs – his father's gold watch.

Chapter Twenty-Two

Highgate Motel, Harmiston.
Present day.

"Have a seat. Can I get you a coffee, some water?"

"No, thanks," Jenna said cautiously, taking a seat at the table and glancing back at the closed door. The thudding of her pulse seemed to rattle the myriad of questions swirling around her mind, and she struggled to bring words to her lips. "It was you, wasn't it?" she finally spoke. "At the funeral? That was you who followed me?"

Owen filled a plastic kettle and carefully wiped out a mug with a worn tea towel. "Yes, I was there. I didn't know your mother well, but I had to pay my respects. I met her in Panama a long time ago, but until last week I thought she had been killed there."

Jenna's jaw was clenched, her pulse easing as she focused upon his mannerisms. There was something so completely humble about the way he prepared his coffee that she found herself strangely trusting. She waited until he faced her again before speaking. "So how did you know that it was her from the news reports? They haven't mentioned her real name on any of the broadcasts."

Owen took a seat at the table, staring calmly into Jenna's face. "Because the day before she was killed she called my office in Canada. She explained who she was, and that she had left a note with her daughter, Jenna Martinez. At first I didn't believe it was her, until I saw the headlines from London the following day."

"Why you?" she demanded, leaning forward and clasping her hands. "I don't understand."

He sighed, avoiding her eyes. "In the 1980s I worked on a story in Panama, which led me to your mother. She had uncovered a secret that threatened to bring down a ring of CIA agents and army officials that spanned all the way to the White House."

Jenna's face remained stony. "Go on."

He again shifted his position, staring into the wood grains of the table. "The man with the most blood on his hands was my cousin, a Lieutenant Colonel who was using the CIA to launder money and traffic cocaine for Noriega. That man was your mother's fiancé. He is now the Director of the CIA."

The loud steaming of the kettle seemed to sweep the blood from Jenna's face, turning her cheeks a ghostly grey. "Joseph Thorn," she gasped.

Owen nodded grimly. "Your mother mentioned him?"

"No, no," she stammered. "She never told me anything about her time in Panama. I only know about Joseph Thorn because… Because he came to see me after a performance in London last week, to congratulate me and –" She shook her head in astonishment. "He knew who I was, didn't he? He asked about my mother, and my father. To make sure – to make sure that…"

Owen bit into his lower lip, his eyes closing.

Another revelation struck Jenna like a punch to the stomach, and she struggled for breath, her emotions unravelling and sending tears down her cheeks. "If he was her fiancé in 1989…" She buried her head in her knees, her sobbing now uncontrollable. "My mother told me that my father is dead, but it's not true, is it? He's my – Joseph Thorn is my – isn't he?"

Owen sighed heavily through his nose and tried to place a hand on Jenna's arm. She pulled away and glared into his eyes. "What was it that she uncovered? What was it that my mother was hiding in her house?"

Owen allowed himself to smile sadly. "Your mother didn't have anything in her house, Jenna. From what I understand she made contact this year with Joseph Thorn, telling him who she was, and that she had a collection of tapes proving his crimes in Panama. Whether it was seeing him on TV after all this time and wanting revenge, or seeing a financial opportunity out of doing it – I don't know, but she tried to blackmail him. Obviously he believed her story, and had her tracked down."

Jenna shook her head, frustration at her mother's actions mixed with horror at the truth. "So the tapes," she asked again, "they never even existed?"

"They certainly did exist." He leaned forward. "But they were destroyed. And without them, there's no evidence of the truth."

Jenna began sobbing again and her hoarse coughing was relieved as Owen placed a glass of water in front of her. He peered through a crack in the curtains and then returned to his seat.

"So the soldier that my mother killed," Jenna eventually said, sniffling, "who was he? They said that they were arresting her for killing a soldier in Panama."

Owen shook his head sadly. "Your mother was feisty, but she was never a killer. I'd say those men – whoever they were – used that story to justify the surveillance over you and your mother, and to raid your house. They were after your mother for the tapes, and when they didn't find them, they must have decided to kill her anyway for fear of what she knew."

"But you obviously know as well," Jenna spluttered. "So why are they not after you?"

"I'm Thorn's cousin," Owen explained again. "He knows that I know the truth, but he also knows that I can't do anything without evidence. Nonetheless, I've been followed since I arrived in England, and they'll no doubt try to kill me if they find out I'm telling you this."

"Well I appreciate you taking the risk, and coming to the funeral." She stood up and wiped the tears from her cheeks. She paced across the room and thinking aloud, murmured, "But what does Rafael have to do with this?"

"What's that?" Owen responded, carefully pouring himself another coffee.

"Rafael Cordoba," Jenna said with a sniff.

It was Owen's turn to look shocked. "Rafael?" he said loudly.

"Yes." She reached into her back pocket and produced the note that her mother had left for her.

Owen spread the paper onto the table. For a few seconds he remained still, then cried out in shock and excitement. "I don't believe it! But it can't be. It can't be!" He turned to Jenna with a wild look.

"I don't understand."

"He's still alive," he laughed. "She found him! My God! But when? When did your mother go to Cuba? When was the last time she left England?"

Jenna's face was wrinkled in confusion. "Um, she went to Central America last year, for a holiday to meet some old friend. She didn't really tell me much. She's like that."

Owen smiled triumphantly. "No wonder Thorn believed her! Your mother wasn't trying to blackmail him with a lie; she was blackmailing him with the truth! Of course! And the reason she contacted me, the reason she left this note for you – for us – was to let us know that she found them, that the tapes must still exist!"

Owen's excited cries drowned out the footsteps shuffling outside the door, and Jenna raised her finger to her lips to silence him. Owen froze. He crept over to the curtains to peer outside. "Get inside the bathroom!" he hissed over the sound of the TV. He crawled over to the door just as it vibrated with a heavy knock.

"Who is it?" Owen called, projecting his voice back into the centre of the room.

There was no answer, and Owen peered through the crack at the base of the door. He leapt back up, pressing his ear to the centre of the door. His eyes closed as he listened fearfully.

It was as if a truck slammed into the door, sending Owen sprawling across the carpet. The frame of a familiar bald-headed man stood in the doorway, his boot returning to the floor as he raised a long silenced pistol and took aim at Owen's head.

Jenna's frantic leap from the bathroom doorway crushed the man's arm against the wall. The gun went off, taking a chunk of mortar from the bricks, spraying Owen's face with grit and filling Jenna's ears with a ringing slap. The man managed to keep hold of the weapon, and cried out as Jenna's teeth sunk deep into his wrist. His left arm was still pinned against the door, and flailed helplessly as he tried to land a punch on Jenna's face. Her bite strengthened, and he finally let the gun slip into Owen's grip.

Owen flung the pistol back into the room and heaved his body into a punch that collided with the man's face. It drew blood from his nose, but failed to keep him from lurching forward and throwing his opponents back into the carpet. Blood splattered from his nose as he came at them, landing his fists into Owen's ribs. Jenna leapt back to her feet, glancing around the room before swiping her hand out to grab the kettle.

The sound of the man's screaming was sickening as boiling water splashed over his naked scalp and down his face.

Owen slipped free of the water and whipped the man's hands behind his back, slamming his pelvis flat against the carpet. "The sheets!" he cried to Jenna. "Pull the sheets off the bed!"

Within seconds a sheet was being twisted around the man's wrists and then stuffed into his mouth, stifling his shouts.

"Go start your car!" Owen cried as he finished, jolting Jenna out of a frozen shock and sending her running out of the door. Owen pulled on his leather jacket and ripped open his backpack to remove a spray bottle of blue detergent and a rag. With adroit speed he wiped over the fridge door and kettle and stuffed his mug and the glass that Jenna had used into his bag. With the rag still wrapped around his hand he pushed the pistol into the front of his trousers and pulled on his backpack. He scanned the empty hallway and swept the broken door shut behind him, leaving the man still gagged and groaning in the darkness.

Jenna whimpered as she fumbled with Molly's keys, finally letting herself in and staring fearfully up at the motel. Molly soon chugged to life, by which time Owen had thrown his bag into the back seat and jumped in. Jenna flicked on the headlights and reversed wildly.

"Your house!" Owen cried as the car left tyre marks across the asphalt. "They won't go there with the press still about."

"They'll have your name at reception," Jenna said anxiously as she drove. "They're going to arrest us, aren't they?"

"No they won't," Owen blurted, pulling the pistol out of his trousers and rubbing it over with a cloth. "This place has no security cameras, and I checked in under a false name."

The growing darkness was a blessing as the car sped undetected through the village and onto a winding country road. Owen's calm was consoling, and his skilful removal of the pistol's magazine in the light of the dash gave Jenna the impression that this was no ordinary journalist.

"What are you going to do with that?"

Owen wound down the window and answered her question by tossing the pistol, then soon after, the magazine, into the tall grass outside.

"Hey! Why did you do that?"

"Because we don't need it. Now it may sound like an odd question," he sighed, checking his watch, "but do you have a passport?"

"I do," she replied, her eyes narrowing. "Why?"

"Because I want you to come with me to Cuba."

Chapter Twenty-Three

Thorn's House.
December 16th, 1989, 9pm.

The jigsaw pieces flew like missiles through Owen's mind, ramming into each other and linking in horrible tessellation. He allowed himself to breathe, then marvelled at his sudden calm, as though somehow he had known the truth all along. His face became stony as he slipped the watch into his pocket and rearranged the photographs back to their original stack. He imagined himself taking the gun, checking that it was loaded and then storming into the dining room, firing like a madman and splattering blood across the carpet. But instead his body became a robot. He locked the drawer, placed the key back on the filing cabinet, then supported himself against the doorway. He took control of his breathing, ran a hand through his hair and then focused upon the wine label as he returned to the dining table.

"Here he is," Thorn declared as Eva removed his plate. "Got lost in there, did you?"

"Of course not," Owen said, forcing a plastic grin. "I've just been admiring the label writer's eloquence." His eyes tried to meet Eva's, but she was ducking into the door of the dishwasher.

"Ha!" Thorn laughed, leaning back in his chair. "Wait for it, wait for it, I've got this one." He closed his eyes, his face morphing into that of a drunken performer. "Sourced from the rich, truffle-laden ridges of the Napa

Valley, where sea breezes cool the grapes at twilight to produce rich, tight tannins. And flying pigs harvest them every morning at the end of rainbows! How did I go?"

"Not bad," Owen rasped, forcing himself to be distracted from the rage that was bubbling through his stomach. "But it's from Monterey. And the tannins are 'soft and silky', not tight."

"I didn't know you were such a connoisseur," Thorn taunted, running his hand over Eva's lower back as she placed bowls of cake and ice cream on the table. "Perhaps you should (hiccup) become a wine label... writer."

Owen shrugged. "I think I've got the vocabulary for it," he countered, finally making eye contact with Eva, "but I'm afraid I didn't inherit your propensity for lying."

The comment seemed to bypass Thorn's attention, but Eva's face became stiff with alarm. Owen hardly knew her, but in that instant he knew her better than anybody else. The boisterous smiles and dainty demeanour were a perfectly executed façade; the mind behind her dark brown eyes must have hidden a thousand secrets – but how long had she known? How long had she kept this up?

The music seemed to become louder as they ate dessert, and Thorn's drunkenness had fully set in as he clumsily dropped his spoon.

"I really should go, I've got a splitting migraine," Owen said with genuine pain, clutching at his scalp. "I'm sorry, but I really should get to bed."

"Ah, come and have whiskey then," Thorn protested. "Give it a few minutes and you won't even feel your head."

"Joe, he's got to ride," Eva argued. "Owen, you'd like an aspirin, no?"

"No, no, it's fine. I better get back. Thanks again, both of you, and congratulations."

"It was great having you," Eva said, removing the bowls from the table and strutting towards the doorway. "Here, I'll show you out."

"Alright buddy," Thorn said, standing up from his seat with a stagger and shaking Owen's hand. "Another time then, you take care heading back now, yeah? Those brown bastards will be all over the streets like they own the place."

Owen stopped, his face inflamed. But Thorn took no notice of his reaction, fumbling towards the kitchen, and Eva dismissed the comment as though it had no bearing upon her. Owen continued through the lounge room, his mind again overwhelmed by images of his pounding fists. He breathed in deeply, controlling his footsteps and allowing Eva to unlock the front door.

The scene moved in slow motion as she stepped outside with him, slowly clicking the door shut and staring downwards like a judge about to deliver a guilty plea. But it was Owen who spoke first.

"How long have you known?"

Eva's top lip quivered, as though trying to suppress a volcano of emotion. "Two weeks," she whispered. "I didn't know what to do, so I photocopied them, those pictures, and I sent them to you. I knew that you would come."

"And you smashed the window," Owen whispered, nodding towards the study. "To make it look like someone else broke in?"

She nodded, her face now filled with fear. "We can't talk about this now. He suspects you know too much, and he has men watching you, and watching me." She stared into the darkness beyond the light of the garage, swallowing deeply. "Meet me tomorrow, at noon, in the park under the bridge."

The night's humidity wrapped its clammy hands around Owen's throat as he tried to accelerate, his lips drawn back like a lion's snarl, his leather shoes pounding into the back of the scooter's floorboard. The engine wouldn't reciprocate the roaring of his emotions, continuing to buzz and whir like a dying lawnmower. The pathetic sound added to the bubbling and frothing of his rage – it was like a viscous fuel with no engine to power, blurring his vision and causing him to ignore the roadblock looming ahead.

One of three Machos cocked his rifle and fixed the headlights of the scooter in his scope. He narrowed his bushy eyebrows and then glanced at the soldiers beside him, waiting for the instruction to fire. They stared back at their companion; their disbelieving expressions followed by amusement as the scooter screeched to a halt. The soldiers laughed, raising their heads and watching as the red-faced gringo struggled to turn the handlebars and retreat.

"Fuera de aqui muchacho!"

Owen's fear and embarrassment quickly pulled him back to reality, and he slid the scooter off the highway and into Avenida A, where the ramshackle balconies were filled with tense families watching the influx of military vehicles. His thoughts turned back to the cause of his white knuckles, and Thorn's grinning face seemed to occupy every dark doorway. Standing in the light ahead was a vision of Eva, the flashes of her ring lighting up a thousand pointed questions. How much did she know? Had Thorn ever suspected her?

The air felt like steam compressed between the slums, adding to a sense of claustrophobia that made Owen more desperate to find the fastest route out of the labyrinth. The streets had grown darker, with some of the street-lights either blown or smashed. He turned a corner into a street bathed in yellow light, where a group of ten or more Machos were congregating at another roadblock. In the next street, the lights of the Comandancia glared like unblinking eyes, and Owen decided that it would be safer to pass through this roadblock than to approach the base. He waited patiently as two sedans coming in the opposite direction were waved through, then felt his body go stiff as another vehicle tried to follow. It was a long beige Chevrolet Impala – the sort of vehicle that would have looked more at home on the streets of New York – and in the street light glow its passengers had the proud look of US marines. They argued with the crowd of Machos, one of whom raised his assault rifle.

Owen gasped as the driver gunned the vehicle, its broad white-rimmed tyres screeching past the shouting men. Gunfire rattled through Owen's chest, and he threw himself into a sunken doorway to his right, cowering behind the cement wall as his scooter toppled into the gutter.

The Impala continued to fishtail down the avenue, its trunk rippling with bullet holes.

Owen remained undetected as the Machos ran after the car like crazed animals, and the rattling of automatic gunfire continued into the next street, where the Impala had mistakenly turned towards the Comandancia. Owen peered out from his hiding place, gasping again as the Machos rounded up a young western couple who had witnessed the shooting. The men ripped at the woman's dress as they dragged her screaming into an open doorway. Her partner tried to resist, his terrified eyes catching Owen's gaze as he recoiled in pain, the fist of a soldier pounding into his stomach. He too disappeared into the open door, and Owen began to feel his knees knocking in panic. He checked his watch and edged out from his hiding place to lift up the scooter.

The street was now clear of soldiers, but the shouts of the young couple had brought families creeping onto the balconies above. A heavily set mother peered down at Owen through a row of potted flowers. She hissed at him, motioning for him to get out of there. He leapt awkwardly onto the scooter, letting it roll off the pavement before revving frantically.

The sound alerted a group of soldiers gathered at the next crossroad. They shouted into their radios and ran forward like a pack of wolves. Owen groaned, hearing the mother's desperate shouts directing him towards a side street. He spun the scooter around and felt the ground suddenly flowing as he sped into the narrow lane, a stack of cardboard boxes crashing in his wake. He emerged onto a main road, and let the scooter purr towards its top speed as the last of the gunshots were lost to the wind.

Across the barrios the beige Impala was roaring its way towards Ancon Hill, where a band of US soldiers were waiting with bated breath. By the time the vehicle reached them the back seat was saturated with the blood of Robert Paz, a twenty-four year old lieutenant. They rushed him through the doors of Gorgas Hospital, but he had already lost too much blood. Twenty minutes later, a US military doctor was slow to emerge in the waiting room; his sombre face bringing cries that would soon be repeated on TV screens across America.

Chapter Twenty-Four

The Bridge of the Americas loomed like a great skeletal dinosaur, spreading its forelimbs onto the shores of North America and shrouding the overgrown park beneath with the shadow of its tail. The silence of Owen's scooter was a comfort as it wound its way cautiously through the dense foliage below the bridge and onto a grassy knoll that overlooked a line of ships.

Eva was visible amidst a craggy outcrop, her black hair tossing in the ocean breeze as she watched Owen hide the scooter beneath a tree and climb onto the rocks. He surveyed the road below before climbing upwards and then wiping the white grit from his hands. He tried to make eye contact with her as he sat down, but her attention seemed to be focused somewhere out towards the ships.

"Joe said you saw the shooting last night," Eva remarked as she continued to stare, her eyes glazed and out of focus. "He said you gave a story, a statement or something, to the media."

"I did," he replied. He could see from the redness in her cheeks that she had been crying, and he shifted uneasily. "I filed a report this morning, and I've got a TV interview about it later this afternoon."

"Entonces," she sighed, her gaze turning to her hands as they fidgeted with her watch, "when Joe got the call last night, he pretended to be upset. But he was too drunk to act, and when he got off the phone he was laughing. Laughing! Sick, don't you think? He's been wanting this to happen for months."

Owen ruffled his hair and sighed.

"And I used to put up with it. I used to be so… endiosar. What's the word in English? Smitten." Her face turned darker as she tightened the strap of her watch, and her accent became stronger as she continued. "I used to dance around like a little girl and tell my friends all about him. I used to say he's so handsome, oh, he's so lovely, you know. But one of my friends, she told me he had been cheating on me, so I started following him, listening in on his phone calls, and going through his drawers." She wiped away a tear and sniffled loudly. "I guess it's funny that I never found any evidence of him cheating."

"So you found more documents than what is in that drawer?"

"Yes. But I never understood what they were about until now, and I never got a chance to photocopy them. He took most of them away now."

"So do you think he suspects you at all?"

She shrugged sullenly. "He thinks I'm an idiot. And I guess I've kept this up for so long that he has never truly known me, or known what I think. He loves talking down to me, calling me 'mi amor' and buying me cute things. So no, I don't think he suspects me, but he's certainly scared of you."

"So he's talked to you about me?"

"Not much really, but he talks about you with Conrad all the time. I sometimes listen in to what they say."

"Conrad." Owen curled his lips around the name.

"They've been friends for a long time. Joe used to be wrapped around Conrad's finger, but now it seems the other way around."

"So why did you say yes to his proposal?" It was a blunt question, but it had been on the tip of his tongue since he sat down.

She chuckled sadly, biting at her lower lip. "Would you have said no to this rock?" She twirled the diamond between her fingers, her eyes drawn into its glittering core. "My mother, she always told me that the best way to destroy a man is to take his money. And this thing is worth a fortune. When he discovers that I was smarter than him it will break him more than any jail, and I cannot wait to see it happen."

Owen whistled timorously, raising his eyebrows.

"Ha!" Eva laughed at his reaction. "Don't you be scared of me, not unless you run off before this is over."

"I'm not going anywhere," he responded firmly.

"Good. So we better plan this. We don't have much time."

Owen frowned. "The death of one soldier doesn't necessarily mean that the US is going to launch an attack. We should try to get hold of more of Joe's –"

"But you know that they will," she interrupted. "And the first target they'll strike is the Comandancia – Joe said so himself – and whatever is inside will be lost. Gone, forever. We need to get in there before that happens."

"But how?"

"You know how."

He stared back blankly.

Her face suddenly brightened and she nodded downhill towards the water. Owen turned to see a red scooter gliding onto a dirt track and whirring its way towards them. The rider pulled to a skidding stop beside Owen's scooter, ripped off the helmet and cast her dark mascaraed eyes upwards.

"Maria?" Owen coughed, bewildered. "But I thought –"

"I told you in that note; I said you were supposed to follow her, nothing else. I convinced her that if she helps us, you will get her son out of Panama. I just need you to confirm that you will do that for her, and also for me."

"Jesus," Owen exhaled. "I'm a journalist, not some sort of diplomat. I can't go making guarantees like that!"

"Si claro tu puedes. Of course you can. If we do this, if we get evidence, it's going to be bigger than the Iran-Contra affair. So much bigger. All of us will have to appear as witnesses. I know how it works. We automatically receive protection."

Owen chuckled derisively, shaking his head. "It's not going to be that simple. What if we don't pull it off? What if there isn't anything incriminating inside the Comandancia?"

"Then you better think up another way to get us out of here."

He clenched his teeth, his eyes flicking back and forth between Eva's and ignoring the figure strutting over the rocks to his right. "Hello Maria," he said with a commanding voice as she reached them. "What a surprise to see you again!"

Maria frowned, her ire relaxing momentarily when glancing at Eva, then returning as she looked at Owen. She placed her hands on her hips as her weight shifted, the movement parting a black leather jacket and revealing a provocatively low-cut top. "Bueno? I wanna to hear it from you in person."

Owen faced her with a rigid jaw. He knew that he couldn't falter in his speech; that she was too good at judging men to be fooled. "How often do you see Noriega?" he asked, deciding that he needed all the facts before committing to help her. "Does he request you, or are you able to turn up to the Comandancia at any time?"

"I see him once a week." She was staring directly into his eyes, and he could feel her suspiciously reading every movement on his face. "Only after 6pm or 11pm for half an hour. Sometimes less, it depends on how much he has to drink. He doesn't tell his guards to expect me. So if I arrive around those times they will always let me in."

Owen allowed himself to smile. "Perfect."

"And? What can you offer me?"

He ignored her, scratching his chin and staring at the ground. "The exit that you take from the back of the Comandancia; according to the blueprint it's directly above a room in the basement. There should be a stairwell down to that room, just before the exit door. Do you know the one I mean?"

Maria continued staring. "I know the room. You forget this isn't the first time I've been asked to do this."

"I see."

"I was promised a way out of Panama. A new passport, a passport for my son, a flight and a home in some other country, a rich country. Promise me again. Promise me, and I will get you what you want."

Owen maintained his stony expression and slowly held out his hand. "Te lo prometo."

Maria shook his hand, her cheek muscles relaxing. It was almost too subtle to notice, but he was sure that he saw a hint of fear crossing her powdered face. "We have a deal."

Chapter Twenty-Five

Jenna's House.
Present day.

"He's addicted to the news channel," Jenna said as she wedged her phone between her ear and shoulder. She finished filling the kettle and glanced out towards the garden. "And he makes his own food – these like, well-healthy salads and fruit juices. And he's finding all these vegetables in the yard that I didn't even know about. He's out there right now gardening."

"Gardening?" Tracey responded distastefully. "He's doing your gardening? Who does he think he is? He can't just pretend it's his house, not after what he's forced you into."

"Hey, he hasn't forced me into anything. And I don't mind the gardening, it keeps him out of my hair."

"But you've only known him for three days!" Tracey retorted. "And you're going to travel with him to some island in the Caribbean? Don't you see how crazy this is?"

Jenna shrugged to herself and began stacking away the dishes. "It's not as though we're travelling together. We've booked separate flights, so that it's harder for us to be tracked. He's going via Canada, and I'm going via Cancun. We'll meet up in Havana for one night, and hopefully after that we'll know what Mum was trying to tell us."

"And how do you know that he isn't another one of those agents? How do you know he's not going to kill you as soon as you leave the country?"

"Ha! I know he's legitimate because I called his office in Canada, and they confirmed who he was, and that he was on extended leave. I also found some of his articles online. And you know that if he wasn't coming with me I'd still be going to Cuba anyway. I'm not waiting around for this inquest."

Tracey was silent. Jenna could almost see her unsatisfied frown. "Do you have a photo? I mean – I believe that this journalist, Owen Ellis, is real – but how do you know that this guy isn't pretending to be the same man?"

Jenna laughed. "I've found pictures of him online. He's genuine, okay. And besides, does he really look like a secret agent to you?"

"Um, he scares me babe, and the fact that he doesn't have a family to call, or a wife, it's creepy. And his accent, and the gardening thing. Oh, and his clothes!"

"Oh, Tracey," Jenna laughed. "If you think you can judge a man by his fashion sense, then your boyfriend proves you aren't qualified."

"Ha ha," Tracey responded sarcastically. "But seriously, I'm scared for you, and I hope you have phone reception wherever you go."

"I can't guarantee it babe, but I'll contact you every day."

"You better. Now do you still want me to come by with those things you wanted me to buy?"

"Yes, please! Oh, thank you so much for doing that!"

"Don't mention it. I'll be over shortly."

Jenna poured two mugs of tea and made her way out to the patio. She carefully scanned a view of the lane beyond the driveway before stepping into the sunlight.

Owen wiped the black soil off his hands and knees as he stood up from behind a pile of weeds.

"Tea?"

"Why, how British of you!" he grinned. "Of course, thank you."

"Wow, you really have transformed this yard."

"I'm sorry, I hope you don't mind?"

"Of course not. But you – I mean, we – are leaving tomorrow, yeah? You're not going to be able to appreciate it."

He smiled as he led the way to a wooden bench that he had assembled in the shade. "That doesn't worry me at all." He took a sip from his tea and sat back to admire his work. "I need to be outdoors to think, and to come to terms with things."

"How do you mean?"

His face was suddenly serious. "I couldn't bring myself to believe that your mother had still been alive all this time. And Rafael – well, that's just another level of shock. But to be in this yard, to be picking up the cigarette butts that your mother had piled up over there; I know it may sound odd, but that really makes it hit home, more so than that man at the motel. This is real."

"Well I wish it wasn't!"

"Oh, oh I'm sorry," he stammered. "I didn't mean to sound –"

"No, it's fine. I understand where you're coming from, I just… I don't need to pick up my mother's rubbish to know that this is real. And I understand you needing to be out here to think. I'm the same with dance studios after dark when no one else is around. And if I don't get that opportunity for more than two days in a row I start to go crazy. Gosh, especially when I was around my mother."

He smiled, the wrinkles around his eyes creasing. "What was your relationship with her like?"

She laughed. "It wasn't terrific. She was very protective, demanding, and hated men."

"That's understandable."

"And she had terrible habits. Like smoking, drinking, and sometimes gambling. And seedy men. And being secretive over the stupidest things. When I was home we were usually fighting, but when I was in London we got along just fine. Things had been a lot different when we found out she had lung cancer, and I guess I had cried enough tears then that there haven't been as many to cry now."

"That still doesn't detract from the shock of what has happened."

"Of course not. And that's why I need to get out of here. I need to know why this happened. And I need to know who she was before she came to England."

"She was certainly a different person, I can assure you of that."

The sound of crunching gravel pulled Jenna's gaze towards the house. "That'll be Tracey," she said, standing up and striding towards the driveway. As she reached the corner of the house her stomach jumped, for leaning against the bonnet of a police car was a familiar female officer, her hair tied back in a tight blonde bun.

Jenna glanced instinctively back towards the garden, her heart slowing as she saw that Owen had already vanished.

"How are you doing, Jenna?"

"What do you want, Sally?" Jenna glowered, folding her arms and looking impatient.

Sally held up a photograph of a bald-headed man with burns across his face "Does this man look familiar?"

"Not at all. I think I'd remember someone who looked like that." Jenna continued to keep her arms folded defiantly.

"Hmm." Sally continued staring at her suspiciously. "He's being monitored in hospital, but he is refusing to talk."

"And what has this got to do with me?"

Sally stepped forward, stopping directly in front of Jenna's face and frowning. "Let's not play games, Jenna," she whispered. "Your car was seen leaving the motel with a man inside on the same night as this attack. I know you think we aren't getting anywhere with your mother's murder, but it's no excuse to take things into your own hands."

"So you are finally calling it murder then? And you're also suggesting that this man was connected?"

"No, I didn't say that."

"But you're suggesting that I was involved in his attack because of my mother's death, correct?"

"Look, I –"

"Don't play games with me either, Sally. Now, if you want to charge me for driving my car at night, then go ahead. But if not, I would like you to stop blocking my driveway."

"Very well then," Sally huffed, slapping on her hat and opening the door of her car. "But be warned, there's no going back if you – or your new friend – do something stupid."

"I don't know what you're talking about. Goodbye."

Sally began to wind up her window, frowning. "Oh, and Jenna?"

"Hmm?"

"Tell your friend that he can stop hiding in the garden."

PART II
CROSSING GENERATIONS

Chapter Twenty-Six

Havana, Cuba.
Present day.

Jenna kept her headphones in after the plane's descent, the loud music keeping her tears at bay. She imagined herself breaking out of her seatbelt, tumbling out of the window and floating across the broth of clouds that blanketed Havana. The last 24 hours had felt like a dream, as though reality had taken a detour through a sequence of memories, the confusion of jetlag only adding to her delusions. She blinked away a tear and then gripped the seat in front of her tightly. The plane bounced uncertainly into the Earth, and she pushed her forehead against the window as she watched the blur of palm trees and tin roofs beyond the airport fences.

Owen's warnings about Latin American men resounded as Jenna waited in line at customs. She had pulled off the cardigan that had kept her warm in Heathrow, and was now feeling her body becoming a piece of meat on display. She adjusted her white tank top and glared at the men in the adjacent line.

Her British passport was received by a female official with a raised eyebrow. She fumbled inside her backpack for a tourist card that she had bought in the airport in Cancun, and the woman again frowned. "Cuál es el propósito de su visita?"

"Um, pardon me?" Jenna responded, her mouth drying.

"What is the purpose of your visit, ma'am?"

"Um, I'm just here on a holiday, by myself." She ran her fingers through her fringe and tucked it behind her ears.

The official continued to frown, eyeing Jenna up and down. "And you have a return ticket?"

"Yes, I do," she exclaimed, the pitch of her voice higher than expected. She again fumbled with her backpack and tried to smile. "Here, I'm flying back to England next week."

The woman carefully scanned her flight itinerary and then stamped her passport. "You take care, señora."

The taxi drivers advanced in a swarm as Jenna stumbled into the morning heat. The air was heavy and dank, swirling with exhaust fumes and tobacco smoke. Beyond the towering airport buildings the sky was a bathwater grey, the sun hidden somewhere in the haze. Jenna turned to the right, wheeling her suitcase and wincing at the purposeful body contact from the male crowd. She pushed at one man as his arm linked underneath hers, then gasped as he tugged her towards the open door of a private taxi.

"Get in, quick," the man demanded, taking her suitcase and closing the door behind her.

"Jeez, I didn't recognise you!" Jenna blurted as Owen jumped in the opposite door. She struggled to pull on her seatbelt as the taxi lurched into the horde of traffic, its horn blasting and the driver throwing his hand violently out of the window.

"Then hopefully no one else did," Owen responded, taking off his Panama hat and replacing his aviators with round spectacles. "How was your flight?"

"Yeah, fine," she smiled, her heartbeat slowing. "I slept most of the way to Cancun, and had a window seat flying over the coral reefs."

Owen seemed to be ignoring her as he flicked the cover off a cheap plastic phone and inserted a sim card. "Take this, I've saved my number under Aaron, as well as the number of tonight's hotel, the British Embassy, and an English line for the Cuban police."

"Aaron?"

He nodded distractedly, his eyes scanning the busy terminal outside. "So that it comes up first when you hit the call button."

"Um, okay."

"I've also setup a tracking app for that sim card, so long as the phone has reception."

She swallowed uncertainly, sliding the phone into her pocket. She noticed the driver staring at her in the rear-view mirror and slinked lower behind the headrest. Her eyes widened mordantly as she stared through the windscreen at the oncoming traffic, then realised with a sigh that it was normal for the cars to be driving on the right hand side of the road.

"Don't make any calls with your own cell phone," Owen continued. "In fact, turn it off."

"Uh, okay."

"I've also decided not to take the bus from Havana this afternoon, it's too easy to be followed. This guy is going to take us directly to a hotel in Batabano."

"I see. How long will it take to get there?"

"Less than two hours." He was staring cautiously out the back windscreen. He called out to the driver in Spanish, then turned to a manila folder of maps and documents.

The streets of Havana flowed past Jenna's window like a faded roll of film, the buildings and cars a dichotomy of pride and neglect. The radio's waning saxophone became a soundtrack to the rows of shanty houses, dangling traffic lights and regal concrete architecture that was now painted a garish, almost mocking array of colours. Ramshackle convenience stores advertised phone plans in the shadow of monuments to communist revolutionaries, and the intersections were a war between polished yellow 'coco-taxis', bicycles and horse-drawn carriages.

Owen noticed Jenna's fascination, and observed her as she stared at a painting of Che Guevara that occupied the entire wall of an apartment complex. The revolutionary seemed to gaze forlornly across the city and ocean beyond, as if looking back to a time when the seagulls landed on fresh paintwork and the waves broke against quays crowded with fishermen and wealthy expats.

"This place was once booming," Owen whispered, just loudly enough for her to hear. "But it's been on a downward slide for the last 30 years."

She gave him a brief smile, appreciating the commentary. She tried to imagine what the streets had once looked like, but the peeling paint and desolate buildings were hard to gloss over with illusion. As the lights turned green a row of antique cars coughed forward, clearing their rusted lungs in a defiant chorus.

"And if anyone asks," Owen said suddenly, "make sure they understand you're from England, not America."

She raised her eyebrows. "Got it."

The bizarre polarity of new and old continued inland, where slick TV advertisements rose out of fields being ploughed by oxen, and modern roadhouses adjoined overgrown colonial ruins. The road became narrower, and Owen finally relaxed as he scanned the open valleys and peered intermittently through the back windscreen.

The sun remained hidden somewhere in the silvery sky as the taxi rolled past the town of Batabano, but the heat was becoming more intense. Jenna felt her eyes closing as she leaned her cheek against the window, then awoke suddenly from a daydream as the taxi bounced across a series of oily potholes. She rubbed the drowsiness from her eyes and stared at a row of dilapidated shanties held up by barnacled fence posts and fishing nets. On the opposite side of the road the muddy flats graded lazily into bobbing brown clumps of seaweed. A corroded wharf pointed out towards the islands beyond, and was flanked on both sides by rock walls leading to a larger dock and marina. The taxi eventually pulled up before a pink concrete building with a brown tile roof and salt-crusted windows. Weeds clung to the base of the walls, trying in vain to escape the overflowing drains where dead insects floated like tealeaves.

Owen continued a conversation with the taxi driver before turning to Jenna. "It appears this is it."

Jenna allowed her eyes to widen.

"He's given me change in pesos," Owen explained as they pulled their luggage off the road and waved to the driver. "So we should be able to buy some lunch. Apparently there's only one restaurant here that operates illegally for tourists."

"Illegally?"

"Yes, they require licences to accept money from foreigners, as does the hotel, but they get by as long as no one says anything."

She remained wide-eyed, her cheeks dimpled. "Right."

Owen kept his Panama hat on as he strolled into the wooden foyer of the pink hotel, his flowing white shirt damp with perspiration and his yacht shoes squeaking on the tile floor. His conversation with the receptionist lasted five minutes, after which they were allowed to ascend the creaking staircase.

"So there is definitely going to be a boat from here to the island?" Jenna asked as they reached his room first.

"Not a tourist boat," he shrugged, opening his door and staring in at the aged decor. "But apparently there is a fisherman at the dock who accepts American dollars to give backpackers a ride there."

"Ha!" she laughed sarcastically, pushing her key into the opposite door. "Sounds promising!"

To Jenna's relief the receptionist had allowed them to hold onto their passports, and she tucked hers carefully into her shorts as she parted the curtains and stared out to sea. The thick smell of fish and rotting seaweed seemed to penetrate the window, but it was more intriguing than unpleasant, and the added wafting of spirits and clinking of glasses from beneath the floorboards evoked images of bounty ships and pirates anchored on the other side of the docks. She turned on her phone to take a picture of the view, but within seconds the chime of text messages pulled her out of her imagination. She glanced at the closed wooden door, quickly scanned the messages and switched her phone back off.

The shower rose trembled like a waking animal as Jenna waited on the cracked bathroom tiles. Finally the water gushed out, and she stood in the lukewarm flow. She tried to pull the cap off her shampoo bottle, but her soapy fingers fumbled and allowed the bottle to fall, cracking open on the tiles and leaking a green swirl into the drain. She reacted with a short whimper, bending down to pick the bottle up but then finding herself buckling, her knees pressing into the cold shower tiles. She tried to hold back the tears but eventually the weight of anguish was too heavy. Her hands slid down the shower frame as she cried, her eyes closed from the stinging of soap and her tears bubbling down her eyelashes and into the flow.

Chapter Twenty-Seven

Panama City.
December 18th, 1989.

The barred shopfront finally opened to customers and Owen traipsed forward, nodding at the cheery Asian attendant and then scanning the isles of electronics. Less than a minute later he placed a set of UHF radios onto the counter beside a pair of binoculars. As the attendant packed them into a bag he glanced over his shoulder, surveying the street outside before handing over a wad of notes.

The clear morning sky was losing its battle with a twisted array of clouds, and the mood on the streets seemed to follow the uncertainty above. The magazine and breakfast stands that occupied the financial district of Panama City were still hidden behind closed roller doors, and the few businessmen walked briskly, clutching their morning newspapers and trying to ignore a ubiquitous sense of anxiety.

Owen passed a fruit stall where a huddle of children stared suspiciously from behind a rack of pineapples. He tried to ignore them, but their paranoia was contagious, and he stared back over his shoulder to realise that it wasn't him they were cowering from.

"It's an interesting shopping list you have there, Owen," the man said in a low voice, stepping onto the footpath and tipping down his black fedora hat. He was chewing on a toothpick, his thick lips bent into a roguish smile. "Anyone would think you were trying to be a spy."

"Conrad," Owen gasped, his footsteps buckling. "What a surprise."

"A surprise? I'll take that as a compliment, as I've been behind you since you left the hotel."

"Um, okay, that's a bit unsettling." He tried to laugh, but it came out as a nervous stutter. "Um, why are you following me?"

"Joe was concerned about your safety." He peered suspiciously down an alleyway. "I'm not the only one following you right now, but I am the only one willing to protect you."

"I-I don't understand."

They had arrived at the foyer of the Marriott, and Conrad slipped a package into Owen's shopping bag before walking away. "Those women have deceived you, oh yes they have. Have a read of that report, and everything will make sense."

Owen's confusion caused him to bump into the doorman as he entered the hotel, and he clumsily pulled the package out of his shopping bag as he stopped beside a line of couches. He took a seat, ripping off the brown paper to reveal a file held together with thick black bindings. The front cover was marked with an ominous red "CONFIDENTIAL" watermark. He glanced around the empty foyer and slowly opened the front page.

"Canton Song: An Investigation into the Sale of CIA Recordings of Panamanian Officials Involved in Canal Treaty Negotiations to Manuel Antonio Noriega".

Owen shook his head as he flicked through the pages. This case had already been revealed to the media, but never in this much detail. And never had the media been aware that one rogue CIA agent was blamed for the entire scandal – an agent whose name filled an entire section of the report. Owen gritted his teeth, still shaking his head as his eyes remained fixed on the chilling letters: RUBUS, "also known as Hector Goldstein, discharged from the CIA in 1977 with no formal charges laid".

Owen's heart was pounding as he left the foyer and stepped into the elevator. This didn't make any sense. Surely Hector was too old for this. He slipped the loops of his shopping bags down to his elbow and awkwardly juggled his room keys. He pushed the door inwards with his foot and was about the throw the bags onto the mini bar when they fell to the floor, the binoculars bouncing across the carpet.

Thorn sat dressed in crisp military attire, his blonde hair spiked and the right heel of his polished black boot resting casually on his knee. He was staring out the window, his hand running thoughtfully over his clean-shaven jaw. On the glass table before him rested Owen's gold watch, taken from his bedside table, and beside it was the distinctive profile of a plane ticket.

"What the hell are you doing here?"

"I can't believe how easily you've been deceived," Thorn said matter-of-factly, turning to face his cousin. "They tried to set me up, Owen. The gold watch, the photographs – they were planted to frame me. And what's worse, they deceived Eva as well. But they won't get away with it. Please, take a seat, and let me explain."

Owen was frozen, his face white. He heard the door clicking closed behind him, and felt his knees shaking in fear.

"Come on," Thorn demanded, his voice louder. "Sit, sit, come talk to me. I'm your cousin, Owen, and you've known me all your life. Don't tell me that your trust in your own family is really that weak?"

Owen felt himself shifting to the couch opposite Thorn, his body drifting into the same robotic movements he had experienced in Thorn's house. He sank into the suede cushions, his eyes trying to focus on the watch and its reflection in the glass table instead of making eye contact. But below the watch's reflection was that of Thorn's face, and he met Owen's gaze in the glass.

"I remember your first girlfriend," Thorn said pensively. "Amelia, wasn't it?"

Owen's face screwed up in surprise at the question, but he continued staring downwards.

"She was pretty, you know."

"What are you talking about?"

"But she never liked me. And you took her side when we were in high school. But eventually you realised that she had been cheating on you. You were shattered, and who was there for you? Who had been right all along?"

"Don't bring that bullshit up," Owen shook his head spitefully.

"I had been right, Owen. I was also right about your father, and what he –"

"I said, leave it!"

"And now it's happened again. You've fallen for someone else's lies, and you're blaming me. I can understand it, people have always envied and in turn despised me, but surely you're not that short-sighted?"

"Don't try and play this game, Joe. Don't try and blame this on Eva."

"Oh, I'm not," he smiled spookily. "Eva is just like you. She's gullible, easily manipulated. Hector has turned her against me. Hector had that watch placed in my desk; he made Eva believe that I had taken those photographs of you. He's infected her, and now he's infected you. But don't worry, I've talked sense into her."

Owen gritted his teeth. "I'm sure you have, I'm sure your fists spoke very well."

Thorn sighed. "You've got no idea, do you? She's carrying my child, Owen. Do you really think I'd hurt her?"

Owen blinked in surprise. "What?"

"That's right, I'm going to be a father." He grinned uneasily, folding his arms behind his head. "And I'll be damned if I let that man break up my family with his lies."

Owen was shaking his head. "I don't... I don't know what to believe right now."

"It's all there in those pages." He nodded towards the report folded between Owen's tense fingers. "And you were right all along. Hector is RUBUS. He had my phones tapped, he recorded my conversations with you, and he used that information to organise Spadafora's death. He ordered those men to attack you, to steal your watch, and to steal the doctor's notes. He sent you those photographs."

"That's not true."

"Hector's plan is to use you, along with that whore, to get into the Comandancia and steal Noriega's tapes. And even if you get to them, Hector will make sure they're destroyed, along with you and everyone else helping him. But I'm going to make sure that doesn't happen. I've organised a flight for you out of Panama this afternoon. Conrad has a vehicle with your bags in the concierge bay, and he'll take you straight to the airport. I know you're not going to want to leave, but you'll thank me for this afterwards. You're going to be killed if you stay here any longer. And don't worry about the tapes; my team will go in for them with force as soon as we get the orders to strike Noriega. And I promise that you'll be the first journalist with access."

Owen's senses had become numb, and Thorn's words were becoming soft vibrations lost in the cold blue depths of his eyes. The sounds of the city street below resonated with greater clarity than the words, and his mind wandered through a series of memories. He watched as Thorn rose to his feet and motioned for him to follow. He reached for the watch on the table, snapping it onto his wrist and slowly standing up.

Thorn began picking up the shopping bags, still talking, and led the way out the door to the elevator. The loud ping as the silver doors opened brought Owen back to reality, and he found himself nodding at Thorn's suggestions. They moved inside together, where a young lady dressed in gym clothes was adjusting her hair in the mirrored wall.

The elevator descended quickly, causing Owen to steady himself against the wall. Thorn had stopped talking, and the silence continued until they arrived at the 'ping' of the first floor. The young lady waited until the doors had fully opened before strolling out towards the hotel gym.

A short, sarcastic laugh escaped from Owen's lips. "You used his codename, didn't you?"

"Huh?"

"You used the name RUBUS so that if you were exposed, you could frame Hector."

"What the fu –"

It seemed to be happening in Owen's subconscious, until he realised that he was actually performing the manoeuvre that he had been visualising. With the elevator doors beginning to close he launched his palms into Thorn's shoulders, heaving him back against the wall. At the same time his right knee jerked forward, collecting with Thorn's groin and driving upwards with a burst of power.

Thorn's eyes were wide more from shock than pain. He reacted with a shove that sent Owen sprawling into the closing gap in the door, and as the pain fully struck he recoiled, collapsing to his knees and bellowing.

The elevator doors collided with Owen's legs as he tumbled through the gap, but he continued to scramble, his feet finding their grip on the tile floor and propelling him down the corridor.

Chapter Twenty-Eight

Batabano, Cuba.
Present day.

Like the hotel, the marina was a tribute to past glories. Swollen wooden planks groaned as Owen and Jenna sauntered past plastic fishing crates and corroded railings, descending down creaking steps onto a lower deck. Jenna grimaced as her shoes crunched on the thousands of fish scales that had crusted onto the floorboards between orange nets, broken foam floats and oxygen tanks. A circle of dark fisherman smoking hand rolled cigarettes surrounded an old transistor radio that blared out Spanish music. They were blocking the narrow walkway, and were slow to shift their wooden chairs to allow the strangers to pass.

"I'm assuming that's the boat," Owen said to Jenna out of the side of his mouth, his expression tense as he saw the stares of the fishermen creeping over Jenna's body.

The boat was a blue and white panga, no more than twenty feet long, and rocked in the shadow of a weather-beaten yacht. Standing on the ramp down to the ferry was a dark fisherman in a stained white muscle shirt, his thick dreadlocks tied back with a blue bandana. His square jawline was tense with concentration as he skilfully filleted a crate of red snapper. Jenna struggled to disguise the focus of her stare as she watched the man's broad shoulders and forearms rippling with each flick of the knife, the intricate tattoos around his biceps almost blending into his veins. Her chest tightened as he looked up, his intense black eyes connecting with hers. A thin smile crossed his thick lips.

"Pardon," Owen said with a wavering voice. "Queremos ir a La Isla de Marfil."

The fisherman studied Owen carefully, his eyes moving from the foreigner's yacht shoes up to his nervous face. He stared into Owen's eyes for a second, his expression unchanging.

"Uh," Owen stammered, suddenly flustered.

"Why you want to go to the island?" the fisherman finally asked in a deep creole accent, his tone accusing.

"Uh – we, we'd like to have a –"

"We're looking for Rafael Cordoba," Jenna interrupted, seeing that honesty would be the only route through the fisherman's obvious suspicions.

The fisherman's expression remained unchanged, and he let out a sharp clicking sound as he stabbed his knife into the head of one of the fish. Within seconds the other fishermen had surrounded Owen and Jenna. Owen gulped, raising his arms as he was frisked. The men then moved to Jenna, but the fisherman held up his hand and they backed away obediently.

"Explain yourselves," the fisherman ordered, wiping his hands on a rag and tossing it backwards into the boat. He advanced towards them, his nostrils flared. "And if you full o'sheet I'll know, and you'll be leavin-ere in the same crates as these snapper."

"My name is Jenna Martinez," Jenna said boldly. "And this is my friend, Owen. My mother was recently murdered in England, and she left me this note."

The fisherman's face became even more intense as Jenna handed him the folded note from her pocket. He scanned it with a curious expression, flipping it over and slowly handing it back. His dark eyelids were half-closed as he studied her face, and he again appeared to smile.

"I believe my mother wanted me to come here, and I believe that Rafael – if he's on the island – can help us find something that my mother had been searching for. Something that she was killed for."

The fisherman turned his head to the side as he stared into Jenna's eyes. "You know who Rafael Cordoba is, no true?" His expression was almost mocking. "He is a wanted man, and he is not welcome here. I'm sorry ma'am, but you gonna have to look somewhere else."

Owen was first to let out a depressed sigh, pinching the bridge of his nose in frustration.

Jenna pressed through her concern. "Is there no one else here that could help us? No friends of Rafael's? I believe my mother may have come here last year, and –"

"For forty American dollars I'll take you to the island," the fisherman said gruffly. "But only you."

"So he is on the island, then?" Jenna's eyes were narrowed, her stare into the fisherman's eyes competing with his elusiveness.

"Uh, I'm sorry," Owen interrupted. "But –"

"You sound American," the fisherman growled, his face clouded and his eyes wide as he enunciated his words. "And she don't. So it's either her, or nunna chu."

"You didn't answer my question," Jenna pressed, ignoring the tension. "Is Rafael on the island or not?"

"That depends which island you're referring to." The fisherman's eyes were still wide but his mouth was curving into a satirical smile. "Lots of islands out there. Now you wanna come with me, or you wanna stay with Mr America here?"

There was something in the man's jesting that had Jenna convinced. She mirrored his smile as she replied, "I'll pay you forty dollars to take me to Rafael."

"Sixty."

"Fifty."

"Okay señorita, vamos!"

"Hang on, hang on," Owen interrupted again. "Jenna, you can't go with this man alone, you've got no idea where he could be taking you."

"What else am I going to do?"

"We can find someone else to take us, I've come this far with you and I'm not letting you go on alone."

"Seriously, Owen?" Jenna's glare was standoffish. "I appreciate your help, I really do, but I would have come this far anyway. I'll make sure that he gets me back here before dark."

Owen looked genuinely scared. He seemed to cower at the fisherman's mocking smile and the chuckles of the men still spectating from behind.

The fisherman clicked again, and the other men moved forward, collecting the fish crates from the boat and standing back as the fisherman whipped the mooring line from its bollard. Owen tried to catch Jenna's gaze after she boarded the boat, but she sat beneath the shade sail and searched though her handbag for a large pair of sunglasses that veiled her expression.

The old panga spluttered and spat its way into the dark green water. The shadow of the yachts slipped away and hot sunlight flooded onto Jenna's back. It wasn't until they were in open water that she finally looked back, seeing Owen's figure still waiting at the dock. He was quickly becoming smaller, and the dock soon became a cluster of yacht masts protruding from the shantytown. She continued to stare, then realised with a jolt that she didn't have any money to pay the driver. He had caught onto her concern, but continued to smile as he relaxed against the outboard motor, his dreadlocks shaking gently in the wind.

Across the bow a flock of cormorants were leading the way towards the row of islands, where white domed hills were sparkling almost supernaturally in the afternoon sun. Giant pine trees competed for attention below the domes, and were buffered from the beaches by a thick line of yellow coconut palms.

"Those hills – they're made of marble," the fisherman said over the sound of the motor. "That's what makes 'em sparkle."

"I see," Jenna responded, making out multiple wharves on each island, and what appeared to be a row of thatched holiday villas on the islands to the left. "Which island are we going to?"

The fisherman took a moment to respond. She could feel his eyes moving over her, and sensed his expression changing. "Furthest on the right, where them gulls are flying over the wharf."

"And Rafael is definitely going to be there?"

"He was this morning."

Jenna huffed, but there was something about the man's roguish expression that comforted her. He turned his attention to a small school of fish swimming alongside the boat, decelerating gently, then glanced back up at Jenna, his expression serious once again. "I'm sorry 'bout your mother. How long ago did it happen?" His voice and accent were different again – still deep and intimidating – but different.

"Thanks," she sighed, searching his eyes to confirm his sincerity. "It's been two weeks."

The fisherman frowned. "You're a brave girl coming out here like this."

"Woman."

"Sorry?"

"I'm a woman, not a girl."

The fisherman chuckled. "Gotcha."

She allowed an awkward silence to lengthen as she stared into the water, her eyes out of focus.

"So you from England, no true?"

"Yes." She drew her knees closer to her chest and leaned her chin on her folded arms. "And yourself? Your English is very good."

He was about to reply, but chuckled again to himself.

"Gee, that sounds like a fun place to be from."

His smile slowly became more serious. "And what do you do in England?"

"I'm a dancer, in London."

"Waah, that is very cool." His eyes sparkled with enthusiasm. "So you know how to salsa, no?"

Jenna's frown was almost apathetic, and her response was clearly sarcastic. "Uh, yes."

"Chooh, it's like that, hey?!" He repositioned himself, flexing his shoulders. "Princess think she gonna show the Cubans 'ow it's done, no?"

"Ha!" she laughed, her cheeks reddening. "And I suppose you also fancy yourself as more than just a fisherman?"

"Just a fisherman! Chooh! Watch who you offending, woman!" He was trying to look insulted but his shaking head was contrasted with a broad grin, his bright white teeth exposed for the first time. "I'll show you up on the dance floor any day."

"Ha! I doubt that."

"Sure thing I will. I know that you don't have no money to pay me, so I will strike you a deal."

Jenna flinched, her eyes darting as though looking for a way to escape, but he continued to grin roguishly. "I guess I have no choice, do I?"

"You do. You choose for me to turn round right now, or you let me show you how to dance when we get to the island. I organise judges, and if you lose, you don't get back to the mainland til mañana."

Jenna scoffed. "Til tomorrow, you mean? And if I win?"

"Then I will take you to Rafael."

Jenna pursed her lips, her eyes responding to the sparkle of his. "It's a deal."

The fisherman accelerated sharply, grinning proudly as the bow lifted and bounced, creating a spray of water that threatened to strike Jenna's face. As though in tune with her emotions, the engine began to cavitate loudly in the whitewash. The fisherman eased off again, steering the boat in a wide arc as it approached a rugged corner of the island.

The cormorants had ended their flight atop a granite spire that rose like a crystalline statue from the calm swell, marking the transition into shallow turquoise water and a neon blue reef. Jenna peered overboard like an eager tourist, her eyes wide at the schools of striped fish and slow gliding rays.

The island was barely a kilometre long, and much of the inner pine forest had been turned into a thatch-roofed building with a smoking chimney. Wrapping around the far side of the island like a lazy snake was a wide strip of volcanic sand and a quaint row of driftwood huts. Palm trees meandered from the beach up to a series of granite boulders that supported a barnacled wharf littered with fishing crates and nets. The sound of reggae music became louder as the boat idled its way up to the wharf, and the fisherman called out in a foreign language.

A tall, spidery man in tattered cargo shorts seemed to materialise from a stack of nets, his dark face beaming. He leaned over to shift a row of buckets, exposing the scars across his back. The fisherman eased the boat carefully against a steel ladder and tossed the mooring line up to his waiting friend. Both men began speaking rapidly in their peculiar language, their conversation obviously about the female guest.

"She proppah like a snappah!" the stranger was shouting.

Jenna hesitated before accepting the man's callused hand, his wide, intense eyes passing over her as he pulled her up the ladder and onto the wharf. "Maddah fiyah! Weh gaan ahn?" he asked with a toothy grin. "Mi naym da Cesar."

"I-I'm Jenna," she responded, confused about what he was asking. She stepped backwards onto the wharf and pulled her handbag tightly over her shoulder. There was something about his elongated limbs and twitching eyes that gave him the look of a cartoon character. She felt that she should be afraid of him, but the bright sun and perfect sandy beach beyond the wharf made the scene far from intimidating.

The fisherman remained in the boat, throwing a stack of nets onto the wharf and then tugging two canvas bags out of a compartment in the bow. He placed the bags atop the wharf, winking at Cesar.

"Pleez to meet you," Cesar said, rubbing his hands together and grinning at Jenna. "We got sum bunk beds in de main dorm if you wahn. They kaas ten US dollar first night, or if you wahn hammock they fo free. We gahn bash tonight too, start 'bout seven."

"Uh, I'm not staying," Jenna responded. "I've come to see Rafael; Rafael Cordoba. Is he here?"

Cesar tried to keep a jovial facade as he shot a stare at the fisherman. "Sorry Jenna," he said, turning back to face her, the corners of his lips twitching. "Rafael gone dis morning. Maybe he here layta, I dunno."

Jenna's frowned gallingly. "I was told –"

"So before then," Cesar interrupted as his spindly body skipped off the back of the wharf and onto the wet seaweed below, "pleez, lemme give you a tour of our wonderful island!"

Jenna bit into her lower lip and then slowly turned back to the fisherman, who was preparing a jerry can to refuel the boat. When she caught his eye he nodded slightly, as though encouraging her to go.

"I guess I don't have a choice," Jenna sighed. She made her way down a creaking wooden ramp, slipping off her sandals and letting the wet sand swirl between her toes.

"So how long you bin in Cuba?" Cesar asked as he scaled the large boulders and arrived on the sand beside her.

"I flew in this morning."

"Chooh! You dahn mess round!"

She ignored him, dodging a row of empty tequila bottles scattered about the remnants of a campfire. The smoke of another fire drifted between the palms to her left, and the haze masked the faces of a circle of Creole men playing acoustic guitars. The men were so absorbed in their strumming that they barely noticed Jenna and Cesar passing through the clearing.

A wide trail led through a thicket of sugarcane plumegrass and into a shallow orange lagoon. The hot, sticky water teemed with baitfish and dragonflies, and Jenna was glad to wipe her feet on the mown grass on the other side.

Before them stood a giant log building, its thatched roof blending into the pine trees that lined the vast bay behind. Cesar led the way through racks of inflatable boats and kayaks, and around to the front of the building where a second storey veranda provided a view of the vast archipelago beyond. Yellow coconut palms shaded a barbecue area and log tables stretched all the way down to the beach. Wooden wind chimes and conch shells swung lazily from the veranda, and a group of Caucasian travellers appeared to be asleep in a row of hammocks.

"It's beautiful," Jenna gasped.

"Upstairs is da bar," Cesar announced, "We be cookin up sum seafood 'bout an hour, so why donchu take out wun de kayaks?"

"Uh, I don't think –"

"You can join us if you like," came a female voice, her accent hard to pick, "we were just about to head out."

Two tanned girls in bikinis emerged from a downstairs entrance, their multiple tattoos catching Jenna's stare. "You just arrived, ya?"

"Yes, but I'm not staying."

"Of course you are," one of them grinned, pulling on a lifejacket. "The last boat for the day just left!"

Agnes and Karen certainly weren't kayaking experts, but what they lacked in ability was made up for by enthusiasm. A small set of waves had broken over the coral reef, concentrating in the curve of the bay and swamping the kayaks with whitewash. Somehow they remained upright, and the girls hooted with laughter.

Jenna watched alone from the shoreline, the scene of laughter, haphazardness and the backdrop of a tropical sunset conflicting with her mood. She focused on the water, urging the churning mass to unravel the knots in her mind. Soon all thoughts of her mother, of Owen, of England and of the plane trips that had landed her in Cuba only this morning seemed to bubble into the breadth of the bay.

"Hey Jenna!!" Karen cried, her face dripping as she pulled her kayak to shore. "Why so serious?"

Jenna smiled meekly, but her mind was too slow to produce a reply.

"Cheer up!" Agnes puffed, dumping herself beside Jenna.

"How long have you two been here?" Jenna asked.

Karen tipped the water out of her kayak and joined them on the sand. "I don't know. Maybe a month?"

"It can't have been that long!" Agnes exclaimed, wiping the wet hair from her eyes. "Although, yes, maybe it has been."

Karen grinned, her nose ring gleaming in the low sunlight. "So why did you want to leave earlier? You looked like you were on a mission."

Jenna leaned back and stared at the horizon pensively.

Karen seemed to recognise the expression, and she grinned again. "You just broke up with your boyfriend, didn't you?"

"Oh, that sucks," Agnes blurted. "Don't worry, we both went through the same thing in Denmark before we came here too."

"So Jenna," Karen started, "have you met Toby and Al?" She nodded back towards the beach, where two tanned Caucasian men were staring at them. "They're from Australia!"

Jenna shook her head, smiling apprehensively. "No, I haven't." Her expression suddenly changed, and she bit at her lower lip thoughtfully. "I don't suppose either of you have heard of a man here called Rafael?"

Agnes shrugged, starting to drag her kayak further up the shore. "Is he one of the fishermen?"

"He's probably that creepy dive instructor from the other island!" Karen blurted, her eyes theatrically wide. "No wait, his name was something like Javier, or Juan."

Agnes shook her head. "You idiot. No, I haven't heard of any Rafael here."

Toby and Al helped the girls drag their kayaks back up the beach. Jenna returned their smiles, but her attention was focused on the men back at the bar. She brushed the sand off her legs before helping Toby carry one of the kayaks back through the palms. Karen and Agnes stayed behind on the beach, keen to take a puff of Al's joint.

"I hope those two didn't embarrass you?" Toby asked, his voice low and steady.

"Ha!" Jenna laughed. "No, no, they're fine. Are there any showers around here?"

"Sure, I'll show you."

Now dressed in a Hawaiian shirt, Cesar grinned as he passed them with a tray of chopped vegetables. He turned up the speakers strapped to the veranda pillars and swayed rhythmically as he lit one of the barbecues. "Mi hope you like seafood, Jenna!"

"I don't suppose Rafael has turned up, yet?" Her lips were pursed dryly, and she raised her eyebrows as he pretended to be burnt by the barbecue.

The palm shadows had soon lengthened across the beach and a southerly breeze was swaying the mast of a lone yacht anchored beyond the reef. The woody taste of coconut shells and barbecued crabs failed to cleanse the pungent smell of marijuana that had nested in the bar upstairs, and Jenna leaned over the log veranda to inhale the fresh air.

"So I hear you challenged El Guapo to a dance off tonight?" The husky voice came from Al, who was carefully rolling a pile of joints.

"You mean the fisherman with the dreadlocks who brought me here? That's what he calls himself?" Jenna laughed, turning around and leaning against the railing. "Doesn't that mean 'the handsome one'?"

"I believe so."

"What a tosser."

"Haha," Karen chuckled from inside the bar. "I think you might be surprised by his abilities, Jenna!"

"Pfft," Jenna scoffed, her attention turning to the sunburn that had crept over her shoulders.

"And is it true that you dance professionally in London?" Toby asked.

"Wow, this certainly is a small island!" Jenna laughed. "Yes, that is true."

"I better go and charge my phone," Al mused. "This could be worthy of filming."

Jenna's grin was suddenly wiped into a concerned frown. She strode inside, ducked behind the bar and pulled out her handbag. Running her hand nervously through her hair, she waited as the phone that Owen had given her flashed on for the first time.

Chapter Twenty-Nine

Marriott Hotel, Panama City.
December 18ᵗʰ, 1989.

The screeching of Owen's shoes silenced a group of men lounging in a bar opposite the hotel gym. They sat up to attention as he dodged a network of pillars and pot plants, the sound of his shoes ceasing as he reached the carpet of a hallway bordered by an indoor pool. He sidestepped a corpulent man in a bathing suit and sprinted to the end of the hallway, throwing aside the swinging doors and tumbling into a dimly lit massage parlour. The receptionist called out in surprise, but Owen ignored her, pushing through another doorway and then ripping open a sliding door to an outside balcony. The leaves of a palm tree shaded a concrete ledge, and he clutched at them as he quickly judged the fall.

The loud tearing of a palm frond alerted a nearby security officer, who paced towards the hotel garden in time to see Owen crashing into a bed of ferns. The officer was too slow to catch up, and instead shouted into his radio as Owen clambered out of the garden and began running down a paved footpath.

Owen stalled outside the entrance to the hotel car park, his fingers running hesitantly over the keys to his scooter. He decided to go with his instincts, leaping over the tollgate and panting through the dark maze of cars.

The scooter started with a protesting kick, but squealed up to the tollgate with unexpected vigour. Owen was leaning over to swipe his card against the gate when a mad shout erupted from behind him.

"Stop! Owen, stop!" It was Conrad, his stocky frame moving swiftly between the rows of cars. "Owen!"

Owen tried to ignore the shouts, spinning the scooter's wheels as he left the tollgate. His knuckles were white on the handlebars as he rounded the corner of the exit and screeched into oncoming traffic.

Thorn's street was even quieter than the surrounding suburb, and Owen rode unnoticed up the empty driveway of the sprawling white house. He dumped the busted scooter against the front door and banged his fist against the stained glass. There was no movement inside. He clambered around the side of the house, pressing his forehead against the windows. The first few rooms were too dark to see anything, but when he arrived at the barred window of Thorn's office he could see the desk thrown violently onto its side. Papers and documents were strewn across the floor and the chaos continued out of the door and into the hallway.

The back sliding door was locked, but a line of dried blood leading downwards from the inside handle was enough evidence Owen needed to slam the heel of his shoe into the glass. His foot rebounded with a sharp jab of pain, and he limped away to a stack of roof tiles against the side of the house. Insects scurried from beneath the first tile as he pulled it free and he limped back to the door, thrusting the tile forward.

The tile rebounded back onto the pavers, but left a small hole surrounded by strings of cracking glass. The glass continued to crack like a spider web towards the corners of the door, then caved inwards as he thrust his leg into the growing hole. He kept pushing, his shoe projecting thousands of glass chips onto the floorboards inside. Eventually the hole was large enough for him to reach his arm inwards and flick up the latch.

A soft moaning seemed to be resonating through the living area, where wine glasses, pot plants and ornaments were shattered against the walls. Owen followed the moaning towards the kitchen where a splatter of blood against the fridge appeared black in the fluorescent light. The eerie white glow then revealed two legs protruding from behind the kitchen counter.

Owen sprung forward, gasping in horror. Eva's feet and hands were bound with masking tape, her forehead was cut open and she was crying weakly though a bloodied tea towel gag. He ripped off the gag, allowing her to splutter, then searched the benchtop for a knife.

"In the drawers," Eva moaned, her voice hoarse and cracking. "Second drawer."

Owen searched through the cluttered kitchen utensils before removing a large serrated knife.

"Where is Joe?" Eva rasped as Owen cut hastily into the tape.

"I don't know," he wheezed, ripping the last of the tape from her leg and then helping her to her feet.

"Water, please," she moaned, her arms floundering at the tap.

"Here," Owen said, finding an unbroken wine glass and flicking on the tap. "Are you okay to stand? Shit, you need to get to a doctor."

"I'm fine," she spluttered, filling the glass again. "How did you get here?"

"On my scooter. Joe and Conrad tried to corner me at the Marriott. How did they know?" His expression had turned from grave to angry. "Has Maria said something to them?"

She shook her head, flicking on the tap again and splashing the dried blood from her lips and forehead. "Conrad. He's following you. Has been since you arrived in Panama. He followed you to the bridge yesterday. Joe asked where I was. I lied to him. And so, he knew."

He sighed heavily. "At least you're okay."

"We got to get to Hector's house," she huffed, limping across the kitchen and ripping open the pantry. "We'll be safe there. Go into the garage. There are keys for Joe's car there. I think the keys are inside the door. Meet me out the front."

"Are you sure you're okay?"

She ignored him, spinning the lid off a bottle of vodka and splashing the alcohol over her wounds.

Owen dodged a fallen bookcase as he made his way down the hallway and into the garage. He flicked on the light, his expression grave as he stared at Thorn's imposing red BMW, its polished bonnet reflecting the racks of tools and camouflage camping equipment at the back of the garage. He studied the car keys and nervously pressed a button on the keychain to open the massive front door of the garage.

Sunlight began flooding across the concrete floor as the door grated upwards, but the screeching of unoiled metal was being overpowered by the rumbling sound of a diesel engine outside. Owen quickly jumped into the driver's seat of the BMW, pushing the key into the ignition and gasping as he stared into the rear-view mirror. The garage door was reaching the top of its ascent, and the glare of the afternoon sun was being refracted by the murky beige outline of a US military Hummer. The massive vehicle was idling at the foot of the driveway, and from its passenger door emerged the hulking frame of Joseph Thorn.

Owen turned on the ignition so forcefully that he nearly snapped the head off the key. He flipped the manual transmission into reverse and ducked in terror as the sound of gunshots blasted like exploding bombs through the hollow of the garage. The BMW fishtailed out of the driveway; the front left headlight smashing and spraying shards across the concrete as it clipped the side of the Hummer. Owen's eyes opened to see that the gunshots hadn't come from the Hummer, but from Eva, who stood defiantly against a pillar beside the front door, her arms outstretched as she continued to fire Thorn's black Beretta pistol. Her bloodied hair bounced like braids as she ran towards the BMW, and her bruised face seemed to glow with rage as she took one last shot at the Hummer, blowing apart the passenger window and forcing Thorn to duck out of view.

The driver of the Hummer slammed on the accelerator, cutting off Eva's route to the passenger door of the BMW and making her scramble towards the cover of the garage. Another round of shots rang out – this time from Thorn – who purposefully aimed high over the house. Owen revved the BMW onto the front lawn, its tyres spinning as it lurched around the side of the garage and into the fenceless back yard.

Thorn climbed back into the passenger seat of the Hummer and shouted for the driver to pursue around the side of the house. Eva emerged from the back door of the garage, scrambling across the lawn with her head down. Owen spun the car towards her, leaning across to push the passenger door open and crying out as the Hummer launched into the yard, its massive wheels throwing up clumps of grass. Eva dived in, slamming the door closed and tugging at her seat belt.

"Faster!" Eva cried, shoving at Owen's hands and forcing him to turn the wheel sharply.

A row of geraniums splattered against the grill as the BMW bounced across a drain and into the neighbouring yard. Owen thrashed the steering wheel back to the right to avoid a septic tank, then aimed the car at the middle of a paling fence. The Hummer continued to follow; crushing the side of the neighbour's garden shed and then ripping a clothesline clean out of its concrete base.

"Keep going!" Eva cried as the car ploughed into the fence, tossing shattered palings and wood fragments into the playing field beyond. Owen again accelerated, his grip relaxing as the car gained traction on the freshly mown grass. He watched in the wing mirror as another section of the paling fence erupted, and the monstrous vehicle thundered across the field behind them.

The BMW skidded onto a bitumen road with a cloud of burning rubber, the front bumper bouncing against the road and then shattering apart beneath the wheels. It was as though the car had coughed its lungs clear, and it responded to Owen's stamping foot with a salubrious roar. The Hummer was soon lost in the distance as they raced towards the border of the Canal Zone.

"Nice driving," Eva said anxiously. "You gotta slow down though. There are always soldiers around the next corner."

Owen gasped as they rounded the corner. A row of troop carriers were moving to block the road, and a crowd of armed soldiers ran from a line of barracks to the right.

Owen again mounted the gutter and revved onto a field, aiming the car towards the highway bordering the Canal Zone. He glanced desperately at the jungle that strangled the hill beyond, and realised with a sinking stomach that the roadblock had been the only route up to Hector's mansion. With no prospect of turning back he continued speeding towards the opposite end of the field.

The ground soon became muddy and the car spun out, its wheels choking and spluttering beside a goal post. Owen managed to ease the vehicle back onto dry grass, but just as he began to accelerate he felt the rear end slumping, the back wheels digging themselves into a trench. At the other side of the field the Hummer again appeared, swerving around a small grandstand and grunting like a wild animal.

"We've got to get across the highway!" Eva screamed as they both splashed out into the mud. "They'll be forced to follow us on foot. Vamos!"

The end of the field was a maze of puddles, and they both gave up trying to sidestep them as the Hummer advanced, mud spurting like a brown fountain from its front wheels. They reached the edge of the highway and leapt like hurdlers over the low railing, landing at the roadside six feet below. Four lanes of traffic blasted horns as they ran blindly, their heads ducking in fear of gunfire from the field behind. Eva tripped at the final lane and Owen clung to her bloodied shirt, dragging her off the road and heaving the both of them towards the dense vegetation. The gunfire only started as they were clear of the road, and they bounded into the wet undergrowth as a swarm of bullets shredded through the leaves above.

Eva scrambled ahead, tossing aside ferns and peering zealously towards the top of Ancon Hill. Ethereal strings of mist seemed to rise through the leaves around them, coalescing in the canopy and drizzling droplets of water back to the forest floor. The mist quickly became an opaque white that bleached the highway below, and Owen's pounding chest eased as he glanced back down the cliff. He gathered his breath, pinched at a cramp in his stomach and then powered onwards.

"There's a back entrance," Eva panted, "behind the aviaries."

Owen acknowledged her with a heavy puff. "How much further?"

Her response was cut off when two silhouettes spawned from the fog above. A sudden hiss of Spanish brought a waving hand from Eva, who called back and pointed towards Owen.

The men were obviously Machos, their wild eyes and thick beards blending into their ominous black weapons. The fear churning through Owen's body was apparently lost to Eva, who whispered angrily for him to catch up.

"What's going on?" Owen puffed as he clambered over the last few rocks to catch up. "Are we turning ourselves in?"

"Of course not," Eva scoffed. "These men work for Hector."

A third Macho waited at the base of a rocky wall enveloped by ivy. He pointed to a gap in the vines, where an open iron gate revealed the entrance to a tunnel.

"Come on," Eva panted, motioning for Owen to follow her into the darkness.

One of the Machos spoke loudly into his radio, nodding to the other and then swinging the gate closed.

Owen's heartbeat continued to race as light globes fizzed on in front of them, casting shadows against a series of low wooden archways. He bumped his head on one of the arches, gritting his teeth in pain and then stumbling blindly up a flight of concrete steps.

"Eva!" came a high-pitched female voice.

Owen opened his eyes wider to see Hector's daughter Sarita embracing Eva at the top of the steps.

"My goodness, look what he's done to you!" Sarita's face was awash with fear as she examined the extent of Eva's bruising. "Papa is going to be furious!"

"I already am!" came a booming shout from further down the corridor. Hector stormed through the shadows, his face a picture of wrath. He pulled Eva into a quick hug, his eyes continuing to flare as he glanced at Owen.

Owen shifted uneasily, patting down his crumpled shirt.

"Sarita," Hector growled, "take Eva upstairs and have her seen to. Owen – you come with me."

Chapter Thirty

Isla de Marfil, Gulf of Batabano.
Present day.

The text messages from Owen continued throughout the evening, and Jenna eventually responded with a rushed string of abbreviations. She had resisted the attempts made to get her to smoke, but a glass of champagne eventually made its way through her stubborn lips. The jetlag struck hard, and she found herself increasingly tipsy as she drifted between the groups of fishermen who had gathered around the barbecue area.

The smiles were infectious. Everyone, everywhere seemed cheerful, and Jenna decided that it wasn't just the food and whatever else they had been consuming. The same trio of guitar players were still strumming away after nightfall, and were joined by another Creole man with a set of bongo drums. Two men emerged from the side of the building with armfuls of firewood, and a bonfire was quickly licking at the palm fronds above.

Cesar's giant arms grabbed both Agnes and Karen around their waists and the three of them performed a comedic dance that they had obviously been practising together. Their performance had the crowd falling over each other laughing, and Cesar somehow dragged Jenna into the middle of the circle. His massive hands clapped above them as he sang, and Jenna downed her latest glass of champagne so that she could join in the applauding.

The fisherman – or 'El Guapo' as Al had called him – had spent much of the night away from the main crowd, drinking spirits and chatting with a group of Cuban men. He had removed his shirt, and paraded a body that had made Agnes and Karen giddy. Jenna had been purposefully ignoring him, and was startled when she felt a rough palm land on her bare shoulder.

"You remember our deal from the boat, princess?" the fisherman asked, his dreadlocks sweeping against her hair. "You said you was gonna outdance me."

"Hey! Don't call me princess!"

"Waah, so passionate!" he grinned mockingly.

Cesar and his entourage had dispersed into the crowd, and the drumming slowed to a low rumbling. The circle had grown wider and with a sudden strumming of guitars the crowd began clapping and chanting in Spanish. Jenna's back straightened, and she instinctively skipped backwards into the middle of the circle, her expression intense. The fisherman had turned his back to her, his bandana now removed and his dreadlocks bouncing rhythmically. He began revving the crowd up with a boisterous display of clapping, turning to give Jenna a wink.

Jenna was still stationary as he turned, and in just a few movements she realised that she had completely misjudged him during their boat ride earlier in the day. After a perfect backflip his fingertips were linked with hers and she was thrown into a spin, pulling away from him and then whipping back into his clasp.

The strumming of the guitars seemed to urge the flames higher, and they thrashed at the sparks that framed each of Jenna's fervent twirls. Her eyes glowed yellow in the firelight, and her hands began to slip over the veining muscles of the fisherman's shoulders, her black fingernails sliding down his forearms and linking with the grip of his powerful hands. He directed her with firm control, and seemed to dance with a calculated effort-lessness that added to the pounding in her chest. The intensity in his eyes pulled her into the bulge of his pectorals, the ripples of her ribcage sliding across the taut ridges of his abdomen. He pulled her tighter, the roughness of his jaw prickling at her cheeks and his hands sliding over the firm curves of her lower back. She had no idea of the meaning of the Spanish that he was mouthing into her ear, but the thick vibrations of his tongue locked her tighter into his embrace. She knew that she was on display, and that this was a competition, but she was so absorbed in their dancing that all else became a blur.

They spun as one, and it wasn't until they shared a smile, the tips of their noses almost touching, that Jenna heard the cheering of the crowd surrounding the fire. Their chests separated, and their smiles turned into beaming grins as the guitar players bounced to their feet, dancing and singing as they strummed. The sea of music brought tears to the corners of Jenna's eyes, and she laughed elatedly, her hands linking again with the fisherman's as they retreated to the shelly sand outside the circle.

"I guess you won't have to pay me for the boat ride," the fisherman whispered as they slinked into the darkness.

"I don't know about that. You are seriously talented!"

"Waah, leave it for the crowd to judge. But you, Jenna, you're something else!" He winked at her as he pulled away and strode back towards the light, his voice almost trailing away as he called back. "Almost a better dancer than your mother was."

Jenna's heart flipped, and she remained frozen as he disappeared into the crowd. "Hey!" she shouted. "What did you just say? Hey!" She clambered over the sand to reach him.

He turned to face her, his expression serious. "You heard me. I'm sorry for what happened to her. But I can't help you."

"My God!" Jenna gasped. "You're Rafael, aren't you?"

He didn't respond, but his eyes told her that it was true.

"But..."

A sudden flash made her stumble.

"Todos abajo!" came a scream.

Jenna spun around to see Cesar's face above the crowd, his eyes wide with terror. He flung his arms around Karen, pulling her to the ground as the onslaught of gunfire began. The deafening roar shook the shell fragments between Jenna's toes, but she continued to stand, paralysed with shock.

The crowd tried to disperse, but without knowing the source of the gunfire they dived to the ground, their faces illuminated by flashes of white and yellow. Four men emerged from the vegetation around the fireplace, their faces hidden behind black ski masks as they sprayed bullets into the treetops.

The gunfire ceased, and through the smoke came a booming shout with an American accent. "Rafael! Where is Rafael?"

Another light appeared in the sky above the bar, swaying slowly from side to side and then flashing directly onto the roof. The ground shook with the vibrations of a chopper, and one of the men stepped into the light.

"I said, where is Rafael?" He locked his assault rifle and then pointed the barrel at the cowering bodies beneath him. "I will start shooting each one of you until –"

"I dare you," came a response from Cesar. He slowly ascended to his feet, raising his arms in the air and glaring at the man.

The man turned his masked head to the side, aiming his gun at Cesar. "So we have a hero, do we?" He suddenly flinched as two of his companions were swept off their feet from behind, their guns ripped from their grasps by Creole men. He tried to shout out, but his voice ended in a sickening gurgle as a bullet ripped through his jaw, splitting apart the mask. The last of the masked gunmen fired into the palm trees in fright, but he fell limply to the ground as another shot rang out from the darkness.

Cesar took the opportunity to leap forward, grabbing the dead man's weapon and crying out for the crowd to run for cover. A white light washed over the crowd as the chopper began to lower, and Cesar took cover beneath the veranda as he fired upwards.

"Get up!" came a deep voice as Rafael powered out of the palm trees. Jenna was hurled to her feet as he snapped his arms around her waist. He threw her forward as he ran, forcing her to start running and then tugging on her outstretched hand. Jenna's stumbling became a sprint as they disappeared behind the back of the building and then splashed through the dark lagoon. Beyond the reeds a dim light was visible from the wharf at which they had arrived earlier in the day. Rafael let go of Jenna's hand as they reached the other side of the lagoon and dropped on all fours to peer at the wharf.

Jenna's heart was heaving her entire body into shudders, and she swallowed in fright as a round of gunshots erupted from behind the building and created a surge of sparks at the base of the chopper. She wanted to scream, but her mouth was wired closed, her breathing non-existent.

"Come on," Rafael ordered. "Stay behind me."

Jenna wanted to respond – to ask what was going on, what he was doing, but no words came out. Within a few seconds she found her wet feet pounding across the shelly beach towards the eerie glow of the wharf. Just as they reached the ramp she saw what had made Rafael hesitate back at the lagoon – a large black shadow bobbed at the end of the wharf where the panga had earlier been moored.

A string of shots blasted out of the palm trees to their right, and Rafael sidestepped, collecting Jenna in a tackle that propelled both of them beneath the nearest pylon. Jenna ducked into the inky blackness, feeling his hands guiding her between barnacled stilts, her bare feet splashing in the ankle-deep water.

"Shhh!" He pressed his palm over her mouth and then crept back towards the foot of the wharf. Jenna clung onto the pylon and tried to make out his silhouette as he paused, peering out towards the source of the gunshots. She felt her breathing speeding up, then gasped as the distant thatched roof of the bar was struck by a ball of fire. The roof erupted into flames as the chopper pulled back, and the entire beach was suddenly awash with orange light. Sparks sprayed across the stars overhead, followed by long burning strings and balls of ash.

The sound of heavy shoes on the slats above Jenna's head made her duck, and she saw that Rafael had disappeared from his hiding place. Her racing mind told her that he had not been wearing shoes, and the terror that enveloped her was pierced by a man's long, hair-raising scream. The cracking of metal on bone directly above her head was followed by an inaudible buzz from a handheld radio, and the body of a man tumbled lifelessly into the water.

"Rafael!" Jenna screamed, diving towards the body. She reached out towards a sinking foot when a shout from behind her tossed her stomach sideways.

"Up here!" Rafael called, his hand hanging over the edge of the wharf and his dreadlocks orange in the light. Numb with shock, she linked her arm into his and pushed her feet against the pylon, heaving her slender frame upwards. He pulled her towards the end of the wharf, his running lopsided as he adjusted the strap of a rifle.

The reflection of the flames glimmered in the paintwork of a black 30-foot speedboat that shoved against a tyre-lined pylon. Rafael swore as he stared at the machine, and pointed the rifle cautiously as he surveyed the deck. Satisfied they were alone, he tossed the rifle onto one of the rear seats and then glanced back at the mass of buckets and nets strewn across the wharf. He grabbed at two large jerry cans and panted as he dragged them to the boat. "Get in," he moaned, lowering the cans individually onto the transom.

"Wait," Jenna whispered. "Whose boat is this?" Her voice became louder. "Where are you taking me? What is going on back there?"

"Get in!" he shouted. He glanced at the base of the wharf as another explosion threw flames up like fireworks from the centre of the island. "Get in!"

She took the ladder, carefully stepping aboard as he ripped the rope from the mooring and tossed it behind the rear seats.

"Get in the front seat, get that seat belt on ya."

Jenna scrambled into the front passenger seat as Rafael checked below deck. He emerged moments later, rattling a set of keys.

The low rumbling of the engine seemed to vibrate the entire ocean. Illuminated dials were reflected in the windscreen, and lights flicked on between Jenna's legs. She cowered as the engines began to purr, the vibrations growing stronger and then heaving into a crackling roar.

Rafael stood confidently at the helm, his face menacing in the light of the dials as he tilted the speedboat into a wide curve, bending around a buoy. He switched off a radio that buzzed beside the controls.

"What are you doing?" Jenna cried. "Where are we going?"

At the opposite end of the island the spotlight continued to scan, and the outline of the chopper became visible against the flames. The light swept ominously across the trees and lagoon, then focused on the empty wharf.

Rafael threw his weight into the throttle and the speedboat launched like a rocket, hurtling around the granite spires at the end of the island and into open water. Jenna screamed as they skittered sideways above the surface, seemingly out of control until the keel ripped into the swell. Rafael somehow remained standing through the whiplash, and gritted his teeth as he struggled to keep away from the chopper's spotlight. He pulled the boat into a tight zigzag and then let out a tirade of Spanish cursing as they accelerated freely into the blackness of open ocean.

The flames became smaller as the boat began to plane, its hull drumming rhythmically across the crests of the calm swell. The purring of the engines seemed to be coming from inside Jenna's head, and she bowed into the wind that thrashed around the windscreen. Nausea took over her breathing, and she threw up over the port side. A mess of hair was tossed over her tearful face, sticking to the champagne saliva and tangling into her mouth. She coughed and spluttered, falling back into her seat and hyper-ventilating.

"Pull yourself together!" Rafael shouted.

Jenna's response was incoherent, and her body was overcome with pins and needles as she tried desperately to calm her breathing. Rafael turned on lights across the bow, searched through an anchor locker and tossed her a crusty towel. She wiped at her face, pulling back her hair and trying to see through the windscreen.

"You gotta focus." He turned the lights back off.

"People are dead," she wheezed. "I saw them. My handbag! I left my handbag in the bar!"

He ignored her as he scanned the sky behind them, his eyes squinting. "That chopper has gone. We got a few hours maybe, that's if they were coming from Florida. But I reckon you gotta better idea where they're coming from than me, no true?"

She blinked at him through her tears, her breathing stalling.

He shook his head again. "This is why I never helped your mother." He eased back the throttle and slumped into his seat. "I knew this was gonna happen."

Jenna coughed, tears streaming over her chin. "I've got nothing to do with this, honestly!"

"Puppycho! I saw you using that phone tonight. You were talking to that man: Mr CIA. Tell me it ain't true."

"What? I –"

"It's still in your pocket, too. It was rubbin' up against me when we danced. Give it to me."

She glared at him.

"Gimme the goddam phone!"

His anger sliced cleanly through her nerves, and she clumsily pulled the phone from her pocket.

Barely a second passed before fragments of plastic and metal glinted across the dark floor of the boat. Jenna gasped in horror.

"I wanna believe you. But I need to protect myself first."

"But he had nothing to do with this! He's a journalist."

"You full-o-sheet, and you don't even know it! You're just a puppet. He was CIA, he had it written on him like a billboard."

"Agh!" Jenna cried, swiping the hair out of her face in frustration. "He's just a journalist. He knew my mother, and he –"

"And how long have you known him?"

She sighed angrily. "Just shut up. Please, take me back to the mainland."

"He set you up to get me, didn't he? And you want me to go and take you back to him. So he can put a thousand bullets in me? No princess, it ain't happening."

She rubbed at her temples, her tears replaced by frustration and confusion. "I'm here for the same reason my mother was. You know that much is true. And you know that she wasn't trying to set you up, she just wanted your help."

Rafael focused on a small screen beside the engine dials, his eyes narrowing as he brought up what looked to be a satellite map. He zoomed in and out, running a hand over his clenched jaw. "Previous places in this thing; they're all in US waters. This boat, it's gotta have one of them GPS trackers. I gotta work out how to turn it off."

Jenna huffed.

"I knew your mother wasn't loco," Rafael finally sighed, turning around to face her. "But it was too dangerous. She wanted me to take her to Panama. That was not gonna happen."

"Panama? Why?" She was ignoring the GPS screen, trying to gain his attention again. "The tapes? They're in Panama, aren't they?"

He turned around, searching the black sky. "Gonna be backup, always is. Another chopper. Or planes. We need to get to land."

"You didn't answer me."

"Huh?"

"The tapes? Where are they?"

"Chooh, I dunno what you fussin' bout."

"Yes you do. My mother would have asked you about them." She leaned towards him, her eyes suddenly alive with anger.

"Sit back down, yo! Lemme think. Whatever you're talking about – it doesn't matter."

"Of course it matters!" she spat, her face a luminescent green in the light of the dials.

He pretended to ignore her, and pushed past her as he searched compartments around the helm, shaking his head in frustration. "There ain't nothing here. Go look below deck. See what's in them cupboards. See if there are any guns, ammunition, somethin' like that."

"You're used to this, aren't you?" She leaned over him, her voice low and reproachful. "You don't stay in one place. You just get up and leave, you become a new person, you call yourself 'El Guapo' like some sort of celebrity. So why did you save me back there? If you think I set you up, why are you helping me?"

"Go down, look for me. I can't leave these controls."

"They were after you, not me. And what about the others? Why save me instead of them? Or do you know something that I don't?"

"Stap yo rass goddam it, you drivin' me mad."

"Hey, I'm not the one being secretive!"

His face became rigid as he glared at her. "You're pissing me off. If you don't do what I say, I'll be throwin' that pretty little body of yours off –"

Jenna was shocked at the speed with which her hand flung outwards, collecting with his cheek in a tremendous slap. The sound seemed to shock him more than the sting, and he tumbled away from her, his eyes wide. He reached upwards, and with a fumbling hand he cut off the engine.

The rushing of foaming water abated, and within a few seconds the only sound was the gentle rippling against the bow. Jenna stood over him, her teeth grinding together. "Don't you ever threaten me again! Now get up, and tell me how far this boat will take us."

He ascended, his face still smeared with shock. He rubbed at his cheek and leaned backwards against the helm. "You're crazy."

"You think? Now, how far will this boat take us?"

He glanced at the gauges and shrugged his shoulders. "Bout one hundred gallons in her tank, another fifty in them cans." He sighed as he scratched his head and pulled back his dreadlocks. "I've used a Baja like this one before – same engines, same length. If we keepin' her over fifty knots, then maybe two hundred miles. But slow her down to thirty knots, maybe double that. But we'd be pushing it."

She stared back blankly. "And where will that get us to?"

"Mexico perhaps, or Belize." He clenched his jaw. "But we may as well shoot ourselves now if we're gonna be goin' west. Same with Jamaica, and without passports we're good as dead. Well, you are."

"What about south?"

He rolled his eyes broodingly. "If we're lucky we maybe make it to Honduras. I can buss out past the patrol boats there, but we gonna be sitting ducks til mornin'."

"And how far is it from Honduras to Panama?"

"Ha!" he laughed. "Don't even think about it. I be takin' you as far as Honduras, no further."

"And then what?"

"Then I get fuel." He stared at the GPS for a second before turning to face her. "And you get yo' ass back to England."

Chapter Thirty-One

It was five in the morning when Jenna emerged from below deck wearing a bright orange life jacket. She had been drifting in and out of sleep, and a distant whirring had turned into the blades of a chopper in her scattered dreams. She calculated the time in England and rubbed at her aching forehead.

The sky was now a patchwork of ghostly grey clouds and clusters of stars, and the lights of an airline jet slowly blinked out of view. A fragmented moon was descending behind a line of cargo ships, and their silhouettes were reflected as abstract shapes across the stagnant black water. The taste of seaweed in the air mixed with the smell of the boat's new vinyl seats.

Rafael was bent over the helm, his dreadlocks swaying like snakes over a black T-shirt that he had found. Jenna sidled up to him, steadying herself against the front passenger seat and rubbing the sleep from her eyes. She was almost beside him when her stomach fluttered, for the thick stubble over his jaw was glistening with what looked like tears. He stared forward like a statue, but as he turned she saw that the glistening was just sea spray.

"Waah!" he laughed as he stared her up and down. "Princess found a life jacket! Waah!"

"Pfft, I'm not too proud to care about my safety."

"How's the bed? Sorry bout the bumping earlier, swell's been havin' a bash."

She sighed. "The bed's fine. Did you want me to take over?"

He turned towards her, a slight smile dimpling his cheeks. "You wanna take the wheel?"

"I'm offering, yes."

"Chooh! Come on, then."

"Do I just steer towards the south?"

"Yup. Got her set at thirty knots." He stood over her, guiding her hands to a position on the wheel and explaining how to use the throttle and shifters. "There's spose to be a quarter of a tank left, but I don't trust the gauge. Gonna give her some more, keep her steady and shout if you have any problems."

"Will do. Did you want some crackers and cheese?"

"Huh?"

"I found some food in the compartment under the bed."

He took a moment to respond. "You find anythin' else?"

She shrugged casually. "Just the life jackets, flares and a first aid kit. And someone's sunglasses. No more guns, if that's what you wanted?"

"Hmm." He scratched at his stubble and slipped below deck.

Jenna huffed and turned back to the helm. Breathing steadily through her nose she listened to him moving around below. Finally his movements ceased, and she carefully bent down to search for Owen's sim card.

Fingers of fog crept across the putty-coloured waves at sunrise, masking the three islands that had appeared to the south. Rafael took over the helm once more, increasing the speed and donning a pair of sunglasses as he scanned the sky.

"You think they'll see us through this fog?" Jenna asked as she slumped into the passenger seat.

"Already have."

"Huh? What do you mean?"

"Drones," he said matter-of-factly, staring upwards at a white glimmer dancing at the edge of a cottony cloud. "Bastards."

Jenna cried out in shock. "Are you serious?"

"Only problem for them is us bein' in Honduran waters now." He stared around the boat and frowned again. "But then I spose this fog will help cover up whatever they do, no true?"

"Could it just be a plane?"

He ignored her, reaching into a compartment below the wheel and pushing his hand deep inside. After a few seconds of searching he pulled out a small rectangular plastic package. "Stuff this in your pocket, we may be needin' it."

She took the package hesitantly. "What is this? Where did you get it?"

"Just put it in your pocket!"

She eased it into the back of her shorts, making sure Owen's sim card was buried beneath before doing up the button.

"I put that rifle down below. On the bed. Grab it, quick."

"Um, okay."

"Fasta!"

She ducked below deck and emerged soon after. "It's really heavy!"

He gritted his teeth in aggravation. "Give it to me. Take the wheel."

Within moments Rafael was positioning himself over the transom as Jenna gripped the throttle. The islands were in the GPS map now, and she turned the boat directly towards them.

The chopper appeared like a black insect, humming up behind them and then piercing the air with a chilling whirr. Jenna screamed, her hands trembling on the wheel as Rafael shouted for her to zigzag.

"Waah, not that much!"

She straightened the boat and turned to see the chopper descending into the frothing wake behind. Another terrified scream escaped her lungs.

Rafael began firing, but he was thrown sideways as an explosion launched a wave over the transom. Jenna grimaced as she pulled herself back up. She spun the wheel and threw her weight into the throttle.

"Here's another!" Rafael screamed.

She ducked as fragments of fibreglass sprayed past her cheek and the windscreen cracked. Bullets instantly pockmarked the bow. Tears of terror swelled in her eyes as she continued gripping the throttle, her eyes glancing at the GPS screen just as the boat sped clear of the fog.

"Look out!" Rafael screamed. Before she realised what was happening his shoulders collected with her thighs. She was thrust high over the coaming panel, whitewash whipping through her hair as she tumbled overboard.

Rafael's body seemed to cocoon Jenna's as they rolled, the blinding spray followed by a bone-crunching impact with the water. Rafael's shirt was torn apart as his hands were ripped like broken straps from her hips. Her body bounced across the surface as his was sucked underneath, and a delayed pain jolted from her bare feet and elbows as she sank into a prickling mass of seaweed. She felt herself being dragged under, but the life jacket pulled her back into the bright sun.

The sound of an explosion never came, and it took a moment for Jenna to realise that it wasn't a rocket that Rafael had thrown her overboard to avoid. The boat had flipped as it struck a shallow reef, and the chopper was descending in a low sweep as it sprayed bullets into the upturned hull. The shock of what had just happened numbed her emotions, and she could barely feel her feet and hands as she struggled to tread water. The whole situation felt like a scene in a movie, and she could almost feel the fabric of a couch, her eyes slipping in and out of a television screen as the stinging of salt water forced her eyes to shut.

The rocks of a small cay loomed over the waves to her right, but the view was fleeting as she sank below the surface. At the crest of a wave she kicked herself high above the water, scanning the swell behind and then choking in dread.

Rafael still hadn't surfaced.

Chapter Thirty-Two

Hector's mansion, Panama City.
December 19th, 1989, 10am.

"I see," Hector said solemnly into the phone, pacing back and forth on the balcony. "Yeah, that's fine. Thanks again, hasta luego." He stared out across the gardens below with a pensive frown, his fingers stroking the end of his white beard.

"Well?" Owen asked, looking up from the scope of Hector's rifle.

"Two PM," the old man responded, pulling out a cigar. "Bush has called a meeting with senior officials. I'll get another call afterwards."

"Hmm." Owen positioned the rifle once more over the side of the railing.

"Both eyes open," Hector instructed, flicking Owen's ear. "That's it, now you can see what's around you while you're aiming. Okay, take off the safety. That's it. Now fix the crosshairs on your target, and whenever you're steady, pull the trigger."

A thin limb was blown off the fig tree opposite and Hector chuckled with approval. "You've done it again, very nice! And to think you've been hiding this talent all these years!"

"I still don't like guns," Owen responded, flicking the safety back on and leaning the rifle against the railing. "And I'll only use this thing if there's no other option."

Hector smiled, puffing at his cigar. "I used to train with an Israeli man who believed that the best way of getting shot is to carry a gun. He fought in the War of Attrition for three years with just a knife."

"And did he get shot?"

Hector continued to smile as he stared down at the aviaries. "No. He got stabbed."

Owen laughed. "I'll take that message on board!"

Hector grinned. "All ideals must be flexible. You may not like holding a rifle, but you have an incredibly steady hand. Use that talent."

Owen stared back with a concordant frown.

"Now, the radios." He rummaged through a collection of electronics on the balcony table. "They have a range of a few hundred metres, but if everything goes to plan we shouldn't have to test that. We'll carry this one in the car, and Maria will have the other in her handbag. It will be on the whole time, so we can hear everything from her end, but the guards won't be able to hear us until she turns this dial up and uses it as a normal UHF."

"And what do we do if she is caught using the radio inside the building?"

Hector stared at him before pointing at the rifle. "You've made the promise to protect her, so it's on your shoulders to get her out alive."

Owen sighed heavily. "Wonderful."

"Hector?" came a voice from inside.

Both men turned to see Eva pushing through the flowing curtains onto the balcony, her head wrapped in fresh bandages. "Maria is on the phone downstairs."

Both men froze. "And?"

"Noriega is in Colon, but he's returning to Panama City late tonight. She said they might get suspicious if she turns up at six and he's not back, so she wants to push it back to eleven."

Hector scratched at his ruffled hair. "I guess we've got no choice. Tell her that's fine, and that we'll meet her in the car park behind her place half an hour beforehand."

Eva nodded, disappearing once again into the house.

Hector sighed, glancing at Owen as if something pressing was on the tip of his tongue. He was about to say something when he decided against it, burying his emotions in his cigar. "We'll be fine," he finally mumbled, his voice unconvincing. "We'll be fine."

Chapter Thirty-Three

Bay Islands, Honduras.
Present day.

Jenna spluttered desperately as she tried to hold Rafael's dead weight above the seaweed. His face had turned a dark blue-grey, and his left shoulder was spreading an inky trail of blood into the water.

"Wake up!" Jenna cried, slapping at his cheeks and whacking like an anxious child at his chest. Her shouting descended into sobbing as she slid her body beneath his, lifting him upwards and trying to kick against the seaweed. She gave up, sliding back out from underneath him, treading water and using his dreadlocks to tilt his head back. With her other hand she pulled open his jaw, inhaling and then blowing forcefully into his mouth. The air came straight back out his nose, and so she tried again, pinching his nostrils closed and feeling his chest rising above the water.

The buoyancy was short-lived, but it allowed her to drag him clear of the weeds and over the top of a shallow reef. She began treading water again, positioning herself to give him another breath. She was beginning to inhale when her lungs recoiled in pain. Her foot had stabbed into the coral, but relief quickly overcame the pain as she placed both feet down and held Rafael steadily above the water.

Another breath filled his lungs, but still there was no response. She wiped the tears from her eyes and scanned the vacant sky. Ahead, the reef was rising above the water and onto one of many sandy cays. A grove of palm trees occupied the first cay, and the image of safety caused her to kick once again, guiding his body over the coral and onto another reef. Another breath, another bout of kicking and she had reached the sand.

"Come on!" Jenna cried as she dragged his body out of the water. She tilted his head to the side, peering into his mouth and then giving him another breath. She rolled him onto his back, positioned her hands over his sternum and threw her weight into compressions.

Blood was seeping onto the sand, and Jenna's squeamish stomach was threatening to throw up. She leaned over to give him another breath when a deep gurgling vented from his mouth and nose. She pulled away as his back lurched upwards and a gush of vomit splashed onto the bloodied sand. The shock caused her to vomit as well, but the acidic taste and smell couldn't hold her back from shouting out with relief. Rafael rolled onto his side, coughing and spluttering and curling into a foetal position.

"Breathe!" Jenna cried, pulling his dreadlocks out of the mess and allowing him to suck in air. For several minutes he said nothing, continuing to cough and wheeze until he had enough energy to shift himself onto dry sand. Jenna left his side, washing her mouth out in the seawater and slumping back onto the shore, exhausted.

"Agua," Rafael croaked, rolling onto his back.

"I don't have any water," she panted, her forearms sinking into shells as she tried to sit up.

"Where's..."

"Where's what?"

"Where's the chopper?" His eyes had flicked open, but the sun had blinded him and he shaded his face with his arm.

"I think it's gone. Come on, let's get up." She rubbed at her bloodshot eyes and shaded her face with her hand. The series of cays followed a reef for the next few kilometres until the sand met a heavily forested headland. The humid air seemed to warp the view into a mirage, and she blinked, again rubbing at her eyes.

A flock of seagulls cast fluttering shadows over the cay as they swooped onto the shoreline nearby, their inquisitive squawking becoming louder as they approached. Rafael grumbled at them and shifted painfully into a crawling position. Blood started flowing from his shoulder, seeping between sand grains and trickling down his arm. Jenna tore at the ragged remains of the shirt that was now scrambled around his waist. The black fabric came free, and she tied it forcefully over the wound.

"Thank you," he spluttered, losing balance and falling headfirst back into the sand.

"Come on," she groaned, heaving him back to his knees and then pulling him clumsily to his feet. She wrapped her arm beneath his shoulders and guided him in a staggering walk towards the shade.

The coarse, crusty sand was heating up as they finally collapsed beneath the palm trees. Jenna had been eyeing the clusters of green coconuts hanging from above, but found that there were already plenty lying amongst the leaf litter. She took off the life jacket and used it as a pillow for him. He quickly fell asleep, and she limped back to the water to wash the blood from her hands and pull out a collection of jagged rocks.

Rafael continued to sleep as she hacked through the husk of one of the coconuts. She managed to get down to the shell, but no amount of hacking would pierce it open. She ventured deeper into the trees, her footsteps crunching over thick mats of dead palm fronds.

Rafael awoke suddenly as moisture poured over his chaffed lips. His eyes met with Jenna's as she stood over him, and he reached up graciously to take the cracked shell. His face relaxed as he drank, and he was smiling as he finally pulled it away from his mouth.

"The chopper did a lap of the islands, but I think it's gone again."

He nodded, closing his eyes and breathing in through his nose. His exhaustion and helplessness was strangely warming to Jenna as she studied the lines on his face.

"The land at the end of these cays looks like it has buildings on it. I think the tide is coming in though, so we'll have to get moving soon if we want to get out of here."

He nodded again, opening his eyes. "You're a smart chica, I'm impressed." He reached his hand up to link with hers, but she hesitated, pulling away.

"What?" He looked up at her innocently, his eyes foggy.

She swallowed, blinking as she tried to suppress an upwelling of emotion. "I-I just saved your life. I know that you did the same for me earlier, but…"

He sighed, his expression sinking into a deep frown.

"I pulled you out of the water, I gave you CPR." She was crying now, her body shaking as she continued to stand over him. "I got covered in your blood, and I held your hair back while you threw up… I – Look, I'll help you up now, and I'll help you to the next island, but I'm going to need you to promise me something."

He exhaled heavily, grabbing hold of the palm trunk and pulling himself to his feet. His stomach was caving inwards in pain, and he steadied himself on her shoulder. "Don't worry," he whispered, his eyes narrowed sincerely. "I'm going to take you to Panama."

Chapter Thirty-Four

Hector's mansion, Panama City.
December 19th, 1989, 10pm.

The bottle of rum was shaking as Owen unscrewed the cap, the clinking of the glass creating an echo through the silent dining area. He carefully returned the bottle to its shelf, his face as white in the mirrored cabinet as the quartz bench tops behind. He closed his eyes tightly as he drank; trying to imagine standing in a bar in Canada around the corner from his apartment.

The alcohol acted quickly, and he felt his hands relax as he stepped into the dark living room, the glimmering of Panama City decorating his reflection in the glass walls. He ran his hand over the white fall of a grand piano, placing his glass down and then spying a collection of instruments in the corner of the room. He carefully removed an old Tanglewood acoustic guitar from its case, closing his eyes as his fingers navigated their way across the frets.

The sound reverberated loudly through the living area, but he continued to play, taking a seat beside the piano and finishing the rest of his glass.

"There you are!" came Eva's voice from the top of the staircase. She strutted into the light of the kitchen, her black outfit and baseball cap giving her the look of an FBI agent. "Is that you playing?"

"It is."

"Impresionante!"

"Gracias. Is Hector ready yet?"

"Not sure. He's still talking to Sarita. He's got one of the guards to drive for us, so you won't have to worry about that anymore."

"Oh, good. Which guard?"

"Javier, the quiet one."

"Okay, good. Good."

She smiled at him, taking a seat on the leather sofa opposite. "Don't look so stressed, we've got this sorted. In two hours we will be back here drinking, and you'll be on the phone with your editor organising the biggest pay check of your life."

"Ha!" he laughed, his shoulders relaxing. "I hadn't even thought about that."

"No, I didn't think you would have."

He moved his fingers back up the frets, his strumming slowing into a low-pitched dirge. "Joe told me that you were expecting a child." He looked up at her solemnly, continuing to play.

Eva swallowed in shock and her eyes darted uncomfortably.

"I made a promise to both you and Maria, and this only strengthens that commitment. The child may be Joe's, but he's still my family. So if anything happens to me tonight –"

"Owen, I –"

"Shh," he whispered. "Let me finish. I've left a diary in my room down the hall. If anything happens to me, go to the last page. All the details you need will be there. Just promise you'll let the people listed on that page know the truth about everything."

Tears began welling in her eyes and she turned away. "Of course I will. Thank you, Owen. Thank you so much."

Music returned as they marched into the auditorium, their faces dark. Owen removed his SLR camera from his backpack, inserted a new round of film and adjusted the ISO and shutter speed. If there was ever going to be a time to get a front page picture it would be tonight.

"Torna A Surriento," Hector announced as he emerged from the tapes room backstage. "I used to listen to this with Noriega, back in Peru. He liked the Carreras version, but my favourite has always been Pavarotti."

Owen began taking photos, smiling cautiously in response to Hector's grin.

Eva had stopped in the centre of the auditorium, her face smoothing into a strange expression as she listened. "I've heard you play this before, Hector." She barely noticed as Hector crossed the floor with a spritely prance, and seemed surprised as he took her around the waist.

Owen grinned as he stood back, allowing them to move around in a slow Waltz.

Sarita emerged at the back of the hall, her lips threatening to grin despite the redness in her eyes. She moved around the border of light, standing beside Owen and whispering to him loudly. "Please look after him tonight. He's not as young as he thinks he is."

Hector's face became serious as the song finished, and he stared at Owen and Sarita with a grave frown, his eyes becoming shadows in the stage lights. "It's time."

Panama City glittered peacefully through the tinted windows of a black Land Rover as it rolled silently down Ancon Hill, its headlights turned off. In the backseat Owen and Eva stared tensely at the Canal Zone, their imaginations creating images of troop carriers and helicopters rising out of the barracks. They were so consumed with looking to the right that they failed to notice a small beige hatchback tearing out of Chorrillo and onto the highway directly in front of them.

Javier spun the car to the right as the hatchback swerved past, the glow of a streetlight illuminating the round, pockmarked face of the man inside.

"Imbecile!" Javier cried, pulling the Land Rover back onto the road and turning into a narrow street.

The streetlights became less frequent as they zigzagged through a network of silent slums. Javier clearly knew the streets better than any of them, and it came as a surprise when the headlights washed over the red dress of a lady standing in a deserted car park. A small boy was clutching to her leg, his eyes wide and anxious and his reflection playing eerily over the brick wall behind.

"Sad, isn't it?" Hector sighed as the car pulled to a stop beside her. "When hookers are more reliable than your closest friends."

Eva and Owen stepped out of the car, smiling encouragingly at Maria as they approached.

"You're a woman of your word," Owen said, pulling a UHF radio and small torch from his jacket and handing them to her.

"Siempre," Maria said brusquely, tucking the radio into her handbag. Continuing in Spanish, she whispered, "I trust that I am going to be saying the same about you."

"Don't worry," Eva responded first, "he's nothing like his cousin." She bent down and then spoke playfully to the boy in Spanish, her hand squeezing his shoulder.

"Owen," Maria said hesitantly, motioning towards the boy. "I'd like you to properly meet my son, Rafael."

PART III
CHASING THE TRUTH

Chapter Thirty-Five

Bay Islands, Honduras.
Present day.

Seagulls offered the only shade as they floated like kites in the glare above. Their squawks circled lower as Jenna and Rafael lumbered through a bed of coral. Jenna's feet were leaking blood into the water, and a school of baitfish followed the scent as she staggered towards the next sandbar. Rafael had taken another route through the reef, wading into deeper water and pushing his way through mats of prickly seaweed. Every so often he flinched as his feet struck coral or hermit crab shells. They reached the sandbar together, and as tempting as it was to collapse and rest, the sight of forested land over the next stretch of water dragged them onwards.

"It's deep," Jenna moaned as she pushed past the sandbar and into a growing current. Her chest was suddenly underwater, and she winced as she realised that she could no longer see her feet through the murkiness. She had left the life jacket back on the island so that they would be harder to spot from above, but was now regretting that decision.

"Gonna have to swim across." Rafael let go of the remains of his coconut shell and linked his hand with hers. His face still had a dark bluish tinge but he was moving with surprising energy. "Hold on, else this current will separate us."

Jenna's face was filled with fear as she lost contact with the sand and began kicking. Rafael's fingers readjusted into a tighter grip and he pulled her forwards. He leaned his head back and closed his eyes, his kicking becoming a steady rhythm.

"We're drifting really fast," Jenna gasped. She began to panic, her breaths rapid as her face bobbed between the ripples.

"Hey," Rafael huffed. "Chill, it's just water." He eased himself to a standing position and held her above the swell. "Come on chica, relax. You were winning back there. You don't want me showin' you up again, do you?"

"What?" she scoffed, spitting out a mouthful of water and momentarily forgetting her fear. "How can you even think that's funny? You nearly died back there. We both did. That's not funny. There's nothing funny about this at all!"

He chuckled to himself, rolling onto his back and gently kicking. "We're still alive, ain't that somethin' to laugh about? And you know that fear costs energy, too."

She began swimming freestyle, breaking away from him and battling against the current. Her burst of energy faded, her shorts weighing her down and forcing her to convert to breaststroke. Rafael remained somewhere nearby, his strokes barely making a splash.

The water became darker, and the unknown depth again sent Jenna's heart racing. Black shadows seemed to morph into ominous shapes, and her movements became more chaotic. Rafael caught up with her, linking his arm beneath hers and pulling her gently.

"Leave me, I'm fine!" She gritted her teeth, again trying to swim freestyle but finding her legs sinking into the black depths. The thought of her bloodied feet attracting unwanted attention kept her paddling through the pain, and a sudden clearing in the seaweed revealed a shallow sandbank. She blew out a mouthful of water in relief, touching down on the sand and then clambering against the current. Rafael rolled onto his front and steadily waded after her.

"Come on, 'El Guapo'!" Jenna huffed, her knees breaking free of the water and her legs pushing her stiffly towards the shore. She felt a sudden dizziness, and images of home took over her vision. She stumbled, the glare from the sand in front stabbing like knives through her corneas.

Rafael began wringing the water out of his dreadlocks and then waited for a wave to propel him towards her.

The colour had drained from Jenna's face, and the dizziness was becoming too much. She threw up what remained in her stomach and sunk to her knees.

Rafael lifted her cleanly out of the water, carried her over the last stretch of shallows and then dumped her abruptly onto the pebbly sand. As he collapsed beside her he saw that her face was scrunching like a child about to cry. She coughed as she tried to suppress the tears, but the mixture of sand and sun, fear, isolation and anxiety swirled upwards and splashed over her eyelashes. The tears carved tracks through the crusted salt on her cheeks and she looked up at him as though he was a stranger in a dark alleyway. "Don't touch me. I hate this. I hate this place, I-I don't know why I'm here. I just want water, I want my phone, I want to go home." She coughed again as she sobbed, her hair matting against her cheeks. "Don't touch me. Just go. Go away!" She slapped at him and he retreated.

"You're going loco from the sun. Just chill. I'll find us some water."

Two seagulls strutted up the beach to watch Jenna's outburst, but they quickly took to the air as she threw a handful of sand at them. "Go away! Everything, just go away!"

Rafael edged through the trees in search of a creek, but his face was quickly swamped by sand flies. He swatted at them and hobbled back towards the beach.

Jenna had moved further up the shore and was now slumped in the buttressed roots of a manchineel tree. She tossed a handful of the tree's fruits into the water and wiped away the last of her tears.

"Hey!" Rafael cried. "Don't go rubbin' your eyes after touching those things. They'll blind you."

"I don't care."

He dropped to his knees beside her, breathing out heavily through his nose. "Chica, listen to me. You're not thinking right, and you're gonna hurt yourself. Wash your hands, and listen to me."

"Where are we?"

"Somewhere in the Bay Islands. Probably another thirty or forty miles to mainland."

She tried to swallow but her throat recoiled in pain. With a vacant expression she reached into the front of her shorts and then cried again as she pulled out her soaked passport.

"Chill. Let it dry before you open the pages. You still got that package I gave you?"

She was about to respond when a distant whirring revealed a bright spec hovering above the cays. The midday sun reflected off the white body of an aircraft, its low-mounted wings slowly taking form as it glided towards them.

"Come on, get up." He tried to grab her hands but she pushed him away.

The plane continued to descend, the whirring becoming louder and turning into a roar as it passed over the jungle nearby.

"It's a Piper Cherokee," Rafael remarked as he hid under the foliage. "I flew one of them once in Guatemala."

"You fly?" Her daze was lifting, and she staggered to her feet.

"Yeah, I do."

"Hmm. Where do you think that plane is going?"

"Must be a landing strip through there. Come on, I'm thinkin' I know where we are." He wiped at his face and then pushed a path into the jungle. "You still got that package?"

"Yes, it's been digging into my ass." She stumbled sideways as she pulled the small parcel from her pocket and he grabbed her arm to steady her. "What is in it?"

"Money." He took the parcel, slipping it into the side of his tattered shorts.

"In what currency?"

He laughed, pushing against a small tree and then bending its branches for her to duck through.

"What's so funny?"

He continued to ignore her, his attention caught by a clearing ahead.

A recent storm had turned the jungle canopy into a mesh of broken vines and splintered limbs. Spindly branches had crashed through the undergrowth like toothpicks ahead and littered the now sunburned ferns. A well-worn track crept between the logs, passing by a mangrove swamp and then into a bulldozed clearing. Overgrown oatgrass bordered a crumbling tarmac that stretched into a steaming mirage.

"I'm so thirsty," Jenna croaked. "Where are the buildings? What is this place?"

Rafael's bare feet ran into one another as he tried to avoid the hot gravel poking through the grass. His face brightened as the mirage melted into a small brick building with a corrugated iron roof. A line of light planes appeared on a tarmac off the runway, and a Honduran flag flapped sluggishly in the breeze.

"Thank God," Jenna wheezed, her pace quickening as the building came into full view.

"Be careful," Rafael murmured, his dry lips cracking. He jumped painfully across the burning asphalt, staring intently at the building. Jenna passed around the tarmac, dizziness threatening to trip her over. Somehow she navigated her way through the shade of the planes towards a suspended water tank. She turned on a tap at its base, burying her face in the jetting flow and swallowing until her stomach cramped. She left the tap running as she slumped into a sitting position, her body tingling with relief. A pair of colourful birds landed nearby, waiting until the splashes of water trickled towards them before drinking eagerly. She watched them dazedly before wiping back her wet hair and breathing in like a fish out of water.

The car park beside the terminal building was empty except for three golf buggies parked in the shade of banana trees. Jenna scanned the line of planes, spotting the Piper Cherokee that they had seen earlier and narrowing her eyes. She rubbed at her nose and then felt herself drifting to sleep.

"Enjoying yourself, princess?" Rafael called from around the side of the building.

She looked up to see him grinning as he held up a bright blue bottle of sports drink. "Hey!" she cried. "Where did you get that?"

"Helados there too if you want 'em. Ice creams, I mean."

She rose stiffly to her feet, limping past him and around to the front of the building. Glass doors opened into a humid terminal decorated with faded posters of the Honduran mainland. A lone man in a baseball cap was shuffling through drawers behind a small check-in desk, his thick moustache vibrating from the force of a desk fan. He nodded at Jenna with a slight smile as she paced up to a fridge stacked with drinks.

Rafael sauntered back into the terminal and the man winked at him, closing the drawers once again and taking a seat behind the desk.

"So where are these ice creams?" Jenna glowered.

Rafael shrugged his shoulders. "How else was I getting you off your ass?"

She huffed, shaking her head and reaching into the fridge. She paused as she pulled out a can of Pepsi. "Um, how do I... I don't have any money."

"It's been sorted," Rafael said, downing the last of his sports drink and tossing the bottle into a nearby bin.

The man behind the desk continued to smile, typing something into his computer and then opening a cash register. He spoke in Spanish to Rafael, then produced a handful of American banknotes.

"Gracias compadre," Rafael said, counting the notes and stuffing them into his shorts.

They continued a conversation in Spanish, the man making hand gestures and pointing through the windows towards the row of golf buggies.

"Si, si. Muchas gracias."

"Buena suerte."

"We'll take a golf buggy downtown," Rafael explained as he opened the glass door for Jenna. "There are rooms at a hotel he says. Next to a diving shop. We can buy clothes and food nearby after the siesta. He also says no flights til Friday. But there will be a ferry to La Ceiba on the mainland in the mornin.'"

"Great." The relief seemed to bring on another wave of tiredness, and she was almost asleep as she slumped into the sticky passenger seat of the golf buggy. Her eyes flicked open as the engine started. "They leave the keys in the ignition?"

"This is an island, chica. You can't steal anything here, unless it floats."

The road from the airstrip wound downhill through swampy farmland and thickets of banana trees. The golf buggy protested as it struggled up a heavily forested hill where advertisements for Pepsi and Coca-Cola marked the outer suburbs of the town. Rafael slowed as children and dogs blocked the narrow strip of bitumen that squeezed through rows of shacks built from cement blocks and driftwood. Car tyres and broken furniture were used to hold down flat tin roofing, and the power lines were a chaotic artwork knitted between crooked antennas.

Soon the shacks grew into brightly coloured weatherboard houses separated from the road by proud balconies and tall iron fences. Themed tourist bars traced the road into the centre of town, where street stalls surrounded two small supermarkets and signs in English pointed towards diving schools and accommodation.

"This looks like it," Rafael announced, prodding Jenna and pointing through the open wooden gate of a resort. A tropical orange building was suspended on wooden stilts above a channel of water, with an enormous sign advertising seafood dinners. Rows of thatch-roofed huts could be seen through the stilts, and a sandy path lined with date palms provided a glimpse of a secluded bay.

Rafael parked the golf buggy beside the open gate, leaving the keys in the ignition and scanning the street warily. The steps up to the building's reception were lined with orange and blue lifebuoys, decorative mooring rope and intricately painted oxygen tanks. A swaying curtain of fishing nets led into a dark reception where photographs of yachts and dive ships lined the walls.

Somehow the receptionist already knew who Rafael was, and she spoke in hushed whispers as he leaned over her desk. He winked as he tapped her on the back of her hand and pointed to a set of keys. She smiled timidly, handing him the keys and then explaining a map of the grounds.

A passageway at the back of the reception led through the side of an extravagantly decorated restaurant, where crabs and lobsters tapped against the glass of their aquariums. Rafael seemed to be distracted as they stepped out of the back of the restaurant onto a driftwood bridge, the bright blue water of the bay sucking away his cognizance.

"You've been here before?" Jenna asked, trying to decipher his expression.

"Our hut is the last one up there, on the left."

Jenna's exhaustion took over as Rafael unlocked the quaint yellow door and allowed her to stumble in first. The nautical theme continued, with old canoe oars and a ship's wheel decorating the wall behind a whitewashed dining table. Blue and white curtains adorned the window of a modern kitchenette, and Jenna was quick to shut away the light reflecting off the white sand outside.

"Hey!" Rafael barked. "Don't close them, leave them open."

"Why?"

"Because I wanna see out."

She shrugged and stumbled towards the bathroom. It wasn't until she emerged several minutes later that she noticed that there was only one queen bed in the room.

"We are not sharing this bed, if that's what you're planning!"

He entered the bathroom, splashing his face with water and studying himself in the mirror. "You think that's what I was planning? Chooh!" He turned around, his mocking grin becoming serious. "Don't worry. She's gonna bring a fold-out bed for me."

Jenna twisted her face into an exaggerated pout, ruffled her pillow and then fell instantly asleep.

The distinctive smell of Thousand Island dressing tingled through Jenna's dreams, and she saw herself sitting in a restaurant in Mayfair, the silver dinnerware glinting as she carefully separated the moist flesh of a lobster from its crisp orange shell. She raised the fork to her lips and awoke suddenly, finding her pillow wet with saliva. Her eyes blinked in surprise at the scene before her, and she groaned as she sat up.

The round dining table had been pulled up to the bed and supported a large tray of seafood and lemon slices; the pink of crab shells matching a tropical milkshake topped with strawberries and pawpaw. Her eyes blinked repeatedly as she swung her legs beneath the table and stared.

At the foot of the bed was a large canvas backpack surrounded by tins of beans and spaghetti, packets of crisps and biscuits, toiletries and glossy bags of clothing. Jenna shuffled disbelievingly through the clothing, finding a long flowing sash, T-shirts and a pair of jeans. An opaque plastic bag contained women's underwear, and she bit at her lower lip, both uncomfortable and impressed at the fact that he had gotten the sizing correct.

The bathroom door slowly creaked open, and Jenna tucked the bag into the pile. She flicked back her hair as Rafael finished drying his face with a towel and emerged into the light.

"Oh my goodness!"

"You think it suits me?" His grin was more timid than cocky, and he ran a hand over his finely clipped scalp as her mouth dropped wide open.

"I-I... Wow, yeah, it looks good."

"It ain't about looking good, but thank you." He pulled on a white linen shirt and ripped off the price tag. "I was gonna buy some bleach for your hair, but I thought it prob'ly best if you try lookin' like a local."

"Um, okay."

"So I bought you a straw fedora. And some leather sandals. I'm thinking they ain't what you would usually wear."

"Aren't," she corrected him.

"Huh?"

"The proper word is aren't, not ain't."

"Yeah, okay princess. Now dig into the food before it goes cold. I was thinkin' 'bout taking you into the restaurant, but it's prob'ly safer we remain inside."

"I agree." She took a long sip from the milkshake, her eyes beginning to lose their tiredness. "I need to call someone. I need to let people know where I am."

"No you don't. You need to rest until you can think straight."

She wanted to argue, but she didn't have the energy. Instead she watched as he struggled to do up his buttons and then smiled to herself as he lay out a napkin.

"There's some soap and shampoo in the bathroom, and I bought you some sunscreen, cos you aren't very dark." He fumbled with a capsule of tartare sauce and smiled awkwardly. "See? I used 'aren't'. And I put your passport on the windowsill up there, it should be dry by now."

"Wow. Thank you." She wanted to compliment him further, but she held her tongue. She still hadn't decided if she could genuinely trust him.

He continued to smile modestly as he cracked the pincers off a crab. "Your passport says you were born in Kent, England, no true?"

She felt a sudden chill run through her. "I don't like you knowing so much about me."

"Sorry, but I like to know who I'm dealing with." He carefully wiped his lips with the napkin. "What's it like in Kent?"

"I don't know. I've never lived there."

Her abrupt answer didn't seem to faze him, and he let the silence linger as he patiently peeled a handful of prawns for her.

"Oh fine. I live in a small town outside of London. Kent is where my mother first went when she arrived in England. She found a husband there when I was a toddler, but their marriage didn't last very long. We moved around a fair bit until she married another man near Harmiston, where she currently lives. I mean, lived." She took a deep breath, avoiding eye contact with him before continuing. "I guess I still live there, but I spend most of my time in London."

"So you're a city chica, then?" He shifted the plate of prawns towards her and leaned back.

"My mother is, but not me. Ironically she still lives in a country cottage – a place that I miss far more than my flat. Now that all this has happened it's making more sense why we never lived in the city – she must have been scared of being recognised."

"And have you travelled much outside of England?"

"Not really. And again, probably because of my mother's fears. I've only travelled around England and France really, and France was during winter."

"Chooh! So is this the first time you've ever been sunburnt?"

"I suppose so, yes." She shifted the straps of her bikini and frowned at the conspicuous lines.

"You'll be black as me soon!"

"I don't think so," she smiled. "But I'll certainly appear more like a local."

"You will. Except for that terrible accent."

"Hey!" she laughed. "Leave me alone. I can sound like a local if I want to!"

"No you can't. Don't even try."

"So what is your first language?"

"Don't know," he responded quickly, as though he had been asked the question many times before. "Depends where I am, who I'm around. Used to be Spanish, but these days I talk more Creole, or Patois, or English. Just depends."

"What is Creole? And Patois?"

"Like pidgin English, but more... how do you say; like, official. So around here Creole has come mostly from English and Spanish, but also through the native Miskitos, and the Mayans." He paused. "And the Garifunas – they're descended from West African slaves. So it sounds a lot the same from here to Belize, but then changes when you go to the islands like Jamaica where they speak Patois, which sounds more like English."

"Gosh", she sighed, perplexed. "So what language was Cesar speaking?"

"Cesar and most of the other boys were talkin' Belizian Creole. But they could all talk Spanish and English too. So when someone like you comes along with that proper princess accent we know that we can prob'ly rip you off, even if you do look like us."

"Ha! So how much was that boat ride supposed to cost then? Not forty dollars?"

"Maybe twenty for men, ten for women."

She laughed. "I see. So were you and Cesar close? How long had you known each other?"

He frowned and rubbed at his scalp. "Not close."

She waited for him to continue – she knew that there was more for him to say – but he was obviously more comfortable with silence than she was. "And how long had you lived there for?"

He shifted uncomfortably and turned away, pretending to be distracted by something outside.

"Um, okay. Where did you live before there, then?"

"Doesn't really matter, does it?" His tone was innocent enough, but his words seemed to cause a rush of heat through Jenna's blood.

"Hey! Don't get stroppy with me for asking questions that anyone else would ask. It's the only way that I'll find out something about you. Hell, I've been happy to tell you everything you want to know about me because I can see that you have a serious issue trusting people. Don't you think I deserve the same respect? I'm the one who's come halfway across the world, who's –"

"Okay princess, calm down, chooh!"

"No, I won't calm down! And don't patronise me by calling me 'princess'! Do you have any idea how scared I am here? I don't know any of these languages, I don't know where we're going, and I don't even know who you are!" She threw down her fork and slammed her hands down on the table. "All I know is that you're some kind of serious criminal, and that doesn't comfort me! I had someone who I could trust, and I left him at a wharf in Cuba for you! No, don't turn away! Sit up and look at me you asshole, have a look around. You've gone to all of this effort to impress me tonight, but what for? To make me like you, to make me trust you? You've got no idea, do you?"

He suddenly left the table and began pacing around the kitchen area, pinching at the bridge of his nose.

"What, you're just going to stay silent?"

He continued pacing, glanced at her for a moment and then unlocked the front door.

"Hey! Where are you going?"

"To get some rum. And a fold-out bed."

Chapter Thirty-Six

El Chorrillo, Panama City.
December 19ᵗʰ, 1989, 10:59pm.

Maria Cordoba emerged from the shadows of the slums, her gliding steps giving her an aura of elegance as she cavorted into the ghostly yellow light of the Comandancia. Her smile was playful as she nodded at the guards, but they moved to block her with grave frowns.

A collective gasp fogged the dark windows of a black Land Rover that was parked through the wire on the opposite side of the building. Hector turned up the volume of his UHF radio, and they all leaned in to listen to the muffled Spanish conversation.

The tone of Maria's voice dropped an octave, and her playful arguing became a seductive whisper. Her hands moved slowly over the guards' arms, finishing at both their hands with a well-practiced flick of her wrists. They slipped the notes into their uniforms and parted, allowing her to glide once more up to the dark front doors.

Owen leaned closer to the radio as Maria's high heels could be heard clapping onto a tile floor.

"She's in," Eva breathed. Spotlights on the building's roof had illuminated the sweat over her cheeks, and were imprinting the shadows of barbed wire over her chin and neck. Owen gave her a quick smile as he settled back into his seat, his fingers running nervously over the automatic rifle that lay on the seat between them.

The sharp sound of high heels became rapid, then halted as another set of footsteps approached and then passed. "That was close," Maria whispered into the radio. "I'm taking off my shoes."

Five minutes passed before Maria's rings could be heard clinking on a metal rail as she descended a staircase. A ruffling in her handbag was followed by a loud click.

"She's turning on the torch," Hector whispered through the darkness.

Several more clinks and she had reached a basement that resonated with the sound of her heavy breathing. "I'm here," she whispered. Then switching to Spanish: "I've found the door. It's made of steel, and there's a metal wheel. It's heavy. I don't know which way it's got to turn."

"Shit," Hector growled, his face wrinkling in the dim light.

"I can't open it," Maria hissed. "Hello? Can you hear me?"

"Yes, we can hear you," Hector responded, his eyes closed in concentration as he held down the button.

"Agh, muy fuerte! That was really loud!" Maria gasped. "Just let me... there... Puedes escucharme? Can you hear me? I can't open it!"

"Si, te escucho," Hector whispered. "Tranquilo, stay calm, turn it clockwise. If you try too hard it won't open."

The sound of Maria's heavy breathing was followed by a long piercing ring.

"Oh, God," Owen wheezed. "She's set off an alarm."

"I don't know what to do!" Maria cried into the radio. "Wait." The ringing stopped, and was followed by a loud clunk. "Funciono! It worked! I'm inside!"

The car bounced with nervous excitement, but the four froze once more as Maria's voice hissed through the radio. "Someone is coming!"

"Get inside," Hector said calmly. "Close the door and make sure any lights are turned off."

"Okay, the door is shut. I can't turn off this light. Wait. Okay, the light is off."

The sound of heavy boots stomped down the metal staircase outside the room and then stopped close by. Maria's breathing became louder as someone pushed at the door. Five seconds passed before the footsteps faded further down the corridor.

"I think he's gone," Maria whispered.

"Good work," Hector said. "Now, use the torch. What do you see?"

"It's a long room. The walls – they are made of metal, and there are metal cabinets. It looks like a morgue. There are letters on the drawers. I'm pulling one open. It's all just files. Darien Ayala, vice foreign minister... Telegrams, in alphabetical order. Invoices and photographs. So many photographs."

"Photos of what?" Hector asked, his eyes closed tightly as he clutched the radio.

"People in cafes. Police photos of dead bodies. More files. Diary notes, all handwritten. A ledger. Photocopies of some sort of court transcript."

"Okay, move onto the other ones. Are they labelled?"

"Yes, I've moved onto 'B'. Here, there's one on... Dios mio!"

"What is it?"

"George Bush."

"You're kidding me," Owen gasped.

"What's in there?" Hector demanded excitedly.

"More photographs. Noriega and George Bush, in a meeting room. George Bush at the beach. More photocopies of some sort of ledger. And plastic boxes. So many plastic boxes, with plastic lids. Inside there are rows of cassette tapes. Oh, there are rows and rows of them."

"She's not going to be able to carry all this stuff," Eva whispered into the darkness. "Get her to move on."

"Maria, keep going," Hector instructed. "You know what we're looking for."

"I know, I know. But... Carter, Jimmy; Castro, Fidel. So many tapes. And letters. Something about the Paredes election. Dukakis, Owen. Letters. Bank account details. Escobar, Pablo... Wow, there are hundreds of tapes with Pablo Escobar!"

"Keep moving," Hector instructed. "We are not here for Escobar. He doesn't matter."

Owen raised his eyebrows in the darkness.

"Okay, I'm moving towards the back of the room. Moss, Ambler. Documents with FBI and CIA letterheads. Some more tapes. N, O, P... Here it is, T."

"What's in there?"

"Um... Torrijos. Omar Torrijos. Four drawers of tapes and photographs. Telegrams from 1968 about the coup. Reel-to-reel tapes. There are stickers, price tag stickers on the tapes."

"Go back, you've gone too far."

"Moises Torrijos... Omar's brother. Love letters, so many letters. Photos of him with a woman in a nightclub, photos of them in bed through a window."

"Keep going. You want Thorn."

"Here it is. Thorn. Joseph Thorn."

"What do you see?" It was Owen this time, his body shivering with excitement.

"Photos. Photos of him with Conrad Ramirez. They are at the Union Club. Talking to Eva. Talking to Hector, shaking Hector's hand. At Hector's house, photos taken over the back wall."

"Bastards," Hector breathed.

"Photos of Thorn's house. Through the windows at night, with the curtains open. Photos of him kissing a woman, I don't recognise her. Photos through the bedroom window."

Owen sensed Eva's body stiffening beside him, and he leaned forward. "What else? Other than the photographs?"

"The drawer goes back a long way, it's still all Joseph Thorn. Oh wow, there are cassette tapes. Muchos cassettes!"

"Do they have labels?"

"Yes. There are names and places. Most say they are telephone recordings with Conrad Ramirez. But there are also some with Hector Goldstein written on them, and one with Owen Ellis."

Owen froze, his fists tensing.

"And there are four tapes at the back with red stars on them. They are all dated September, 1989. And they all say Muerte del Dr Zhivago."

Owen's gasp made him jump from his seat, and the shaking through the car was lost in his dizziness.

"Spadafora's codename," Hector breathed, his eyes wide as he turned.

Owen clumsily grabbed at the radio, holding the button down as he struggled to clear his throat. "Take them," he demanded. "Take those tapes, all of them, and get out of there! Vamos!"

Chapter Thirty-Seven

"I've put them all inside a plastic box," Maria said calmly. "It fits in my handbag. Okay, I'm heading back to the door."

Sweat was beading over Owen's face as he slumped backwards into the seat, his head spinning. He turned to face Eva, who was smiling at him through the darkness. "This is it," she whispered.

"Um. I... Oh, no!"

The tone in Maria's voice made Hector grab up the radio in concern. "What is it?"

"I can't open this door. There's no handle."

"Stay calm," Hector responded. "There must be a button. Some sort of lever?"

Javier was the first to notice the movement outside the Comandancia. "Hang on," he whispered loudly. "What's going on over there?"

Shouts erupted through the silence as three guards ran out of the building, joining a circle of Machos at the back gate who were aiming their rifles up the street. The congregation grew as more guards burst out of the emergency exit at the back of the building and ran towards the open gate. Spotlights on the roof of the Comandancia swept quickly over the Land Rover and scanned further up the street in the direction of the guards' eager pointing.

"Someone's sent them a warning," Hector growled, his back straightening.

More guards continued to pour out of the building, and an array of spotlights swept vigorously over the slums. The crowd took formation, spreading along the boundary fence and kneeling in preparation for an attack. The upper floors of the building came to life with guards lining the railings, their weapons aiming down at the street.

A distant boom sent a shiver through the slums, and doorways across the suburbs were quickly illuminated with light. Another boom, closer this time, brought a chorus of shouting from the guards. Two heavily armoured vehicles burst out of the Comandancia's open gate, their tyres screeching as they rounded the corner and thundered up the avenue.

"Shit," Hector cried, turning around to make eye contact with Owen. "We're too late!"

Maria's fearful voice crackled back onto the radio, again in Spanish. "I can see light outside the door. There are footsteps. Loud. I think they're running away. What's happening? What's happening here? Hey! Help me, somebody help me! Ayudame!"

"Tranquilo!" Hector shouted into the radio. "They're not after you."

"What's happening? I can't get out!"

Owen's tongue had dried into sandpaper, and he fearfully grabbed at the rifle, his mind unable to make a decision.

"Stay where you are," Hector instructed, loading the magazine into his own rifle. "It will be suicide if any of us step outside." He picked the radio back up and carefully wound the dial through the channels, his face pale in the ruddiness of the streetlights.

"What are you doing?" Eva spluttered. "We won't be able to hear her!"

Hector ignored her, continuing to wind through the channels until a loud crackling of Spanish filled the car. He put the radio to his ear, his face grim as he concentrated on the incoherent shouting. "American gunships," he groaned in translation. "They're moving over the airport, heading over the top of Fourth of July Avenue. They're coming here!"

It was as if all of Chorrillo had heard his words; fear seemed to freeze all movement as two Spectre AC-130 gunships floated into view like fire-breathing galleons, green flames creating a supernatural glow across the charcoal sky. The guards atop the Comandancia seemed to be paralysed in horror, their guns slumping to their sides as jets of fire leapt from the gunships in slow motion. The flames gained speed, combining into balls of light as they struck, pulverising the roof of the Comandancia and incinerating the guards. Great sparkling shards of concrete rained down over the slums, tearing apart roofs and splitting cars into twisted scraps of metal.

Owen's ears were filled with a piercing ringing as he screamed, his eyes wide and unblinking as green tracer bullets erupted from the surviving guards. The green lines were joined by streaks of red that whizzed upwards from the Canal Zone. The gunships breathed another round of fire, tearing apart the remaining fragments of the Comandancia's roof and filling the air with great gusts of smoke. The wire security fence was blown outwards, smashing into the side of the Land Rover and shattering the right side windows. Eva's screams could barely be heard as she threw herself down to Owen's feet, her hands covering her ears and her body convulsing with terror.

Through the smoke emerged the silhouettes of at least twenty guards and Machos. Their shouting was frantic as they scrambled away from the crumbling building and fired indiscriminately up the street. Two of them were thrown backwards by a mortar, their charred bodies fragmenting across the asphalt and bubbling into pieces. The mortar was followed by a series of grenades that had been launched from the next street, and the revving of four M-113 armoured personnel carriers vibrated through the ground. They exploded like charging bulls over the blockades set up by the Machos, their tracks ripping up the road as their armour was pockmarked by Panamanian gunfire.

Hector had switched the radio back to Maria's channel, and her wailing sent a jolt of electricity through Owen's stomach.

"She's going to be trapped in there!" Owen cried as the tanks began blowing chunks out of the Comandancia's back wall. "We've got to help her!"

"Don't you move!" Hector shouted, grabbing Owen's arm as he fetched the rifle and struggled to open the door.

An onslaught of grenades launched from the slums behind the building, disabling three of the tanks before return fire transformed the slums into balls of flame. Sparks became thicker than smoke, and Owen's face was met with a gust of searing heat as he pulled free of Hector's grip. He slammed the door shut, gripping the rifle's magazine and taking off into the burning swirl.

The smoke moved upwards in a churning swale as Owen moved across the street, his eyes squinting through the ash particles and his nose clogged with the smell of burning rubber. The air was turning a poisonous green as he reached a break in the fence, his feet crunching over mangled wire as he surveyed what was left of the building. The roof had all but collapsed, and flames were thrashing upwards from giant holes in the southern wall. The emergency exit at the back of the building was blasted open, and the gaping hole pulled at Owen's attention. He ran forward, leaping over the body of a guard and barely noticing the two men emerging from the smoke to his left.

"Owen, get down!"

Owen spun around, falling to his knees as automatic gunfire whizzed past his ears and shoulders. Something collected with his chest, and he clutched at himself in shock. Between blinks he saw Javier running for the hole in the fence, his rifle raised as he fired into the smoke. Two guards retreated behind a line of skip bins, failing to return fire.

"Keep moving!" Hector cried over the radio on Owen's hip. "We've got you covered!"

Owen stared down at his chest, his eyes wide. The camera strapped around his neck had been struck by a bullet, and a smear of battery acid leaked down his chest. He staggered back to his feet, ripping off the camera and letting it fall into the ash. He scrambled over another body and ducked behind a burnt-out troop carrier. From this position he surveyed the expanse of concrete, aiming his rifle into the smoke before sprinting for the hole in the back of the building. The troop carrier behind him caught fire, and a deafening explosion blew chunks of cement past his legs. He imagined himself screaming, but no sound was reaching the plasticine feel of his ears.

The heat was stifling as he clambered into the building, flicking on the torch attached to the riflescope and waving the light through the smoke. He coughed, covering his face with his hand as he found the stairwell. Two bodies blocked the first few steps, and he cringed as his shoe sunk into the open wound of a man's stomach. The blood made him slip down the remaining steps, tripping into the railing and stumbling onto the basement floor. The corridor lights were flickering, and sparks were spraying intermittently from the steel door.

The power flickered off for a moment, and his torch scanned the metal door as he yelled, "Maria, it's Owen!"

"Ayúdame!" Maria cried back, banging at the door.

He tried to turn the wheel, but his fingers recoiled from the heat of the metal. He sucked at them painfully and then used the barrel of the rifle.

"Ayúdame!" Maria cried again as sparks spat out from the top of the door.

Owen stood back; sweat dripping through the soot that had smeared across his face. "Come on!" he cried, staring fearfully over his shoulder and back up the stairwell. The sound of footsteps made him turn back towards the corridor, his eyes meeting those of a terrified guard.

"Quien es?" The guard cried, his face dripping with perspiration. "Quien es?"

"Esta bien," Owen stammered, raising his hands. His instincts told him to aim and fire, but his hands seemed to involuntarily do the opposite. The guard raised his pistol, taking aim at Owen's head.

"She's trapped," Owen said shakily, pointing at the door. "She's trapped in there. Please help me open the door, or else she'll die." He let the rifle strap slide off his shoulder before bending down and resting it on the floor. "Please help us."

The guard continued to hold his aim, but without a gun Owen hardly appeared a threat. He slowly returned the pistol to its holster and called out, "Quién está ahí?"

"Maria!" she called back. "Ayúdame!"

The guard swallowed uncomfortably before approaching the door, his eyes also monitoring Owen's movements. He pointed to a rupture in a pipe that extended behind the metal door. Electrical wires were exposed within the hole, and Owen watched excitedly as the guard removed a knife from his belt and wedged the blade beneath the wires. The wires snapped cleanly, and a sudden clunk was followed by a gushing of gas. The door rumbled, holding tight for a second before flinging open.

"Cabrón! Bastardo!" Maria floundered out of the door, her shoulder charging into Owen's chest. He caught her around the waist, preventing her from falling as she punched at him furiously.

"Calm down!" Owen cried, pulling her tightly to avoid her flailing fists. "Stop it!"

"You bastard!" Maria cried again, her face glistening with tears and sweat.

The guard watched in confusion, unsure whether to apprehend them or to run away. Owen nodded to the rifle on the floor. "Take it," he said. "And get yourself out of here!"

The guard obliged, picking up the rifle and then leading the way back up the steps.

"Do you have the tapes?" Owen hissed to Maria. "Are they on you?"

"Of course I have them!"

"Alright, let's go!"

The building shook with another explosion, and chunks of concrete collapsed down the stairwell as the guard disappeared from view. Owen grabbed Maria's hand, pulling her over the bodies at the base of the stairs and holding his breath as powdered concrete filled the air.

A high-pitched whizzing was followed by another explosion, which sucked the air pressure from the room and shot pins and needles through Owen's chest. A sea of flames cascaded through the holes in the roof, dripping like lava onto the dust below. Maria was screaming as Owen pulled her upwards into the doorway of the emergency exit, avoiding the flames but exposing them to the gunfire outside.

"Oh my God!" Maria gasped, her eyes wide with panic as she took in the scene outside. She stared downwards and screamed again, for lying at their feet was the charred body of the guard who had helped them.

Red and green tracers had ignited the sky once more, and a band of American tanks had gathered at what remained of the back gate.

Both Maria's and Owen's radios buzzed to life, and Hector's voice joined the gunfire. "Run, now! Both of you; get out of there!"

Javier emerged from behind the burnt-out troop carrier, his stout frame shuffling into the open and spraying bullets in a sweep. His gunfire was reciprocated by a jet of flame and a grenade that seemed to dissect Owen's legs before exploding into the building behind. Owen's grip around Maria's arm tightened as he pulled her behind Javier and dived for the safety of the troop carrier.

In the last moment before taking refuge Javier whipped the butt of his rifle into his shoulder and fired towards one of the tanks. His efforts were in vain, as another jet of flame shot through the smoke towards him like a cannonball. He was thrown upwards, his body spinning in the air before thumping into the concrete.

"No!" Owen cried, rolling behind the troop carrier and gasping for breath. His eyes cast upwards into a swirling, sulphurous sky. A helicopter was firing into the slums nearby like a hovering wasp, and was soon joined by a transport plane. The plane seemed to hover in slow motion as a band of paratroopers spun like spiders into the light. They descended quickly, their weapons drawn as they landed silently on the other side of the Comandancia.

"This way!" came a voice to their right.

Hector emerged through the smoke, grabbing Maria by the hand and pointing towards the road. Another explosion struck the concrete in front of them as they ran, shattering through Owen's ears and causing him to trip. Maria rushed ahead as Hector's legs also failed him. The old man stumbled, flinching in pain, and Owen wrapped his arm underneath him. The warm stickiness of blood seeped over his arm as he dragged Hector through a gap in the fence.

The Land Rover seemed to leap like a caged animal out of the flames of the slums, the front wheels bouncing against the gutter as it rocked to a halt. Maria was about to dive into the passenger seat when she hesitated, turning back and then helping Owen drag Hector behind the car. Together they lifted him into the back seat, Maria tumbling in after him as Owen slammed the door. He rounded the car, taking a last glance into the smoke before jumping into the passenger seat.

Eva shifted the car into reverse and skidded back onto the street. She turned and looked at them briefly, her face a pale grey. "Where's Javier?"

"He's gone," Owen cringed, turning around and trying to examine Hector's wound.

"I'm okay," Hector wheezed, attempting to smile. "It's gone straight through, I'll be fine."

Maria had pushed him to an upright position, and padded a cloth into the wound as the car sped through Chorrillo.

"The tapes?" Eva asked as she studied Hector in the rear-view mirror. She flung the car around a corner to avoid a burnt-out truck and glanced back into the mirror. "Do you have the tapes?"

"Maria has them," Owen wheezed. "Don't you?"

"Yes." Her fervour had turned into anxiety as she watched the burning outside, and she suddenly erupted in a high-pitched shriek. "Rafael! Rafael! We have to go back!"

"We can't go back!" Eva retorted. "He'll be fine, Maria. Casco Viejo hasn't been hit."

"Cómo sabes? We have to go back!"

"No, Maria!" Eva insisted. "We'll go back soon, okay? We need to get Hector to safety."

The argument continued as Eva navigated her way out of Chorrillo, speeding into the smoke that crept along the highway. The suburb to the left was now fully alight, and civilians were running like ants across the road in front. Eva slowed, flashing the lights and revving. They allowed her to pass, staring with terrified eyes into the tinted windows.

The road was clear until the next bend, where the Canal Zone came into full view. Red tracers were still ejecting from the barracks, and a row of tanks was blocking the line of demarcation. Eva was about to spin the car into the road up the hill when she skidded to a halt and swore.

Blocking the road was a distinctive beige Hummer, its passenger smiling smugly as he eased the barrel of his rifle out of the open window.

Chapter Thirty-Eight

Eva spun the Land Rover across the highway, trying to avoid the bullets that rippled into the doors and trunk. As she directed the car back towards the slums, the Hummer crept forward, moving slowly down to the highway to a position where Thorn was able to take aim.

"Quick!" Hector cried. "Go back, cut them off!"

Eva did as she was instructed, revving the car onto two wheels and screaming as bullets shattered the windscreen. Owen pushed his hand through the glass, clearing it away as Eva accelerated towards the road up the hill.

The Hummer was slow to turn around, and Thorn was unable to take aim from his window as the Land Rover crashed into the driver's side door. The impact threw Hector forwards through the hole in the windscreen, and Owen ripped him back inside the car as Eva reversed and rammed the Hummer once more. The driver had been thrown over Thorn's lap, and the two of them were cowering as Eva reversed wildly and then flung the front of the car into the side road. She flicked the transmission back into drive, screaming in fear as she accelerated up the hill.

Hector was shouting into his radio as they ascended, and his instructions appeared to be received as a line of guards parted at the top of the hill. The bronze gates were rumbling open, and Eva slowed as she eased the car towards safety.

Maria was groaning as they turned into the driveway, for the entire city was now visible below. Flames had engulfed Chorrillo, and were snaking into Casco Viejo. Assault helicopters were circling the Comandancia, and another planeload of paratroopers was being dropped into the slums.

"Stay calm," Owen placated as the car crunched over the white-pebbled driveway, illuminated now by a series of floodlights.

Sarita emerged from the foyer, her face blank with fear as she pulled open the car door. "Papa!" she screamed, pulling him out and screaming.

"I'm fine," Hector resisted. "But they got Javier. Come on. Let's get these tapes inside, we're not done until we hear what's on them."

Owen was slow to emerge from the car. The pain throughout his body was finally seeping through the numb of adrenaline. Eva joined him, staring at him before pulling him into a relieved embrace.

"Come on," Owen smiled after they pulled apart. "Let's hear what's on those tapes."

Sarita had bandaged Hector's neck and shoulders by the time they emerged into the bright lights of the downstairs bar. The sound of gunfire was growing closer outside, and a red flash appeared to ignite the back garden.

"Estoy bien!" Hector protested, pulling at Sarita's grip as he drank desperately from a bottle of whiskey. On the marble table beside him was a distinctive plastic box, which Maria was staring at like a hawk from the other side of the room. Her face was smeared with ashes and tears, and she was staring nervously at Owen.

"Thank you," Owen called to her. "Thank you so much."

She nodded at him, her fingers fidgeting.

"Have a beer, Owen," Hector demanded. "Go on, and get one for the ladies too. You all deserve one. We're all extremely lucky." His voice trailed off, and he swallowed coarsely as he took another sip of his whiskey.

"Alright," Owen sighed as he opened the fridge, taking out three bottles. He was about to hand one to Eva when he pulled back. "Maria?" he called.

"I'm fine," Maria responded, rubbing at her temples.

"Well?" Hector said suddenly, nodding towards the box. "Are we just going to stand around, or are we going to listen to them?"

Owen moved forward, staring at the box carefully and allowing his swollen fingers to slide over its polished cover.

"Oh, come on!" Hector cried, his words slurred. He swiped his hand out, picking up the box and rising unsteadily to his feet.

"Papa, sit down," Sarita demanded.

Hector ignored her, tottering towards the door to the auditorium. A trail of blood followed his footsteps, and Eva and Owen stared at each other in concern. "Stay there, mis amigos!" he cried. "I'm going to put this through the speakers for you!"

Owen stared at Sarita, whose face was grim. "He's lost a lot of blood," she said tensely. "We need to get him to a doctor."

Owen nodded, and was about to follow Hector out to the auditorium when a haunting crackle resounded through the entire house. Maria had slinked further to the back of the room, and shared their frightened stares as a tape began to play.

Chapter Thirty-Nine

The voice was in Spanish, wavering and uneven. "September 13, 1989, 9:55PM. Recording number 11." The man cleared his throat and continued.

"That's Noriega," Eva said, breaking Owen's concentration as he stared at the nearest speaker. "That voice is Noriega's."

The speakers began to ring with the sound of a telephone. Another distinctive voice answered.

"Si. Yo soy RUBUS."

"That's Conrad!" Eva cried. "That's Conrad's voice!"

"It's me," Noriega replied in Spanish. "Do you have an update?"

"All is in place," Conrad answered. "Joseph Thorn has the dog in the kitchen."

"And have you turned on the recorders?"

"Oh yes, all is done as you've asked."

"Good. I want you to make Thorn talk while it's happening. Get him to call me in five minutes. The tape will be number 12."

The tape crackled for ten seconds before Conrad's voice returned. "September 13, 1989, 10PM. Recording number 12. La Concepción, Panama."

A phone began to ring once more. Owen stiffened as another distinctive voice spoke into a reverberating room.

"I'm being put through to the General," Joseph Thorn rasped in Spanish.

A nervous shuffling could be heard in the recording, and the sound of a man struggling against his gag sent shivers through Owen's spine.

"General?" Thorn grated. "We have the rabid dog."

The muffled sound of someone on the end of the phone broke through the silence, and Thorn could be heard nervously tapping the telephone cord against a bench.

"What does one do with a rabid dog, you ask? Well. One kills it." Thorn voice was menacingly. "Yes. I will make sure it happens. I will kill Spadafora."

Thorn hung up the phone, his breathing becoming louder.

"Well, Joe?" Conrad asked in English. "What did he say?"

"He wants us to –"

"He wants us? Or, he wants you?"

"I..."

"You're the one who owes him, Joe."

"I don't owe him a thing. He always gets his share. And besides, if it weren't for me, he wouldn't have dirt on Bush. He wouldn't have dirt on Carter. He wouldn't have the money I've cleaned for him. And he certainly wouldn't have Hugo Spadafora."

"Are you going to do it, or aren't you? Remember, he's going to ask me what happened."

"Fine then. Give me the God damn knife."

Owen cringed as Spadafora's gag was removed, and the sound of his torture suppurated through the speakers.

"It was him," Owen cried. "Thorn killed Hugo Spadafora!"

The tape eventually went silent, but soon the sound of a man in pain continued through the house.

"Papa!" Sarita cried, running towards the doorway, her red sash flapping behind her. Owen hesitated, scanning the room suspiciously for Maria. He darted into the next room, his eyes searching desperately as he made his way towards the auditorium.

A mournful wail echoed through the house, and Owen's pace quickened as he rounded the final corner and pushed through the black curtain.

Hector lay writhing, one hand over his wound and the other grasping at his forehead. "Let Maria go," he wheezed. "Let her go."

"Ella tiene los cassettes!" Sarita cried, staring up at Owen. "She took the tapes from him!"

"Pavarotti," Hector gurgled, his eyes rolling back as they tried to make contact with Owen's.

"What's he saying?" Owen cried, attempting to keep the old man's eyes open.

"Papa!" Sarita sobbed, trying in vain to pull him upright. He slumped forward, the nerves in his legs giving one last kick before he was still.

Eva fell to her knees with a wail, clutching at the old man's legs as Sarita buckled over his chest.

Owen pulled away, his eyes bloodshot. "Maria!" he roared, running to the back of the stage and then through the auditorium. "Maria! Where are you?" He returned to the others who remained over Hector's body. He shook his head as he stared at the large stereo system. The cassette tape player was open, but there were no tapes inside. He searched frantically over the unit, his heart thundering. Eva wiped at her tears as she clambered to her feet and joined him.

Owen's body was thrown into action as a loud bang came from the front of the house. He scrambled across the stage, ducking through a corridor and into the dimly lit foyer. He stopped abruptly, feeling the draught flowing through one of the front doors as it rested ajar.

"Maria!"

The air was thick with smoke as Owen threw aside the doors, his face dark with fear.

"I need to get Rafael!" Maria's voice cried through the purple gloom. Her face appeared in the lights of the water fountain, then disappeared from view as she slammed the driver's side door of the Land Rover. The engine started, and she held the box of tapes out of her open window as the car began skidding across the pebbles. "I'll be back! I'm sorry! Lo siento!"

"Stop!" Owen cried, sprinting across the pebbles. "Maria, stop! Détente!"

The Land Rover bounced out of the open gate, the guards looking stunned as Owen collapsed onto the pebbles.

"She's smart," Eva panted, stopping beside him and resting her hands on her knees. "She's taken the tapes, so that we don't abandon her."

"But she's going to get herself killed! She's playing into their hands!"

Chapter Forty

Bay Islands, Honduras.
Present day.

Sheets of rain washed away the view of the marina as the ferry departed, its double keel crashing heavily into the bubbling waves. Jenna adjusted her sash as she took a seat beside Rafael at the back of the boat. She tipped down her straw hat and smiled at two children pointing at the surge of water erupting from the stern. Their parents took them by their hands and led them upstairs, leaving Jenna and Rafael alone.

"If you want us to act like a couple then you better stop avoiding me."

Rafael raised his eyebrows. "I'm not avoiding you, I'm just tired."

"No, you're not tired, you're still drunk."

"Oh, chooh! You know what, princess? I think we look just like any other couple, you yellin' at me and all." He tried to get her to reciprocate his smile, but she was not impressed.

"So I take it you've been to Honduras before?"

He laughed. "Of course. But I always steer away from La Ceiba."

"Oh yeah?"

He frowned, folding his hands on his lap. "Too many police."

She pretended to laugh. "I won't ask any more questions, then."

"It's cool. I just can't be recognised here."

"Well you certainly don't look like the person I spent the day with yesterday."

"Hope you're right."

It was barely an hour before the ferry began to arc towards to the shore. The misty outline of a mountain range was visible through the rain, the jagged peaks looking more like something from Transylvania than Central America. Jenna gripped her backpack tightly as the crowded wharf took form and faces become visible through the rain.

"Wait til all these people have gotten off," Rafael instructed. "If anyone is waiting for us, they gonna be easier to see."

Jenna became stiff with anxiety, and began rubbing at her forearms.

"You cold? You want my jacket?"

"No, no, I'm fine."

Rafael stood up to survey the crowd as they drifted off the boat and through a covered waiting area. A Spanish announcement came through the boat speakers, and he nodded at her. "Come on," he said, grabbing her hand. Together they walked around to the side of the boat, smiling at two sailors who held the bridge steady as they stepped onto the platform.

"Around the side," Rafael breathed, continuing to hold her hand as they passed around a toilet block and into the back of the shelter. The sound of taxi horns and shouting mothers was overtaken by the pounding of rain on the iron roof, and in just a few minutes the terminal was drained of the crowd.

Rafael was preparing to wave down a taxi when a young couple in identical black hoodies stood up from a bench at the far end of the terminal. The girl's vacant eyes stared directly at them as she reached into her front pocket. Rafael's grip on Jenna's hand became tighter, and he guided her briskly behind a pillar. "Something don't feel right. Let's go the other way."

Shouting followed a sudden screeching of car tyres on the wet bitumen. Rafael motioned for Jenna to retreat, but as they stepped out from behind the pillar a loud shout echoed against the concrete walls. Jenna gasped, her body turning to jelly as Rafael pulled her behind a second pillar. More shouting came from the direction of the car, and rapid footsteps were followed by the sound of a scuffle. A loud crack rang through the terminal.

"What the hell?" Rafael hissed, peering out from behind the pillar.

The car was a police wagon, and the shouts were coming from two officers as they slapped handcuffs around the hooded man's wrists. Beside him, the girl lay facedown in a splatter of blood, knocked unconscious by a baton.

"Holy shit," Jenna gasped, her legs pumping with adrenaline.

"You see why I don't like this place?" Rafael cried as they sprinted to the back of the terminal, busting out a back exit and running across an empty dock.

"What the hell just happened?" Jenna cried. "Those police just knocked her out!"

"Why do you think?" Rafael took her hand and led her around a rusted boat shed where they stopped to catch their breath. "They thought them two were us."

Jenna's face turned white. "Oh my God. They could have killed her," she groaned, her mouth wide open.

"Come on." He pulled her out from under the shelter of the shed's eaves. "Let's get out of the open."

Jenna swallowed her sobbing and followed him up to a tall wire fence at the back of the shed. He tested its sturdiness before pulling himself up and over, landing on wet chunks of boat ballast. Jenna followed, swiftly flipping her body over and landing silently.

"We gotta get through this marsh, then the river on the other side should lead us into the city."

Jenna nodded, rubbing at her eyes as she followed him down a muddy track where tall reeds hid them from the roads and industry in the distance.

The rain continued through the morning, soaking through Jenna's clothing and causing friction between the straps of her backpack and her sunburned shoulders. She tried to ignore the pain; closing her eyes as she trudged through the mud and imagining herself back in front of a fireplace in England.

The river eventually twisted towards the sounds of the city, and the banks opened up into a small community where three or more families lived in ramshackle tin shacks. Jenna kept her head down as she passed by two fishermen and followed Rafael hurriedly beneath a busy causeway.

"This place is giving me the creeps."

Rafael smiled matter-of-factly. "This ain't the tourist route."

"Did you want some fruit?" she asked as they clambered over the top of the riverbank and onto a muddy playing field.

He took awhile to respond, studying the outskirts of the city and rubbing at his sore shoulder. "Honestly, I want Burger King."

She scoffed at him before noticing the row of western fast food outlets along the highway. "Are you serious?"

"It's gotta be the last place anyone will expect us to go. And besides, they don't have Burger King in Cuba."

"Whatever you say."

Rafael's attention was fixated on a group of teenagers and their dirt bikes in the restaurant car park. He bit his lower lip as they stepped over a small wall bordering the field and into the restaurant's drive-through lane. He reached into the side pocket of his shorts, handing Jenna some US banknotes. "Just get me whatever you're eating. Meet you in there soon."

Jenna eyed him distrustfully as she kicked the mud off her sandals. She adjusted her hair and strutted towards the main entrance, her eyes scanning the faces of the men sitting outside. She could feel their stares moving over her.

The queue inside wrapped around two dividers, and was filled with teenagers wearing American surf brands and playing with noisy cell phones. Jenna's envy was forgotten when she noticed Rafael patting the back of a young man outside. The group of motorcyclists had surrounded him, and were looking over their shoulders warily. Her eyes narrowed as she saw Rafael reach into his pocket and remove the package that she had carried for him through the cays. It looked smaller than she remembered, and the frayed plastic revealed something white that was quickly slipped into the hand of one of the boys. Rafael caught Jenna's eye through the glass, his face suddenly abashed as a set of keys were tucked into his palm.

He nodded at the boys, bowed his head and slowly traipsed into the restaurant.

"What was going on out there?" Jenna asked tautly as she placed a large tray of food onto a vacant table.

Rafael mumbled a response, digging through one of the paper bags and pulling out a handful of fries.

"Oh come on," Jenna scowled. "What was in that package? Seriously?"

He shook his head in frustration, stuffing more fries into his mouth.

"You told me that it was money."

The silence continued. Rafael disappeared into the toilets and re-emerged, his face flushed. "You know what it was," he griped, slumping back into his chair. "You know who I am."

She swallowed uncomfortably. "And that man at the airstrip? You sold drugs to him too, didn't you? That's how you paid for the resort, and the seafood, and these clothes, and the ferry?"

"Don't try givin' me a guilt trip, princess. You known this all along."

"No I haven't." She slapped down the remains of her hamburger, shaking her head. "I believed you when you said it was money!"

"Even if it was money, where d'ya think that money woulda come from?"

"From fishing? From that hostel on the island? Those backpackers? Giving people a ride between the island and Cuba, like you did for me? That's all money, Raf. That's legitimate money. And last night, I mean, I was almost convinced that I had been wrong about you, that perhaps you were actually a good person. That you weren't just a criminal."

"Oh come on, don't go making things black and white! Look where you are. You're sittin' in a Burger King in a country where most of these people are livin' in poverty. Before you judge me, why doncha judge the people payin' for those billboards along the river, where those families you saw are now spending all their money on coke and hamburgers and dyin' of diabetes? How about you judge the westerners selling these kids cell phone plans and forcin' their parents to work in tobacco factories for two dollars a day? That, Jenna, is criminal." He wiped his lips with a napkin, his face now flushed. "What you're talkin' about is us selling a product back to those very people who exploit us. Those people – they make a choice to use that stuff, knowin' full well what it's gonna do to them if they go stupid with it. Most of 'em get a lot of joy out of it, but it's their fault if they happen to kill themselves doin' it."

"You've been practicing that speech, haven't you?"

"Huh?"

"And besides, people wouldn't make that error if you didn't make drugs available for them."

"And those people out there wouldn't have diabetes if Americans didn't make this shit available for them either. But they do."

She bowed her head, pushing at the last of her soggy burger. "I agree with you, but that's no justification."

"If it makes you feel better, I don't sell drugs. I've just worked with people who do. None of them articles you went and read about me are true. All a load of shit."

"What do you mean, you don't sell drugs? How do you explain what I just saw you doing outside?"

"Wasn't my package. I found it in the boat."

"Oh, you are so full of shit."

"Believe what you want, princess. I'm just trying to make you understand where I'm coming from, just like you wanted."

"Then tell me where you're coming from! And I'm talking about you, not those families by the river. You're more than happy to talk about others, and about me. But I still haven't the faintest idea about you, where you've lived, how you learnt English, what those tattoos on your arms mean, your family..."

He turned away, his throat twitching.

"Don't turn away, and don't pretend that you're offended. None of us have perfect lives, and maybe if you told me about yours, I'd actually have some sympathy for you."

"Chooh," he breathed, shaking his head and trying to hide his emotions with a smile. "You don't let up, do ya?"

"No, I don't."

He shook his head again, running a hand over his scalp.

"Fine then, be like that. But if you want me to get on that bike out there with you..." She held out her hand, raising one eyebrow expectedly.

Rafael frowned. He slowly reached into his pocket, pulling out the last remaining corner of the white package and handing it to her.

She took the package, rolling it between her fingers and then stuffing it into the oily wrapper of her burger. She picked up the tray, stared at him and then dumped it into the bin. "From now on, we do things my way."

Chapter Forty-One

"Are you gonna hop on or aren't chu?"

Jenna pulled the straps of her backpack tighter, her eyes moving apprehensively over the green Honda motorbike. It was certainly no prize; its boldly stickered fairings were faded and cracked, and its engine was caked with tacky brown mud. Rafael revved the throttle, smiling impishly as the worn tyres carved a wide black mark into the car park bitumen.

"Here, put on this helmet," he said, skidding alongside her.

"Is there only one?" Her face screwed into a pout as she tapped the mud from the inside.

"Looks like it, yeah."

"Then what about you?"

"Don't need one," he shrugged. "Got enough foam in my head already."

"Ha ha. I'm not sure what that means, but okay." She carefully lifted her leg over the back of the seat, her face creased awkwardly as she wrapped her hands around his waist.

"You good?"

She responded with a tight squeeze of his hips and he leaned forward eagerly, accelerating across the gravel and bouncing onto the highway.

"Do you know where you're going?" Jenna shouted as her hands took a tighter grip on his shirt. She imagined herself losing balance, and tried not to stare down at the blurred pace of the road.

Rafael pushed his sunglasses further up the bridge of his nose. "You doubtin' me, princess?"

She squeezed him tighter. "Don't play games with me, Raf. Where are we going?"

"Gonna cut through the mountains towards Olanchito, then head south to the border somewhere near El Paraiso. Gonna be a longer route than going by the highway, but there's less chance of us runnin' into trouble. We'll also be avoidin' customs in Nicaragua."

The town names meant nothing to Jenna, but his obvious knowledge of the country was comforting. She leaned forward, resting her chin at the back of his shoulder as the bike grunted through a quiet Garifuna village and then followed a wide stony river towards the mountains.

"Looks like we won't be bothered by rain after all," Rafael observed as the bike rumbled onto a soft gravel road. "Should clear up more when we get to the top of the mountain."

"You mean we're going all the way up there?" Jenna's eyes were cast upwards to the jagged cliffs overlooking the coast.

"Didn't I say we were gonna take the scenic route?"

She huffed, then pulled tighter as she glanced down at the billows of dust churning around her dangling feet.

The jungle seemed to close in on the narrow road as they left the river, and the speed at which Rafael navigated his way around the bends caused Jenna's eyes to close in fear. When she opened them again they had passed through the clouds and into a clearing atop a towering basaltic peak. Sunlight poured across a lush valley to the left, and the ocean to their right glistened through swirling holes in the mist. She pulled away from Rafael's shoulder, twisting her head back and forth to take in the entire view.

"The city don't look so bad from up here, no?"

"It's beautiful!" she exclaimed.

The road continued to follow the contours of a ridge that stretched like a serpent towards a broiling horizon. The midday sun burned streaks of light through the jungle canopy, drying up the puddles and dissolving the clouds to the left into views of foaming rapids below. The heat also stirred up the sounds of insects and birdlife, casting Jenna's attention into the treetops.

The road reached the end of the ridge, and the vegetation became so thick that it was impossible to distinguish the leaves of the trees from the vines that entangled them. Dark shapes fluttered from the road ahead, and the silhouette of what looked like a toucan passed into a clearing of light, its beak igniting with colour.

The Honda bounced across a wooden bridge, the tyres darkening with the spray from a cavern below. Jenna maintained her tight grip on Rafael's torso, and his muscles tensed as he accelerated into a long shaded strait.

"Not long now," Rafael announced, prodding her from a daydream. "Stay awake there princess. Don't want you fallin' off!"

"I'm fine," she said dazedly, pushing her face back into the collar of his shirt. There was something strangely relaxing about the vibrations of the bike, and the smell of damp earth and fallen leaves pulled her into a peculiar sense of security. She nuzzled closer into him and then suddenly pulled away, her eyes widening in surprise at her apparent comfort.

Rafael's lips curled into a slight smile, and the bike drifted momentarily onto the wrong side of the road.

The Olancho Valley provided the first sign of civilisation in over an hour. Banana plantations spread across the slopes and into the valley, where hundreds of dairy cattle dotted the bright green plains. The roofs of farmhouses reflected the afternoon glare, and the smell of maize stubble and hay evoked an array of images in Jenna's mind.

"Gonna need fuel," Rafael explained as he turned onto a tarred road and accelerated towards a village. A small airport was visible to the left, and Jenna stared impassively at the steaming runway as three men inspected a small red Cessna.

"You want anythin' from the store?" Rafael asked as he turned into a fuel station and dismounted beside a rusted bowser.

Jenna stumbled off the bike and onto the oil-stained concrete, stretching her arms with a yawn. "No, no, I'm fine, thanks. We've still got a lot of food in the backpack. Do you think there's a bathroom here?"

"Go inside and ask," he responded, plunging the nozzle into the bike's fuel tank and staring at the bowser reading.

"Um," she hesitated, staring back at him with a sheepish frown.

"Just say, 'hay un baño?'"

"Hay un baño?" Jenna repeated, grinning at him before approaching the store.

Rafael replaced the fuel nozzle and stooped down to check the oil. A distant whirring became louder as he pulled out the dipstick, and he turned his head to see a white spec swooping over the mountains at the end of the airstrip. He shrugged, replacing the dipstick and then walking nonchalantly towards the store to pay. A sudden thought made him spin around, his face darkening as he saw the plane in clear view – a distinctive blue and white Cherokee. It landed with a puff of rubber, and two men rushed out from the small terminal to meet the men inside.

"Hay un baño?" Jenna whispered to herself as she pushed through the plastic slit curtains draped over the doorway to the store. A young bearded man behind the counter stared at her stiffly, his cheeks flushed and shining with perspiration, as though he had just been running. He was unblinking, his jaw swelling as he clenched his teeth.

Jenna was about to speak when something in the man's appearance made her stall. He wore a tight black shirt and camouflage pants, which certainly didn't suit someone working at a fuel station. She shot a glance down one of the isles to her left, gasping as she saw a smear of fresh blood and the feet of someone lying on the floor.

The bearded man put a finger to his lips, motioning for her to be silent as he steadily reached beneath the counter.

"Raf!," Jenna screamed, ducking behind a bread stand as Rafael barged through the doorway.

Jenna screamed again as packets of chewing gum and chocolates were strewn across the counter and over the floor. She remained frozen as Rafael pinned the man against a cigarette stand, backhanding a sawed-off shotgun from his grasp and whipping his hands into position around the man's neck. They shouted at each other in Spanish, the man's words reducing to a gurgle as Rafael tightened his grip. The seconds crawled by; Jenna paralysed amongst a sea of spinning M&M's as the man wheezed and spluttered.

"Quien eres tu?!" Rafael demanded.

The man refused to speak, his hand slowly reaching between Rafael's legs for the gun.

"Look out!" Jenna shouted.

Rafael's efficiency was frightening as he ripped the man's arm from between his legs and snapped his wrist backwards like a stick against his knee. The man bellowed in pain, his eyes popping as Rafael used the butt of the gun to knock him unconscious.

"There's someone else here!" Jenna shouted, running to the fridges at the back of the store. She knelt down beside the store attendant, an elderly man with a white moustache that was stained with blood. He was conscious, but with a painful wave of his hand he indicated that he didn't want to talk.

"Leave him," Rafael said anxiously. "We gotta get out of here."

"He's beaten up badly." Jenna gasped. "He needs an ambulance."

"So will we if we don't leave! Vamos!" He grabbed her by the arm and pulled her towards the exit, his other hand clinging onto the shotgun.

"Stop, we have to pay him!" Jenna struggled. "We have to pay for the fuel!"

Rafael stared at her disbelievingly. With a sudden huff he reached into his pocket to remove a wad of cash.

"And the gun," Jenna said with raised eyebrows. "Give him the gun too. We can't carry it on the bike."

Rafael shook his head but complied, leaning the shotgun beside the shop attendant and placing down a handful of notes.

A dark brown Chevrolet sedan had left the airport terminal. It created a trail of dust as it soared through a paddock towards the road. Rafael let go of Jenna's hand as they left the store, leaping onto the bike and kicking it to life. "Get on!" he cried.

The bike rocketed out of the fuel station, leaving skid marks on the bitumen as it approached the village. Jenna's tears were blown across the side of her face as she turned, staring at the Piper Cherokee parked on the tarmac to their left.

"It's the same plane," Rafael shouted back at her. "Must've been on the island with us."

She shuddered, turning her head further to make out the dark brown car swerving onto the road behind.

"We're gonna have to go backabush! Hope we got enough fuel to get us over the border."

"That car is gaining on us," Jenna shouted, her fingers digging into his waist.

Rafael adjusted the bike's broken rear-view mirror and frowned.

"What are you doing?" Jenna cried as he relaxed the throttle, letting the bike slow as it reached the centre of the village.

He ignored her, pulling on the brakes and easing the bike into a lane bordered by flowering hedges. He allowed Jenna to dismount before pushing the bike deep into a hedge and motioning for her to hide.

She ducked out of site, aware of a group of children watching them from the veranda of a nearby house.

The Chevrolet slowed as it approached the lane. The men inside came into view as it rolled past an empty store across the street. The driver could be seen scanning the houses as the car pulled up suddenly against the gutter, nudging a row of garbage bins.

"Go!" Rafael hissed, motioning for Jenna to abandon her hiding place and run. But she resisted, frozen as she stared at the Latino man getting out of the back seat. His face had turned towards her, revealing a set of scars mottled across his neck. His beady eyes made contact with hers, and he quickly reached inside his windcheater.

"Come on!" Rafael shouted, pulling the bike from the hedge and starting the engine.

Jenna blinked, unable to pull away as the man produced a long silenced pistol.

"Jenna!" Rafael screamed.

She finally pulled her eyes away and leapt on behind him, squeezing herself into his back as he revved towards the end of the lane.

"What's wrong with you?" he shouted, turning the corner and speeding onto a dirt track.

"I'm sorry," she blurted, her face still white with shock. "But that man."

"What man?"

"The one in the back seat of the car."

"What about him?"

She swallowed hesitantly.

"Shit!" he cried, jolting the bike sideways as a gunshot cuffed through the buildings to their left. He revved through a large puddle, splashing mud across both their faces and ducking as they roared beneath the branches of an overhanging fig tree.

The track wrapped around the border of the village and back to the main road. A mob of dairy cows watched as the bike flung around the final corner, knocking the leaves off a row of saplings and skidding sideways onto the bitumen.

"We got two options," Rafael shouted as they passed the entrance to a cattle ranch. "First is we hide now. Second is we keep going into the mountains."

"Keep going," Jenna cried, clinging onto him desperately as the bike hurtled downhill.

"The next town is a long way south if we stay on this road. But I know another way."

The road proved to be quiet, and the only traffic for the next hour was a wide cattle float that struggled up the winding slopes of a densely forested mountain.

The sky dimmed over the peaks to the east, swirling the last of an orange sky into a deep lilac canvas. Rafael turned on the headlight, the stars beginning to ignite as he searched for a landmark at the side of the road.

"Where are we going?" Jenna asked as the bike rumbled onto a gravel track.

"Backabush."

"Okay then."

The faint flickering of a village was lost in the thickening undergrowth. Wet leaves slapped at the bike as the track meandered around the mountainside. Echoes of the engine seemed to bounce around the darkness to their left, indicating that they were riding along the base of a cliff. Jenna felt herself lapsing into a dream, her eyes starting to mimic the blinking of the moon above the forest canopy.

Chapter Forty-Two

Jenna awoke with a shudder, the curious sound of howler monkeys piercing through the moist morning air and bouncing between the limestone walls of a rock shelter. Her eyes blinked repeatedly, and she pulled back from the wall to feel that the side of her face was imprinted with the texture of the rock. She held back a yawn as she brushed white chalky powder off her shirtsleeve and then rubbed at her cheek. Her mouth was dry, and vivid dreams were slow to leave her mind.

"Good mannin," came Rafael's spritely voice. He was snapping up a pile of sticks and building a fire at the edge of the shelter. He wore a striped linen shirt that was crinkled from being stuffed at the bottom of the backpack, and his leather boots were white from the limey dust throughout the cave.

"What time is it?"

"Bout eight. But you was thinking it was midnight just before, no? You talk n' doze."

"Hey!" she blurted, her face flushing with red. "Was I talking? Gosh, what was I saying?"

He shrugged. "Not much."

She pouted, stretching her arms.

"I was gonna go and fill the water bottle from the stream down there, but you were layin' on it, and I was thinking you might snap at me if I tried shiftin' you."

"I probably would have. I'll go fill it." She rubbed her eyes, stared over the edge of the rock ledge at the motorbike tucked into the ferns below and then scanned the rustling canopy above. Two monkeys stared down at them, chewing on berries and spitting the seeds over the bike.

"Creek is just through them trees," Rafael pointed. "Take some soap too. You need it."

She laughed in feigned offense, collected a change of clothes from the backpack and slipped on her sandals. "I'll be back soon then."

The monkeys watched as she crept into the undergrowth, her eyes wide as she followed a rocky track downhill. A hummingbird became a third spectator to her stumbling and followed her merrily through a mass of red flowers that screened a grassy clearing. She ducked beneath a branch, her face brightening as she saw a wide stream of water tumbling out of a mossy wall of stone. The stream became a patchwork of connected pools below her, and through the trees she could see the flow plunging into a wide canyon.

Back at the shelter Rafael carefully edged a cigarette lighter beneath his pile of kindling and waited for the flames to catch. He smiled triumphantly as the cave behind was filled with light, and quickly finished snapping the rest of the sticks. He searched through the backpack, peeling back the lids from two cans of beans and prodding them into the fire.

The monkeys returned, watching with interest as he settled back against the wall and stared into the fire. A cracking of twigs made him look up, and he burst out laughing.

Jenna was shivering, her hair dripping wet as she pushed her way through the undergrowth. She glanced up at Rafael and pouted dramatically.

"Forgot we don't have a towel, you did! Waah!"

"Shut up!" she groaned, clambering up into the shelter and huddling in front of the fire.

"Poor chica," he grinned. He was about to throw another splintered branch into the flames when she pulled her shirt upwards, peeling it away from her shoulders and holding it above the fire. His eyes blinked in surprise and pretended to look away.

"What? I'm soaked!"

"Oh, I-I ain't. I was, see, I made some breakfast."

"Beans? Ugh, from a can? Is that all we have?"

"Yeah, I – waah, you know. Could have got you a monkey, I spose. But they don't taste any better, so –"

"I'm just teasing," she smirked. "I don't really know what that stuff is, but I'm starving."

"Good."

She smiled to herself as he turned away. "I'm sorry," she said. "I'm not much of a morning person."

He ignored her, his mouth producing a smile as he handed her a plastic spoon.

"How far are we from the border?"

"Bout an hour." He allowed his eyes to move back to hers. "After that I say we take the road to Granada. See 'bout someone who can help us get past Costa Rica."

She narrowed her eyes. "Oh yeah? How do you mean?"

"Gotta go by boat, cos there's no tracks like this across the border. And if we go by highway through Costa Rica… Waah, we're dead. It ain't happenin."

"I see. But are you sure this friend can be trusted? I thought we were trying to avoid people?"

He frowned. "She can be trusted, yes."

"And what if, at some stage, we get separated? What am I going to do? You still haven't told me where we are actually going. I still don't know where the tapes are, or anything about them."

"We won't get separated," he said resolutely.

"Hmm."

She watched as he tossed his empty can of beans in the fire and rolled up the sleeves of his shirt. He settled back against the wall, staring once more into the flames.

"Those tattoos on your forearms," she said. "What do they mean?"

He took a moment to look up and rubbed at his arms self-consciously. "Swallows," he eventually said. He turned his arms over to show her the intricate artwork. The dark ink was hard to distinguish from the colour of his skin, but after staring intently she saw them – numerous small birds were woven between thorns and vines. He pulled the sleeves up to his shoulders where the once confusing pattern now made sense.

"They're beautiful," she remarked genuinely. "What do they represent?"

He smiled, rolling his sleeves back down. "Birds."

"Well, obviously!" she scoffed. "How long have you had them?"

"I was sixteen. Got them in Belize."

"Belize? Is that where you grew up?"

"Come on, gotta get moving. Sounds like someone is coming."

"No one is coming, we're in the middle of nowhere."

He smiled uneasily, knowing that she was right. "I moved around. Never had, you know…"

She frowned. "Owen told me about your mother. I understand that she knew General Noriega, and that you lived in Panama City. But he has no idea what happened to you after the invasion. He thought you were dead. So where did you go?"

Rafael raised his eyebrows. "Why you askin' me? Sheesh, you seem to know more than I do."

"But I don't. I only know up until the invasion. Then what?"

He sighed. "There was a family in Granada. They lived in a farmhouse, 'bout two miles outside of town. They looked after a few kids like me. We're going to see one of them today. She's going to get us to Costa Rica."

"I see."

"I lived there until I was twelve, maybe thirteen. Then I had to leave. So I lived around the border towns, in Panama and Costa Rica, helpin' on the buses, sleepin' wherever. Then in Nicaragua – on the buses in Managua. Then in Puerto Cabezas, on the piers, workin' on the fishing boats, cargo ships, a few times round the Caribbean, Guatemala, Belize. Eventually made some good money and got myself into flyin' lessons. Wanted to be a pilot, or a ship captain." He sighed, but her obvious interest made him continue. "I love the ocean, the smells, you know. I love the coast. So that's where I tried to stay. But then I had to disappear again." He breathed in deeply, shaking his head slightly.

"Disappear from who?"

He ignored her. "Swallows are a good omen for men on the ships. You see them; you know you're close to land. And they can fly thousands of miles. All over the world. They're on every island, every continent, you know? Anywhere they want to be."

Jenna mirrored his slouched pose, her hand resting on her chin as she stared at him. After a few moments her solemn expression turned into a warm smile. "Thank you."

The track wound its way down the mountainside, emerging from the rainforest into a rolling plantation of short, broad-leafed plants. The bike wrestled with a stretch of mud, emerging onto a dewy hill that overlooked the plantation and a swollen river beyond.

"Criollo tobacco," Rafael announced, his hand panning across the plantation. "For making cigars."

Jenna screwed up her nose. "Yuck."

"You no fan of cigars?"

"No, not at all."

"Your mother smoked, no?"

"Yeah, she did. And it gave her cancer. And you?"

"Me? Nah, too addictive. Makes men weak."

"Ha! Really? Or are you just saying that because you heard it from someone else?"

"What do you think of me, waah!"

"Relax," she laughed, squeezing his waist. "I'm just kidding."

"So am I. I can't say no to a good cigar!"

"Oh, you ass!"

"Hey, stop it!" he laughed as he squirmed away from her prodding. "You wanna end up in that river?

"Very well." She moved her hands back to his hips as they rolled down the side of the hill, the track passing into a grove of pine trees and tracing the banks of the river. A scurrying made her sit upright, and she watched as a deer retreated tentatively into a mass of wild cashews.

"Apagüíz mountain," Rafael announced in a husky voice, pointing towards a distinctive peak in the distance. "We're nearly at Danli."

Sure enough, the outskirts of a large town came into view over the next rise. A stone bridge stumbled across the river, and Rafael slowed to take in a view of the buildings rising through the fog. A maze of terracotta roofs bordered white colonial villas, leafy avenues and rich green playing fields. Tall date palms poked out from quaint courtyards, and bright pink bougainvilleas clambered up the walls of whitewashed churches.

Rafael pulled the bike to a stop beside the river, stretching his arms and pointing to the water. "It's fresh. Good idea to fill more water." He disappeared into a thicket of trees and she gladly took the opportunity to brush her teeth and remove the taste of breakfast.

"I hope you like bananas!" Rafael called.

"Gosh!" Jenna laughed, spitting out toothpaste and glancing up as he lumbered into the open. "I think you're going to give me potassium poisoning!"

"Dunno what that is, but it's gotta be better than those beans!" He weaved a string between the stack of bananas and secured them to the back of the bike.

The river continued around a coffee plantation where they turned onto a wide dirt road. Landslides had taken out much of the side of the mountain, and the road soon became a narrow track that wound between wooden huts.

"Sierra de Dipilto," Rafael announced, pointing across a valley to a mountain range in the south.

"Pardon?"

"And Cerro Mogoton, over there, highest peak in Nicaragua. We're almost there."

The track ran abruptly into a giant wire fence. Rafael jumped off the bike and inspected the base of the wire. He pulled at a tussock of grass, sliding his hand beneath the wire and then ripping it upwards.

"Wow," Jenna said. "You really do know this place, don't you?"

"Hold it up. I'll get the bike."

She took the wire, pulling it high above her head as Rafael shuffled through the gap. He leaned the bike against a fencepost and then took the weight of the wire, ushering her through.

"Bienvenido," he smiled, taking her melodramatically by the hand, "to Nicaragua."

"Gracias," she chuckled as she stepped across the border.

The rumbling of traffic could be heard through the trees, and a closer view revealed a busy highway below. Exhaust haze rose in a cloud from the back of a lone fuel station that seemed to float at the edge of a great expanse of steamy marshland. Two trucks bellowed out black smoke as they joined the queue for a diesel pump at the back of the building.

"Could dump the bike and take a bus," Rafael said as they wheeled the bike onto the edge of a rocky lookout point. "Or else the Pan American Highway is maybe a half hour ride south. We make it there and we should have avoided the checkpoints. What d'you think?"

She shrugged. "At least on a bike we can get away from anyone."

"Tis true." He adjusted his sunglasses, frowning. "Either way there will be men, boys, sittin' by the road, driving vans, on the buses, sellin' sweets… Eyes are cheap here."

Jenna frowned thoughtfully, squinting as she watched the truck drivers come out of their cabins and light cigarettes. "How much money do we have left?"

Chapter Forty-Three

Every bump in the road produced an echoing clang as the motorbike bashed against the metal wall of the truck. Rafael tried to wedge it between a stack of foam boxes, but a line of empty plastic crates toppled over and bounced like rubber against the rear doors. Jenna closed her eyes tightly as she tried to stop herself from being sick, but the bumps soon subsided on a smooth stretch of highway and the truck grunted its way into overdrive.

Rafael shuffled through the darkness to the front of the cargo, his body illuminated by thin spears of yellow light. He positioned himself in front of one of the holes, sucked in the fresh air and began peering outside.

After two hours the water bottle was empty, banana skins littered the floor and the inside of Jenna's mouth felt like a crusty towel. Dust had mixed with the sweat on her forehead, and dark gritty specs were slowly flowing into her eyes. "I've had enough!" she shouted, banging a crate against the wall of the truck. "I need to get out!"

"Not yet," Rafael called back. "Still too dangerous."

"I think there's a bigger risk of us dying of thirst! Make him stop and let us out!"

Rafael sighed heavily and began rapping his knuckles against the metal wall.

Fresh air never tasted so good as Jenna climbed onto the back of the motorbike and waved to the truck driver. He nodded, stuffed a wad of cash into his trousers and climbed back inside.

They sped quickly out of the truck stop and into a hoard of traffic. Exhaust and flecks of mud added to the grime on Jenna's forehead. She peered over Rafael's shoulder, craning her neck to see a fleeting view of Lake Managua to the south.

Thinly forested hills regressed into swampy grasslands, where naked coral trees and ramshackle wooden huts bordered the highway. The city of Managua came into view across the lake, marked by a grey-brown haze that seemed to be rising from the afternoon shadows. They turned left at the village of Tipitapa, avoiding the city and continuing southwards through copper-coloured fields of harvested maize.

Rafael became tense as he navigated his way into Granada, his shoulders flexing as if in preparation for an ambush. A swirling breeze rustled liquidambar leaves out of the gutter in front of them, leading Jenna's eyes up the intricate white pillars and terraces of restored Spanish buildings. She imagined the streets pulling her back in time, the hooves of a draught horse echoing between weathered basalt sculptures and grand stone archways blackened by historic fires. Her marvelling turned to awe as they rolled into the light of the central plaza, the sun's yawning rays sweeping over a giant yellow cathedral whose brilliant red spires gazed watchfully into a stained-glass sky.

"This place is beautiful."

Rafael nodded, his lips pursed as he glanced cautiously into the passing lanes.

The majestic streets gave way to colourful stone and timber houses and quiet corner stores. The sky continued to grow darker as Rafael took a sudden left turn, a churning mass of cloud sweeping gushes of cold air through a bus station to their left. A group of young boys watched from the shelter, one of them running out with a cap gun that he fired at them jokingly. Jenna laughed, but Rafael was in no mood for humour. He clenched his teeth as he surveyed the road ahead and then took another sudden left turn.

"Where exactly are we meeting this friend of yours?" Jenna asked.

"We'll meet her soon."

The road ended back at the town's central plaza, and Rafael carefully parked the bike against a wrought iron fence. He led the way into the plaza, and to Jenna's surprise he casually put his arm around her shoulders, his body suddenly moving with more of a swagger than a walk.

"What the hell are you doing?" Jenna hissed. She was about to push his arm off her – more out of shock than not wanting his body contact – but realised quickly what he was doing.

"You're not very good at acting, are you?" Rafael mocked as they passed through a group of teenagers on pushbikes.

"Yes I am!"

"Then relax!"

Jenna breathed in deeply through her nose, closed her eyes for a moment and then slid her arm around his waist. He began speaking rapidly in Spanish and she responded with feigned understanding, smiling and nodding up at him.

"That's better," he whispered.

The central plaza was full of life despite the threatening storm, and they had to sidle between kiosks and crowds of children to get to the base of the cathedral.

"Are you hungry?" Rafael asked.

"Uh, yes!"

A grey-haired woman sat cross-legged on a colourful mat at the base of the cathedral, her neck adorned with shell necklaces and her dark eyes looking up at Jenna with strange warmth. "Un poco de pan?" she asked, pointing to a basket of bread and pastries beside her.

"She asked if you want some bread?" Rafael explained.

"Si, por favor," Jenna smiled.

Rafael gave the woman an assortment of coins as she whipped a large flat loaf into a brown paper bag. They exchanged a short conversation in Spanish before Rafael took the bread and passed it to Jenna.

"God, it's dense," she exclaimed.

"What else do you want to eat?"

"A quesadilla?"

"Sure. Take these coins."

Rafael stood back and watched the square like a policeman as Jenna continued shopping. A group of teenage boys kicking a ball caught his attention, and he eyed them suspiciously as their ball rolled towards him. He juggled it between his feet and kicked it back skilfully. He held his stare with one of the boys until he looked away.

"Come on," Rafael whispered as Jenna returned, grabbing her by the hand and directing her towards the bike. The eddying wind was now drawing rain, and specs of moisture began to create a patchwork across the paved plaza.

"Wait, are we done?"

"Yes, we're done."

"But what about your friend? Aren't we meeting her here somewhere?"

His grip tightened, and he was scanning the passing faces carefully. "Look in the bread," he whispered.

"What do you mean?"

"Exactly what I said."

She wedged it out of the paper bag as they walked, annoyed that it was getting wet from the rain. "It's bread. I'm confused."

"Tear it open."

Jenna gaped as something metallic was exposed in the soft dough. Rafael motioned for her to pull it out, and she eased out a set of keys on a labelled key ring.

Rafael read the address on the key ring and frowned.

Jenna turned back towards the stall where the elderly lady had been selling the bread. She had disappeared. "That lady, she was –"

"Yes, she was," Rafael nodded. "Come on, we gotta go. That address is in the next village."

Twilight marked the end of the shower, the remaining droplets of water now dancing like cottony sleet in the beam of the motorbike's headlight. Jenna's naked legs tingled with goose bumps, and her wet ponytail slapped rhythmically against the back of her neck as Rafael accelerated out of Grenada. She clung on tighter as she leaned sideways, taking in a view of a vast inland lake. Two volcanic peaks rose proudly out of the water, and seemed to be mustering the last of the rainclouds into a threatening ball between them.

Rafael slowed as they entered another village. Industrial buildings gave way to ramshackle apartments that seemed to stare down at them through hollow black windows. Wisps of steam swirled off the wet sheen that matted the potholed road, and the motorbike skidded as it turned into the parking lot of one of the apartment buildings.

"Here?" Jenna gasped.

Two men in grey hoodies watched from beneath a flight of concrete steps as the bike rumbled to a stop. Rafael flicked off the headlight. He stared warily into the windows above.

Chapter Forty-Four

The apartment was furnished, but far from being anyone's home. The only picture on the wall was a large map of Nicaragua covered with pins, and the heavy grey curtains were tightly drawn. An old fridge buzzed noisily, and the brown carpet gave off a dusty musk. On top of the dining room table was a handwritten note beside a handgun, a stack of ammunition and a white cardboard box. Rafael pulled open the box, smiling as he held up two smartphones.

Jenna's eyes widened.

"Here, take one. Should have a sim in it. But be careful, yeah? It can be tracked if anyone finds out the number."

"Rightio."

The fridge was empty, but the freezer contained stacks of frozen packaged meals. Jenna gleefully piled three pasta dishes into the microwave and began searching for cutlery.

Rafael returned from inspecting the rest of the apartment, clenching his jaw and picking up his new phone. "Gotta bad feeling about this place," he said as he looked up. "Too many people hanging outside."

"I agree. Do you want to leave?"

"No. Wait til mornin'. We'll leave before sunrise for San Juan Del Sur. Then get a boat to Costa Rica. But right now I need to make some calls."

"To who?"

He motioned his hand around the room. "Who do you think?"

"All right, well I'm going to have a shower while this food heats up."

Rafael slumped into the couch, putting the phone to his ear.

Jenna closed the bathroom door behind her, dumping the backpack on the cream tile floor and rummaging for her toiletries.

The feeling of hot water was incredible, and she leaned back in delight as shampoo tumbled in great bubbling clouds over her body. Her fingers were finally able to stroke through her hair without running into knots, and the sensation of clean shaven legs had never felt so good. She wrapped herself in a towel, rubbed a circle into the mirror and then stared at the black smartphone sitting on the vanity. She clicked her tongue against the back of her teeth, glancing at the door and running a hand through her hair indecisively.

The temptation became too much. She ripped open the front of the backpack, tossing out a pack of chewing gum and then pulling out Owen's sim card. She steadied herself against the sink, taking a deep breath before flipping the phone over and swapping the sim cards. Time seemed to slow as the phone eventually gained reception, drawing her thumbs into a rapid dance across the screen.

A muffled shouting became louder, and a sudden thump caused Jenna to gasp. She quickly dressed herself and then cowered as a deep voice boomed through the walls. It was difficult to tell if the voice was coming from an adjacent apartment, or within the one she was in. She glanced at the frosted window, realising with a jolt of fear that it couldn't be opened – and even if it could be, she was three storeys up. Her hands trembled as she slipped the phone into her pocket and crept towards the door.

Silence. She swallowed tensely as her fingers carefully turned the doorknob. She edged the door open, her ears prickling in anticipation, but there was still no sound. A sector of light from the bathroom beamed outwards, casting her shadow across the floor as she peered into the hallway.

"Rafael?"

The living room was dark, the only light coming from the muted television. She stepped out of the bathroom, her eyes wide as she turned towards a bedroom to her left. A gentle draft was flapping the curtains against an open window, and a soft yellow ruddiness flowed across the bed from a streetlight. She crept towards the room and was about to peer in when two hands passed over her forehead, ripping a hard nylon rope around her neck. She choked, and her attempts to scream were suppressed as a roll of duct tape was slapped across her mouth. The rope loosened as a black cotton bag descended over her head, followed by a drawstring that was spun into a tight knot.

The horror seemed to have reached a threshold, and by the time her hands were bound she had drifted into a state of semiconsciousness. The rope had been pulled from her neck, and she breathed steadily through her nose, the starchy smell of the bag filling her mind with bizarre, dreamy images. Her eyelashes flickered uncontrollably against the fabric, and she put up no resistance as she was carried through the living room and into the night air. Her captors were silent as they descended the steps, carrying her briskly across the parking lot. The door of a van slammed shut behind her, and her body became limp as the engine started.

Jenna's consciousness continued to drift, brought back only by the low wheezing of a man beside her. Her eyelashes flickered again, and her jaw muscles swelled as she recognised Rafael's breathing. She rolled herself over, trying to make out the shape of his body through the black fabric. He seemed to be curled into a foetal position, his legs shaking as if in agony.

Reality hit with a powerful bounce as the van rumbled onto a dirt road. Jenna's head shivered in horror. She quickly edged her fingers upwards. She groaned, her abdominals straining as she flexed sideways, trying to force her fingers into the pocket of her shorts. She rolled onto her stomach, flexing backwards, but the phone was wedged too tightly against her thigh to be removed.

The road became sealed again, and the van accelerated onto what sounded like a highway. Passing lights blinked rapidly through a crack in the back door, and the reverberating sound of a truck seemed to shake the dust from the floor. Jenna sneezed, her nose beginning to run. She rolled back over, her heart becoming an irregular drumbeat as her nostrils struggled to suck in air.

The van slowed, turning onto another sealed road. The crack in the back door became dark, and the sound of traffic was replaced with the pattering of rain on the metal roof. The smell of water vapour rising from the hot bitumen outside was strangely comforting, and Jenna was finally able to steady her breathing. Her eyes flicked back and forth as she tried to imagine scenarios less frightening than those fizzing through her nerves. Surely they would already be dead if the intention was to kill them? Or were they simply being transported somewhere away from the town for their bodies to be disposed? There was no record of her having entered Nicaragua, or even Honduras, so there was little hope for their bodies ever being recovered. She closed her eyes tightly as tears stung, the black fabric sticking to her cheeks.

The pattering soon became a downpour. The van slowed as the sound of water gushed against the underside of the chassis. They turned again, the sound of gravel crunching under the tyres followed by that of another vehicle parking beside them. Jenna's tears were streaming now, and she shivered uncontrollably as the back door was ripped open.

Rafael groaned as he was pulled out first. His legs slammed against the back door. Two men spoke loudly in Spanish, and sounded as though they were puffing as they carried Rafael through the rain towards a large shed lit by a floodlight from high above. Another loud conversation followed as a metal door was opened at the base of the shed, and a man could be heard laughing in a large, echoing space.

The men returned for Jenna, heaving her out of the van like a piece of furniture and guiding her into the light. Her foot banged against the wall, making a sharp tinny sound. The distinctive sound of an aeroplane could be heard through the front of the building, which must have been open to the air.

The industrial smell of hydraulic oil and damp canvas tarpaulins clogged her nose, and she struggled for breath as the heads of her captors swayed below a high ceiling of round fluorescent lights. The men readjusted their grip, edging her around a row of metal drums and then dumping her into a hard wooden chair.

266

The two men pulled her hands between the slats at the back of the chair and bound her wrists against the wood. She whimpered, her eyes flickering again as the sound of another aircraft whirred through the roof above. A high-pitched blare was followed by the puff of rubber tyres on an airstrip, and the two men stood up to attention.

"El esta aqui."

"Si. Ve a saludarlo."

The men walked away from her, the sound of their footsteps on a concrete floor resonating through the vast open space. As they opened a far door the sound of the plane was piercing. The plane's lights passed through a glass wall dividing what she figured must be an aircraft hangar.

The plane idled for a minute, its high pitched beeping echoing through a network of struts crisscrossing the curved roof. Jenna's eyes were blinking against the black fabric, and her hands and feet were trembling as the idling came to an abrupt stop. The door at the base of the glass wall opened, and a set of determined footsteps tapped through the silence.

"Donde esta Rafael?"

"En la habitación de al lado, con Bruno."

"Bueno. Vamos a empezar con la perra."

The drawstring was suddenly loosened, and the bag was ripped off her head. She blinked. Her eyes took a moment to adjust to the light before her body convulsed in horror.

"Hello, Jenna," the familiar Latino man rasped, his mottled neck quivering with excitement. "So good to see you again."

Chapter Forty-Five

Hector's mansion, Panama City.
December 20th, 1989, 2:10am.

Eva carefully slid a pink pocketknife into her jeans as she joined Owen on the dark driveway. She threw her leg over the seat behind him, gripping him tightly around the waist as he revved Hector's black Ducati. The engine crackled into a thunderous roar as the bike sailed across the driveway, through the open gates and around the guards. The tyres gained traction on the bitumen and the bike seemed to float as it turned sharply down the hill and powered into the smoke.

A great spiral of fire was rising from within Chorrillo, twisting its way into the mephitic sky and spreading plumes of undying sparks across the suburbs. Ash rained down like snowflakes across Ancon Hill, and the film across the road was swept up in powdery gusts as the Ducati glided like a shadow onto the highway. A line of tanks was moving steadily across both lanes, but they barely had time to react as the motorbike weaved its way clear and then skidded into the suburbs.

"She's obviously gotten this far," Owen called back to Eva.

"Take the back way!" Eva shouted into his ear. "There's no way we can get through that fire."

Owen clenched his jaw, staring up at the flames and then pulling his visor down as he veered back towards the highway. The bike's speed was dizzying as they accelerated into the left lane, passing two troop carriers before knifing through the side of a US roadblock. Bewildered soldiers fired shots from a machine gun, but the bike had already disappeared around the corner and onto the cobblestones of Casco Viejo.

Owen knew the area well enough to swerve almost unnoticed through the alleyways, dodging a crowd of shouting civilians and then skidding into Avenida 4a.

"Stop!" Eva cried as she saw the scene ahead.

Hector's Land Rover was parked at the front of the red door. Its tyres were blown out and its back window spread like crystals across the cobblestones. Surrounding the vehicle and aiming their weapons at the house were a dozen US soldiers in bulletproof vests, their faces disguised with masks and their shoulders strapped with great swathes of ammunition. Parked against the back of the Land Rover was Thorn's beige Hummer, its windscreen shattered and the passenger door buckled inwards. From the roof of the vehicle beamed three spotlights, their white rays blazing a path through the open red door.

The distinct sound of a helicopter was becoming louder, and a blinding spotlight cast directly onto the bike.

Owen hesitated, revving the bike before steering into an alleyway. He felt Eva's grip tighten as they bounced between ferns and broken fence palings, eventually emerging into the light of the next street. He steered to the right, accelerating into another alleyway and stopping above the steps at the back of the brothel.

Green tracers lit up the next block as they jumped off the bike, and Owen ducked instinctively as though they were about to be shot. The helicopter's spotlight had drifted towards the tracers, reflecting off the tin roof of a burning house.

"We're fine," Eva huffed. "There's no one here."

"Shh! Did you hear that?" Owen stood up again, staring tensely at the glowing curtains in the windows above. "Come on!" he hissed, parking the bike and rushing down the steps. He pushed at the steel ingress but it held strong. He repositioned himself sideways, took a deep breath and rammed his shoulder into the door.

"Don't be an idiot!" Eva hissed. "Get the bike!" She began searching the tall grass beside the steps and retrieved a broken awning. The sound of her knife cut through Owen's confusion, and when she held up a length of fibrous cloth he understood her plan. He worked quickly, wedging the bike against the metal door and opening the fuel cap.

Chapter Forty-Six

Casco Viejo, Panama City.
December 20th, 1989, 2:26am.

Rafael opened his eyes, his senses on alert. He crawled silently towards a gap in the rafters, his face an iridescent purple in the light of the waiting room below. The whirring of a helicopter vibrated the roof above him, but it was the screeching of tyres outside that had pulled him from his hiding place. He flattened himself in anticipation as the front door rattled, then pulled backwards in fright as the room was awash with white light.

"Rafael!" Maria screamed as she scrambled through the doorway. She tried to slam the door behind her, but it rebounded off the steel-capped toe of a man's boot. She kicked at him, but a machine-like punch to her cheek sent her sprawling across the floor.

Rafael was frozen in horror as the spotlights atop a vehicle outside created a silhouette out of a tall, hulking soldier. He stepped forward, rubbing at his fist as the light refracted off his spiked blonde hair. Two masked soldiers emerged around him, blocking off the entrance and scanning their weapons cautiously around the room.

The blonde man took another step forward. Rafael's eyes widened, recognising him as a man who had come to the house before – a man his mother had called "Thorn".

Thorn grinned as Maria flicked a knife from her dress. She held up the blade with a shaking hand, and staggered backwards towards the maroon curtains dividing the waiting room from the hallway. Thorn began to chuckle, turning his head to the side almost mockingly as he reached for a radio strapped to his bulletproof vest. "We have her," he announced.

"Get back!" Maria screamed as the radio crackled a response. "Rafael, run!"

Rafael flinched, pulling back to the mezzanine behind as Maria ripped at the curtains, sending the metal curtain rod crashing to the floor.

"Oh, Maria!" Thorn boomed as he marched after her. "Where are you going, now? We have the place surrounded. It's only going to hurt more if you try to escape!"

Maria had disappeared down the hallway.

Rafael's light frame leapt nimbly through a gap in the rafters and into a slanted tunnel that traced around the side of the house. He slipped silently into an upstairs bedroom, ducking beneath a bed and scrambling towards a sheepskin rug in the corner. He flipped the rug over, his fingers digging into a gap in the floorboards. Within seconds he had slid into a foil-lined vent, and was peering through wire mesh into his mother's office below.

Maria moaned as Thorn pulled her by the hair from behind her desk, her face hidden in the torn front of her red dress. Thorn smiled as he reached a hand beneath her chin, pulling her bleeding face into the light.

"Not very good at hiding, are you? Now where are the tapes?"

"Go to Hell!" Maria screamed.

The two other soldiers entered cautiously, once again scanning the room and then flanking the doorway.

"Ha!" Thorn laughed. "Rafael? Su hijo, si?"

"Let me go!"

Thorn's radio crackled again. His face turned grim. "You better start talking, because my friend isn't going to be so kind if he has to come in here."

"I don't have the tapes! They're with Hector! I came back for my son, let me go!"

"Oh really? I thought you were smarter than that, Maria. Do you really think Eva will help you now if you don't have those tapes? Of course not! She's just as deceitful as you. And you know that. So hand them over."

"Stand back, Thorn," came the voice of a beady-eyed man in the doorway, his stubby fingers wrapped around a pistol. He was shorter than the soldiers beside him, but his scarred face and flattened nose gave him a more intimidating appearance. "Let me handle this."

Thorn smiled somewhat timidly as he looked up. "All yours, Conrad."

"So you came back for the boy, did you?" Conrad asked casually as he stepped forward. He seized Maria by the hair, pulling her upwards and throwing her across the desk. "So where is he? He has the tapes, doesn't he?"

Maria's throat growled, sucking inwards for a moment before she spat forcefully into Conrad's eye.

"Bitch!" Conrad recoiled, slamming his palm into her cheek so forcefully that a streak of blood traced across the floor. He squashed her face into the desk before looking upwards, his eyes studying the vent in the corner of the room. "Rafael!" he cried, his voice unnaturally high. "Sal ahora, niño, o tu madre morirá!"

Thorn began swiping his hand across the bookshelf. Files and diaries tumbled to the floor. He turned to the drawers, pulling out a bottle of tequila and a stack of folders before emptying the rest of the contents across the desk. Cigarettes and coloured lighters tumbled over the desk like candy.

Rafael's grip on the wire mesh became tighter, and his eyes widened as they made contact with his mother's.

"Where are the tapes, Maria?" Conrad continued calmly. "Tell me, before we blow this place into the bay."

Maria's gasping finally ended and she took a deep breath. She was about to speak, but stopped herself as her eyes pulled away from the vent.

"Speak!" Conrad demanded, pressing the barrel of his pistol into her temple. "Where is he, bitch?"

Maria screamed, "Rafael, huye! Escapa!"

"That settles it, Joe," Conrad sighed with exaggerated coolness. "We'll just have to light a match and see how well that little boy burns." As his grip on her hair relaxed she suddenly pushed forward, her arm heaving from underneath her chest and flinging the pistol out of his hand.

"Bitch!" Conrad cried as Maria's hand swiped across the desk, grabbing the bottle of tequila and swinging it as she pirouetted to her feet. Conrad was too slow to react, his eyes popping as the bottle smashed into his nose. The glass shattered, cutting into his lip and splashing tequila across his neck and the bookcase behind. He stumbled backwards, and was still off-balance as Maria's hand flicked the top off one of the cigarette lighters.

Thorn launched forward, knocking Maria backwards before the flame was able to ignite Conrad's chest. The lighter rebounded off the bookshelf, spinning like a Catherine wheel to the floor.

Conrad spat blood as he staggered to his feet. Blue flames hungrily licked over the bookshelf beside him. "Stand back, Joe!" he roared, reaching for his pistol.

Maria's eyes were wide with terror as she crawled backwards to a wooden chair beneath the vent, her eyes focused on the long barrel of Conrad's pistol. She took one last look upwards, her eyes making contact with Rafael's as she screamed a string of words in Spanish. The bullets ripped through her neck, spraying bright red blood across the wall as blue-green flames leapt at the base of her dress.

Rafael's scream was ear piercing as he tumbled through the vent. The chair below split apart, and he stumbled over its broken legs as he dived onto Maria's bloodied chest. He continued screaming, his hands pulling the hair away from the holes in her face.

"Shit!" Thorn gasped from the other side of the room. "Shoot him!"

"What are you doing?" cried one of the soldiers as he stepped backwards. "He's a child, you can't shoot him!"

Conrad hesitated, wiping the blood from his face and glaring at the soldiers. Both of them had now retreated to the hallway, unsure where to aim their weapons. He turned to Thorn, an ugly frown smeared across his face. "You do it."

"Goddam it, just shoot him!" Thorn edged clear of the flames rising from the desk. "Shoot him!"

Flames advanced over the broken chair as Conrad reloaded, his bloodied face wrinkling into a grimace as he took aim.

"Do it!" Thorn cried.

The sound of hurried voices drifted up from somewhere below. Conrad blinked in hesitation, his finger yet to pull the trigger. In a moment of confusion Rafael vanished. He reappeared over the desk, his agile body lunging forwards and thrusting a burning chair leg into Conrad's tequila-soaked chest. The chair leg fell to the floor, but the flames swooped like orange snakes over his neck. He stumbled backwards, his wailing inhuman as he clutched at his throat.

Rafael dived beneath the desk, his hands wrapping around a plastic box. Conrad flailed a burning arm at him but Thorn pulled him back and heaved him towards the door. The two soldiers helped, rolling Conrad into the hallway and trying to douse the flames. He pulled against them; his shrieking stifled as the bookshelf erupted, sparks gushing like a crashing wave into the hallway.

"Shoot him!" Conrad gurgled through the smoke. "He's got the tapes!"

Thorn was temporarily blinded, and his hands caught only sparks as Rafael clambered through a hallway to the right. The chase continued down a metal staircase, which Rafael descended like a swooping bird.

"Bastard!" Thorn cried as he tumbled into the basement below and squinted into the dark. He removed his pistol from its holster, firing shots to ignite the darkness. The flashes revealed a room full of broken toys and a steel ingress. He was about to fire another shot when an explosion tore the metal door clean off its hinges and propelled a buckled motorbike wheel across the floor.

The concentration of the sound in the room was paralysing, and Thorn dropped his pistol as he clutched at his ears. He tried to shake off the ringing, clambering across broken figurines as two figures barged through the crumpled doorway.

The flames of the explosion quickly dissipated, and the only light in the room now came from the concrete steps outside. The light caught the sweat on Rafael's naked back as he emerged from beneath a stack of toys in the corner. He blinked in fright and then rushed over to the handle of a trapdoor.

"You little shit!" Thorn thundered as he dived forward, ignoring the two figures that peered into the darkness. Dust was thrown upwards in a choking cloud, and the target of Thorn's aggression again disappeared. He clawed blindly across the floor for the trapdoor, but a kick to his ribs sent him sprawling back through the dust.

"Let him go!" Owen roared, picking up Thorn's pistol. "Show me your hands!"

"Ha!" Thorn puffed into the dust. "Get out of here, Owen."

"What have you done with his mother?"

"It wasn't me, she killed herself." His hand slipped over his radio, and he glared up at Owen's blackened face as he held down the button. "Back of the house, now!" he shouted. "Man down!"

"I'll kill you!" Owen roared, kicking the radio out of his grasp. He pressed his finger against the trigger of the pistol, his lips quivering with rage. "But I'd rather see how big you think you are when you're on trial." He kicked him again in the stomach, then turned to see Eva lifting the handle of the trapdoor.

"Rafael!" Eva shouted into the hole. "Yo soy Eva! Ven, esta bien!"

A loud crashing upstairs was followed by a gust of sparks from the stairwell. An orange wavering became brighter, and a chunk of smouldering wood shattered into flames as it tumbled into the basement.

"Rafael!" Eva cried again, her voice echoing in the hole. She looked back up at Owen with a fearful expression. "I can't see anything!"

Owen hesitated, his eyes still locked into Thorn's. "Okay, take the gun. I'll go down there."

"How valiant," Thorn jested, his grin revealing strings of blood across his teeth. "I'd love to watch you try to get out when this place falls in."

"Drop the weapon!" came a shout from the open doorway. Torchlights blazed into the room, and Owen stumbled backwards in shock. The pistol fell from his grasp, and he found himself slammed into the dust, his hands bound behind his back.

"Good work!" Thorn laughed as he climbed to his feet.

Eva was pushed up against the wall, and Owen spat dust in protest as her hands were also bound with cable ties.

"Leave the trap door open," Thorn growled as a soldier was about to kick it shut. He unbuckled his vest, allowing his chest to puff out. "Get them outside, everyone get outside! Phelps, get me another grenade."

Chapter Forty-Seven

Managua, Nicaragua.
Present day.

"I don't suppose you've seen the news reports?"

Jenna winced, her lips burning from the removal of the duct tape. She looked up at his black beady eyes, her mouth curling with hatred. Behind him, the hangar was awash with stark white light, and through the murky glass wall she could see a familiar blue and white Cherokee parked diagonally across the vast concrete floor. The front of the hangar was open, and the lights of a runway punctuated the darkness beyond.

Out of the corner of her eye she made out two men in grey hoodies straddling rifles as they leaned against the metal door in which she had entered. A network of pipes, vents and electrical leads occupied the walls around them, and an array of tool cabinets, workbenches and gas cylinders littered the floor all the way to the glass wall. At the other end of the space was a mezzanine floor, beneath which an office had been built within white chipboard walls and grimy windows. A man could be seen guarding the office doorway, his face concealed by shadow as he stared towards them.

Jenna turned back to the man before her. He paced towards the glass wall and then spun on his heel. He adjusted the collar of his suit, raising his chin and staring at her down the twisted hump of his nose. "Apparently you've been kidnapped," he said with a sarcastic tone, spinning again and kicking dust over his polished black shoes. "Which I suppose is true, isn't it? You haven't had any role in this. It was all him, wasn't it?"

"Sorry?" She cleared her dry throat. "What are you talking about?"

"A Cuban drug lord and a famous dancer, what a pair! Indeed, you are famous, are you not? Certainly famous enough for the media to pour over your life. So for you to disappear permanently would be… well, a real problem. But him –" He motioned towards the office, speaking gruffly. "No one will even notice if he's gone, will they?"

Jenna snarled, her wrists going numb as they pulled at the chair.

"You're not stupid, Miss Martinez. Neither was your mother. But we managed to keep her quiet, didn't we? Oh yes, I'm sure we can do the same with you. After all, you know exactly what will happen if you decide to open your mouth."

"Who are you?"

He ignored her, continuing to pace like an actor delivering a soliloquy to the glass wall. His voice bounced through the hangar, and he seemed to take delight in hearing its echo. "Journalists," he declared, talking in quick bursts. "So underrated, aren't they? I always knew it; I always knew I needed to control them. But I was never a charmer, you know. I was a bully, oh yes, I've always been that, but never popular. And I never had the looks." He licked his lips, staring back into her eyes. "That's why I used Joe. Oh yes, he was handsome. They loved him, didn't they?" He leaned back in, his eyes narrowed as if trying to draw out her thoughts. "People always go on about how Noriega had control over the politicians, the lawyers and the police. But do you know where he fell down, Miss Martinez? The media! He thought he owned them, but he certainly didn't. Across the world, they hated him. If you want to influence people, if you want to destroy little birds, you need to own the journalists."

"What are you talking about?"

"They can make a policeman a thief; turn a scientist into a fool, and – my personal favourite – turn a young ship worker into a ruthless drug lord! Oh, don't worry Jenna, your boyfriend was never innocent. He's always been bad, but I made him terrible!"

Jenna shook her head incredulously.

"A street rat, the offspring of a whore, the bastard son of Panama's most notorious criminal. Do you really think anyone would have believed he was a decent man, that anything he had to say about his past might be true?"

Jenna's face had turned white, and she clenched her jaw in shock.

"Oh, you didn't know?" He leaned forward, studying her face before chuckling malevolently. "He hasn't told you that he's Noriega's son, has he?"

"Liar!" Jenna screamed. "You lying, ugly, hideous –"

"Ha! That won't work, my dear. I'm not as vain as Noriega was about appearances; I enjoy being ugly! I'm afraid, however, that you're going to have to learn to change the object of your hatred. Oh yes, you're going to have to learn to conform to what is written in the newspapers, the blogs, on social media. Because the only way that you're going to survive is if you tell the story that I ask you to. And don't worry, it's a good story. And I don't want you to fail, it would be such a shame to waste your talents like the creature I'm about to waste in that room over there."

Tears began streaming over Jenna's cheeks. She coughed violently, and her nose turned a burning red.

"Rafael is going to be given two options," he said calmly. "His first is to stay silent, and to therefore be killed, along with you. His second is to talk, to tell us where those tapes are that your mother was trying to find, and to allow you to live."

Jenna's sobbing was uncontrollable now, the chair vibrating against the dusty floor as she struggled for breath.

"So before we go and see to him, what has he told you?" He knelt down beside her, his voice turning to a whisper. "The tapes are still in Panama, I know that much. But I'll be honest; I don't know all of his secrets. And he has never been one for talking. But he speaks to you, he tells you things, I know he must. So, what do you know?" He leaned in closer, snarling. "Tell me what you know."

Jenna swallowed her choking, her face suddenly calm. "There are no tapes. They were destroyed; you know that."

The slap sent Jenna's tears spraying into the dust. "Don't try to fool me, Jenna Martinez! You wouldn't be so determined to get to Panama if there wasn't a reason!"

She looked up with a dark glower. "Your name is Conrad, isn't it? Owen told me all about you."

Conrad raised his eyebrows. "Oh, did he now?"

Jenna turned her head to the side, her eyes mocking. "You're Joe's mignon, aren't you? Even after all these years, you're still the guy who cleans up for him. But why?"

Conrad ignored her, staring out beyond the front of the hanger.

"A little mignon, that's what you are. And I can tell by the way you describe him that you envy him, don't you? Don't you, Conrad? You envy his looks, and a lot more than that, don't you?"

"You're treading a very thin line, young lady."

"I think there's more to it. I think it's more than envy. The way you talk about him. Owen certainly had a theory about you." She smiled jeeringly. "I bet these guards probably joke about it behind your back. I bet everyone does!"

Conrad ran his tongue along the front of his teeth, his eyes boring into hers before breaking away. "I gave you a chance. Now let's see if Romeo is as kind to you." He reached into his blazer, removing a pair of plastic surgical gloves. He winked at her as he pulled them on and traipsed towards the office in the corner.

Rafael's reflection could be seen in the glass of the open office door, his body slumped like hers in a wooden chair. Conrad rubbed his gloved hands together, nodding at the guard standing behind Rafael's covered head. The black bag was loosened, then ripped off suddenly as if exposing a prize.

Rafael's eyes blinked as his bloodied face moved upwards. Conrad edged closer, leaning over and grinning mockingly.

It was as if a volcano had erupted inside Rafael's chest. He launched forward, his eyes bursting with rage. He tried to shout through the gag, his arms quaking as they strained against his bindings. Conrad continued to grin, his gloved fingers pausing beside Rafael's mouth before tearing off the tape.

"You!" Rafael roared. His face was a picture of wrath; his teeth snapping together like a wild animal as he thrashed his head. "Conrad! I'll kill you!" The slats at the back of the chair splintered apart, but Rafael's lunge ended when a metal rod crashed over him.

The reflection of the scene vanished as someone kicked the office door shut. Jenna slumped forward, shaking in despair.

Rafael's cries continued through the night, his body pounding in agony against the thin wall that divided him from Jenna. Her screaming was ignored, and her voice was eventually too hoarse to make a sound. She thought she heard the sound of a motorbike, but her concentration on the sound was interrupted as the back door to the hanger opened behind her. She looked sideways to see a man in black lumbering past, his arms straining as he carried a metal bucket of water and a towel.

Rafael's cries became gurgling moans, and the horrible sound seemed to twist Jenna's insides into a bursting knot. Tears mixed with her dripping nose, strings of moisture forming a blurred puddle at her feet. She rocked sideways, then winced in panic as the chair toppled, her head cracking sickeningly against the concrete.

"You're a lucky girl, Miss Martinez." Conrad leaned in, grinning proudly. "Oh yes, you are, Romeo's decided to keep you alive!"

Fluorescent globes pierced through Jenna's eyes, and she blinked in pain as someone heaved her upright. She focused her eyes upon Conrad, then drew back in horror as she saw the blood dripping from his gloved hands.

"What have you done to him?!"

"Oh, calm down! He's fine. We haven't even opened him up yet."

"Oh God! Oh, please, oh please, don't hurt him anymore! I'll give you anything; I'll do whatever you want, please! Please!"

Conrad raised his eyebrows, using the back of his wrist to wipe a splatter of blood from his forehead. "Oh yes? Keep talking."

Jenna couldn't stop herself from shuddering, and the involuntary movement seemed to prevent her from being able to think.

"Come on, I'm listening. Rafael has told us where the tapes are. So if you can confirm the location that he has told us, I might just ask Thorn if he is willing to let the both of you walk away."

Jenna tried to concentrate, but something was happening through the glass wall. Conrad caught onto her distraction, and turned to stare into the darkness beyond the plane. He raised his hand for silence, his back stiffening. "Shh!"

"Señor, está todo bien?" The voice came from the guard behind Jenna's chair. She turned her head, scowling spitefully at him.

"Shh!" Conrad hissed, pacing towards the glass. "Bruno, échale un vistazo."

"Si, señor." The guard named Bruno moved out from behind Jenna, holding a pistol as he crept towards a door at the left side of the glass wall.

The other two guards stepped out of the office. Rafael groaned as they left, and strained to make eye contact with Jenna through the crack in the office door. He was bloodied and wet, but still alert.

It initially sounded like a gunshot – a low boom followed by a high pitched whizzing through the humid night air. Fireworks were exploding at the front of the hangar, one of the crackers crashing and exploding against the inside of the metal roof. The guards stared, dumbfounded, as Bruno opened the door and stepped into the front of the hanger, his pistol aiming at the tarmac beyond the plane. Jenna squinted as she tried to see through the glass wall, but there was only darkness.

More booms continued, a high-pitched explosion of light, then the sight of a body lying still beside the plane. Bruno had been shot cleanly through the chest.

Conrad cried out in horror, stumbling backwards before gaining his footing and running for the office. The other two guards separated, one taking position beside the open door at the base of the glass wall, the other moving back towards Jenna. Their eyes were wild as they scanned the front of the hangar, their weapons aiming shakily.

Conrad emerged from the office, one hand grasping a long silver handgun and the other holding a phone to his ear. He began shouting in Spanish, instructing the guard beside the door to move into the front of the hangar. The guard stepped forward hesitantly, peering through the open door and then diving for cover as a round of gunfire sent shards of glass crashing and skittering like crystals across the floor. He scrambled towards Jenna, his eyes closed and his face bloodied with glass fragments. Wailing filled the hangar as he clawed at his eyes, dropping his gun and then slumping forwards, exposing the hole in his shoulder. Within a few moments he was still. His companion was about to run forward, but Conrad motioned for him to stop.

"Stay with her!" Conrad hissed, staring back at Jenna accusingly. "Put the gun to her head."

The guard did as he was told, and Jenna winced as she felt the metal make contact with her scalp.

"Get them here now, Thorn!" Conrad was shouting into his phone. "Two of my men are dead. Shots are coming from the tarmac, I can't see a thing!"

Another gunshot burst through the top of the glass wall, and Conrad ducked as the shards rained down on him. He fired back, taking out three panels at the base of the wall and marching boldly through what was now a gaping hole. "Come on, you assholes!" he screamed madly, firing two more shots as he scampered for cover behind the plane.

An abrupt silence sent a chill across the surface of Jenna's skin – she could feel herself shivering with fear and anticipation, yet found that her fingers would not budge from their grip on the back of the chair. She focused on Conrad, who could be seen reloading behind the wheel of the plane, his gaze set on something in the distance.

Jenna's guard stepped forward, trying to gain a better view through the cracking wall. Another panel collapsed, and the hole was now half the width of the hangar. Jenna turned towards the office, her eyes widening as she saw that Rafael was writhing his way out of the door, his hands and feet bound heavily with tape. He surveyed the scene before fixing his eyes on the nearest panel of broken glass.

The silence continued. Conrad crept stealthily to a position at the plane's rear fairings. He glanced back into the hangar before falling over in shock. Another eruption of fireworks, further away this time, sent multi-coloured sparks spraying across the tarmac. Conrad began firing indiscriminately, the sound of his weapon like a hammer against Jenna's ears. She closed her eyes tightly. When she opened them she saw that the guard beside her had tumbled like a deck of cards, his limbs folding over one another as his gun clattered against the concrete. A bullet had passed through his head, and the contact of his upper body with the ground was marked by a nauseating splash.

Another silence ensued. The smell of burning – either from the fireworks or the gunshots – had nested in the hangar. Conrad was trying to reload beneath the plane, but his hands were trembling and a series of dropped bullets clinked loudly against the floor. His phone began to ring. It dropped out of his grasp, its blue screen creating flashes against the roof.

A cool breeze ruffled Jenna's hair, and a soft creaking alerted her to the back door of the hangar being opened. A man in a navy-blue bomber jacket advanced through the doorway, his grey hair tucked beneath a baseball cap.

"Owen!" Jenna gasped.

Conrad fired two bullets that thundered into the rear of the hangar. Owen jumped sideways, positioning himself out of Conrad's view and easing the blade out of a distinctive pink pocketknife.

Conrad stood up. He was about to stalk towards the back of the hangar when another round of gunshots from the tarmac forced him back to his position beneath the plane. Again, his phone began to ring.

"Are you hurt anywhere?" Owen hissed.

"No," Jenna shook her head.

"Okay, stay still." In a flash he had moved behind her, sliding the pocketknife deftly between her wrists and then her feet. He was about to turn back to the front of the hangar when two booms shook the air. Owen fell forwards, crying out in pain and clutching at his left shoulder.

"Owen!" Jenna screamed. She tore herself away from the chair and leapt over the top of him.

"I'm fine!" he cried. "Get down! Quick!"

The shots continued. Jenna screamed as she saw Conrad kneeling beside the plane, the barrel of his gun like a black hole, sucking at her vision and – for a moment of terror – paralysing her entire body.

The next shot crashed into the wall behind her and she finally ducked, grabbing at Owen's waist and dragging him forcefully behind a workbench. From this position she could see Rafael, still in front of the office, his teeth clenched on a piece of glass that he used to tear at the tape around his wrists. His efforts were clearly futile, and he was staring across at them desperately.

"The knife," Owen wheezed, his face fraught with pain as he pointed to the pink pocketknife at her feet.

Jenna flung the knife across the floor, a little too forcefully, and it clattered into a wooden crate at Rafael's feet. He curled upwards and flipped himself on top of the blade, flinching as the knife cut into his wrist.

Conrad bounded to the other side of the plane, but was unable to see Rafael unless he moved through the hole in the glass wall. He hesitated, taking aim towards Jenna as she helped Owen to his feet.

Owen staggered and then found his balance. He allowed Jenna to guide him behind another workbench. A bullet rocketed into the pipes behind them, but instead of ducking Jenna moved back into the light, scampering towards the rear door and slamming her palm down on the light switch.

Another bullet struck somewhere near the door as the rear of the hangar was cast into darkness. Conrad's elongated shadow now stretched across the floor, ending at the body of one of the guards.

Rapid gunfire resumed from the tarmac and Conrad retreated again beneath the plane.

Rafael had cut through enough of the tape to now tear it apart, his body finally free. Conrad tried to fire into the hangar, cursing as he realised that he was out of ammunition. He scrambled backwards, his eyes wide with terror as he saw Rafael stepping into the light, his hands curled around an iron bar.

"Conrad!" Rafael boomed, tightening his grip on the bar before striding forward, his shoes crunching on the glass and his nostrils flaring.

Conrad let out a short, high-pitched scream, tripping over his feet before leaping onto the wing of the plane. He scrambled for the cockpit door but realised that he was too late.

Rafael swung the bar over the top of the wing, clipping Conrad's ankle as he dived back to the ground. He landed awkwardly, but managed to avoid another blow as he stumbled forwards, his limping turning into a lopsided run.

The silhouette of a third man appeared in front of Conrad on the tarmac and calmly aimed a giant rifle. The man was short, dressed in dark camouflage and wearing a beanie. He ignored Rafael and called out into the hanger, "Owen, you okay?"

"I'm fine," Owen called back.

"Do you want me to shoot this one?"

But before Owen could respond Rafael had struck. It was as though his body was so full of loathing, so knowingly close to vengeance that there was no need to draw it out. The anger churned and frothed through his veins, his muscles tightening; almost seizing with pressure as the iron bar came down.

The sound of Conrad's death caused the tears to finally flow over Jenna's cheeks. She found the light switch and ran to Owen's aid.

"I'm fine," Owen said. "It only clipped me. Were there any other guards?"

"No. Just the three of them. And Conrad. But I think more are coming. Who is that guy out there with the gun?"

"Hired help." They both looked out towards where the man had stood, but he had disappeared.

"Can you stand?"

"I think so, I'm just dazed." He struggled into a sitting position against the workbench and sighed heavily. "You two were damn hard to track."

She let out a short sigh. "That was the idea. How did you find us?"

"The sim card. I've been behind you since you left Honduras, but it wasn't until you turned on your phone that I could see you were in Granada. Come on, we've got to keep moving. Help me up."

Silence was again punctuated by the ringing of Conrad's phone. Rafael picked it up from beneath the plane as the call ended. He staggered towards the back of the hangar and tossed the bloody iron bar to the floor. For the first time Jenna could see the patchwork of bruises and cuts across his body. She wanted to run to him, but his expression was standoffish as he stared at Owen.

"Rafael," Owen acknowledged, nodding his head towards him, "I'm –"

"I know who you are," Rafael nodded back, relaxing his shoulders. Again the phone rang and he held it up, showing the caller's name: "Joseph Thorn."

Owen stared. His face was suddenly awash with anger. He reached out, taking the phone and answering the call.

"Hello?" came the voice. Owen turned on the loudspeaker.

"Hello, Conrad, are you there?"

"Hello," Owen answered, his voice husky.

"Conrad, is that you? What's going on? Talk to me."

"Tell me, Joe," Owen said slowly, his voice low and threatening, "what does one do with a dog that has rabies?"

The call abruptly ended.

Owen slowly looked up at Jenna and Rafael with a determined grimace. "Let's go. We'll take that van parked outside."

"No we won't," Rafael shook his head. "Follow me. You can strap your shoulder on the plane."

Chapter Forty-Eight

Casco Viejo, Panama City.
December 20th, 1989, 4:20am.

The soldier readjusted his grip, flipping Owen's face into the cobble-stones and forcing his eyes to tightly shut. His brain seemed to be bouncing inside an oversized skull, and each bump against the laneway clamped his teeth down on his tongue. His neck muscles strained as they tried to keep his head from bouncing. He soon gave up, letting his mouth squash into the ground. The taste of gravel mixed with grass, dead banana leaves and soil. Gravel arrived again, followed by mud and then bitumen. Blood flowed over his lips and eyebrows as the soldier tossed him into the gutter, allowing his eyes to finally open.

Eva whined in pain as she was dumped beside him. Her pupils dilated scarily as they made contact with his.

The thick night air was filled with the choking smell of gunpowder, and the bitumen vibrated with the sound of nearby explosions. American soldiers were running back and forth, their shadows dancing like insects over Owen's half-closed eyes. The sound of a diesel engine made him turn, and he winced in panic as the rear of Thorn's Hummer slowly rumbled backwards, the reverse lights beaming aggressively.

"Steady!" One of the soldiers cried, thumping his hand against the back of the vehicle as the exhaust pipe moved over the top of Owen's head. "That'll do, Thorn!"

Thorn stepped out of the vehicle, slamming the door and instructing the lingering soldiers to move across the street. "Un-ass!" he yelled. "Move everything out of the way!" He glanced momentarily at Owen and Eva, his upper lip curling.

Between the Hummer's wheels Owen could see further down the street. Smoke swirled in ghostly strings from the gutters, rising up towards the firelight that radiated from the roof of the brothel. A sheet of tin roofing bowed inwards, sending a gush of sparks back down towards the street. Owen narrowed his eyes, his throat swelling in fear as a dark American tank trammed slowly around the intersection beyond the brothel.

"Hat up!" Thorn cried, leaping away from the front of the Hummer. "Get back you fools!" He ran forward towards the tank, waving his arms and pointing towards the burning building.

"Are you okay?" Owen asked hoarsely, his eyes flicking back to Eva.

She closed her eyes, her tongue struggling to wet her mouth with saliva.

There was a flash of innocence and helplessness in her expression that gave Owen a sudden verve. He curled his chest upwards, his wrists cutting into the cable ties as his fingers steadied themselves on the concrete gutter. The soldiers had moved out of view to the other side of the street, now spectators to the rumbling of the tank across the cobblestones.

Owen eased himself into a position against the Hummer's rear wheel, his eyes blinking repeatedly as he stared in the opposite direction. He could make out the buildings at the end of the headland, and saw that the roof of the Union Club was on fire. Two helicopters hovered over the flames, their spotlights scanning the streets below as they slowly moved towards the distant roof of the Presidential Palace.

"My knife," Eva whispered to Owen. "It's in my left pocket."

Owen gulped, staring back between the wheels of the Hummer. The legs of the soldiers were visible across the street, their feet still pointing in the direction of the tank.

"Come on!" Thorn was shouting into his radio as he pointed at the brothel. "Let it blow!"

Owen shuffled, his backside wedging between Eva's legs. His hands pushed against her thigh, and his heart vibrated through his ribcage as he tried to lift it higher.

"Keep coming back," Eva urged. "Higher." She leaned forward, her chin resting between his shoulder and neck as his elbows splayed outwards and his hands moved into her pocket.

"Okay, can you feel it?" she asked tautly.

The world seemed to heave upwards as the tank fired, bouncing cobbles across the street like exploding popcorn. What was left of the brothel's roof imploded, and the adjacent buildings all lurched sideways.

Eva pulled back in shock and Owen's hands were torn free. A sudden pulse of fear subsided as he heard the knife rattle onto the cobblestones.

"Just behind your hands," Eva whispered excitedly. "That's it, you've got it."

Owen lifted the pink pocketknife upwards and pulled the blade open. He shuffled over the top of her leg and moved alongside her.

"What are you doing?" Eva hissed.

"You first," he responded, closing his eyes in concentration as he traced the blade down her wrists and into the cable ties. He pushed downwards forcefully, but the plastic held strong.

"Is it working? Is it cutting?"

The tank fired again, blowing what remained of the front of the building into sparkling splinters. One of the soldiers laughed, lifting his radio to his mouth. He was about to speak when an onslaught of gunfire erupted from further down the street. A wide troop carrier roared into view, and a band of Machos formed a line across the intersection behind the tank. Automatic gunfire rattled through the Hummer and Thorn dived into the gutter, shouting desperately into his radio.

Owen dropped the knife and cried out in angst as he tried to pick it back up.

"Leave it," Eva wheezed, "I've got it."

The tank reversed backwards, blocking the road as its turret rotated towards the Machos. Three of the American soldiers moved into the middle of the street, aiming their rifles and firing either side of the tank. A fourth soldier hesitated. He cried out in horror as one his comrades was cut down beside him. The tank rocked backwards as it was struck with a grenade, then fired towards the troop carrier. The two Machos atop the vehicle were thrown into the air, their bodies engulfed in flames.

Owen closed his eyes tightly, imagining that the scene was just a dream. His nerves relaxed, and he felt a numbness spreading across his body.

Thorn moved back into the street, crouching on one knee and skilfully taking out the remaining Machos on foot. He shouted into his radio as the other soldiers surrounded their fallen comrade.

"Help me!" the soldier cried, clutching at his leg.

The two helicopters had left their position above the Presidential Palace. They flew low overhead, firing at a target beyond the Macho's burning troop carrier. Thorn ducked shakily as they passed, then clambered over to his men. "Where's he hit?" he cried.

"In the thigh. He's losing blood fast."

Thorn again shouted into his radio, staring back up into the sky. A crackled response came through, and he glanced back at the soldiers grimly. "They can't land a bird here. Wheeler and Phelps, get him to the plaza. Tell them I'm black on ammo as well."

"Roger."

"Sanchez, stay here. We'll deal with these two."

Sanchez nodded, his young face staring back at Owen and Eva nervously. "What are we going to do with them?"

Thorn pulled the empty ammunition straps off his shoulders, dropping them into the gutter and cracking his neck. "We're going to teach this traitor a lesson in loyalty."

Owen scoffed. "Sanchez: this man just killed an innocent mother and her child. You saw what happened in that –"

Owen's head was thrown backwards as the side of Thorn's boot swiped against his jaw. "You killed them both Owen, and you've corrupted my fiancé with your lies."

"Ha!" Owen cried before he was struck again.

"Get off him!" Eva screamed.

Thorn snorted like a caged horse, turning to Eva. "Oh, you're trying to protect him now? You believe this liar, do you? The only reason you're still alive is because of my child, and I'll be damned if –"

"Idiota!" Eva spat. "Eres un tonto!"

Thorn tilted his head to the side in confusion.

"You don't see it, do you? I knew that you wouldn't kill me if I was pregnant." She laughed caustically, shaking her head. "You're too proud. That's why I made it up."

Thorn jolted backwards, his face twisting into a stunned scowl. "What did you say?"

"I made it up, Joe," she laughed madly. "I'm not pregnant, and I never have been!"

Thorn stared.

"Vamos!" Eva grinned wretchedly. "Go ahead, hit me! Hit an innocent civilian in front of this soldier, go on!"

Thorn's face flushed with a bright red rage. "You are not innocent!" he roared. His fist came down towards her face but she dodged sideways. His knuckles cracked against the wall behind and caused him to topple over her. The pressure of his body on hers helped break through the last cable tie, and her wrists flung outwards from beneath her. She pushed at Thorn's arms as he tried to strangle her, squirming out from beneath him and flipping adroitly to her feet.

"Bitch!" Thorn roared, grabbing at her ankles. "You lying whore!"

"Run!" Owen screamed to Eva. "Go, now!"

Eva stalled, dodging another of Thorn's punches and trying to clamber back.

"Leave me!" Owen cried. "Just run!"

Eva sidestepped again, her face filled with hesitation as she jumped backwards into the middle of the intersection.

"Shoot her!" Thorn cried back at Sanchez. "Damn it lieutenant, shoot her!"

Sanchez remained still, his face rigid. He glanced down at Owen and then looked up again, stamping his feet with resolve and pulling his rifle closer into his chest.

"I'll have you for this, Sanchez!" Thorn turned and began chasing after Eva. His fingers clenched into fists as he ran, his lips drawn back. His gait was lopsided, as though his anger was so great that it took away his coordination.

Owen shuffled backwards, grasping the pocketknife and cutting desperately into his cable ties.

"Here," Sanchez said nervously, shuffling over to Owen. "Let me give you a hand."

Chapter Forty-Nine

Caribbean Sea, Costa Rica.
Present day.

The shadow of the plane swept towards the Costa Rican coastline, fracturing against the rocky beaches and coalescing once more over the dark blue ripples of the Caribbean Sea. Purple-grey clouds bobbed like buoys out to the horizon, and the plane shuddered as it pushed between them and into the sunlight above.

Rafael's pain and exhaustion was obvious, but he maintained his concentration, his hand gripped tightly over the yoke as he guided the plane steadily out of the turbulence. He pushed back his headset, turning around and making eye contact with Jenna as she peeled her cheek from the window. She smiled. Beside her, Owen had locked his teeth around the collar of his shirt, his eyes closed as he tried to ignore the pain in his shoulder.

"The tunnel," Rafael shouted, "it goes under the headland. It snakes around, under a few houses, a few streets. I remember trap doors in the cellars, at the bottom of maybe three houses. But the houses, they're gone now, blown up. Two of 'em got built again, and the entry to the tunnels under got cemented up. I'm thinkin' the only entrance now is a drain. It's next to the Club de Clases y Tropas, the old Union Club. You can see the entrance only at low tide."

Owen opened his eyes. "How wide is it? How easy would it be for us to get down there?"

"Jenna will fit, fo' sure. Don't know 'bout you and me."

Owen turned to Jenna, his face sombre.

"I'll do it," she said confidently. "Just as long as there aren't any rats."

Rafael laughed painfully. "Dunno 'bout that."

The plane continued to float across the mat of cloud, its gaps revealing a stormy horizon over the ocean. The darkness seemed to spread like a plague through the clouds as they flew further east, and the plane struck turbulence once again as they passed into Panama.

Owen stared tensely down at the mountains, his fingers tapping nervously as if recognising memories that he didn't want to recall. He turned, his green eyes meeting with Jenna's and sending a strange jolt through her stomach. He reached into his jacket and removed the pink pocketknife, handing it over the seat to her.

Jenna smiled, confused. "Thanks. But –"

"It was your mother's," he said.

She could feel the prickle of tears, but her interest in the knife kept them suppressed. She turned it over, examining the scratches and dents in its pink resin handle. She was about to question why he had the knife – and had kept it for so many years – but suddenly she smiled.

Rafael's voice was distinctively altered as he spoke into his microphone, and all that Jenna could catch from the fast flow of Spanish was a combination of numbers.

"Chooh! They've gone and blocked the airstrips," Rafael shouted as he pulled away his headset. "This will not be a friendly landing!"

The plane lifted over a heavily forested hill, providing the first view of Panama City. Rafael's emotions lifted away as he locked himself in concentration, guiding the plane anxiously down towards the Canal. His eyes flicked back and forth over the skyline before fixing determinedly on a strip of green north of the city.

Rain pelted against the windows. Jenna felt herself shivering from both fear and cold. She closed her eyes tightly, gripping onto the sides of her seat.

The plane swooped over another hill and then descended sharply.

"A golf course?!" Owen shouted disbelievingly.

"No arguing, just chill!"

The plane narrowly missed a pine tree as it tilted towards the longest fairway, the windscreen a wall of water.

A loud pounding of rubber on wet grass sent jets of water into the bottom of the fuselage. Jenna forced her eyes open and screamed as they bounced clean over the top of a bunker. The end of the fairway rapidly approached, and Owen cried out as the propeller shattered through a tall wire fence. The plane bounced through the fence, claws of wire tearing at the windows and grappling onto the landing gear.

Jenna's screaming continued as the last of the plane's momentum was absorbed by a vast reedy swamp. The landing gear gurgled into the mud, and the wings groaned as they released the remains of the straining fence.

"Pull down on the door!" Rafael cried, ripping off his lap belt and cringing in pain.

Jenna groaned as she forced the door open, her face speckling with rain. She began to shuffle through the gap when Rafael pointed frantically. "Not here, too deep. Go up the end of the wing!"

Owen was next to clamber outside, and took hold of Jenna's hand as he stepped onto the right wing. She held him steady as they shuffled forwards. He let go of her hand, leaping over a ball of wire and into the reeds. He sunk to knees, losing balance and splashing into the mud.

"Go!" Rafael cried to Jenna.

She hesitated, her legs quivering before she launched over the wire and into reeds. She spun sideways, rolling into the base of a rotting cabbage palm. Owen looked up and then clambered away as Rafael crashed into the mud beside him.

A shrill siren bounced between the rain droplets, its source a mystery until they had clambered further out of the swamp. Blue and red flashes lit up the pine trees at the end of the fairway, and Owen wiped the mud from his face fearfully.

"Come on," Rafael hissed, pushing forwards into the swamp. Jenna felt her stomach tighten as he stumbled painfully, and she sympathetically linked her fingers into his.

"I'm good," Rafael protested.

"No, you're not."

The sound of a passing truck broke through the sirens. Owen powered eagerly ahead, flattening a path through the reeds and into a thicket of tall pine trees. He kicked the mud off his boots before parting a gap in the hanging branches.

A small pickup truck roared past, slowing across a wooden bridge and then turning into the entrance to an orchard. Rolling green paddocks continued into the distance, ending in the hazy outline of an industrial estate.

Two sedans came from the other direction, splashing puddles of water into the trees.

"They aren't going to stop for us," Owen declared.

Jenna huffed, letting go of Rafael's hand and stomping into the open.

Barely a minute passed before a brown Dodge pickup truck rumbled off the road and grunted to a stop beside her.

The driver was an elderly Panamanian man, his straggly grey hair splaying out of a faded cap. He wound down his window, his bushy eyebrows raised expectedly. "Qué necesitas que te lleve?" His eyes moved over her slowly, and his yellowed teeth made her cringe.

"Si. Por favor... Into the city. But I have two friends. Do you speak English?"

He turned his head to the side, indicating that he knew enough English to understand. "Dinero?" he asked. "You have money?"

"Owen!" Jenna shouted. "We need money!"

Owen hurried into the open. "Here," he said, pulling out his wallet and removing a handful of American notes. "Here you go. Can you take us to Casco Viejo?"

The driver stared at the notes in awe. He suddenly grinned and then nodded.

Owen pulled down the tailgate and dodged the excited licking of a young German Shepherd. He painfully shifted a crate of watermelons and made a hiding place underneath a bulging hessian bag.

Jenna joined Rafael at the back of the truck, wrapping her hands around his waist and helping Owen to pull him upwards. His legs smeared a fresh streak of blood over the tailgate, and he groaned as Owen flipped him over and steadied him against a crate.

The cabin had the smell of the old man's oilskin jacket, and the floor beneath the passenger seat was a jumble of wrenches, spanners and rags stained with grease. The man smiled at her curiously as he wound up his window and pulled the truck back onto the highway.

Jenna gasped as she saw a mass of police cars blocking the intersection ahead. Two officers waved through a line of sedans and then motioned for the pickup truck to pull over.

The driver turned to Jenna with a disapproving frown.

Jenna flipped down the sun visor, pulling out her hair and fluffing it in the scratched mirror. "Thank you, sir. Really, thank you."

He scoffed, his tongue running along the front of his teeth.

Two officers ran in front of the truck, one of them glancing into the back while the other motioned for the old man to wind down his window.

"Si?" he said casually. "Qué es lo que quieres?"

The officer responded with a string of Spanish, staring past the old man at Jenna. She raised her eyebrows impatiently then continued ruffling her hair in the mirror.

The driver sifted through his jacket pockets and the officer watched cautiously. Two American notes were passed swiftly through the open window and the officer nodded at the driver with a smile. He moved onto the car behind, calling for his companion to stop the cars coming in the other direction.

Jenna let out a relieved gasp as they accelerated. She glanced through the window into the back of the truck, spotting Owen's grey hair poking out from beneath one of the hessian bags.

The Panama City skyline drifted in and out of the rain. Finally the skyscrapers came into full view, and Jenna gaped at the size of the city. A rapping on the rear window made her turn.

Owen looked like a drowned rat, and he pushed the dog away as he pointed to the right.

"Could you please turn right up here?" Jenna asked.

The driver nodded.

Owen continued directing them through the glass, and was soon joined by Rafael. His face was a pale blue-grey, the skin around his eyes sallow and dark.

The truck rolled slowly onto a narrow cobblestone street lined with quaint three-storey Spanish townhouses. Jenna pressed her forehead against the window as she stared up into the layers of balconies, then swallowed cautiously as they stopped before the entrance to a modern Italian restaurant. Two black Mercedes were parked out the front, and a man in a black trench coat stared suspiciously at the truck.

Rafael and Owen ducked below the crates, and the dog barked aggressively at the man. A hand moved up to the back window and pointed towards the next side street.

"Keep going," Jenna instructed, trying to hide her face from the man. "Turn right up ahead."

The truck grumbled to the next corner, revealing a construction site against the rocky shores of the ocean. The skeleton of a once majestic building rose from the layers of scaffolding, and two men in yellow helmets and raincoats allowed the truck to squeeze through to a view of the water.

"This is it!" Rafael shouted over the sound of the diesel engine.

Jenna turned to the old man, a sudden thought creasing her forehead. "Um, sir, I don't suppose you have a torch?"

His face crinkled and he pointed behind the seat. "Torch is there. Money?"

"Oh, thank you. Uh – Owen, more money please!" She pulled open her door and reached behind the seat, her fingers eventually bumping into the handle of a dusty torch.

Owen shuffled around her and passed more notes to the driver. They exchanged a short conversation in Spanish before the truck reversed away.

Rafael hurried around the scaffolding, stopping suddenly as he took in the view of the bay. He scanned the street behind and then led the way down a flight of crumbling concrete steps. He ran his hand along the rusted railing and then cringed painfully as his feet stumbled at the bottom.

Jenna jumped down the steps and steadied him. "Are you okay?"

He ignored her, his eyes spying a vast bougainvillea creeping over a crumbling wall at the base of the old Union Club. He shuffled forward in front of the bush, bending to his knees and pulling back the thorny stems. Owen joined him, and stepped back grimly as the rusted entrance of a drain was exposed.

Jenna's chest pounded as she saw the cobwebs spread across the corroded grill. The space was barely two feet wide, and the gaping black hole seemed to be sucking at her churning stomach.

Owen wedged a stick between the grill and levered it cleanly from the sandy bricks. It toppled loudly onto the cement path, fragments of rust quickly washing into a dark brown flow.

"I can probably fit," Owen breathed, pushing his head and shoulders towards the hole.

"No," Jenna argued. "I'll do it."

Rafael looked up at her with a pained frown. "You sure?"

She nodded, her nose twitching nervously. She held up the torch, blinking away the beads of rain flowing down her forehead.

Owen was shaking his head anxiously. He leaned against the wall and ran a hand through his wet hair, glancing up at the road above. "I really don't feel good about this."

"She was my mother," Jenna responded matter-of-factly, sliding the phone from her pocket. "I've come this far, and I'm not going to fail. Now, this phone still has batteries. If there are any problems, I'll call you."

Owen pursed his lips, continuing to scan the area for anyone watching. "Rafael, how much did you let them know? Do they know about this entrance?"

Rafael shook his head. "All I told them was the tapes are in a tunnel under Casco Viejo, beneath where I used to live. They knew where I was talking about, but they don't know how to get down there. And they don't know exactly where the tapes are kept."

"And exactly where are they?"

Rafael tore a stick from the bougainvillea and began to draw a map on the sandy path. "Only one way. Comes out here, it's a big drain. You can stand up, walk around and everything. Over here on the right, there's a whole row of cellar doors. Just keep goin' straight, and maybe ten steps before the end of the tunnel you see a trap door – it goes up into the basement of that restaurant, where we stopped at just before. Go left at the trap door, then there's a culvert, wide enough for a kid. Just inside it, up on the left there should be this loose brick. It's red, but all the other ones are black. Behind the brick – that's where my mother got me to put all her money and jewellery. I checked there a few years back, those tapes were still inside. No reason why they won't still be there, I was the only one who knew 'bout this place."

Jenna closed her eyes as she envisaged the route.

"Got it?"

She pulled the torch into her chest and took a deep breath. "Got it."

Chapter Fifty

Casco Viejo, Panama City.
December 20ᵗʰ, 1989, 5:35am.

Sanchez threw his water bottle to Owen as he clambered to his feet. He caught it gratefully, shouting out his thanks as he began running eastwards down Avenida A. The water splashed through his mouth and over his face, giving his strides an extra burst of energy as he rounded the corner into another deserted avenue. The streetlights passed by in a blur, and the sound of gunfire faded into the distance. He glanced desperately into each passing alleyway, his running reducing to a jog as he arrived at the burning Union Club.

To the right the French embassy was shrouded in shadow, and cars were piled into a roadblock. He turned to the left, jogging into the light of the burning club and gaping at the destruction.

"Eva!" he cried, his pace quickening as he passed into the heat of the flames. "Eva!"

The sky beyond the club appeared to be soaking up the flames, but the light was instead coming from the beginnings of a sunrise, the fiery light shimmering off a calm Pacific Ocean. Sand and shells stretched outwards from the club, flowing over a rippled outcrop of mudstone and into the lapping water. Owen glanced briefly at the view, and was about to turn around when a shrill scream erupted from behind the flames.

Two silhouettes burst onto the sand. Owen gasped, leaping over a low barrier and arming himself with a brick from a pile of rubble.

Thorn's arm reached out, grabbing at Eva's top as she sidestepped to the right. He failed to keep hold of her, skidding across the sand and shouting. His boots gripped onto the rocks, swivelling him back to his feet. Eva had stumbled onwards towards the ocean, and was about to leap over a rock pool when her shoes slipped on the wet surface. She fell forwards, her chest crashing into layers of seaweed as her feet splashed into the water.

"Ha!" Thorn cried, grabbing her legs and flipping her over.

Eva spluttered with terror, her eyes flickering like a broken machine as Thorn gripped his hands around her neck.

A wave of power had swept up through Owen's legs, pulsing through his core as he launched himself forward. The scene seemed to move in slow motion as he brought the brick downwards, but he was too late.

Thorn dodged the blow, backhanding Owen into the rocks like swatting away a fly. "You!" he roared, standing up and clenching his fists.

Owen scrambled to his feet, picking up the brick again and using it almost clumsily to block Thorn's punch. The brick exploded over Thorn's right fist and he cried out in shock. His eyes popped with pain as he grabbed at what was clearly a broken wrist.

Owen took the opportunity to land a punch, his fist crashing into a solid iron jaw. The pain from his knuckles hung somewhere above, and he continued to fight, swiping away Thorn's attempted block and connecting with his cheek.

Thorn bared his teeth, his eyes burning as he used his left hand to push Owen back. "Go home, Owen!" he spat. "You're done here. You've got no tapes, no evidence. It's just your word against mine."

Owen scoffed, his face glowing in the light of the sunrise. "Your word against *ours*."

"Ha!" Thorn laughed, blood running down his chin. "Not when I'm done with her." He pretended to stagger, waiting for Owen's punch before pivoting on his heel and striking Owen's chin with his left fist.

Owen's head was thrown back with a spray of sweat, his jaw rattling loudly. He stumbled backwards, gasping as Thorn charged forward like a bull. Owen was too slow to move out of the way, and buckled in pain as Thorn's head crashed into his stomach. The air was knocked clear of his lungs, escaping in an agonising cry as Thorn tossed him like a sandbag into the rocks.

"Give up!" Thorn cried, wincing again as he clutched at his broken wrist. He turned back to Eva and puffed out his chest. She tried to crawl backwards, and cried out as he lunged at her.

Owen ignored the blood dripping from his forearms, jumping back to his feet and ripping at Thorn's shoulders. His face was struck with Thorn's elbow but he continued to wrestle, grappling him around the neck and pulling him away from Eva.

"That's it!" Thorn roared, swiping out with a backhand jab that failed to make contact.

Owen again struck him in the jaw, stepping back and then landing a fist in his eye. Thorn staggered backwards, wiping blood from his cheek and swallowing in surprise.

Owen marched forwards confidently, his right arm towering above his body and preparing to come down with furious force. Thorn threw up his forearms to block the punch but failed to see that it was a bluff; the force of Owen's body was instead heaved into his left arm. His fist ripped upwards, colliding with the bridge of Thorn's nose and dropping him to his knees.

Owen pulled back, flicking the blood from his fists and tensing his shoulders. He swayed once again, leading with his left arm as he jabbed continuously. His eyes were wide with concentration, and he waited patiently for Thorn to push forward. But the retaliation never came, and Thorn's arms floundered hopelessly. Owen gripped him around the neck, forcing his face upwards and into the brassy sunlight. His eyes were swollen over, and bright red blood cascaded over his jaw.

"I always envied you," Owen whispered, pulling him further upwards by his neck. "But not anymore. You're nothing but a fraud, a liar and a murderer."

Thorn tried to speak, but the sounds became a gurgle. He dropped back to his knees, his head leaning. For several seconds he hung motionless, his eyes flickering before he slumped, unconscious, into the sand.

Eva staggered to her feet. Tears rolled down her chin as the warm morning air expanded into her lungs. Her eyes blinked slowly as they met with Owen's.

Sunlight had swept across the rocks, coalescing with the flames that curled at the remains of the Union Club. Hidden beneath a charred archway, a grubby boy peered outwards. He shuffled away from the heat, pressing his body against a small bougainvillea. He squinted, recognising Eva and Owen, then vanished into the smoke.

Chapter Fifty-One

Casco Viejo, Panama City.
Present day.

The slime was cold, its stringy brown fibres licking over Jenna's stomach and forearms and dripping into thick icy fingers over the back of her neck. Her lungs refused to hold onto the putrid air, jerking out wet coughs that echoed through the blackness. The torchlight fell upon a moving shape, and she moaned in horror as a large water rat scurried casually towards her. It stopped barely a metre ahead, rising onto its hind legs and sniffing at her curiously.

"Go away!" Jenna coughed. "Please, go away!"

The rat appeared to shrug, falling back on all fours and then scurrying further down the drain.

Jenna snivelled softly, closing her eyes and continuing to crawl. A grilled culvert ahead spewed out a gush of black water, and it flowed gently down the drain, running beneath Jenna's torso and soaking into her skin. She sneezed, her shuddering body throwing the slime off her neck and allowing it to slide slowly down her front.

The drain began to slope downwards, and the slush that had ploughed against Jenna's chest spread outwards to the walls of the drain, removing all friction as she tried to prevent herself from sliding. Her efforts were in vain, and she drifted steadily around a sharp corner and then tumbled out into an open space. The torch slipped out of her grasp and splashed into a puddle of sludge, its dim light illuminating a wide, brick-lined tunnel. She stood up slowly, her spine crackling.

Just as Rafael had described, numerous tunnels and inlets branched off to the right. Some were blocked with rusted iron bars, while others were filled with crumbled bricks and cement. The torchlight swept over broken glass bottles, blackened leaf litter and what appeared to be dog bones. Jenna held back the urge to vomit, keeping the torchlight low and easing her sandals across the tacky mud.

A dim glow illuminated the end of the tunnel ahead, and Jenna approached cautiously as she saw a wide metallic stepladder beneath an open trap door. She aimed the torchlight to her feet and shuffled forwards, peering hesitantly up into the hole. A single light bulb flickered against the walls of what appeared to be a wine cellar. Her view was restricted, and she breathed unsteadily as she debated whether or not to walk around the ladder.

A distant gurgling came from the tunnel behind, and Jenna crouched, pressing her back against the slimy brick wall and edging away from the light of the trap door. The gurgling became louder, followed by heavy breathing from the direction she had come. She turned off her torch and froze, her eyes wide as a thin light appeared at the end of the tunnel. Footsteps moved warily through the sludge, and the dark outline of a man took form. The light was coming from a phone, which swept steadily across the floor. Jenna's legs began to quake in fear, and she was about to run for the trap door when the man's face became visible.

"Owen!" she hissed. "What are you doing?"

"We were getting suspicious stares," he whispered back, brushing the slime off his front. "And besides, I wouldn't be able to forgive myself if something happened to you down here."

She allowed herself to smile, knowing that it was too dark for him to see her expression. "What about Rafael? Is he okay?"

"He's hiding in the construction site, he's fine."

"Okay, good."

"What's that trap door? Have you been up there?"

"No. I think it's the one that goes into the bottom of that restaurant Rafael was talking about."

"I don't like it. Is there any way that we can get around it without going underneath?"

"Only if we squeeze around that step ladder. And we don't have another choice, because we've got to get to the culvert on the other side."

"Hmm."

Jenna rose to her feet, leading the way silently towards the light. She stooped, staring once more into the cellar and making out an open steel ingress. She edged closer, her body leaving the shadows and entering the sector of light.

Owen stayed behind, his eyes wide. He peered forward at the steel ingress and gasped. "I know that door."

"Huh?"

"Keep going." He motioned for her to continue past the stepladder. She nodded, creeping on all fours and then flattening her body against the wall.

The stepladder rocked slightly as she squeezed past, her frightened face directly beneath the light. The cellar appeared empty, except for a rack of cardboard boxes. She exhaled with relief as she shuffled onwards into the darkness, fumbling with her torch until it exposed a narrow culvert on the left. Peering over her shoulder she ran her hand across a wall of loose bricks. She lifted the torch up steadily, her eyes flicking back and forth as she searched.

Something moved in the tunnel behind her and she clenched her teeth, peering back towards Owen. He hadn't moved, and continued to crouch below the cellar. She turned again to the bricks, her eyes widening as she found what she was looking for.

The brick scraped loudly as she pulled at its rounded edges, and her hands shook uncontrollably as it pulled free. She placed it on the ground and pulled up the torch, continuing to shake as the light passed over a collection of gold jewellery and a plastic box behind. She edged the jewellery aside and carefully wedged the box out of the hole, glancing back towards Owen as her fingers pried off the lid. The torchlight flickered, then bounced excitedly over five curious cassette tapes. She pulled one out, her eyes narrowed.

"What do you see?" Owen asked excitedly.

"I'm confused," Jenna responded, barely loud enough for Owen to hear. "This looks like a music tape. I think I recognise the singer."

It began with a vibration – something or someone moving in the room above. Jenna held her breath, pulling out of the culvert and gasping as she saw Owen creeping backwards, his arms tense as he searched the ground for a weapon.

A loud rattle of metal on brick echoed through the tunnel. A moment of silence followed before a high-pitched gushing of gas. Owen flinched, glancing at the metal tube rolling past him and crying out in horror.

Smoke hissed through the tunnel, forming a dark grey cloud that enveloped Owen's silhouette. He tried to kick the metal cylinder back down the tunnel but he floundered, keeling over and coughing.

"Owen!" Jenna cried, scrambling towards the ladder and tripping over her torch. She pulled the tapes close to her chest as she squeezed around the stepladder, but her lungs erupted in protest as she tried to clamber onwards. She fell to the floor, her free hand flailing against the base of the ladder.

"Get up!" came a shout.

She turned her face upwards, her body encircled with smoke. Her fingers wrapped automatically around the first metallic step, and she screamed as someone jumped nimbly over the top of her and into the tunnel. Owen let out a vehement wail, his fists trying to fight back as he was thrown into the wall beside the ladder.

Jenna groaned, her body numb as she slowly pulled her head up to the light. Her left hand gripped the wooden frame of the trapdoor, and she imagined herself screaming as a man's grip heaved her through the hole. She tried to flip herself onto her stomach, squeezing the tapes against her chest, but her left arm was snapped backwards. Her eyes glimpsed an empty cellar, and two Latino men flanking the closed steel ingress. They were dressed in tight black tee shirts, their bearded faces devoid of expression. Another man moved behind her, helping to drag Owen's writing body upwards.

"Search him!" ordered a gravelly voice. "Make sure he isn't wearing a wire!"

The trapdoor was kicked shut, and the last of the smoke swept upwards into the corners of the cellar like ink swirling in water. Two men ripped at Owen's shirt, tearing the buttons off before prying his phone out of his pants. The phone was passed to a Caucasian man with glasses who skilfully ripped off the cover and removed the sim card.

Jenna let out a coughing scream, thrashing against the man's grip as he pinned her against the cold bricks. She could feel the plastic box loosening from her grip, and she swiped out her fingernails, missing his face as the man pulled the box free.

He was wearing a tan blazer and a white business shirt pulled tightly over a broad barrel chest. His trousers glistened with the slime of Jenna's legs, and he wiped disdainfully at the mud smeared across his white Rolex. He pulled back from her, his spiked white hair shining in the light of the single dusty bulb as he held up the plastic box. His face slowly came into focus. Jenna screamed.

"You bastard!" Owen wheezed, his naked chest slamming against the floor as a man's boot dug into his back.

Joseph Thorn smiled, tossing the box playfully between his fingertips. He stared for a moment at Owen, his smile fading, then turned his attention to Jenna. "Nothing ever gets done unless you do it yourself, does it?"

She launched herself at him, her fingers clawing at the box, but she was thrown back into the corner. One of the men held her down and pressed the cold barrel of a pistol against the side of her head. She could feel him frisking her, and winced as her phone was removed from her back pocket.

"So violent!" Thorn said with mock surprise. "So passionate!"

She wanted to erupt, to hurl abuse and swipe at the pistol. But instead she remained motionless, her eyes unblinking as they bore steadily into his.

"Certainly your mothers' daughter, aren't you? And I hear you've also inherited her talent for using men. So tell me, were you planning to abandon your new beau once this was over, just like your mother abandoned your father?"

Jenna's shoulders relaxed, and she glared at him with haunting eyes.

"She didn't tell you that bit, did she? Didn't tell you how she left him, that it broke him, and that after everything that happened, I was the one who got him back on his feet again?"

Owen's face had turned pink, tears welling in his eyes as his chin pressed painfully into the bricks. "Jenna," he wheezed, tears now tumbling down his cheeks. "I wanted to tell you earlier, but I –"

Thorn's face was suddenly awash with amusement. He bent down, cocking his head to the side melodramatically as he grinned at Owen. "What's this? You haven't told her, have you?"

"He didn't need to tell me," Jenna said boldly, closing her eyes and then nodding affirmatively at her father. "I already figured it out."

Owen's body shook, his face crumpling as he sobbed. The emotion was suddenly overcome with rage, and he kicked frantically at his captor, growling savagely as he tried to break free.

"How touching," Thorn mocked, turning back to Jenna. "But he never learns, does he?" He held up the box once more, his eyes narrowed as he pried off the lid and glanced inside. "Funny, isn't it? To think that such a small package started a war." He narrowed his eyes, nodding to himself with feigned contentment. "And to think that without it, this man will come back begging for my help. Again, he will realise that I'm the only one who can get him out of jail. But you, Jenna, you're too much like your mother. You worry me."

"Let her go," Owen wheezed. "She's no threat to you. Please, burn the tapes, do whatever you want with me, just let her go."

"Burn them, you say?" Thorn laughed heartedly. He reached into his blazer, removing a cigarette lighter and holding it beneath the plastic box.

"No!" Jenna screamed, thumping against her captor. "No!"

Thorn clenched his jaw, raising his eyebrows in mock consideration. He ignited the lighter, glaring at her as the bottom of the box turned black.

Jenna suddenly relaxed, her eyes fixed into Owen's.

The box began to melt, a single flame licking over its blackening surface. Thorn let it drop, grinning as it spun like orange silk into a bright ball of flame.

Jenna felt herself writhing free, her body thrashing before something crashed into the back of her head.

Chapter Fifty-Two

She moved to the side of the bed, her smile genial as she studied Jenna's sleeping face. Her fingers traced over the purple bruising, her other hand moving downwards to pull the crisp floral sheets upwards. Jenna stirred, her nose twitching as the familiar smell of her mother's thyme incense dispersed through the room. She rolled onto her side, reaching out her hand and slowly opening her eyes.

No one was there.

The back of her head was throbbing, and her limbs were uncomfortably numb. She blinked at the bright taupe walls, her face scrunching as he stared through the open bedroom door and into an empty hallway. She moaned in confusion, her swollen head floating like a balloon as she stared up at the intricate cornices and chandeliers that decorated the ceiling.

Lacy peach curtains flapped gently against an open sliding door, and a jasmine vine rustled within the white iron railing of a balcony. She rubbed at her eyes, sitting up and blinking as she took in the view.

A Romanesque water fountain sprouted proudly from a pond of lilies, a gentle morning breeze blowing the mist over a white pebble driveway. Two giant bronze gates framed a view of Panama City, its skyscrapers speckled with the glare of a glinting bay.

She shifted her feet out from beneath the sheets, dangling her legs over the side of the bed and examining the strange bruises crisscrossing her wrists. Her attention turned to the unfamiliar white nightdress, her eyes closing in frustration as she struggled to revive her memory. Fleeting images of boats, palm trees and motorbikes spun together in disarray, imagination indistinguishable from reality. She rubbed at her temples; her mind filled with the image of a distinctive cassette tape. It was white, with the face of a bearded singer imprinted on the side.

Her fingertips rubbed indignantly at the silky fabric, and she continued to blink as she glanced at the wall above the wooden headboard. Her eyes came into focus, and she doubled back in surprise.

The dancer seemed to leap from the photographs adorning the wall, her jet-black hair tied into a familiar double bun. Jenna stood up shakily, her fingers moving towards the closest photograph – an image of her young mother standing proudly beside an elderly Margot Fonteyn.

"They were both as cheeky as each other," came a female voice from the doorway, the accent oddly familiar.

Jenna spun around, her eyes remaining wide.

The lady must have been in her sixties, her slender frame accentuated by black tights and a dainty three-quarter top. She moved forward into the room, smiling warmly and continuing to admire the images. She stopped before Jenna, her eyes sparkling affectionately. "And just as beautiful as you. How are you feeling, my dear? You've been out cold for the entire night."

"Uh... I...."

"My name is Sarita Goldstein," the lady smiled, taking Jenna's hands in hers. "I was your mother's dance teacher, and will always be her biggest fan." She gazed around the room airily, continuing to hold Jenna's hands. "My father also loved her dearly, and invited her to live here when things took a bad turn. This was her bedroom for almost five years. Everything has been kept the same since she left."

Jenna's face flushed with colour as she stared about the room, and the numbness in her legs was overcome by tingling. She shivered, clutching at the back of her head, her face suddenly taut with dread. "Owen? Rafael?" Her voice had dropped an octave lower, and her eyes were stretched fearfully.

"They're both downstairs. Querida, relax. They're fine." She took Jenna by the shoulders, trying to get her to sit back down.

Jenna stared forward, memories flooding back. Tears quickly traced down her cheeks.

"It's okay, sit down, it's okay."

"Oh, thank God!" Jenna sobbed, rubbing the tears across her swollen cheeks. "But how did... I mean, what happened?"

"You and Owen were both locked in the tunnels. Do you remember?"

"I-I think so. I'm not sure." Her voice cracked, her throat dry.

Sarita grabbed a bottle of water from the bedside table and helped Jenna take off the lid.

"Owen dragged you to the drain where you came in, but he couldn't pull you through. So he tied his shoelaces to your wrists, and dragged you behind him. That's how you got those bruises. God knows how he stayed conscious; he was barely breathing by the time he reached us outside."

"He's strong as an ox," came a distinctive husky voice.

"Raf!" Jenna cried. Her tears continued to smear as he rounded the bed, pulling her into a tight embrace.

"Nearly died waiting for ya," he whispered. "Think you've given me claustrophobia!"

"Haha," she grinned, pulling back and then pressing her forehead into his. "Well I won't be crawling into any more drains for a long time to come!" She tried to stand up, but the dizziness sent her falling back onto the mattress.

"Here," Rafael said softly, wrapping his arms around her shoulders and pulling her back up. "Lemme help you. Come downstairs and get some food, you gotta be hungry, no?"

"I'm starving," she acknowledged, groaning in pain as he guided her away from the bed.

Sarita fetched a thick robe, wrapping it over Jenna's shoulders and following them into the hall.

The smell of incense grew stronger, as did the sound of classical music from downstairs. Black and white images of the Panama Canal during construction followed the railings down a giant cedar staircase, capturing Jenna's gaze. The landscapes switched to portraits halfway down, and Jenna's footsteps were stalled as she took in the antique images of ballerinas and their cavaliers. Her dizziness lifted, and she allowed Rafael to take her by the hand as they passed through the foyer and into a modern dining room. Rows of glass panels were pulled aside, connecting the room with a sunny Mediterranean garden.

"Jenna!" Owen exclaimed, trying to lift himself out of a plush white sofa. His right arm was in a sling, and his shoulder and neck were heavily bandaged.

"Tranquilo, Owen," Sarita warned. "You should really be in bed."

"I'm fine," he retorted, his face filling with joy as Jenna carefully sat down beside him. Rafael moved away, allowing her to place her palms into Owen's. "And thank God you are, too."

"You're the one I should be thanking," she said, squeezing tighter and frowning at the cuts over his forehead. Her lips suddenly twisted into a pout, her eyes again swelling with tears.

"Hey."

"I'm so sorry that I gave him the tapes. I could have run, I know that I could have gotten through the smoke, and –"

"You couldn't have done anything more. You had no choice."

Jenna exhaled heavily, wiping at her cheeks. Her face became rigid, and she blinked repeatedly. "He's going to have you arrested, isn't he? Both of you, and me, for what happened to Conrad and the others?"

Owen smiled meekly. "Conspiracies are always louder in a court room than they are on the street. Thorn will make sure everything we did is swept under a rug."

"But you're a journalist. And I've already been all over the news. Whatever we say will attract attention. Surely he knows that."

"We don't have any evidence, Jenna. It's as simple as that. Thorn has done this to me before. He knows he's untouchable."

Morning turned into afternoon, and as Jenna finished her third helping of fruit salad she finally recognised the image of a bearded singer that had imprinted in her mind. "Pavarotti," she whispered to herself.

"What's that?" Owen asked as he wiped his mouth with a serviette beside her.

"Take me through that night again," Jenna said, shifting uneasily in her chair. "Where was Hector when he gave Maria the tapes?"

"He didn't give them to her," Sarita said abruptly as she began clearing the table. "She stole them from him, and knocked him down."

Rafael stirred uncomfortably at the end of the table.

"I'm not so sure about that," Owen retorted, staring intently at Sarita. "There was something he was trying to tell us when he lay there dying. He said to let her go. It was as though he wanted Maria to have the tapes."

"No recuerdo. I don't remember," Sarita shrugged, "but I do know that she took the tapes from him and left him there to die."

"But where was this?" Jenna persisted. "Where were they when she took the tapes from him?"

"The auditorium," Sarita said as she walked towards the kitchen.

"Auditorium?" Jenna asked, perplexed.

"Claro. It's where your mother and I used to train. Along with hundreds of others over the years. I still open it up for functions sometimes."

"It's through there," Owen pointed.

"Can you show me?"

"Sure," Owen said. "Rafael, can you give me a hand please? I'll give you both a tour."

Rafael helped Owen to his feet, then linked his arm under Jenna's as he escorted her. Owen hobbled painfully behind them.

"You'll see a set of glass doors," Sarita called from the kitchen, drying her hands on a tea towel and pointing. "Go through, and it's the first door on your right."

Photographs of an elderly man with a silver beard lined the hallway, his soft grey eyes following as Jenna's bare feet pressed softly over the cold wooden floorboards.

The smell of old books wafted through an archway on the left, and she gazed curiously into a dark library. A large botanical book was spread out on a wooden desk, the borders of the book framing a thick layer of dust and cobwebs. She stared, noticing the light reflecting off the polished surface of the adjacent desk.

Sunlight illuminated the end of the hallway, the shadows of palm fronds swaying gently over a tall set of glass doors. She breathed in deeply as Rafael pushed the doors aside. The familiar appearance of red carpet against a line of black doors sent a flutter through her stomach.

The door on the right led into a cluttered backstage area where instrument cases were gathering dust behind a row of red curtains.

"Wait up," Owen called.

Jenna ignored him, her eyes narrowed in concentration as she studied the room, her hand subconsciously squeezing Rafael's. "You only hid them," she murmured, finally staring into Rafael's eyes.

"Huh?"

"You never played the tapes, did you? You never used them for anything?"

"No. I didn't have any use for 'em. I just knew they were important."

"Jenna, what's going on?" Owen huffed. "What am I missing?"

She turned and led the way onto the stage area, her mouth gaping as she took in the size of the auditorium. "Where did Hector play those tapes?" she asked, her voice echoing.

"Through there," Owen pointed into the darkness.

Jenna walked to the far corner of the stage, pushing through a black curtain and gawking.

A soft yellow glow illuminated a giant wall of records. Her eyes slowly adjusted to the darkness, and her fingers traced excitedly along rows of cassette tapes.

"These are all Hector's old tapes," Owen explained. "Exactly as he left them. And right there is where we found him. That's where he died."

Dust accumulated on Jenna's fingertips as she traced along the rows of tapes. "Guys, can you shine a light on here please?"

Owen edged past Rafael and flicked on a light switch. "I'm still confused."

"Pavarotti," she whispered, nudging Rafael to help her search.

The confused look on Owen's face suddenly collapsed, leaving his jaw hanging and his eyes like saucers in the shadowy light. Vivid flashbacks of Hector's death consumed his senses. His hands trembled.

Jenna was about to start on another row when one of the labels sent her heart racing. She pulled the dusty cassette case into the light, smiling back at the distinctive face of Luciano Pavarotti.

The tape inside was certainly not meant for the case – it was a dull grey, with a red star drawn on the side and a handwritten label in Spanish.

"He swapped the tapes," Owen stammered, his eyes still wide with shock. "Hector swapped the tapes!"

The old stereo system flickered to life, and Jenna's heartbeat pounded through to her fingertips as she transferred the power to the cassette player. She turned up the speakers, holding her breath as she gently pressed play.

Made in the USA
Monee, IL
03 April 2021